The Rosetans

The Rosetans

An Italian Clan

Anna Marie Ruggiero

VANTAGE PRESS
New York

This is a work of fiction. Any similarity between the
names and characters in this book and any real persons,
living or dead, is purely coincidental.

Cover design by Polly McQuillen

FIRST EDITION

Published by Vantage Press, Inc.
419 Park Ave. South, New York, NY 10016

Manufactured in the United States of America
ISBN: 0-533-15116-3

Library of Congress Catalog Card No.: 2004099567

0 9 8 7 6 5 4 3 2

In loving memory of parents
Fausto and Mary

Literary Advisor   Marilyn Rettaliata
Technical Advisor   Stephen Rettaliata

The Rosetans

Part One

1989

Nicole noted a touch of autumn as she peered through the living room window. It was mid-August. Soon the hickory trees, plentiful in Roseto, located in northeastern Pennsylvania, will begin turning to display the autumn foliage of golden leaves. Squirrels scampered up and down the large grayish trunks. A huge supply of nuts was expected by October. Martha was an elderly German woman whom the Italians had called "a Vecchi" (old woman). Owner of an extensive amount of land, she had reminded the early Italian immigrants, who founded the borough of Roseto, in 1882, that an abundance of nuts foretold a cold winter.

Chrysanthemums, dahlias and other colorful flowers looked radiant in the early morning sunshine. Evergreens surrounding the stone and brick ranch style home were lush and deep green from the ample amount of late summer rain. The large living room window presented Nicole and her family the opportunity to enjoy the wild life, especially deer and fawns foraging for food. A birdfeeder attracted a variety of birds and competed with squirrels for a share of seeds. She and her husband Dan had purchased the home fifteen years ago. The crisis that had developed within the past few days have made her immune even to the beauty of her surroundings on this particular Sunday morning.

Nicole and Dan Grasso were seniors at Penn State University when they first met on a blind date. The chemistry between the two was instant. Bonded by Italian traditions and cultural similarities the relationship flourished. In June 1972, only two years after graduation, they were married in the Our Lady of Mt. Carmel Church. A huge reception attended by 350 guests followed at Hotel Bethlehem. The groom's family lived in Hoboken, New Jersey. Distance was no obstacle and most of them had joined the bride's relatives to celebrate the marriage. Friendships had developed easily and remained close; even the occurrence of obstacles that ordinarily siphon the love of close relationships did not split the deep ties existing between the two families.

The bride and groom had departed in their 1970 Oldsmobile after a tumultuous celebration and headed toward the New England states. Their honeymoon trip was a happy and memorable one. During September of that year both returned to their second year of teaching. Nicole taught first grade in the Bangor Area School system. Dan was employed as a Chemistry teacher in the Easton High School and remained there until 1980, when he decided to join a pharmaceutical company as a sales representative.

Their first child, Lisa, was born in 1975, Andrew in 1977, while Matthew arrived in 1979. Nicole remained at home during their early childhood and returned to the classroom in 1982.

As a sales representative Dan traveled within commuting distance. He was seldom away from home longer than a day. He enjoyed his role as a husband and father. Tall, handsome, with olive skin, he was an imposing figure and well respected by friends and business associates. He was one of four sons born to Stella and Victor Grasso.

Attractive, five feet-four inches tall with brown hair and eyes, Nicole was a caring and friendly person adapting well as mother, wife and teacher. Through the years her love for Dan had not wavered. Like her mother, grandmother and most Italian wives, she catered to her husband. Her parents, Mamie and Domenic Donatelli, were blue-collar workers. Mamie was a seamstress in the local blouse factory. Domenic, or "Tom" as friends called him, worked at the Bethlehem Steel Plant. Besides Nicole, there was a son Peter and daughter Elizabeth (Beth).

One evening after work, Dan presented Nicole with the news of a possible job promotion.

"It will mean a substantial increase in pay. That's the good part."

"So what is the bad part?" She was almost afraid to ask.

"I might have to be away for a week at a time. It may present a greater burden for you."

Nicole hesitated momentarily. There was an apparent look of indecision and surprise. Many things had to be considered.

"Let me mull this over awhile, Dan."

"No problem honey. Take your time."

Nicole wrestled with the pros and cons of a job change throughout the evening. It was obvious that Dan was excited about this opportunity. To stifle it would indicate a selfish attitude on her part. They certainly could use the additional income. In a few years they would be confronted with the problem of a college education for their children. Tuition was steadily increasing. On the other hand, Dan's absence would require adjustments. Children nine, eleven and thirteen years old ideally benefit from the presence of both parents, and Nicole was well aware of that fact. Knowing her parents were always more than willing to help, she finally decided to give her approval.

Dan began his new job, traveling by car and sometimes air, south, along the east coast. Several times he flew to Texas. Happily his presence at home was for longer periods of time than first anticipated. Adjustments were minor. Nicole's class of twenty-two first-grade children was a well-disciplined group. She was home usually in time for her own children. They were instructed to spend after school hours with their grandparents if occasions warranted it.

Two years passed without incident. Gradually Dan began to spend increasingly less time with his family. The lawn and evergreens he meticulously trimmed were often neglected. Eventually a neighbor's son was hired to mow the grass. Repairmen were called whenever necessary. It had to be that way he informed Nicole. An intense work schedule prevented him from coming home more often. She acquiesced but with intense reservations, pondering whether or not his absence was worth the extra money.

It was June 7, 1990 when Dan made a surprise visit. Nicole and the children had commenced their summer vacation only two days earlier. Andrew and Matthew were erecting their large tent in the lawn. It was a hot day and the boys planned to sleep outdoors that night. When they saw their father coming down the narrow walk toward them, sheer pandemonium erupted. They rushed to embrace him while shouting. Sensing the commotion, Nicole rushed outdoors, shocked and bewildered to see Dan. He was still embracing his sons with obvious love and affection when she ran up to him, her face gleaming with joy. He smiled and placed a perfunctory kiss on her forehead.

"This is a wonderful surprise, Dan. But why didn't you call in advance as you usually do?"

"The company is opening a plant in Mexico City, Nicole. In three days I am expected to fly down there. I can only stay until tomorrow. It was a last minute decision," he replied sheepishly while mopping his brows with a white handkerchief.

"I am terribly disappointed, Dan. This job is taking precedence over family obligations." Disgust was clearly visible in her demeanor. Patience, one of her many attributes, was suddenly losing its hold. She wanted to unwind completely but stopped short of doing so. "Suppose you freshen up while I prepare some lunch for you." Nicole was quick to reveal her priority. She became the traditional wife and mother, always concerned about the needs of her family.

"Thank you, Nicole, but I had breakfast on the plane. Perhaps later." Aware of her frustrations, he nevertheless chose not to pursue the subject.

Upon returning to his rented car parked in front of their home, he retrieved one large piece of luggage from the trunk. On arrival he had noted that the landscaping was perfect. Nicole was a stickler for neatness both in the home and outside.

"Dad, would you like to sleep in the tent with us tonight?" yelled Matthew as Dan was turning the corner. "We have an extra sleeping bag."

"That sounds like fun. Let me work on it. By the way where is Lisa?"

"Swimming at her friend's place. She is lucky. We have to go to the park. Why can't we have a pool?" Inquired Andrew.

"Perhaps some day," Dan replied nonchalantly.

Nicole was tidying up the kitchen when he entered the room. It was cool indoors. The air conditioner kept the house very comfortable. He felt the need of a shower, shave and a change of clothes. It was excessively hot in Texas when he left during the early morning hours, probably exceeding one hundred degrees by the end of the day.

"Nicole, don't prepare anything for supper. Perhaps we can go out for supper."

"Suits me fine. However there is plenty of food in the refrigerator."

Dan headed for a quick shower. She felt frazzled and dismayed. This short visit only added more fuel to the fire. She could blame it on the need for a much needed rest. Yet, a certain feeling of insecurity haunted her. Meanwhile she decided to call Lisa at her friend's home to tell her that her dad was home and that they would all be going out.

In record time Lisa appeared. Her long black hair was still wet. She wore a pink, print bikini to barely cover a perfect youthful figure. Vivacious with an electric personality, she was the ideal cheerleader, reflecting her mother's friendly disposition, her ready smile displayed perfect teeth, the latter achieved following braces, frequent visits to the orthodontists, plus a chunk of money. When the tall figure of her father emerged from the hallway, she dashed to meet him. He enveloped her in his strong arms and squeezed her. He was proud of his attractive young daughter.

"Dad, why can't we see you more often. Don't you know we miss you?"

"I miss you guys too, sweetheart. Sometimes I just can't get away as much as I would like to. How are you doing with the swimming?"

"It won't be long before I'll be a full fledged lifeguard. Should be taking my test soon. Andrew and Matthew are pretty good swimmers too. Both can jump off the high diving board. Maybe we can all go to the pool this afternoon and you can watch us."

"That sounds like a pretty good idea."

"Are you going to sleep in the tent tonight? The boys said you might. You won't be getting much sleep."

"I can get a few winks on the plane going back tomorrow."

Nicole did a double take but remained calm. He wasn't even staying for a day.

Dan enjoyed the afternoon at the public pool with his family. They were all excellent swimmers, including Nicole who looked trim in her black one-piece suit. One of her former students dashed to embrace her. The pool was getting too overcrowded with youngsters so Dan retreated to one of the lounge chairs.

*   *   *

Supper was at "Johnny's." It was a unanimous decision. Hamburgers, chicken nuggets, French fries, salad and soft ice cream topped with chocolate syrup and whipped cream were readily consumed. *How great it would be if only they could do this more often*, thought Nicole. They returned to their car. Then began the endless chattering as each competed to be heard.

As promised, Dan slept in the tent with the boys and had very little sleep. By nine that morning, after repetitive hugs and kisses, he was on his way east towards New Jersey to visit his parents. He hoped to be at the airport by 2 P.M. The short visit with his family and parents had energized him.

Mexico was wearisome but productive. Progress was rapidly being made. A sizable number of workers had been hired. The plant would be in full swing within weeks. He was anxious to return to the comfort of his apartment in Houston. There was a slight turbulence but thankfully the plane landed safely at the airfield. Two large pieces of luggage were retrieved. He hailed a cab, deposited his suitcases in the back seat, sat back and heaved a sigh of relief. The short drive to his apartment was relaxing. After declining the driver's assistance, he paid him and made his way into the foyer of the three floor apartment building.

Several people were milling around. The lingering heat wave discouraged any unnecessary efforts by those who contemplated leaving the comfort of their home A cool drink in front of the TV was a lot more satisfying. He walked up the stairs to his apartment. No elevator. It was not a luxurious building. It served the purpose. He placed his luggage down in front of the door, turned the key and entered the cool apartment. Nothing had changed. It was exactly as he had left it two weeks ago. Three rooms and a bath was all he had and needed. They were usually clean. As one of four boys, his mother trained him well. Nicole followed suit. He knew all about dusting, scrubbing, vacuuming and disinfecting. A tiny nook off the kitchen served as pantry and laundry room with washer and dryer.

Before unpacking, he showered. After covering himself with a light robe, he marched to the refrigerator and reached for a cold beer. He drank half. The rest he placed on a small table next to the recliner into which he effortlessly abandoned himself. The sound of the telephone awakened him. He glanced at his watch. It was almost seven P.M.

"Hi! You're home at last. I've been trying to reach you all day. How did everything go?"

"Just great. As usual it's always good to get back. Missed you very much."

"May I come over?"

"Why ask. You know I'd like nothing better."

"Hope to be there in twenty minutes."

He rushed to get dressed. Stacy should arrive in a heartbeat. It was only a short distance from her home. Speedily he donned a pair of tan slacks and a white sport shirt. During the last eight months a business friendship had developed into a clandestine relationship. Never would he have condoned such action in others yet he made little effort to control his own desires. "It's something like using drugs and alcohol," he told himself; you get hooked. Even if you have the perfect wife and children, you sometimes flip. Maybe it's the demons. He rationalized about his relationship, as any do.

Statuesque with long blond hair and a steady smile, Stacy soon made her appearance. No healthy male would refrain from a sustained look. Dan had left the door slightly ajar. He rose abruptly for a quick embrace and an affectionate kiss on her pink rouged cheek.

Slightly taller, her gray-green eyes searched his freshly shaven face for assurance that nothing had changed in their relationship. Obviously it had not. He placed his arms around her shoulder, kissed her again and led her to the navy sofa. It contrasted well with the white slacks and blouse that covered her slender body.

"You're looking great as usual, honey. Sure missed you."

"Thanks, same here. So how did your trip to Mexico go?"

"First how about a cool drink?"

"Vodka will be just fine. How was the tequila and of course the food?"

"That aspect of the trip was tops. The work and intense heat were not. Besides I missed you terribly." He placed a warm kiss on her cheek and a cold vodka in her hand. "Pardon me a minute. I have something for you." He dashed from the bedroom and drew out a tiny box from the still unpacked suitcase. "Happy birthday. Only three weeks late." She was twenty-nine and seven years younger than Dan. The box contained a silver charm bracelet made by the Mexican Indians. She was delighted and carefully examined every little charm.

"Thank you so much, Dan. It is beautiful. I will think about you every time I wear it."

"Hopefully it will be more often than that." He bent down to kiss her again.

Stacy, a broker for the Ellis and Williams firm, was smart and calculating. Once married to Richard Adams, she divorced him after a three-year marriage citing irreconcilable differences. Truth of the matter was he was only a bookkeeper at a small textile factory who enjoyed his work. "Dick" had no big ambitions. He did not contest the divorce. Her life now was a lot more fulfilling. The fact that her lover was a married man with three children didn't even make a dent She spent the night, left Dan's apartment at eight the following morning and was at her desk by nine.

Two weeks away from Houston required a lot of catching up. Dan stopped at the post office to pick up his mail and then kept an appointment with the barber. He bought a few groceries at the small Italian market. Benny welcomed him back with a big toothless smile. He wanted to know all about his trip. Dan was in a hurry but gave a few details. Benny put a couple of free oranges into his bag.

Back at the apartment Dan made a call to his family. It was late morning and they were all still at home. Nicole answered. She was out hanging clothes.

"Dan, you're home at last."

"Got in late last night honey. How are you and the kids?"

"We are fine. Had to drive the boys to the dentist this morning for a regular checkup. No cavities, thank God. Shirley invited us over to her place to swim. It's the children's favorite pool. Tell me about Mexico."

Dan went into a prolonged discussion and told her he

would be making that trip more frequently. She flinched but was happy he found time to share his experiences in a lengthy conversation.

"Are the kids around?"

"Yes. I'll call them. They are going to be very excited. Hold on."

Each of the siblings gave their take on the summer vacation. No one was eager to hand over the receiver to the next. After an hour they all said their final good byes. Dan was relieved. They were all healthy. He called at least once a week. In an emergency they were instructed to call him. He traveled a great deal but was usually in his apartment by eight P.M.

Stacy called. "We've got to talk, Dan. I will explain when I get there," and hung up while he wondered what had ruffled her feathers. Within twenty minutes he would know. That was when Stacy made her hurried entrance. Looking gaunt, devoid of make up and her hair pulled back in a ponytail, her appearance sent a message before she even opened her mouth. It indicated rough seas ahead.

"What the hell happened?"

"Dan, I'm pregnant."

It was like being hit by a left hook out of nowhere. She practically collapsed on the sofa. He sat next to her. His head slumped backward in total dismay. After a brief pause, he asked, "When did you find out?"

"I was suspicious so I made an appointment with Doctor Stuart. He suggested I see Doctor Samuel, a gynecologist. He confirmed my suspicion I am pregnant with what he now believes are twins."

There was a long silence. Dan, looking quite puzzled, wondered what had gone wrong. They had always taken necessary precautions. The consequences could be enormous. Right now his mind was a total blank. Best to take time and give it some rational thought. He prided himself in always being in control. Not this time. How about Nicole and the children? A philandering husband and father was too often history, especially in a small town. He put his arms around Stacy. He had never seen her so vulnerable.

"I love you, Dan."

"I love you too, sweetheart. Tomorrow is another day. Let's get some sleep."

Bright sunshine filtered through the window early the next morning. It was going to be another scorcher. Stacy was sound asleep. She was beautiful. Her long blond hair spilled about her peaceful face. Soon she would again have to face the reality of her pregnancy just as Dan must deal with its probable effects. He sauntered into the bathroom. The small mirror did not belie the fact that he had spent a sleepless night. His usual handsome face bore the ill effects—dark circles and puffy eyes. Thankfully it was Saturday morning and neither of them had to work.

Stacy slept until nine. Meanwhile Dan read the morning paper but not quite digesting its contents. His head was still spinning wondering how everything would fall into place. He wasn't too optimistic. The sound of running water from the bathroom indicated that Stacy was up. Twenty minutes later she walked into the living room appearing refreshed from a restful sleep; she was also relieved from the burden of having to inform Dan about her situation and hoped it would not affect their relationship. Now they must confront their limited options. Past discussions confirmed they both opposed abortion. That obviously gave them time to consider the other choices. These did not require an immediate solution.

"Stacy, let's take a break and go out for brunch. We are mature adults who should be able to reach a satisfactory conclusion." Dan tried to give the impression of the wise male in complete control.

The weekend wasn't a total loss. Dan's boss had given him tickets for an Astro–N.Y. Mets baseball game. Neither was his team. He was strictly a Yankee fan from way back. Joe D and Yogi had always been his idols. They were "paisans." Practically the whole Italian section of Hoboken was loyal to the "Yanks." Radios blasted with the team's games during the summer. Stacy wasn't a baseball addict but was apparently happy with a change of pace. She had never been in the Astrodome and found the indoor stadium comfortable on this July night. The obvious male attention of the blond beauty did not go unnoticed by Stacy. She relished it and so did the male admirers.

Life began to again fall into a satisfactory routine although not devoid of its headaches and adjustments. If co-workers were aware of Stacy's pregnancy they simply ignored it. She was a bit of a free spirit. Without much thought she decided that no one else must have her babies. A nurse would be hired to help her. She could afford it. Her parents lived in Minnesota. No help there. Dan would help solve the problem. She had no doubt about it now.

In mid-August on a Sunday morning while Dan was showering, there was a loud knock on the door. Stacy, dressed in white slacks and black sweatshirt, hurriedly slipped into her white loafers to open the door. Standing there was a strange couple, probably in their early forties, staring at her. They looked bewildered.

"Pardon us, we must have the wrong apartment," said the tall rather handsome man. "We are looking for Dan Grasso." They were surprised at being confronted by this unexpected tall beauty.

"No, you have the right apartment. May I ask who's calling?"

"I am Angelo Grasso. This is my wife Maggie." His reply was crisp.

"Please come in. Dan is taking a shower." She tried to remain indifferent.

"My name is Stacy Edwards. I am a close friend of Dan and will tell him you are here." She registered no apparent emotion. Angelo and Maggie did. They were on the verge of a minor stroke. Stacy delivered the terse message, heard his instant reply, "Oh hell," bid Dan's relatives a speedy good-bye and left. Angelo and Maggie looked at each other in utter disbelief. They waited for Dan's entrance. It was a short wait. He appeared in minutes wearing jeans, a white T-shirt and smiling like the proverbial cat that ate the canary. His black hair was still wet. It was an awkward meeting to say the least. The three embraced and exchanged pleasantries.

"This is one hell of a surprise. What are you guys doing in these parts?"

"We are on our way to Dallas. Maggie's sister and brother-in-law are having a big shindig this evening to celebrate their twenty-fifth wedding anniversary. We expect to stay a few days."

"I finally got your brother to get away, Dan," added Maggie. " We drove down the east coast to visit friends in Orlando. Decided to stop here before heading north." Maggie was still ill at ease.

"Tried to call you last night, but you were probably out on a hot date," added Angelo with a sly grin on his face. The implication did not go unnoticed by Dan. He could not mask his guilt.

"Went to visit some friends," replied Dan. He regretted the absence. Had he been home to take the call Stacy would have slept at her own home and no one would have been the wiser.

"What's with this dame?" Angelo laid it right on the line. He was eight years older and took on the paternal role. There was strong resemblance between the brothers. Angelo had a construction business requiring the use of heavy equipment. His white sport shirt displaying sinewy arms and deeply tanned skin easily confirmed the fact that he worked outdoors. He always expected straightforward answers from workers or anyone else. This supposedly intelligent brother was no different.

"She came on to me and perhaps I was weak," he replied meekly.

"Dan, you have a devoted family. Are you nuts? For their sake drop this bimbo."

Maggie felt most uncomfortable. Although she was a legal secretary with wide experience in this facet of life, she would have preferred not to be a part of the conversation. A dark-haired beauty in her youth she still maintained a fashionable appearance. The few pounds added to her figure over the years did not bother her. She was the mother of four children. One of her two boys was in business with his father. The other was a sophomore in college. The girls were still in high school. Maggie was very perceptive about many things. Right now she knew Dan was hoping his brother and sister-in-law could evaporate. It was clear to her that he wasn't about to suddenly drop this sexy blonde babe. Women sense such things.

An hour later, Dan suggested they go out for breakfast. He thought Angelo might not come on so strong in a public place. Besides he did not have answers to his questions. More than anything he was sure the demons were in solid control.

Breakfast was pancakes, sausage and scrambled eggs. They drenched everything with maple syrup. Maggie left a few wedges of pancakes on her plate. The men cleaned their plates and raved about the coffee. Angelo picked up the check. They walked a few blocks to the car, stopped to embrace and exchanged well wishes.

"Do some serious thinking, brother. Take care and go to confession," were Angelo's final words. They drove off in their Mercedes. Well up the highway to Dallas Maggie dropped a bombshell.

"Angelo, I think Dan's hot shot is pregnant."

"Are you crazy or what?"

"I'm only giving you my honest opinion. Take it or leave it."

"Holy Gees, I hope you're wrong. That would be a tough break for Nicole and the kids. Also Mom and Pop would flip."

Stella Grasso would not take it sitting down. She had always been a strict disciplinarian. The boys called her "coach" when she was in the proper mood. Field hockey and basketball were high on her agenda during high school. She encouraged her sons to play all sports including football, baseball and basketball. The Grasso boys always made the sports page when they were in high school. From their early childhood she was in the back yard with a catcher's mitt teaching them the game. She and her husband attended every game in which they were participants, criticizing any botched plays. Stella was still muscular with a Santa Clause face and short black hair tinged with gray.

Vito Grasso graduated high school and immediately got a job as a garbage collector. He married Stella four years later. They were pretty thrifty. In just ten years they had built an eight-room brick home. Eventually he bought his own garbage trucks and called the business The Hoboken Waste Management Company. It sounded a lot more refined than garbage collectors. Vito kept his sons under toe by threatening them with his trouser belt. He seldom used it.

Angelo and Maggie continued on their motor trip towards Dallas.

"Do you think this blonde dame would intentionally plan to get pregnant if such is the case?" inquired Angelo after a brief silence.

"It's not unheard of. It might be a way of claiming him, although her sexy body might also do the trick." Many things were bombarding Maggie's mind.

"You sound like Sherlock Holmes. Perhaps we should drop this whole discussion. It is depressing you know." They continued toward Dallas.

Meanwhile Dan had walked back to his apartment. It was only a short distance away. His head was spinning. He expected stressful days ahead. Fortunately he would to be in the Houston area during the next couple of weeks.

Stacy called. She was feeling rotten physically and mentally. The unexpected encounter with his brother and wife was upsetting. She was going to take a short nap. An appointment with her hairdresser was scheduled for that afternoon. Saturday night was a dinner and dance date. They were excellent dancers.

Angelo and Maggie arrived home on Thursday night after first making a short stop in Nashville. Both of them had enjoyed country music so they visited various interesting sites before heading home.

Friday afternoon, his brother Frank stopped casually by at his office. He was a probation officer, slightly shorter than Angelo but heavier. Not the type of guy you would mess around with. Nights he could be found slumped in a recliner. He watched all the wrestling matches television offered. His wife Nettie finally bought her own TV for the bedroom to watch favorite movies.

"Wasn't sure you were back. How did it go?"

"Tiresome. Always good to get back," was Angelo's blunt reply.

"And the anniversary party?"

"The band was too loud and the pyrotechnics are for younger people. The food was pretty good though. Lots of drinks! Glad I didn't have to drive anywhere. They put their guests up at the same hotel. Guess where else we stopped." Angelo eyed his brother carefully.

"Don't have a clue."

"Dan's joint in Houston."

"I thought he was in Mexico."

"He probably wished he had still been in Mexico." Angelo flashed a wicked smile.

"Yeah, why?"

"A blond chick opened the door when we got there. Our brother is cheating." Frank looked shocked. His large rough hands clutching his head.

"Holy mackerel! You must be kidding. Not Dan?"

"Yeah. Dan!"

"He didn't know you were stopping?"

"We called the night before. There was no answer so we took a chance hoping we would find him home."

"Maybe it's only a brief joy ride."

"Doubt that very much. He seems to be hooked." Angelo did not dare bring up Maggie's theory.

"Boy if Coach gets a load of this there will be hell to pay." By now Frank was almost beside himself. "And those poor kids and Nicole. He's nuts."

"Bet your bottom dollar Mom will find out soon enough."

"I'm getting out of here. I have an appointment at eleven." Frank checked his watch. "Sure hope next time I see you things will not be as bleak." He left in a hurry. The

20

thought of his brother fooling around haunted him all day and night.

The Grasso gossip grapevine quickly went into action until its tentacles reached the top echelon. Stella and Vito refused to believe it. They questioned the source. *Since Angelo had traveled through Texas he may have visited him*, thought Stella. She called him at home. Maggie answered but wanted no part of the situation. She refused to discuss it and signaled for her husband. Angelo decided it was senseless to refute it. Besides she might be able to get through to Dan. He certainly had not. On the other hand, Dan was old enough to be responsible for his own actions; he advised his mother to act accordingly.

"He is my son. Damn it! I'll get my two cents in. You know that." She hung up abruptly.

Angelo was not surprised. His mother would not be dissuaded. She was not only a coach but a general as well.

Promptly the following Sunday morning she put in a call to Texas.

"Danny, this is your mother. How are you?" She tried to sound as natural as possible.

"I'm fine Ma. How are you doing?"

"So, so." She wasn't going to start by telling him how disgusted she felt about him. "And your trip to Mexico, how was it?"

"Good but always happy to get back and sleep in my own bed."

"Do you know why I'm calling?" The adrenaline was beginning to flow. She couldn't wait to get her message across.

"No tell me." He had an idea. Angelo was spreading the word.

"What is going on with you and that 'putana' you are seeing?"

His mother could be irritating and aggravating. He did not enjoy having Stacy called a tramp. He wanted to tell his mother to knock it off. His friend was pregnant with his twins and he would not abandon her.

"I think I'm old enough to make my own decisions."

"Yeah. Even old children need to listen and wake up. You have a good family, Danny. Don't blow everything."

"Then it's my fault. You tried your best." Dan was getting more irritated by the minute.

"If you want to make a spectacle of yourself go right ahead. Good-bye!"

Stella hung up fearing her blood pressure was exceeding its limit. That possibility became even more threatening when news of the pregnancy began to circulate.

News of her husband's infidelity would soon envelop Nicole and her relatives. At first it was gossip that reached the ears of her sister Beth. A friend of the Grassos called to alert her to some indiscretion by her sister's husband. Wives often sense a mate's change in attitude before it becomes common knowledge. A talk with her sister might be in order. It could avoid sudden and unnecessary accusations. Beth was an art teacher at the Bethlehem school district. It was mid-August. She and Nicole would be returning to their respective schools in three weeks. Not exactly the right time to be rocked with this kind of news, as if any time was suitable.

Beth called her sister and explained she was in the area and would like to stop in a minute. "Get the coffee brewing I should be there in about twenty minutes." She got into her red Toyota and noticed she was low on gas and made straight for the nearest gas station. While the attendant was pumping, it suddenly occurred to her that she had not seen Dan in weeks. His type of job had made her immune to his absence. She handed the attendant twenty dollars and waited for change. Soon she was on Route 191. Darkening clouds appeared from nowhere. Rain was expected by afternoon. It was now ten A.M., Wednesday. She stopped at the light on Route 512 between Bangor and Pen Argyl, headed for the Slate Belt Boulevard and into Roseto. Nicole's brick rancher was soon visible.

Nicole was waiting on the front lawn, occasionally pulling a weed among the petunias and marigolds. Blue jeans and yellow top covered a slim figure. Beth parked her car in the driveway and stepped out to meet her sister. They embraced briefly, exchanged pleasantries and walked slowly down the walk to the rear of the home. They entered through the back screen door. The aroma of coffee filled the air. The paneled kitchen with white cabinets and light floor tiles was spotless.

"Where are the kids, Nicky?"

"Andrew and Matthew are at the park. The town is sponsoring a summer recreation program. Lisa and her friend Jennifer went school shopping."

"When did you bake the chocolate chips and fudge bars?" The cookies were in a tray neatly covered with plastic wrap and resting on the kitchen counter.

"This morning. You came in time to take some back with you. Your guys will enjoy them. Incidentally where did you leave them?"

"With our neighbor, Louise."

Nicole set two mugs, sugar, cream and cookies on the table then poured the coffee. They engaged in some idle conversation before Beth asked about her husband.

"How is Dan doing? Haven't seen him for at least a month."

"You are not the only one." Disappointment clearly visible on Nicole's face. "He has been calling less frequently. It has been agonizing. A strange feeling has been

23

haunting me for months. Perhaps he has found greener pastures."

"So what if he is cheating?" Beth tried to analyze her sister's mind.

"I don't remember the exact words of the old proverb; something about 'the truth setting us free'."

"Thou shalt know the truth and the truth shalt set thee free."

"Beth, do you think Dan may be cheating on me?"

"Do you remember Luanne from Hoboken? She called and insinuated that he was doing just that." *Okay better this way,* thought Beth, *than delay the inevitable.*

Nicole's face turned gray. She grimaced and closed her eyes and repeated "Oh my God" over and over again.

Beth rose to put her arms around Nicole. "This is equally hard on me, Nicky. We don't know the truth. Let's wait and find out." Tears began to cascade down her cheeks. Both endured long silence and pain broken by a soft knock and a loud "Anybody home?"

Aunt Zee marched in gingerly on her high heels as usual. She carried a large brown bag overflowing with fresh corn and placed them on the counter top.

"Stopped at Millers' farm and picked up some vegetables. Their sweet corn has been especially good lately. You will find enough here for both of you."

Aunt Zee was Carmela Piccone, their mother's sister. The Italian word for aunt is "Zia." Somehow or other she became Aunt Zee. At 5'7" she towered above most of the local ladies who averaged 5'2" and shorter. Her thick black hair was parted in the middle. She usually wore loops for earrings. Only when working indoors or out in the garden did she wear flat heels. Earthy and bosomy she was often compared to Sophia Loren. Lucille Ball and her friend stomping grapes while visiting an Italian village is a memorable one. Aunt Zee in a similar situation could have excelled. At sixty-four she showed no signs of aging. Fun loving and casual she never failed to speak her mind. Her only son Guido (Guy) worked in California as an FBI agent. He had two children, Justin and Amy, and wife Darlene. Zee rarely saw them. Nicole and Beth were like her own daughters. Her husband, Neil Piccone, was an Easton native and worked at the Dixie Cup plant as a sales manager. He had worked there for twenty-five years.

"What the heck is the matter with you girls? You look like you just walked out of a coffin." Her brows furrowed.

"We feel just the way we look. Sit down and you will be told about it." Beth pointed to a chair and leaped up to get a mug and coffee. Aunt Zee seemed to be suspended in time.

Beth did most of the talking. Nicole kept dabbing her eyes. After the brief details were disclosed, Aunt Zee seemed deep in thought. Her first response was "The son of a bitch. A man of his intelligence to lose his senses! First before we draw any final conclusions, let's try to get the facts straight. Children are involved; God forbid they should be upset over false accusations."

"Luanne seems like a pretty credible person, Aunt Zee."

"Yeah, but maybe the person who told her is less credible. Nicole, what do you think about a phone call to one of the in-laws? Stella is not the ideal person. She may blow her top. One of the others may be better. Let's get it straight from the horse's mouth. What do you think?"

"Right now I am so confused I can't think straight." She placed her hand on her forehead.

Since the children were expected back momentarily, Beth and Aunt Zee decided to leave. They embraced Nicole and promised to keep in touch. Aunt and niece walked back to their cars. Beth opened the door for Zee. The back seat was as new as when it was first purchased twenty years ago. It was rarely used. No one cared to ride with the Aunt, except a neighbor, Theresa. She was eighty and never quite aware of how fast Aunt Zee was driving. She had someone to chauffeur her about. Neil Piccone always drove when they went out together.

The pressure of not knowing the real story about her possible wayward husband began to build. Nicole had to know the truth from a reliable source.

Two days later she decided to call her sister-in-law at four-thirty in the afternoon. Maggie was usually home from her job by that time.

"Hello Maggie. How are you?"

When Maggie heard Nicole's voice the reason for the call was evident. She had heard about Dan.

"Thankfully we are well, Nick. Hope you guys are all doing well. No doubt you are preparing for the new school year?"

"To some degree, but unfortunately that is not what is uppermost in my mind." Nicole found herself squeezing the receiver. Her hands were moist. "There is something that I need to talk to you about."

"Okay, Nicole."

"Several days ago my sister, Beth, was conversing with a friend of hers from Hoboken. During the course of the phone conversation she told Beth that rumors were flying, implying Dan was unfaithful to me. Maggie, I had to muster up a lot of courage to make this call but I have to know the truth. Are you aware of anything like that?"

Maggie cringed. This was a difficult situation, but the truth could no longer be concealed.

"Nicole, you are really putting me on the spot. Unfortunately I must be the bearer of bad news. What you heard is correct. The whole family is sick about it. Mom gave him the business but he shrugged it off. We don't know what to do."

The silence on the other end was deafening. There was a surge of compassion for Nicole.

"Thank you Maggie for giving it to me straight." There was a tremor in her voice. "I will keep in touch." She hung up quickly. Anguish on both ends would continue indefinitely.

Several days later Nicole was on the phone talking to Lisa. Her daughter was at the high school for cheerleading practice and expected to be home slightly later than usual. Her friend's mother would drive her home and asked Nicole not to worry. From the front window Nicole spotted the mailman driving away. It was almost three P.M. and about the usual time for her mail to be delivered. She exited from the front door and retrieved a batch of junk mail, utility bills and magazines. In between was a letter from Dan. After rushing back into the living room and sinking into the sofa she ripped open the letter and anxiously unfolded it.

The news was devastating. The letter explained that she had always been a perfect wife and mother. In no way was what had happened have any reflection on her. Dan had unwittingly developed a romantic involvement with a woman who was now pregnant with their twins. He loved this woman and could not abandon her at this time. Subsequent financial and other arrangements would be made. He preferred that she start divorce proceedings.

In retrospect he obviously thought she was aware of the affair and thus rather curt in his explanation. The Grassos, hoping the nightmare would just blow away, never told Nicole the whole story.

The sordid details left her in limbo and frozen in time

until the slam of the kitchen door delivered her back from oblivion. Lisa returned to find her mother sprawled on the sofa with the letter still in her hand. Nicole immediately sat up. The wrenching sight of her mother's eyes swelling with tears unnerved Lisa.

"Mom, what's wrong?"

"Read this."

"The big jerk. The big jerk." She cried out in despair after reading the note.

"Sorry, Lisa, this news should not have been delivered so abruptly. I would much rather wanted that you not to be shocked this way."

"It's a hard take no matter how you deal it. Dad has been acting weird for a long time. You can bet he will regret this. I don't care to talk to him anymore. Wait till the boys hear about this." Spiraling anger and frustration continued until Nicole reminded her that he was still her father and must be respected as such.

"How can I respect a father who ceases to be one?"

Nicole was too drained and couldn't think straight. She walked outdoors hoping the sunshine would disinfect her thoughts. Her sons would be back from the ballpark by five P.M. How would she tell them? She sat on the patio rocker trying to make sense of it all. Lisa dashed into the bedroom and flung her body on the bed. Half hour later, still wearing a cheerleader outfit, she rose, changed into a print blouse and tucked it into a pair of white shorts. Following a brief search she located her mother on a patio rocker disheveled, staring into space. Lisa looked worried.

"Mom, suppose I call Grammy?"

"Grammy will get too upset. She will also need a ride here. Your grandfather isn't home from work yet. Besides it is close to suppertime, Lisa. Everyone is busy. This can wait. Matthew and Andrew will be home from the park soon. You can place some hamburgers on the grill. I will prepare a salad and heat the macaroni and cheese."

Lisa was relieved. Her mother was getting more rational. They both agreed the boys should be spared the bad news for the time being. A format was needed to avoid maximum disruption in their lives.

When the boys returned home, a friend, Joseph, accompanied them.

"Mom, can Joseph stay for supper?"

"No problem, just make sure he gets his mother's approval." They were not aware of any strain in their mother's voice. The focus was elsewhere.

Nicole phoned Beth late Friday evening. Her sister was not entirely surprised. However the pregnancy was a jolt. Next morning, after gaining some courage, she called her mother. Mamie attempted to control her emotions. Beth had already related the disturbing news to her mother who had been dabbing away tears ever since. The wheels turned into motion. The immediate family was notified and swung into action. They agreed to meet at Nicole's during the afternoon.

Grand-pop John and Grammy Gina were on a trip with the local Senior Citizen Club and were not expected back for a week.

The entourage made its appearance at two P.M. Mamie, Domenic, Aunt Zee and Uncle Neil arrived first. Beth, husband Pat, their two children and brother Peter came later. Bearers of an ample supply of food to soothe body and spirit, the support group entered the kitchen, deposited the casseroles containing sausage and peppers, barbeque, various salads, hard rolls and an assortment of desserts on the kitchen counter. They embraced Nicole and Lisa. The children were already playing outside. Nicole's eyes swelled with tears. The others pretended to be upbeat and engaged in idle talk. Aunt Zee broke the ice.

"No need to beat around the bush, Nicole; that weak son of a bitch will live to regret this. He got himself messed up with a first class bum who should have her neck squeezed in a noose. I wouldn't mind doing the squeezing."

"Hold it, Carmella." Uncle Neil tried to inject a bit of humor. "What am I supposed to do without you when they put you in jail? You know I won't eat anybody else's spaghetti sauce. Besides, who is going to wash my back?" He had learned to employ his excellent sense of humor to offset his wife's sudden outbursts of passion. Neil was easygoing but would never be controlled by Aunt Zee's forceful nature. All he had to do was give her a long stare with his dark eyes and walk away. She loved her husband.

" 'Va fa gula,' Neil." The give and take between them eased a bit of the tensions.

The two had met in 1954 at Antonio's Fish Market in Easton. Neil's uncle owned the market and Neil helped out on Saturdays during the busy season. The busiest was and still is 'pre-Christmas.' Italians observe Christmas Eve by cooking a variety of traditional fish dishes. These include squid in tomato sauce, eel (fried, in stew or baked), and "bacala," dried cod first soaked several days and then prepared for salad, baked or stewed, to name but a few.

When Aunt Zee had pranced into the market a few weeks before Christmas, she had met the glance of the handsome, tall dark-haired Neil. His baptismal name was Neilo, but the "o" was subsequently dropped. She glanced at him holding the gaze a few extra seconds. "Bacala" was the only fish needed. She paid the bill, $3.15. The fresh fish would be purchased later. After one last look and a smile she made her exit but determined to be back.

It was three days before Christmas when the long

awaited reunion occurred. Neil was working near the large fresh eel tub filling out an order for a customer who expected to pick it up in about a half hour. Wearing large white suspender overalls, he was lifting huge handfuls of live eel and depositing them in a small metal container. Italians wanted their eels alive to ensure freshness. Aunt Zee watched from a distance. He had not seen her enter the busy market. The wiggling creatures held his attention. Even so one crept into his overalls. He quickly tried to retrieve it but it was especially elusive. "Damn you," he uttered as the critter kept slithering about. Eels were no strangers to Aunt Zee. She and her grandmother had cleaned plenty of the slippery fish.

"Need any help?" she called out.

Standing before him was the last person he wanted to see. With a menacing look and a wide grin she approached him. He never forgot the vision of the tall woman in a brown camel hair coat with the loosened belt advancing toward him. The rings on her ears were dangling back and forth.

"You don't mind if I help?" She whispered in his ear, "I am an old pro in dealing with eels."

Before he even gave it a thought, she dove into his overalls. Thankfully he had blue jeans underneath. She searched and finally got a good grip on the slimy fish and deposited it back in the water-filled metal tub.

"Thank you." His face was crimson.

"I would like to wash my hands. Where is the bathroom?"

He directed her toward the rear of the store and watched her march down the wide aisle. She wore spike shoes and walked with determined quick steps. He tried to remain composed after an unusual incident that hopefully no one had witnessed. Determined to appear at ease he re-

31

turned to the task before him by completing the order he had begun. The sight of her bouncing back up the aisle infused excitement but he was determined to retain some dignity. When she stood before him, he thanked her again. She continued to smile.

"May I help you in any way?" he asked.

"Yes. May I please have three middle size eels?" Her voice was lowered to a gentle tone. Not exactly her usual style. "What is your name?"

"Neil Piccone. And yours?"

"Carmella Sabatino. I'm from Roseto. You're probably from Easton. Right?"

"That's right. I have been in Roseto a few times, especially during the 'Big Time'." He was beginning to relax.

She wanted to invite him to stop in during his next visit but stopped short. Her grandmother would kill her.

"Is there something else I can get for you?" This time he displayed his perfect teeth.

"No, thanks, I need to walk over to the other department for the rest of the fish. Nice meeting you. Anytime eels give you a rough time give a yell." She smiled. He smiled back.

During the next six months she made several more visits to the market but he was never there. Knowing full well that he only worked in the market on occasions she still made frequent trips to the store but to no avail. Unexpectedly a worker, Tony Sabetti, from the uncles' blouse factory where they both worked approached her one afternoon.

"Carmella, do you know Neil Piccone?"

"Of course. I saved his life when he was attacked by an eel," she replied in a jovial manner. "Why are you asking?"

"He inquired about you. He expects to come up for the

32

'Big Time.' I got the impression he wanted to ask you to meet him there. Probably take you on the rides."

"I expect to be there every single night." She did not want to sound too excited but her heart rate was skyrocketing.

Tony relayed the substance of the conversation and immediately became the primary messenger for the two. They met on the carnival grounds in July 29, 1951 and were married two years later. Tony was their best man.

Aunt Zee and Mamie were sisters. With the exception of some facial features the resemblance ended there. Aunt Zee was vivacious while her sister was reticent and always refined. Mamie was shorter, thin with hair worn short and trim and resembled her mother Gina a great deal. She was a very pretty woman with fine features. The sisters worked in blouse factories from the time they graduated high school. They were excellent seamstresses spending a great portion of their life at a sewing machine. Concern for each other's welfare and family was always evident.

Mamie married Domenic (Tom) Donatelli in 1949. He was a war veteran and worked as a welder at the Bethlehem Steel Company. About five feet eight and built on the stocky side, he appeared Slavic, possessing a bulbous nose, blue eyes and a reddish complexion. The couple worked hard, budgeted their income and educated three children, all of whom earned college degrees.

Divorce in the Rosetan family was still a rarity. Their daughter's sudden thrust into this sudden and difficult position was depressing to say the least. Hopefully it will not cause instability among Nicole's children. Mamie and Domenic would certainly try not to allow that to happen.

The family attempted some normalcy on that particular Saturday afternoon as they sat around the kitchen table making idle conversation. Mamie would frequently pull

33

out a tissue from her pocket to dab her eyes, making a maximum effort not to show her emotions. At times she walked around the kitchen adjusting something or wiping the sink for the tenth time. Aunt Zee continually checked her every move. Nicole was in another world.

Beth, her husband Pat Gallagher, and their two children, Tommy and Lori, walked in with more food. Pat was a red headed Irishman. Tall and lanky, with horn-rimmed glasses, he worked in a real estate office. Each morning Pat attended Mass before driving off to work. His parents had died after an auto crash several years ago. In church he routinely lighted candles in their memory. Tommy, nine, has the same shade of red hair as his father. Lori's hair is black and she has green eyes. She is seven. The children rushed to embrace and kiss their grandparents, sat in their laps awhile, hugged the other relatives and made fast exits to play outdoors with cousins Matthew and Andrew.

"Hi, everybody, I see we are not going hungry as usual. There is enough food to feed an army." Beth deposited her tray and greeted everyone. Sunglasses sat over the top of her head. She wore a long light summer dress.

"Hey, Beth," yelled Uncle Neil, "want to bet we won't have leftovers to take home?"

"I'll take you up on it. How about a dollar? I'm cheap Uncle Neil."

"Fair enough."

Meanwhile Pat slowly meandered over to Nicole, placed his arm around her shoulder and whispered, "Hi, kid. Hang on! Everything will be all right." His eyes displayed compassion. "Trust me."

"Sure hope so, Pat, as this is a real downer." Her face was still drawn and tense.

"Just relax and pray. Remember we are by your side." He continued to make the rounds slowly greeting his wife's

34

relatives with love and respect. There was little doubt that the feeling was mutual.

Domenic quietly slipped outdoors to check out the children and then paced up and down the narrow walk. Lori ran over to him clasped his hand and walked beside him. The boys rejoiced. They were not too excited about having her around while they attempted to throw the basketball in the hoop. She was the first to spot her uncle Pete as he stepped out of his Audi and made a dash towards him. He lifted her up in his arms and hugged and kissed her. She was delighted!

"Uncle Pete," the boys yelled in unison. "Do you want to shoot baskets with us?"

He put down his niece and accepted the basketball that they gleefully thrust in his hands after the high fives. He missed the first shot but hit the basket on the next try.

"Hi, Dad, are you getting some air?" Pete caught a glimpse of his father coming toward him.

"That and also trying to keep an eye on the kids."

Peter Donatelli was a lawyer who worked in the local law office of Renaldo, Miller and Jones. At twenty-eight, he was still a bachelor and enjoyed the status. Five feet nine inches tall with thick black hair, olive complexion and blue eyes, the females considered him a good catch. No doubt about that! The qualifications were indisputable. Only he wasn't ready to be caught. Why? He was having too much fun. Besides Mamie catered to his every whim: washed and starched his white shirts, cooked delicious meals and attended to the tailoring. He loved it. She did too. His future wife would have to adjust. It would be a hard sell.

Father and son walked into the kitchen together. As always Peter's entrance caused the usual playful remarks.

"Hey, Pete, you're late. Over dozing after a wild Friday night?" yelled Aunt Zee.

"Wrong. I had work to do this morning."

"How about that tall dame we saw you with at Mac-Donald's about a month ago? She was pretty nice," echoed Neil.

"Too tall. She towered over me and even had the audacity to wear high heels. Want a date with her, Uncle Neil? Just your height."

"Wouldn't know what to do," chuckled Neil.

"Yeah, I'll bet."

"None of that stuff, Pete. I am a very jealous woman. Don't give him any ideas," interrupted Zee.

The mood in the room became more relaxed. Peter walked over to Nicole and placed a loving punch on his sister's chin. "Heads up. Nick. We will see it through together. You know very well that resiliency is part of our genes." Tears swelled in her eyes; Mamie and Domenic tried to subdue theirs.

"When do we eat, Mommie?" asked redheaded Tommy as he burst on the scene, slamming the screen door behind him.

"Exercise a little patience, honey. It should not be long."

Lisa was the last to make an appearance, bubbling over with enthusiasm. Cheerleaders had an excellent workout. The football team had held a practice session. Local newspapers picked them to win top spot in their league. Observing the people she loved the most boosted her spirits even further. Lori followed her around with obvious admiration as she hugged the family members. Mamie wiped away the tears again. Yielding to pressure from the hungry crew, the ladies hurriedly began to prepare the buffet table. In a matter of minutes they were ready for the onslaught.

To silence the hunger chants, the children were the first to be served. Aunt Zee and Beth did the honors. They already knew their likes and dislikes. Most of them wanted sausage but no peppers or onions. Potato salad and baked beans were acceptable. Several had barbecue. The huge mixed green salad was always a big hit. They had a choice of water or milk. The adults settled down in due time. Cold lemonade was passed around.

"Thank you for my special kind of potato salad, Mom. Just oil as a dressing and no mayonnaise. The cut spring beans make it extra special."

"Now you don't think Mom would forget your special desires," teased Beth. "We made both types just to satisfy you."

"For that I am deeply grateful," Pete smiled broadly.

"Why aren't we having some kind of pasta? I miss not having any."

"You will all be at my home tomorrow for Sunday dinner, Lisa. There will be plenty of macaroni," promised Mamie. She was beginning to relax.

"Make baked ziti, Grammy. Those are my favorite," yelled Andrew.

"No, spaghetti," interrupted Matthew. "I like to twist them around the fork."

"Maybe I should take a vote," Mamie suggested. True to form, she would probably cook both.

Conversations soon began to shift. "How is your neighbor, Michael Shanley, doing these days, Pat?"

"Six months have passed since his wife's death and his outlook hasn't improved one iota, Dad. Of course you know how much they clung to each other. The sight of him pushing her around in that wheelchair toward the end was truly inspiring. Eileen fought a brave battle but the bone cancer conquered her much too swiftly. She was only fifty-six and a wonderful person. Everybody misses her."

"That's a big house he's got. Do you think he'll stay there?"

"As you know, Dad, he has that one daughter, Kathleen, who lives in California. She and Jim have three children. They are constantly pleading for him to join them. He won't have any part of that. Besides it would mean relinquishing a good paying job with decent benefits."

"It takes a little time. He's not old. About Eileen's age I believe. Best to stay put until the hurt eases. It will. Then you decide what is best. Self-pity is very bad. It can stagnate your whole life. Pat, you know that better than I do." Domenic spoke in a very quiet, wise and reassuring manner. He then reached for his second helping of peppers and sausage.

The conversation did not go by Nicole unnoticed. She ingested what her father was saying. He was the rock of Gibraltar. Hopefully her plight would resolve itself with as little pain as possible for herself and the children. The food and the company were a calming influence and as usual a proven sedative.

"What are we having for dessert, Mom?" yelled Andrew.

"You haven't even finished what you have in your dish," responded Nicole rather gingerly.

"I will. But until then I can dream about what I think Aunt Beth baked."

"So what's that?"

"Cream puffs."

"Good guess. Also, how about 'S' cookies with butter icing? Maybe even a gooey ice cream sundae? Can't beat that assortment."

"Love you Mom, especially when we discuss desserts."

The children began an animated discussion among themselves on the virtue of each dessert. Matthew expected to taste each. The rest were expected to do the same. After being excused they rushed for the outdoors.

Psychiatrists have the couch. Italians have the dinner table to sit around, eat, blow off steam and talk out difficult situations that may arise. Nicole's problem was brought to light. The clan would not let her down.

It was nightfall before the family departed. Tomorrow they would reassemble for Sunday dinner. Nicole slumped into a recliner after the children retired for the night. Totally aware that sleep would be hard to come by, she began to take stock of the sudden crisis in what was until a few days ago, a calm and uneventful lifestyle. Thankfully family support rooted in a long history of crisis and resolve would pull her through what no doubt would be an agonizing period. Reflecting on well known experiences relayed through the century, she too would have to pull herself together and remain strong in the face of adversities. Nicole closed her eyes and, as she did so many times in the past, reflected on the history of her close-knit family.

Part Two

1882–1970

During the latter part of the nineteenth century, immigration from the European countries reached new heights. Many braved hazardous ocean voyages and faced the uncertainties of an unfamiliar land to escape impoverished homelands. The Rosetans were among the immigrants who traveled from Roseto, Province of Foggia Italy to America.

In 1882, a group of eleven men sailed from Naples and arrived in New York City. After a rough trip lasting thirty-five days, they disembarked in Castle Garden and began the arduous task of looking for employment. A month later eight of the men were sent to Bangor Pennsylvania while the remaining three found work elsewhere.

The area was rich in slate. The first quarry was opened in 1863 after German farmers who settled in the eastern part of the state during the eighteenth century, alerted the public to the presence of slate. The Welsh were adept at working with slate. In Wales it had been quarried for centuries. Therefore men were induced to emigrate from that country and helped to establish the industry. Where farmers once tilled the land, towns like Bangor, Pen Argyl and Mount Bethel were founded. The area became known as the Slate Belt and were inhabited by chiefly Germans, Welsh and English immigrants.

The first Italians who arrived in the Slate Belt settled in an area of Bangor known as Howell Town. Living there meant tolerating sub-standard living conditions. Homes were mere shacks. Yet fellow townsmen and boarding relatives continued to arrive. Nicole's great grandfather, Lorenzo Sabatino, at twenty-two was among those who arrived in 1883. He left behind his eighteen-year-old wife Maria Giuseppe. These early immigrants were recruited for dangerous and meager paying jobs in the quarries.

Prejudices confronted the Italians. Most were not kindly welcomed by the northern Europeans who considered them uncultured and uneducated peasants. They became prone to punishment for minor infractions of the law. When a young mother was caught trespassing in a wooded area gathering firewood, she was brought before the local judge who handed out a ten-day or ten-dollar penalty. She opted for the ten-day jail term. Her husband earned but a meager dollar a day. Since she had a ten-month-old child, the latter had to accompany her to prison. Fortunately for her the prison warden's wife was a compassionate woman and found more pleasant housing for her during that period.

Regardless of the circumstances of those early years the new arrivals had jobs yielding scanty income and savings.

A year after his arrival, Lorenzo had been able to save enough to pay for his wife's voyage to America. His feisty young wife, Maria Giuseppe, did not take kindly to the miserable life and cold winter in the new country. She made no secret of the fact that she longed for sunny Italy. Yet survival was the name of the game and determination triumphed. Such was the case with any of the other ethnic groups who had the fortitude to see it through and help develop the new homeland.

In 1886 Lorenzo and Maria Giuseppe purchased a parcel of land in the vicinity of other Rosetans. They were expecting their first child and wanted suitable living quarters in a more friendly environment. Within a year, and with the help of fellow countrymen, they built a simple six-room frame dwelling on a dusty and stony road. Most of the property extended beyond the rear of the home. The outhouse and later chicken coup and animal pens were erected along the outer edges. A well and pump provided water. The remaining portion became the all-important garden. Fruit trees and grape vines eventually became part of the landscape.

A summer kitchen referred to as the "shanty" was erected outdoors within a few feet from the house. The immigrants canned enough vegetables and fruit from their gardens to provide for winter use. No better way to keep the kitchen clean during the canning season than to work in the "shanty." The area surrounding it had a bit of atmosphere. Discarded slate was often brought home by the quarry workers via wagon or truck and placed behind their homes to form a crude style patio. Overhead grape vines were arranged for shade. Awnings were not yet popular but if they had been available, the Italians would not have spent the money on a frivolous object way out of character for the times. They preferred to admire the overhanging bunches of grape for eating and wine making. In June or late May the family moved into their summer kitchen. It was like taking a vacation!

Over the years daughters Lucia and Grace modernized the home. The "shanty" was no longer a humble shack. Siding, a new roof, paneled interior and a rug denied the original earthy atmosphere. The heavy oak table and chairs were refinished. The shiny black wood stove was still there but never used. The outside grill replaced it. A recliner and a small TV were added plus an air conditioner, important for summer entertaining. The girls enjoyed retreating there to dream of days and people long gone.

Lorenzo and Maria Giuseppe had ten children, four

boys and six girls. Antonio, Filippe, Michele, Giovanni, Angelina, Concetta, Lucia, Jennie, Grazia and Antoinetta. The baptismal names were Italian and used very infrequently except by the parents and elderly friends. In school they adjusted to the American equivalent.

The nascent town of Roseto developed rapidly. As with most of their countrymen, the Italians were farmers, masons and artisans. A post office became a reality in 1898. New homes, a municipal building, clubs, grocery stores, bakeries, both Catholic and Presbyterian churches, and blouse factories were established rather rapidly. In 1912 Roseto was incorporated as a borough. The Columbus School with eight grades was built in 1913. Until that time, children attended one-room schools. Private schools became popular by mid-century. All this came about because of the efforts of uneducated but wise citizens who achieved much in a short time due to strong work ethics and persistence in the face of many obstacles. They accepted meager jobs in the slate quarries and clothing factories to acquire a decent life style.

Lorenzo and Maria Giuseppe raised their family in this friendly environment and tight knit community. Discipline was strictly enforced and the role of children was hardly that of freedom to follow one's whims. As the century progressed changes gradually diminished those values and even the national education system fostered a lessening of physical discipline in the hope of curbing negative psychological effects on students.

Besides the religious aspects, the church was also the center of social activity. Both Lorenzo and his wife were committed to a religious lifestyle. When quarry work was slow, Lorenzo was seen assisting Father De Nisco repairing the small wooden church. The latter was a very popular priest who came from London, England in 1897 to become the regular pastor of the Our Lady of Mount Carmel Church. His expertise with the English language as well as civic law and tradition made him an invaluable asset in the budding community.

Nicole's great grandfather, Lorenzo, was a quiet and refined man and did more listening than talking. Almost six feet tall and slender, he towered over his diminutive five-foot wife. Like many Italian fathers of that generation, he did not openly display affection for his children, nor did he physically punish them. He simply gave them a long hard look. On the other hand Maria Giuseppe administered the punishment with her quick hands, often causing her husband to teasingly admonish her to be careful lest she injure them.

Their grandchildren Mamie and Aunt Zee related many incidents that were recalled and enjoyed over and over again during family gatherings. Their father John (Giuseppe), Maria Giuseppe's and Lorenzo's youngest son, had experienced many skirmishes with his mother.

On one occasion when he was barely ten years old, he was instructed to lead the family goat, "Chee-Chee," to pasture. He obliged without incident and while approaching a nearby field he saw friends playing hockey with polished wooden sticks and tin cans. After anchoring the goat's leash to a tree stump, he searched for a suitable discarded stick and joined them.

Unfortunately "Chee-Chee" strained on the leash and escaped into Maria Antonia's flourishing spring garden and hungrily consumed the tender lettuce plus a few other delicate plants. Of course Maria Antonia was livid and marched over to her neighbor's home gesturing with hands and arms raised in utter distress. The immigrants continued to converse in Italian although they had absorbed some English through the years.

"Maria Giuseepe 'vene subito'," and explained the situation.

"Madonna mia, Madonna mia." She was hanging clothes and quickly dropped the clothespins back into the basket and explained that Giovanni was supposed to be leading the goat to pasture.

The two plump little women dressed in long print dresses and white aprons waddled as fast as they possibly could back to Maria Antonia's garden. There was "Chee-Chee" dragging her leash and enjoying a good meal while staring innocently at the women. Maria Giuseppe recovered the leash and reassured her neighbor that the lettuce would be replaced and expressed deep regret for her son's lack of concentration.

Thankfully Lorenzo still had lettuce growing in his seedbed. That evening after work, he replaced the missing plants and gave her an assortment of other seedlings as well. Maria Giuseppe did not let Giovanni escape her wrath. He threatened to run away from home. She reminded him to carry something to eat for the journey!

John loved animals, especially their huge red rooster. Although he crowed loudly at four-thirty each morning and woke him from a sound sleep he nevertheless admired this dictatorial fowl and was tremendously shocked to learn of his cruel demise. The fowl became a victim of the Thanksgiving feast. Vowing not to partake of the defenseless bird, he began memorial plans.

Ten friends including two girls were recruited. All necessary arrangements were made. The remains, mostly feathers, were gathered and placed in a box. A Requiem Mass was scheduled for that afternoon. It was cold but they all wore their woolen caps (cupolini) and hand-me-down sheepskin coats. Two boys who were familiar with the ritual, were assigned to be altar boys. John was the priest and tore a slit in a newspaper and placed it over his head as a vestment. The altar was a wooden crate and stones became pews. Two boys carried the remains in a carton with utmost respect and placed it on a burlap bag The ceremony lasted ten minutes and concluded with the singing of "My Country 'Tis of Thee." That was the only song they all knew. Girls wearing black veils over their heads pretended to weep while the procession, with several boys carrying the carton, began with the beat of old tin cans. Upon reaching the final resting place the remains were placed in a small hole dug earlier in the day. Pine branches covered the top. After concluding that the rooster was safe in heaven they marched off to play.

Obviously Maria Giuseppe ruled over her brood with a firm hand. Yet she would have exchanged her own life rather than forfeit the lives of any of her offspring. In 1919 her eighteen year old daughter Jennie died. She was a victim of the flu that had spread world wide claiming millions of lives including those of many local residents. Maria Giuseppe never recovered from that loss. Her children feared that she would someday commit suicide by jumping into the deep well as she had so often threatened; happily she never succumbed to that bleak desire. However she did wear black mourning clothes for a number of years. Family and friends finally convinced her to abandon the dismal clothes by asserting that Jennie was an angel of God and such display of sadness was inappropriate.

Conversely her husband suffered only in silence. During summer evenings, he retreated to his favorite rocker under the grape arbor and smoked a Di Noboli cigar, insisting it kept the mosquitoes away. It was also the ideal place to sit, admire the garden and meditate.

Like many of the other wives of that era Maria Giuseppe catered to her husband. At meals he was the first to be served. The slate quarry took its toll on the laborers, particularly during the hot humid days of July and August. The two mile walk home from work added to the misery. A sigh of relief was heaved as Lorenzo set his metal lunch pail on the patio and slumped into the cushioned rocker under the grape arbor. His wife removed the heavy work shoes and thick socks and placed his feet in a shallow pan of cool water. A tall glass of lemonade rested on the table beside him. Wine and cheese would follow later. Lorenzo began to relax and inhale the delectable aroma of spaghetti sauce emanating from the shanty.

Most of the children were only twelve years old when they began to work. Textile factories including silk mills, blouse, shirt and pants factories, mushroomed in the Slate Belt in the early part of the century. There were no child labor laws until years later. The majority of youngsters had to settle for only a six grade education. The younger children, John, Grace and Lucia, graduated from Columbus School with an eighth grade diploma. They quickly entered the local work force. There were no health or unemployment benefits. Money earned was given to the mother who dealt out small allowances. Most were experts at budgeting income. In fact, many husbands preferred to have the wives handle finances.

Upon reaching their eighteenth birthday the male members of the family retained most of their income. They had to prepare for marriage and their own family. The young girls were less likely to be treated in a similar fashion. Instead sheets, crotchet tablecloths and bedspreads and embroidered household items of fine workmanship were completed and stored in a cedar chest, to be used should marriage be in their future. Bank accounts were meager or non-existent.

Matchmaking for marriage prevailed during the early

years. "Putting on the red stockings" referred to this practice. Maria Giuseppe would often try to nudge her children towards certain individuals who met her criteria. Not much faith was put on their choices. Sometimes the desired effect was lost in a verbal scuffle. When she approached John about the merits of Giuseppina, daughter of Maria "the fat one," he became quite annoyed.

"Ma, I'll choose my own wife." He was reluctant to be disrespectful to his determined little full figured mother as he angrily glared down upon her round face. She glared back in the same way.

"Giovanni, she be a gooda wife. She cooka ana cleana." She was not intimidated by her son's outburst.

"She also has a long thin nose and a flat chest." John made his point and walked away from his mother who had made significant progress with the English language.

As John grew into adulthood his parents were resigned to the fact that they had given life to a free spirit and adventurous son. His love for motorcycles alarmed them. They fretted that his wildness might some day maim him for life. Older brothers Antonio, Philip and Michael, now married with children, were never so worrisome. When comparison was made, "They lived in a different century," was John's immediate response.

The big cities beckoned John, as did the army to escape the dull country life but he remained home.

At the age of twenty John was working as a mechanic for the Lehigh New England Railroad at the Pen Argyl terminal. Unfortunately he had never received an advanced education, otherwise his natural ability may have led him to become a mechanical engineer. After experimenting with several inventions, he did apply for patents which however never succeeded in reaching the industrial world.

Ford Motor Company had begun manufacturing cars

in 1903. Within a short span of ten years, Model T Fords were no longer an oddity in the area. In 1920 John withdrew some money from his savings account and purchased a Ford pick-up truck that required cranking to start the engine.

Until the mid-twenties a trolley snaked its way through the Slate Belt area. The fare was ten cents. It was hardly a surprise that not everyone took advantage of that convenience. They preferred to walk a few miles and save the dime. Possessing a vehicle of any type was a luxury and a curiosity.

*   *   *

Gina DeFranco was no stranger to John. Rosetans were a tight knit group and knew everyone in their small community. Five feet three inches tall with chestnut brown hair, aquamarine eyes that sparkled and a smile revealing a tiny dimple on the corner of her mouth, John had his sights on her for some time. Occasionally he would stop and tease her whenever they met. He was twenty-two and three years older than Gina. Trying to date a girl of that period and culture meant that serious intentions and often a commitment had to be made. It was no accident that he ran into her with increasing frequency of late and finally cornered her after Sunday Mass. The request to visit her was received with a Shirley Temple smile, a blush and a reply to be given later. She had to receive her parents' consent.

Luigi and Rosa DeFranco were products of the same rigid standards as John's parents as were most of the local Rosetans. However differences in personality and stature were evident. Luigi was of average height, rotund and boisterous. Personal opinions relative to religion, politics and discipline were seldom reversible. Gesturing constantly, adamant and stubborn only a disdainful glance from his wife temporarily subdued his testy outbursts.

It was pure folly for Rosa to demean her husband in public lest his ire prove embarrassing. Five feet two inches tall with reddish braided hair pulled pack into a bun on the nape of her neck she was a quiet and dutiful wife. Rosa was also an excellent tailor. The majority of the local women were able to mend and make minor alterations but lacked the intricate talent that she possessed. Hence when difficult situations arose or a complete garment had to be designed and sewed, they would head for Rosa's home. She and Luigi were the parents of four children; Marianne, Gina, Carlo and Dante.

John decided to approach them for permission to visit their daughter. On a warm Sunday afternoon in early August, 1924, he began the short stroll to the DeFranco home. The Sabbath was a day of rest. Practically everyone attended religious services on Sunday morning at either the Catholic or Presbyterian Church. During the afternoons they sat on their porches with relatives and friends. Some walked to the baseball field to watch the game between the Roseto AA and a team from a neighboring town. Others went to the Marconi Social Club or the Columbia Fire Company to play cards or simply "shoot the breeze." No one hung out wash or did manual work. Stores were closed and of course shopping at a mall was a long way into the future.

While approaching the white frame home with the well-trimmed green, edge fence and pear tree already beginning to bear fruit, John's heart rate accelerated. He adjusted his blue bow tie and pulled out a white linen handkerchief from his gray trousers to wipe the perspiration from his brow. After unlatching the wooden gate and sauntering along the side slate walk, he was met with loud greetings from the family members and guests who had assembled on the back porch and under the protective shade of a large apple tree. The reason for the visit was already common knowledge and immediate approval was obvious.

"You're lost, John!" yelled someone.

"What are you up to? Don't tell me you missed the baseball game. Your cousin Larry is pitching," intervened another.

"Yeah, well I thought things might be more interesting up this way."

John spotted Gina's parents and walked over to them. "Hello, Zio Luigi. How are you?" They shook hands and smiled affably. Seniors were addressed as Zio and Zia (uncle and aunt). Never Mr. or Mrs.

"Bene, Giovanni, grazie, e Lei?"

"Bene, thank you." Italian was often interspersed with English since the majority of the Rosetans were bilingual. Of course the older generations still spoke with an accent.

"Howa youa Mama and Papa?" continued Luigi. He appeared rather jovial.

"They are both well. Pop went to the ball game to watch Larry pitch. Mom, Lucia and Grace are visiting Comara Adelina." John was beginning to relax. He greeted Rosa who sat on the reed rocker next to her husband.

"Hello, Zia Rosa. Everything going well with you?"

"Just fine, John." Since Rosa was born in this country she spoke perfect English. She and Luigi were about ten years younger than his parents."Gina will be back soon. She and Marianne went to the cemetery to put a couple of potted geraniums on their grandma's grave. You came just a bit earlier than expected. Sit on that rocker." Rosa pointed to the other reed rocker in front of them.

"I'm glad we were left alone for a few minutes." John was clenching his hands as he spoke softly, desperately hoping to properly articulate his interest in their daughter.

"As you already know I came to get your approval to visit Gina on Saturday nights."

"It isa okay, Giovanni, we knowa you be a gooda boy from a gooda family; you worka hard." Luigi then went into a lengthy discourse about honorable relationships. He expected Gina to be treated with respect at all times. John assured him such would certainly be the case. He had sisters and expected no less from their suitors. Luigi pulled himself up from the rocker and motioned for John to follow him towards the garden.

Passing and greeting the assembled with a smile or pat on the back, John entered Luigi's well-cultivated garden, one much like his father's. There were rows of tomato plants tied to six foot wooden stakes, most derived from strong tree limbs that were plentiful in nearby wooded areas. Healthy pepper, chard, dandelion, assorted types of lettuce, onions, garlic, cabbage and a few other species of vegetables grew well in the carefully enriched soil achieved by including a compost heap in a corner of the garden. Discarded plants, grass clippings, table and animal wastes were components of that organic pile of material that had to be kept moist. A sprinkling of lime was added periodically. Within a year it was ready to be added to the soil. Today the compost heap is essential in organic gardening.

Although there were many masons, the immigrants were basically farmers who never lost touch with the earth. Through the century many residents who entered the professional world or were employed in industrial plants maintained small gardens as an escape from the stress of a regimented routine. Bragging rights to producing the first tomato of the season continued.

Luigi repeated the familiar liturgy about gardening as he and John trotted along. It was one heard so often from his father. The snort of the hog and cackle of the chickens brought temporary halt to their conversation. The older man scooped a handful of feed from a small barrel and dispersed it in the coup where the hens devoured it in record time.

"Zio, that looks like a fig tree." John pointed to a tree along side of the hedge fence. "I hear they do well in Italy where it's warm. Here they need a lot of care or they won't make it through the cold winters."

"Thatsa right, Giovanni. I take care. In late fall I wrap around with burlap, bend tree and put lotsa ground on the top so no freeze. Vene qua (Come here)." Luigi led him to the tree and pointed to the small green figs that had already appeared and would soon ripen. His attention was abruptly directed elsewhere. While walking he motioned for John to approach and directed his attention to the huge zucchini plant. There sprawled atop the lush green leaves lay a garter snake. "He no hurt. Eat lotsa bugs." John agreed.

The welcome sounds from the rear of the house indicated that Gina and Marianne had returned. The two men slowly made their way back to join family and friends who were now in the midst of teasing Gina for keeping John waiting so long.

Both girls wore dresses that Rosa had created for them. Gina wore a loose white cotton sleeveless dress with an ochre sash around her waist. Hair was pulled back and a large ochre bow held it together. Marianne wore a loose light pink print dress. Her long black wavy hair was neatly held in place by a white headband. She was two years older than Gina and engaged to Ralph Martucci from Philadelphia. The wedding was scheduled for late September.

"Hey John, Gina is here at last. She kept you waiting long enough." Dante's voice echoed almost as loud as his father's.

"She plays hard to get." Her other brother Carlo enjoyed teasing.

"Yeah she does that to all the guys," yelled her cousin Joey. It was not easy to subdue her brothers and young cousin. She wanted to squeeze their necks. Instead she only blushed and played the part of a tolerant maiden.

John approached Gina with as much ease as possible. Obviously all eyes were focused on the young couple. He had to remain relaxed though he felt like an actor on a stage.

"Sorry to keep you waiting, John. Hope my family held your interest?" By now Gina's face felt unusually warm. And it wasn't from the hot summer afternoon.

"Didn't mind it at all. In fact, your father here gave me a tour of his garden. Thought I knew all about gardening but he is the expert. One has but to look around and see how well everything is growing." John knew that even a small compliment would go a long way in bolstering Luigi's ego.

"Giovanni you gotta do the right thing for the garden. It's like people; if you eat and drink gooda you feel gooda. Plants, they wanna good food and drink too." Luigi was really puffed up by now.

"You're right there, Zio." John heard enough about gardening procedures and looked forward to the older man's quick exit. However that was as likely as picking figs from Luigi's tree on a cold December day.

"It's my turn to talk to John," Gina interrupted. She was like a fresh breeze on a hot day. He tried to remain calm. Luigi reminded him that he had some basil plants for his father and left to rejoin his wife.

"Hope he didn't bore you."

"Not at all. He understands gardening, that's for sure."

They joined the younger group who were playing

cards or "Scopa"' to be exact. A dish of roasted chickpeas and sliced provolone plus a bottle of Luigi's homemade wine rested on the table. They were among the usual snacks.

"You two wanna join us? We are just about ready for the next game," Joey asked with an amused smile.

"We'll just watch you play for awhile," Gina responded quickly. She preferred to totally enjoy John's company.

Everyone looked up at the sound of clicking heels. Eddie Ronca and his fiancée Rita, were strolling down the slate path. They were frequent visitors of the DeFranco family. Luigi and Rosa were Eddie's Godparents. After the usual exchange of greetings with all present, they approached John and Gina.

"Hey John, never expected to see you here." It didn't take long for Eddie to understand the reason. "This happens to be a bonus. I was going to walk over to your house for a favor."

"What's that?"

"I need a ride to work tomorrow morning. Jerry can't make it. He has some legal matters to straighten out."

"Glad to be of help."

"Didn't realize you worked at the car shop with John," interrupted Dante. "I thought you rode on the trains."

"I do both. It all depends where they need me." Eddie had the reddish hair and complexion common among the Ronca family.

"We get to see each other at nine A.M. for a snack break and then lunch whenever he's around," added John

"Yep, once in awhile I enjoy eating with the Pepper Popper."

"Who's that?" Gina looked interested.

"John. That's what the 'med-e-gons'(Americans) call him."

"Why that name?"

"Because he loves peppers, fried, roasted stuffed, pickled or any way imaginable. He eats them almost every day. One sandwich for a snack and two for lunch. Those 'Johnny Bulls' tease him about it."

"They don't know what's good," replied John. "I like peppers. They like pasties."

"What are pasties?" inquired Dante

"Something like a meat pie," explained Rita. "Janice Jones gave me the recipe. She is English and her mother makes them quite often. They are popular among both the English and Welsh and were first introduced in Cornwall, England, centuries ago and were especially convenient for miners to carry in their pockets for lunch."

"Did you ever make them?" inquired Gina.

"A couple of times. Actually all you need is rolled out pie of dough, cubed potatoes, meat, chopped onions plus a little butter and seasoning. Bring the ends together on top. Crimp and place on greased baking sheet. They are baked at 350 degrees for one hour or until brown."

"Rita, you'll have to write it down for me," suggested Gina.

"Will be glad to do it for you. Some of the churches bake them on Wednesdays and sell them in mills and other work places," continued Rita.

"They take orders at the shop, Gina. I'll order a few and drop them off on Wednesday after work. See if you like them. I have one for lunch occasionally. They're pretty good," interrupted John.

Marianne appeared with the news that she and Gina had baked fresh blueberry pie. The boys and some friends had picked the wild berries in the Blue Mountains. Each serving would also have a dip of ice cream if desired. No one turned down the offer. They all had the combination pie and ice cream. Immigrant Rosetans were less interested than their children in pastry and desserts. Fruit and cheese were preferred. That changed soon enough.

The afternoon sun was gradually setting. Friends and relatives who had dropped in to participate in the weekly reunion gradually said their good-byes. Sunday afternoon was prime time for visiting in all the Roseto households. Over the ensuing years television gradually took precedence.

John was among the last to leave. He would have preferred to stay longer and enjoy Gina's company but opted for a short first visit. There would be other Saturday nights.

As promised, the pasties were delivered on Wednesday after work. Rosa appeared when John knocked on the door. The girls were still working. Just as well. The day's grime and dirt still clung to his clothes and skin. Rosa graciously thanked him. Following a brief discourse on pasties, he bid her well and sped away in his Ford pick-up.

Much to his disappointment he had to work a few hours on Saturday morning of the following weekend. He was up at five-thirty A.M. and saw lights in the shanty. His mother was making initial preparations for the bushels of tomatoes that had to be canned. Purchased from a local farmer during the week they were properly ripened and ready for canning. The tomatoes in their garden were not quite ripe. Perhaps Lorenzo had planted a species that ripened later in the season. It didn't matter. There was always need for more.

John, not fully awake, entered the outside kitchen. Huge pots of water covered the top of the black wood and coal stove. It would obviously be a busy day for the ladies. There was the slam of the screen door. His mother appeared surprised to see him up so early on a Saturday morning.

"Giovanni, you uppa early?"

"I gotta work a couple of hours, Ma." His voice was groggy.

"You wanna I packa you lunch?"

"No thanks. I should be home before lunch."

"You have veal and peppers with tomata when you comma back. I make for everybody. Zia Michelina, Julie anda Nina they come help can tomatoes Lucia anda Grazia they no work today so they help."

"It's a good thing you will have help. Lotsa of tomatoes there."

Maria Giuseppe placed a large bowl on the table before him, poured hot coffee into it and added an equal amount of warm milk. He reached for the large loaf of homemade crusty bread and cut a thick slice, broke off pieces and dunked. He told his mother he expected to visit Gina that evening.

"Brava Giovanni. Nica gal."

"Glad you think so, Ma." John finished his breakfast and placed the bowl in the sink. He completed some last minute chores, bid his mother good-bye and walked toward his truck parked in front of their home. His mother's voice singing an aria from a favorite opera emanated from the shanty. John presumed it was part of a joyous opera.

As expected, Lorenzo found his wife well into the task ahead. He asked if there was anything she needed. Everything was in place she informed him and quickly reached for the pot of coffee. While they sat at the table she informed him that John was going to visit Gina that evening. A smile appeared on his face and both agreed it was a wise choice. They chatted briefly before he left to do a little spading in the garden. Later he expected to help Antonio build a shed.

Lucia and Grace were not working at the silk mill that

day. It was perfect time to engage their help. They did all the household cleaning while Maria Giuseppe claimed priority in the kitchen. Steering their mother into the twentieth century was a monumental and almost daily task. They tried. She turned them off. Only financial matters were finally abdicated. The girls had come of age, were making decent wages, about eighteen dollars a week, and had their own bank account. Aware of her penchant for handling money, a small amount was handed to their mother on payday. She lifted her three petticoats, took out a large worn change purse and added to the other money they gave her.

Most of it was used for food. Excess cash finally ended up in a joint bank account shared with her husband. Often many of these early immigrants amassed substantial savings so that they were able to finance mortgages at lower interest rates than those given by banks. Such transactions existed only among known acquaintances.

Lucia and Grace were ready to begin what they knew would be a hectic day and not at all surprised to find their mother as usual off to a fast start.

"Morning, Ma. Looks like you were up all night and got a lot done." Grace inspected the results.

"Morning. Too much work. Que ora e?"

"It's six-thirty. When will Zia Michelina and the girls be here?"

"They come eight o'clock. We get things ready. You wanna coffee?"

"We'll get our own Ma. I see Pop is in the garden. Did John leave yet?" Lucia looked curious.

"He go pretty early. Giovanni essere inamorato (is in love)." Typically the mother often expressed herself in both languages.

"Gina?"

"Si."

"She will be good for him," Lucia responded while reaching for the coffee pot. "It's time for him to settle down."

"I agree. There has been a rumor around that he was interested in her. Now I call that a good match," added Grace.

The two girls were taller than the average local women. Always neatly dressed, they had bobbed black hair and brown eyes. Lucia was twenty-one. She had a distinct way of looking into one's eyes and seemingly unveiling the true character of the person before her. She could also be unnervingly serious. Grace, nineteen, smiled easily and was generally inclined to second most of Lucia's opinions.

Neither of the girls ever married. A few friends were aware that Lucia and Len Policelli could have been easily involved in a romantic relationship. Only Len was Presbyterian and of course she was Catholic. Religious tolerance was not one of the finer virtues of the Roseto clan. This was particularly true among the older folks. Lucia was pragmatic and dismissed any thought of a serious union. That is not to say she did not reevaluate her decision throughout her life. Len married Lena and they had five children. Life led Lucia and Grace along a different path—one accepted with few reservations.

Lorenzo completed spading the garden and left to help his son Antonio who lived but a short distance away. The women began the canning process by first washing the tomatoes and then dropping them into boiling water to blanch. After less than a minute they were individually removed with slotted spoons and placed into large platters or pans. Next they were cored, peeled, cut in half, seeds removed and placed in a pot. The seeds, peals and liquid were not wasted but were boiled, run through a sieve, and

63

boiled again to make a thick puree. The pulp was cooked about a half hour after reaching the boiling point. The puree and pulp were boiled together for a short time, seasoned with salt and a few basil leaves, poured into hot Mason jars and each topped with a warm lid. Towels or blankets were used to cover the jars until cool.

It was a job that required help especially when processing a large amount of tomatoes. Not only family members but also neighbors helped each other during the tomato season. Vegetables and fruit were also canned but the task wasn't as formidable.

Michelina and her daughters Julia, seventeen, and Nina (short for Annina) fifteen, walked into the summer kitchen about seventy-thirty A.M. All the ladies wore aprons and kerchiefs knotted behind their head. Michelina Falcone was a widow. She and Maria Giuseppe were childhood friends. Her husband had died twelve years earlier in a slate quarry accident leaving behind eight children. Insurance for such a catastrophe was minimal. The older children worked and supported the family.

"Buon giorno."

"Buon giorno, Zia Michelina, Julia and Nina." Grace was the first to greet them. Maria Giuseppe and Lucia quickly followed as they entered the summer kitchen. "Are you ready for the big day ahead?"

"Set and ready to can one hundred jars," responded Nina.

"Wouldn't think of missing the canning," added Julia who possessed a beautiful voice and was an important member of the church choir.

"First how about a cup of coffee and some biscottini? I baked them last night just for us," Lucia asked. Since they already had breakfast they all agreed to indulge after the canning was completed.

" 'Cuora di Zia' you work hard and bake too. Rest a bit." Michalina sprinkled her conversations with phrases like "curoa di zia," (heart of your aunt), "coura di mamma" (mothers's heart), and "figlia bella" (beautiful child). Listening to her talk was enjoyable. She usually held everyone's interest with her dramatic delivery in the use of hands as well as the way she articulated each word.

"You are all special so why shouldn't I bake. How about all the work you will be doing today. It's my pleasure, Zia." Lucia was emphatic in her response.

"Grazia, Lucia. We lika help you. We talk a little, laugh, cry and work. Tima, she go by fast."

"By the way, where is 'mangia polenta'?" inquired Nina.

"Her mother had a small accident yesterday afternoon and she spent the night in Pen Argyl."

"That's too bad. I'm going to miss her jokes. Time flies when she's around. Maybe she'll drop by later."

"Could be. Meanwhile we will try our best to keep you laughing," replied Grace.

Eva Confalone's parents came to America from a small village near Venice. Polenta has always been an important part of the diet of northern Italians. The southern Italians call them "mangia polenta." There is good-natured ribbing between the two about the difference in diets. Venetians and other northerners counter with "mangia pasta" when teased about polenta. Eva Uliana married James Confalone twenty years ago and built a home across the street from the Sabatino residence. They had a childless marriage. The Rosetans easily adopted her as one of their own.

It was almost eleven A.M. when Eva surprised them all by suddenly making her appearance. She was a tall woman with a playful grin that revealed a gold tooth. The older women immediately inquired about the health of her mother.

"Thank God it was nothing too bad. She fell and hurt her ankle. The doctor told her to stay off her feet for a couple of days. Try telling her that!" They were all relieved to hear it was nothing too serious. "Sorry I wasn't able to be here earlier. You are already beginning to fill the jars."

"Eva, guess what?" interrupted Nina gleefully. "We will let you wash all the pots and pans."

"I'm willing. Will you be drying?"

"That's not as bad as washing and scrubbing."

"Just remember a couple of years back when water had to be pumped out of the well and carried in buckets. Now with running water it's much easier," Eva reminded her.

As expected the morning was filled with hard work and pleasant conversation. By noon they had canned one-hundred-and-four jars of tomatoes. Before the fall many more would be canned. Maria Giuseppe placed all the soiled dishtowels into a pail of hot water to soak. Most dishtowels were made from cotton one-hundred-pound flour, sugar or feed bags, cut into desired size and then hemmed on a Singer sewing machine.

It was apparent that the mothers were tired. They sat on the sofa and heaved a sigh of relief. Julia immediately dampened a towel and mopped their sweat-covered faces. The girls cleaned the kitchen until it was spotless.

Grace and Lucia set the table for lunch. Maria Giuseppe had prepared food in advance. There was plenty of fried peppers cooked with veal and tomatoes, pizza with potatoes (flattened bread dough topped with sautéed onions and potatoes and then rolled), tomato pizza and a tossed garden salad. Wine and cold lemonade were the liquid refreshments. Sliced almond toast and fruit were served as dessert. The women began to unwind.

66

"You all know my sister Pia?" Eva inquired.

"Yes we do." Lucia was the first to reply.

"Well her husband's parents are from Philipsburg and visited for a week. Angela and Sammy are really nice people. Pia's youngest son, Vinny, is quite a rascal even though he is only six years old. You remember how he opened the door to our chicken coup and flushed the chickens out?"

"Yeah that was funny." Nina's face lit up as she stared at Eva's gold tooth.

"You will never guess what he did before his 'nonna' took a bath."

All faces were watching Eva as she spun the tale and held everyone's attention. Maria Giuseppe and Michelina looked happy. Perhaps it was the food and wine.

"Pia keeps a wicker basket in the bathroom for dirty clothes. Vinny hid in the basket before she ran the water in the tub. She took her bath and stepped out. Vinny's head popped up. With an impish smile he shouted 'boo'! His grandmother was shocked but not amused. She quickly covered her wet, nude body with a towel and stared in total dismay."

" 'Vergogna' I tella your mamma. Badda boy."

The women burst into abrupt and continuous laughter. Tears rolled down Maria Giuseppe's cheeks. Lorenzo and John made their entrance into the kitchen during the prolonged period of merriment.

"Glad to see you are having fun. So what's up?" John looked puzzled. "I expected you all to be knocked out from all that canning. It looks like you did plenty of it."

"Eva tell them," Nina suggested. She did not mind a repeat performance.

The men reacted with some amusement but did not find it as hilarious as the women. They simply smiled. Maria Giuseppe motioned for them to sit at the table and

67

have something to eat. They washed their hands at the sink and joined the women. Grace placed dishes and utensils before them and spooned out veal and peppers as they helped themselves to the other food already on the table.

The conversation shifted to the work done on the shed. John, as prearranged, had joined his father at Antonio's home after working a few hours at the shop. Four of them including a neighbor had erected the structure within a matter of hours. Antonio's wife, Margaret, pleaded for them to stay for lunch but they declined. Father and son were noticeably and deeply tanned from the hot sun. Their hair was moist and ruffled. They consumed the food with gusto and appreciation. John soaked the crusty bread in the sauce.

The Falcone women were really like family. They squeezed together around the table and talked frequently competing with each other in order to be heard.

"Zia Micelina I hope you did not get too tired today?" asked John.

"Naw, naw figlio mia. We must help you, just like you help me. Tonight we rest."

"You know how it is," added Julia, "everything goes faster when we work together. Canning a lot of tomatoes is hard on a couple of people but fun when friends join in." Julia was from the same mold as his sisters. They were serious-minded and duty bound. Nina was the youngest. She craved action and entertainment whenever possible.

Lorenzo reminded them that the next few months would, as usual, require joint efforts. Not only canning, but also wine making and the November butchering of hogs. It meant an assemblage of neighbors to help each other with the fall routine, handed down for generations.

"Gotta hand it to you guys. Our people did less of that.

But after living among you for so long I understand what it's all about."

"It is a regional thing, Eva. Your ancestors found work in the factories. Our folks depended on the land to care for their families. And the land wasn't even theirs. They usually rented from abusive landowners and had to share the harvest with them. One or two years of school was all they got. There was no hope for advancement."

"They didn't get much schooling, John, but these old folks are pretty darn smart about a lot of things," Eva reminded John.

"You better believe it. They were born with wisdom and a sense of responsibility. This land where the Indians once hunted was nothing but woods. A small village emerged within a span of twenty years."

"We work hard, Giovanni. Lotsa stones to carry when we built house."

"I knowa Zia Michelina. Work was your middle name."

"And the clothes," added Maria Giuseppe, "we wash in the creek. We carry baby in our belly and clothes basket in the arms."

"I heard about those stories over and over again. Thank God I wasn't around. Maybe working in the mill isn't so bad after all. At least I get to earn a little money." Nina giggled.

"I remember a lot more, Nina. But do you know what? I didn't know the difference," added John. "That's just the way things were. We all worked hard. There was always plenty of food and plenty of caring for each other."

Lucia interrupted the serious conversation by suggesting that Grace get her Kodak camera.

"Where did you put it?"

"It should be in the living room. Look in the drawer of the small table."

Grace returned with the square camera and gave it to Lucia. "I have some film that I would like to use up and have developed next week. How about a group picture first?" Lucia directed them to walk outside toward the bench. The mothers, Lorenzo and John sat on the bench while the girls gathered behind them.

"Lucia, suppose I snap the picture so you can pose with your family, at least in this first shot?" volunteered Eva.

"That's a good idea. Thanks Eva."

The group photo and various other shots that were taken that afternoon became an important part of the family album. Granddaughter Nicole enjoyed studying them through the years. That same day would be eventful for her grandfather John. During the evening he would stroll to the DeFranco home for his first date with Gina.

Michelina, her daughters and Eva left about two P.M. Lucia and Grace straightened out whatever else needed attention and then decided to go into the house to wash. Maria Giuseppe scrubbed the towels on the washboard with a strong soap and hung them out on the line to dry. She returned to the summer kitchen to once more admire the day's work. She was very pleased with the results.

*   *   *

The silence of the evening was broken only by the melodious music from the strings of a distant violin as John strolled toward Gina's home. A light breeze rustled the leaves in the trees and a black and white cat darted across the dusty road. Soon the sun would set in the western sky, beyond the Blue Mountains. He looked forward to an evening alone with Gina. The thought of simply sitting together on the living room sofa and enjoying the nearness of her beautiful body had engulfed his senses throughout the past week. To be left alone with her without intervals of intrusion was merely a fantasy. He was well aware of the social limitations of the boy-girl relationship in an Italian family during the early twenties.

Loud chatter and a record with Caruso bellowing out an opera aria resounded as he approached the rear of the house. After he tapped gently on the door Gina opened with a smile and a "happy to see you look." At last he would be in her company regardless of the commotion.

"Sounds like a lot is going on. Are you having a party?"

"No, John. The girls have been working on the bridesmaids' dresses for Marianne's wedding. They're calling it quits and on the way out.

"Mom had completed sewing the dresses but supervised while they stitched the hems. Saturday afternoon is the perfect time because they work during the week."

A loud chorus of greetings met his entry into the kitchen. He knew the girls well and addressed them individually. Marianne and Rosa were still in the sewing room. Gina excused herself and rushed upstairs to put the finishing touches on her hair.

"Don't worry, John. We are leaving. Wouldn't think of spoiling your evening."

"Don't leave on my account," was his quick reply but only a half hearted one. They were not leaving soon enough as far as he was concerned. Dolly, Tina and Jennie were to be the bridesmaids.

"You look pretty neat in that red bow tie and red suspenders."

"Do you know something?"

"What?"

71

"I had an idea you girls would all be here so I did it all for you."

"Yeah John, you are a real 'bugiardo'."

"I never lie."

"I wouldn't bet on that."

"Hey, John," whispered Jennie, "don't be disappointed if the night doesn't go as you dreamed. When Freddy visits me the family sends a spy at various times while we simply sit. Even my little nieces get to become spies. These old folks are all alike. They just don't trust us. Who would even try a peck on the cheek with them around?"

"That means I better be careful, right girls?" John teased.

"You got the message," added Jennie.

"You all remember my sister Tina? She married Philip the farmer. Whenever he visited, little Domenic and Dennis would sneak behind the living room chair and sing 'The Farmer in the Dell'. Poor guy turned red as a beet. Tina had to bribe them to stop. She gave them each a nickel to scat." Dolly always enjoyed repeating that story.

Rosa and Marianne returned after straightening out the sewing room. The conversation stopped. The girls thanked Rosa for help and hospitality. They bid all a good evening. Dolly gave John a sly wink before departing.

Rosa greeted John and led him into the living room with Caruso and Luigi. The latter sat in the middle of the mohair brown sofa. Lace doilies were displayed on the sofa and two matching chairs.

"Buona sera, Zio Luigi."

"Buona sera, Giovanni."

"I see you are enjoying Caruso's record 'Traviata.'" The record was spinning on a phonograph with a huge horn.

" 'Magnifico.' He was and still is the best tenor in the world."

"My sisters bought a couple of his records mostly for my parents. They too enjoy him. It's too bad that he died before he was fifty years old."

"He die in 1921, three years ago." Luigi prided himself in knowing the exact statistics.

"I hear he cheated on his wife and had a few women on the side."

"I no believa," was Luigi's quick response. *Sometimes it is hard to believe that your hero has a dark side,* thought John.

Gina entered the room within minutes and sat on the sofa beside her father. Rosa sat in the other chair and Marianne sauntered in minutes later. Obviously there was one happy family and one disappointed suitor. Dante and Carlo joined them about an hour later. It was a full house but not a game of poker! John reviewed the situation and decided the cards were stacked against him.

Marianne asked if anyone wanted refreshments. Rosa asked for a tall glass of cold water. Luigi crossed his arms over his huge belly and hummed along with Caruso. Gina smiled prettily while the boys grinned. It was tough going. Luigi occupied the space that John had, during the past week fantasized would be his and Gina's alone. It finally got better. Marianne called from the kitchen, "Dessert is ready." All marched towards the long oak kitchen table where lemon pie, almond toast and biscotti were ready to be served.

They sat in unison. John had followed Gina to make sure he did not get cheated out of sitting next to her. It worked. She smelled like lilies of the valley. Her voile green dress matched her eyes and slightly covered his gray trouser. He tried to remain disaffected and participate in the conversation. Instead he stared vaguely at the kitchen cupboard with the glass doors and paper doilies. Luigi was the only one who did not have lemon pie and coffee, preferring instead, biscotti dipped in his home-brewed wine.

By nine P.M. John returned home. The several hours spent at the DeFranco residence was not entirely a bust. He had expected a romantic evening but should have known better. For now he was resigned to the fact that he had at least enjoyed sitting next to Gina at the kitchen table. Tomorrow afternoon he would again seek her companionship. Dating twice a week, Saturday night and Sunday afternoon, was par for the course.

Angelina and Concetta, John's older sisters, were frequent Sunday afternoon visitors. They lived in Bethlehem, approximately thirty miles from Roseto. Angelina and husband Ernesto had four children. Concetta and Stefano had two. The families shared a double home, with six rooms on each side. The men worked at the Steel Company. Prior to the birth of their children the sisters had worked in a clothing factory. John spent a short time with them, and extended his apology for not socializing longer. They understood and gave him their blessing.

"You will have to introduce Gina to us, John. We know the family but I don't believe we ever met her. It's been a while since we left town."

"Of course, Angie. Maybe I can introduce her to you on your next trip here." Angelina and Concetta were in their mid thirties. The children, ranging in age from six to fourteen, were presently playing ball under Lorenzo's watchful eyes lest the ball end up in the garden. Ernesto and Stefano were walking along the garden path admiring the rows of healthy plants. John extended parting gestures and walked away.

Gray clouds were visible along the western skies, pos-

74

sibly signaling the arrival of some much needed rain. Not a drop had fallen during the past few weeks and the land looked parched, while some trees were prematurely shedding leaves. A slow soaking rain would have been ideal but a downpour was more likely. A sudden clap of thunder stunned John as he approached Gina's home. Large raindrops followed by a deluge sent family and screaming guests scuffling for indoor protection. There was no shanty so they all huddled in the kitchen and living room.

"You made it just in time, John." Gina greeted him as he wiped his wet face and hair with a white handkerchief.

"I saw it coming but didn't expect it so fast. Listen you can hear the hail beating against the window. Peek out the back door. They are the size of marbles."

By now everyone was peering through some door or window to witness the onslaught. John towered over Gina as he stood behind her and pointed to some potted plants overturned by the gusty wind.

"Giovanni thesa badda."

John turned to see Luigi, brows furrowed and worried about the fate of the garden. Several of the tomato stakes had already tipped over. They did not escape Luigi's surveillance.

"I press them deep in the ground but they come down."

"Only two are tipping over Zio. Don't worry you will get everything back in shape." Luigi seemed reassured.

The storm lasted an hour and then came the bright sunshine and an evaluation of damage as they all meandered outdoors. A slate had fallen from the roof and fractured into several pieces The trees were dripping with moisture but the fresh fragrance of foliage and flowers filled the air. Luigi's compost and manure pile was much less fragrant. Outdoor furniture needed a bit of wiping.

The young people including John and Gina decided to walk around the neighborhood to look for any additional damages caused by the storm. Gravel roads contained many puddles that delighted barefoot youngsters. Outside of broken tree limbs everything appeared reasonably normal.

Gina informed John that Marianne's fiancé would be visiting the following weekend and a good opportunity to get to know each other.

"By the way what's his name?"

"Ralph Martucci."

"Did you say he is a barber?"

"Yes. His parents immigrated from some village near Roseto, Italy. He and his father have a shop in South Philly. I understand it's a pretty good business and he's well off."

"So that means Marianne will be living in Philadelphia?" John looked down inquisitively into Gina's uplifted exquisite face. "You will miss her?"

"That's for sure. It will be tough for the whole family. She won't be living in the city. He has brothers who are masons and they built a stone home for him in the suburbs."

"How did she get to meet a guy from Philly?"

"We visited relatives. They met and became interested in each other. I can't believe the wedding is only weeks away."

"You will be the maid of honor. Who is going to be the best man?"

"One of Ralph's friends. I haven't met him yet."

John felt a twinge of jealousy as he pictured Gina on the arms of another man. She searched his face as the silence became pronounced.

"I guess you will be pretty busy. What Mass will it be?"

"The wedding is on a Sunday morning at eleven o'clock. Rehearsal will be sometime on that Saturday."

"You will have to make sleeping arrangements for the guests?"

"Aunt Katie and a few cousins are helping out. You know that engaged couples cannot sleep under the same roof."

"I know all the rules, Gina. Remember we both come from the clan with the same unwritten rules."

The walkers returned to the house to find the kitchen table set with cheese, prociutti, tomato salad, green tossed salad, homemade bread and a good supply of wine. The all ate, drank and conversed chiefly about the storm and its effects. Luigi encouraged them to try the supresso, a type of salami made by relatives in Italy and sent through the mail.

*   *   *

John felt a mild despondency as he later walked home on muddy roads with deep ruts made by newly acquired cars. Leaving Gina for another week was sad enough but now the coming wedding began to affect his mental state. The vision of the best man coming from Philadelphia to be with Gina for even a few hours irritated him. Guys from the city were more sophisticated and knowledgeable than the small town "hicks" and might even give him competition. Theaters and fancy clothes were readily available in the cities and, like some Italians, he was no doubt influenced by Hollywood idol, Rudolph Valentino. Perhaps even trying to emulate his style.

John decided to stroll toward the creek and check out the water flow. He expected the water level to have risen considerably following the heavy rain. Sure enough the water was gushing rapidly toward a main tributary that emptied into the Delaware River. His mother and many other immigrant Italian mothers had washed clothes in the

77

pristine waters when they first settled here, and was once the hunting grounds of the Lenape Indians.

John sat on a familiar rock to enjoy the fresh smell of the land. Deer freely roamed the woods and rabbits were plentiful. On the first Monday of November his brother Antonio and he hunted for small game including pheasants. Nellie, their five-year-old beagle, was a faithful companion and skilled at seeking out the prey. At the moment with dark skies, only the distinct and crisp call of the whip-poor-will filled the night air. After approximately an hour spent enjoying the peacefulness of the night, John slowly followed the narrow path home.

A light in the kitchen indicated that a family member had not yet retired for the night. Most homes were dark by nine. Rosetans retired early because they had to be up by five or six in the morning. In most instances it meant walking to factories and quarries. Very few had cars for a last minute dash to work. John found Lucia pressing a garment as he carefully closed the screen door to the kitchen.

"How come you're up so late, Lucia? It's past nine I'm sure."

"It's nine-fifteen to be exact." Lucia checked the clock on the wall. "I wanted to get a few clothes pressed before going to bed. These electric irons make the job easy. Flat irons are a thing of the past. Mom still puts that heavy metal thing on the stove to heat and press. Thank goodness we finally got electricity in town. How come so late, John?"

"I took a walk down by the brook. Checked it out after all that rain. What time did Angie and Concetta leave?"

"About six-thirty."

"Did the storm do any damage?"

"No, but plenty of leaves fell all over the wet slates; nothing bad."

"I'm heading for bed. See you in the morning."

John marched up the dark hallway and stairway. His parents were asleep. He could hear his father snoring. It did not bother the mother who prided herself in falling asleep as soon as her head hit the pillow, probably due to a full day's work. Hopefully it would rub off on him. Force of habit prompted him to retire at nine P.M. even when sleep was elusive. After undressing in the dark with only moonlight filtering through the window, he hopped into bed and hoped for the best. Visions of Gina and the best man marred his thinking. Sleep conquered it within an hour.

When he walked into the summer kitchen the following morning his mother was at her station by the stove brewing a pot of coffee. Small bowls were stacked on the "oil-cloth" covered table and a metal container with forks and spoons retained its perpetual center spot. The weekly Italian newspaper *Stella di Roseto* lay on the corner.

"Good morning, Ma. I see the paper. Where's Pop?"

"Buon giorno, Giovanni. He go opena the coal shoot window."

Homes were built so that a stone-walled section of the basement in the front of homes served as coal bins. When coal was delivered, it was propelled into the bin over a metal slide inserted through a small window.

"So that means you are getting a ton of coal today?"

"Si. We almost out."

"You pay for it with this money." John reached into his pocket, pulled out a five dollar bill and placed it on the table. He was generous when it came to contributing for household needs.

"No, no, Giovanni, we pay. You give enough."

"Ma, don't fight me. You do plenty for all of us."

"Good morning, Giovanni."

"Good morning, Pop. You won't have to water the plants. That rain came down in buckets."

"Too fast, Giovanni. The ground is hard. Tonight I dig around the plants and loosen ground so it can breathe."

"Do you need a ride to work?"

"No, Nick, he drive me."

The three sat together to talk and enjoy their morning coffee. John left before his father. He had to pick up Eddie again. The sun was peeking through the early morning skies. Within minutes he saw him standing in front of his parents home holding a lunch pail.

"Morning, John! Looks like we're in for a scorcher today." Eddie hopped in and they sped away. It was only a ten-minute trip to work.

"Morning Eddie! You can bet on it. About seventy degrees already. How was your weekend?"

"Not bad. Took in a movie on Saturday night with Rita, her brother and sister-in-law. It was a good western. Not too exciting for the girls. Clara Bow or Valentino would have suited them more. Yesterday afternoon we went to the park and watched the Roseto AA play Bangor. Then came the rain. We huddled in the bleachers. The storm came so fast we couldn't escape. It was damn scary. What did you do?"

"Fooled around the truck most of Saturday morning. Picked up some feed for the animals and flour for Mom at Flory Milling Company. Antonio came along. We bought a couple of things at the hardware store. Visited Gina at night."

"How's it going?"

"Alright."

"Alright! What kind of answer is that?"

"Got to compete with Marianne's wedding plans."

"Wishing everybody would take a hike and leave you alone with Gina?"

"Yep!"

"Why so surprised. You have sisters and know the game."

"I was too young to realize what it was all about when my older sisters were courting. In my case it's like admiring pastry in the bakery window, look but don't touch."

Eddie let out a hearty laugh. "Don't let it affect you, John. Believe me if you love each other, it gets better. By the way who's the best man?"

"Some friend of Ralph's from Philadelphia. Why are you asking?"

"Wondering if even the slightest hint of any guy giving Gina a second glance would shake up the Pepper Popper."

"You know damn well I don't like it."

It was a question that made John face the truth. He felt a pang of jealousy that was not hidden from Eddie. A horse and buggy going at a minimum speed forced John to pass. The Lehigh Valley Rail grounds came into view. He made a right turn and parked a short distance away. The two friends wearing blue denim overalls and gray caps and carrying lunch pails headed toward the car shop.

*   *   *

Ralph Martucci was sitting on a kitchen chair when John came into the DeFranco home the following Saturday night. As usual Gina met him at the door and introduced him to Ralph who quickly stood to shake his hands. They joined the family around the kitchen table. Luigi was loud as usual. He couldn't have asked for better future sons-in-law and knew it. He became the leading actor on a friendly stage urging them on to eat and drink. Somebody had to be the life of the party. He was so blessed.

The mental picture John had formed of Ralph before actually meeting him was a bit erroneous. He was shorter and more slender than envisioned. Perhaps five feet seven at the most, he had light brown hair and brown eyes. The soft large hands with well-trimmed nails were undoubtedly an asset for a barber who soaped faces and gave haircuts. He was quiet and unassuming, whether due to present company was not yet clear. At twenty-seven he was president of the Italian Club in South Philly. His clear cultured voice suggested a difference in environment. Local residents not only spoke with an Italian accent but also used Pennsylvania Dutch structured sentences like "throw father down the steps his shoes."

"Ralph, what you charge for haircut?"

"A quarter for a haircut and fifty cents for shave and a haircut, Pop."

Luigi was now addressed as "Pop" instead of Zio because of the imminent marriage of his daughter and Ralph.

"Here we pay about the same."

"Do you know what I wish, Ralph?"

"Tell me, Carlo."

"That Dante and I can come to visit you and Marianne, and then go watch the Philadelphia A's."

"How about opening season of 1925?"

"Wow!" The boys yelled in unison. "We can't wait to see Al Simmons knock the ball out of the field."

"Yes, he is one of the best. It would be nice if John and Gina drove you down. I'll be glad to show you some of the historical things like Independence Hall and the Liberty Bell?"

"How about it, John? No truck, you have to get or borrow a car." By this time Dante and Carlo were highly enthusiastic.

"It suits me fine. How about you, Gina? Wanna see a baseball game and the Liberty Bell?" John turned to Gina who was in full agreement.

"Nothing like watching Roseto AA, right?" Gina looked amused.

"You can bet on big crowds to see guys who love the game and get big bucks for doing what they like."

"Yeah, our guys just love the game." Carl made a true assessment.

"Not to change the subject but how about if we all take a walk to Marty's soda fountain. Marianne's been raving about it. I hear they have delicious sundaes. It's still light so I can learn more about the area." Ralph like John was anxious for some prime time with his fiancée. He was also diplomatic by extending an all-inclusive invitation. Certainly Luigi and Rosa were not about to walk a couple of miles for sundaes. The boys had other plans. John decided Ralph was a pretty smart guy.

"We will be back shortly," Marianne informed her parents as the four casually stepped out the door.

The attractively dressed girls wore light loose dresses with the usual long strands of pearls. John was aware of Ralph's car parked in front of the home. The decision was made to walk instead of riding. He couldn't argue about that although sitting in the backseat with Gina would possibly have offered a moment of bliss. The girls held the men's hands as they walked along, feeling the warmth and protection of their relationship. Ralph pretended he was aware of this Italian village for the first time. It was almost sundown as they walked slowly down the gravel roads to Marty's, located in Bangor.

"I can't tell where the border line between these two towns is located." Ralph was curious.

"You get to know soon enough especially if you're a property owner. It's also like two different countries. They are 'Med-e-cons' (Americans) and we are 'Wops' or 'Dagos.' Most of the people we know from work are pretty nice."

"In Philly we have our ghettos including Italian, Polish, Irish. African. You name it. At the barbershop we get people from a lot of different cultures. Most of them are friendly. We become attached to them as friends and patrons."

"Any Mafia customers?"

"Probably, John, but it's usually a guess. Got to wonder when big tips are stuffed in our pockets."

"In the factory where I work with people who aren't Italian, they seem to think that we are all part of the Mafia." Marianne looked annoyed. Ralph placed his arm around her shoulder and squeezed gently.

"That will disappear when friendly bonds are established. Your people as well as mine come from Apulia, on the east coast of Italy. Mafia control has not been a problem. However, in the extreme sections of southern Italy and Sicily, where through the centuries raids by bandits invaded the country, the Mafia originally established itself as a protective force. Eventually it became corrupt like many political parties." Ralph noticed that they were approaching the bright lights of the business section of Bangor. "I suppose we are almost there?"

"Yep, that's known as the 'block.' Stores are grouped in a circle on both sides of the main streets, Market and Broadway with different types of stores and even a theater. Not many people have cars so they walk into town to shop. In the distance you will see mountains of discarded slate waste from the quarries," John explained as he still clutched Gina's hand.

"A few years ago this town was dim on Saturday nights. Only kerosene lamps lit the area. I can remember it as if it were yesterday." Gina spoke almost wistfully.

"Three cheers for the change. It's a new way of life and it happened within the last few years. Electricity, telephones, piped water and gas, automobiles and record players to name but a few. Ralph, you and others living in the city had all this long before we did."

"True, John. The burst of night lights in the city skies is impressive."

As they approached Marty's the Saturday night influx of farmers and residents from adjoining towns was much in evidence. Young people dressed in their finest clothes were on the prowl. Everyone was bent on looking into store windows, meeting friends and just walking round the block a number of times.

A small bell over the door signaled the presence of customer as they entered the drug store. Marty, standing behind the soda fountain, was wearing his customary white jacket. He immediately recognized John and the girls. Ralph was soon introduced as Marianne's fiancé. Two young girls sitting on high stools were having ice cream sodas at the fountain. John opted for one of the booths.

A heavy-set blonde woman was the single waitress. She appeared at their booth in a few minutes. Gina and Marianne ordered peanut sundaes. John and Ralph settled for tall glasses of birch soda with a dip of vanilla ice cream. Their conversation was soon broken by the appearance of a tall, blond man wearing rimless glasses.

"Got a glimpse of you heading for your booth. How are you doing, John?"

"I'm doing fine. Well I'll be damned if it isn't Elmer Snyder! Didn't recognize you with those glasses." John stood to shake hands and introduced him to Gina, Marianne and Ralph who also stood to extend greetings. "Haven't seen you since you left the car shop a couple of years ago."

"I'm back on the farm, John. My father passed away so I took over. Wouldn't sell the place for anything. Two hundred acres of good rich land that has been in the family for over a hundred and fifty years. Clifford and I do all the plowing; I have twenty-five heifers for milking."

"Who's Clifford?"

"My horse."

"Time for a tractor."

"Too expensive, John. Maybe some day. By the way, how are the guys? Miss the whole bunch of you. Give them my regards. You have a truck, stop over sometime."

"Maybe I will. How do I get there?"

"Go through Delabole and cross the highway. It's about a mile up. You'll see the name on the mailbox."

"Hey that's beautiful country."

"Bet your life! Heaven on earth. Got to go now. My wife and kid are waiting by the door." The two shook hands. All joined in to wish him well.

"While driving in from Philly I was impressed with the well-kept farms. Bucks County and the farmlands between there and here are picture perfect. The red barns with the hex signs dot the landscape. That goes for the Amish territory near Lancaster. I visited there several times. Rural Pennsylvania is beautiful." Ralph's face showed his admiration for the region.

"Did you enjoy your soda?" Marianne asked.

"Even though I'm not a soda and ice cream person, I must admit it was delicious. Of course your presence makes everything better." Ralph squeezed her hand. Marianne looked at him adoringly.

They hung around for a half hour, spoke to Marty for a few minutes and then made the trek up the hill toward Roseto which sits on a hill; Bangor rests in a valley. It is much easier coming down of course. The road back tests one's physical endurance.

The skies were dimming as they ascended the hill. A

fat groundhog waddled across the road after probably having devoured part of somebody's garden. Bats flitted around a street lamp and the hoot of an owl broke the silence of the night. The outline of the girls' home was soon in view. When they arrived and unlatched the gate, the steady hum of the sewing machine meant Rosa was putting the final touches on wedding paraphernalia. They found Luigi sitting at the kitchen table with a bottle of wine and small glass beside it, playing solitaire. "Hey you back." He gave a loud vocal greeting, whipped his cards together and asked them to sit. They obliged.

"Pop, aren't the boys back from the movies?" Gina looked curious.

"Must be a long movie. They come soon, I believe."

Rosa made her entrance wearing her brown sewing smock with the large pockets that were customarily filled with packets of needles, measuring tape and thimble. A threaded needle was pinned to her smock. Just as artists are attached to their canvass and easel Rosa was attached to the Singer sewing machine, material and thread. The girls did the housework and even the cooking when their mother was sewing. It was quite often. She enjoyed it. Nobody fought it including Luigi. He learned long ago that it was futile to thwart an artist.

"Looks like the boys aren't back yet. I thought it was a two hour movie." Rosa surveyed the group and looked at the clock. "Did you all enjoy your stroll into Bangor?"

"It was an eye opener for me, Ma. Nothing like a walk to get a handle on these little towns," Ralph explained with deep conviction.

"After you've lived here all your life you don't want to leave. I'm sure Marianne will adjust because you will be living in the suburbs. We are going to miss her, Ralph, so make sure you drive her up once in a while."

"Will do, Ma. Don't you worry."

"He had better; otherwise I'll take the train to Easton and the trolley here if I get homesick," Marianne said teasingly.

"Having you travel alone will never do. I'll gladly drive you for a visit because I too want this family atmosphere."

"Thank you, Ralph. You will always be very welcomed." Rosa was relieved.

Thankfully the conversation shifted at the sound of the boys' voices. Marianne was already beginning to get depressed.

Carlo and Dante were still excited about the movie when they trotted in. They had seen a Tom Mix movie depicting one of Zane Grey's many novels. Talkies were not yet out. Locally that event took place in the early thirties.

Rosa was the first to greet her young teen-age sons. "I was beginning to worry about you."

"We walked Joey home. That's why we are a little late."

"Did you enjoy the movie?"

"I wouldn't mind seeing it all over again, Ma. Tom Mix is my very favorite," responded Dante. "He always gets the crooks and saves the girls. Wish I had a horse like that."

Marianne was at the sink when Carlo sneaked behind her and with his thumb and forefinger pretended he had a gun pressed against her back. "Alright damsel lady give me the loot or I shall have to carry you away. Your hero will never find you."

"You don't know him, bad cowboy. He will find you even beyond the sunset." Marianne was playing out her role.

"My guys are waiting beyond the Blue Mountains right now. Don't give me any trouble damsel. You'll have to follow me."

Meanwhile Ralph shaped his large white handkerchief

into a triangle, placed it over his face, tied it behind his head. He quietly approached Carlo. "The game is up bad man. I've got you covered. Drop the gun." With that the whole family broke into uproarious laughter.

"Hey that was fun. Let's pretend some more." Ralph had put his arms around Carlo in a tight hold. Rosa thought they had enough of cowboys and guns even if it was only pretense. Luigi wanted to know why girls were damsels, and wondering if it was an unfit word for a lady.

After an additional hour with the family, Ralph and John decided to call it quits. It had been an unusual but well spent evening. They would pick up the girls next morning for Sunday Mass. Ralph drove John home and then proceeded to Marianne's aunt's home to bed for the night.

The girls, looking fashionable in their white brimmed hat and white gloves, were waiting on the porch the following morning. Their dresses were slightly shorter than usual. Marianne had a white print voile dress while Gina's was pink silk. They wore white button shoes and carried beaded purses with chains. John held the car door open for them as they stepped into the back seat.

The Our Lady of Mount Carmel Church sits majestically on the top of the hill overlooking Bangor and Roseto. It had been completed that year, 1924. Many of the local men helped build the gray stone structure resembling a small cathedral. Three marble altars, one main and a smaller altar on each side, were designed to inspire. A vaulted ceiling white pillars and stained glass windows are comparable to many European cathedrals. Semi-circular concrete steps lead up to the entrance.

The basement, during the twenties and thirties, became the center of numerous activities such as plays and graduation exercises. Rented silent films were shown to youngsters after catechism on Sunday afternoon for only a nickel. Churches of all denominations became the center of social life and many still remain such.

Ralph parked the car in front of the church. The men donned their straw hats. Both wore bow ties and suits with vests and buttoned shoes. After assisting the girls out the car they made their way up the dozen or so steps. Gina and Marianne walked together and the men behind them.

They found the church nearly filled to capacity. It was a few minutes before ten. The girls sat in the left middle aisle and the men in the section to the right. Men and women, unless married, were traditionally segregated by choice. The children sat in the front. Nearly everyone had favorite pews which they practically claimed as their own. Attendance at this and the eleven o'clock Mass included largely second generation Rosetans. The older folks attended the early Mass, many wearing mourning clothes for loved ones who passed on years ago. Their children had embraced new ideas and styles energized by such things as movies, work place and modern communication.

Hollywood had no monopoly on styles. The well-dressed also emerged in small immigrant villages and Roseto was no exception. Women relished silks, furs jewelry and beautiful clothes and made no pretense to the contrary. Expensive fabrics and well-designed clothes were high on wish lists. Besides church weddings and other occasional events their use was limited. Yet dressing well, even for a few hours, brightened their lives and improved their self-esteem. The drudgery of sitting at a sewing machine all week required a happy balance.

Rosa was quite aware of this attitude and saw that her daughters were always well dressed. As they sat in church and looked around they saw a sea of fashionable young people, men as well as women. The sixties reversed such gentility, when blue jeans and casual wear became the new trend. Then slowly exiting would be designer flowered hats, white gloves, pearls and furs. Animal rights activists took care of the latter.

The roaring twenties reflected many aspects of both the social, spiritual and economic life. It was a time of immense change much as the sixties would be. Jobs were plentiful and people were earning more and spending it. Automobiles spearheaded the economic growth. That meant highways had to be built. Villages and towns sprung up. The construction industry flourished. The garment and slate industry were working at full tilt. The Rosetans were thrifty and saved much of their earnings although earnings topped at twenty dollars a week.

Mass was over before eleven. Many of the worshippers preferred to do a little socializing in front of the church. John caught a glimpse of his friend, Victor Castellucci, and walked over to greet him.

"Only you would have the nerve to wear knickers and matching cap. Vic, where did you ever find that outfit?"

"Hey, John. Do you like it?"

"Have to think about it awhile."

"Got it in Easton at the men's shop near the square. Is that Marianne's fiancé over there?"

John called Ralph and the girls over and introduced Vic. He knew the girls well. Lucia, Grace and Julia who also had attended Mass joined the group. Vic was the recipient of all their not so flattering comments. Only fifteen-year-old Nina, last to enter the circle of family and friends, congratulated Vic on his daring taste.

"Vic, you are definitely my type of guy. Love that outfit. Even the white shoes are pretty neat for an old guy."

"Old? For your information I'm only twenty-one,

91

Nina." Vic really did not need to confirm his age. Everyone knew the ages and birthdays of everyone in town.

"Yeah well that's pretty old." Nina found delight in teasing; only certain people of course. Vic had too much self-confidence to be annoyed by that label. He regarded her as just a child who still did not quite understand.

"When you get to be twenty-one, you will be old and look like a hag."

"'Canta tu' (keep singing)." Nina giggled and thought she had won that exchange.

They gradually dispersed and John and his group walked towards the car. He asked Ralph to drop him off at his home. As usual he would meet them during the afternoon. Sunday dinner was generally spent with his parents, siblings and their families who decided to join them for his mother's homemade spaghetti, a roast of chicken and potatoes and antipasti.

* * *

Friday of that following week was warm and humid. The quick lash of the whip and screech of cartwheels heralded the approach of Theresa selling her farm vegetables. Neighborhood women gathered around the wagon to inspect the produce. It included tomatoes, red and green peppers, corn, eggplants, zucchini and cabbage. Sweet corn was the most popular because local residents rarely planted much corn. Garden space was limited. Other vegetables received preference. A tug of war often ensued when it came to meeting Theresa's prices for the produce. It was only ten A.M. and Theresa was not about to succumb to price haggling. She expected to sell everything before the end of the day and at her own prices. "Take it or leave it," she declared.

Maria Giuseppe who had gathered around the wagon with the others purchased a dozen corn on the cob and two eggplants for one dollar. With giant loaves of crusty Italian bread still rising, those vegetables were sufficient for Friday night's meal.

Hucksters coming from miles away to sell their wares were a common sight. Clothes and various types of fabrics were included among the merchandise stuffed into their small trucks. Leonard Romano sold meat from a horse-drawn yellow buggy as he canvassed the neighborhoods a few hours on Thursday and Saturday mornings. Ground beef for meatballs, flat steaks for frying or "braciole" were among the items in the buggy. Spaghetti sauce for Thursday and Sunday dinner required those items. The same meat market was within walking distance but residents were given that extra service.

Thirteen grocery stores were located in town. Two were general stores selling clothes, shoes, food and animal feed.

LeDonne Bakery operating after over a century continues in the business of turning out Italian bread and pizzas. In early days women mixed the bread dough and shaped it into loaves and carted them to LeDonne's to bake. In fact it was not at all unusual for people to have roasts and biscotti baked in the brick ovens after the commercial bread was out and while the brick ovens were still hot.

Maria Giuseppe enjoyed cooking. Her children and husband enjoyed eating. Expressions of appreciation was all the thanks she needed.

"Ma, you are the best cook. This eggplant 'parmigiana' is delicious." John was on his second helping.

"Grazia. Mangia! Mangia!"

"Won't be having sweet corn much longer. The later corn isn't as sweet and the field corn isn't my favorite."

Grace relished every bite of her corn on the cob cooked a few minutes in salted water. Early Italians used a minimum amount of butter and seldom on corn.

"Field corn be alright for roasting," Lorenzo informed them.

"I'm not that crazy about roasted corn, Pop; I know you always enjoyed a good corn roast over the low flames of a bonfire."

"Yes! For me that is best, Giovanni."

"Corn on the cob is delicious, but nothing beats fresh bread dipped in the tomato salad." Lucia enjoyed dunking in the eggplant "paramigiani" as well.

The sound of a bell alerted the diners to the fact that it was six P.M. and Pepino, the town crier, was making his weekly tour. Stores paid him to advertise their merchandise. Birth and death notices were also announced. Those he yelled out at no cost. However, by the time he got around it was old news.

"Pop, we should get Pepino here to fix that back wall. A few stones are loose.

"I tell him, Giovanni. He say he come soon."

Pepino was also the town handyman. He and his uncle had arrived in Roseto from Italy about ten years ago and moved into a shack owned by a cousin. Quite skilled at carpentry, they eventually made marked improvements so that the place no longer resembled a shack. Flowers and a small garden surrounded the property. The uncle returned to Italy but Pepino remained. Forty-eight years old, slight of stature, he wore oversized hand-me-down clothes. Whenever he was called upon for small jobs, he was given a couple of dollars, meals and a few glasses of wine that enhanced his merry temperament a notch. Understandably the most fluid singing erupted at such times.

"Ma, you can use a few extra shelves in the basement.

Let Pepino do the job," reminded Lucia. "You seem to be canning more each year."

"I'm sure Mom knows the exact count of every variety of thing canned. Right, Ma?" John smiled broadly showing his square white teeth.

"I tell you. Two hundred and ten tomatoes, fifty-two peppers with tomatoes, forty-eight peppers with vinegar, sixty-seven peaches, thirty-nine sour cherries and twenty-four zucchini. I will can more yet."

"I'm sure about that, Ma. We can't forget the sausage when the pig is butchered in November." Grace knew the schedule well.

"It sounds like a lot but don't forget the Sunday dinners with children and grandchildren. We need the extra jars," Lucia reminded them. "It's a lot of work but Mom loves it. She can relax in the winter while crocheting."

*   *   *

The week of Marianne's wedding had finally arrived and logically nothing else took precedence. Members of the wedding party were in constant contact even over the slightest details. Rosa had completed all the gowns and had overseen the final details. Arrangements with the florist had been double checked. The social aspect of the wedding took place in the bride's home. The use of public halls for wedding receptions was not yet prevalent. Usually a limited number of guests were invited to a home cooked meal. The DeFrancos extended seventy-five verbal invitations. Lorenzo, Maria Giuseppe, John, Lucia and Grace were among the invited.

A group of women volunteered to help with the meal that included antipasti, baked ziti, roast of chicken and potatoes, assorted cookies and Luigi's homemade wine. Maria

Giuseppe baked biscotti and almond toast. A wedding cake was not yet traditional.

When John arrived on Saturday evening he found everyone, including out-of-town guests, milling about, in and out of the home enjoying a buffet. It was a cool September night but some preferred the outdoors especially after the liquid refreshments.

Gina immediately ran to greet John and flashed a dimpled smile as she grasped his hands. Her dress matched her dark-lashed aquamarine eyes perfectly. He smiled back while not wanting to release her hands in any great hurry. Appearing quite handsome in his light trousers, sleeveless white sweater over his white shirt and wearing a red bow tie, Gina promptly introduced him to some of the Philadelphia guests. Ralph edged forward to clasp his hand in a strong grip.

"It won't be long now. Are you nervous?"

"Not really, John, but still worried that I might come off as a bungling idiot."

"No, you won't, Ralph. You always seem to have good sense about doing the right thing. Relax you'll do just dandy." Gina was confident about Ralph's ability to handle any situation.

"Suppose I should accidentally step on your sister's long train and create a minor catastrophe? It could happen you know."

"Like maybe an earthquake hitting the church at the exact time of the ceremony." His future sister-in-law tried to reassure him in her own gentle way. "Women plan these things pretty well. Don't worry, Ralph."

"You've settled all my fears. I shall forever be indebted to you, Gina." They all appeared amused.

"Where are you going for a honeymoon?" inquired John.

"Now that's another thing. What better way to shake off a bit of anxiety than focus on the honeymoon? We expect to drive back to our home after the reception and then the following morning head for Washington D.C."

"I feel sad just talking about life without Marianne." Gina was visibly moved by the reality of soon living without the companionship of her sister. "We always shared the same bed. I will miss her."

"I know you will, Gina. Your loss is my gain. Tough life." Ralph gave her a peck on the cheek. "Besides I'm sure John will pick up the slack."

"I'll will be glad to help this sweet lady in her misery." They were all receptive to the good humor. John placed his arms around Gina's shoulder and drew her closer.

The three separated and greeted the noisy guests. Someone had activated the player piano while a chorus of young people sang along to the tune of the recorded music as the roll kept spinning around. Ralph had rejoined Marianne and together they graciously milled among bridesmaids, ushers, flower girl, the Philly guests and a few friends. It was an event much like the present-day rehearsal party.

Luigi was in high spirits encouraging everyone to eat and drink. After spotting John and Gina he made a quick dash to join them. He held the arm of some dark, curly haired man with a parrot nose, apparently from the Philly connection.

"Giovanni meet Donato Martucci, Ralph's papa." The two shook hands and made small talk. He had arrived that afternoon. Gina had met him several months ago in Philadelphia. In his late fifties, he was a soft-spoken man. Blue eyes contrasted with his dark skin. Luigi yelled out "Madalena" and motioned for her to join them. Madeline Martucci was a small, dark-haired woman, rather plump, with a broad smile, a fuzzy black mustache, a good sense of humor and the mother of six. With that many children, humor was definitely an asset. She extended her hand when introduced.

"This is a good looking man you have here, Gina. Don't let him get away. What do you do for a living, John?"

"I'm a mechanic," replied John enjoying her flattering remarks.

"Yeah, let me look at your hands."

John extended his large strong hands for inspection. Madeline looked them over with her own less than perfect hands; almost like a man's hands from years of hard work.

"Clean hands and clean nails, keep them that way. You are pretty tall for an Italian man. Where did that come from?"

"My father. My mother is about your size."

By this time more guests had joined the group, knowing full well that Madeline was entertaining by merely being her natural self—asking questions and giving advice. She was a self-proclaimed matriarch of all Italian young people—flattering them and also advising them not to stray from the proverbial right path. "And Sonny isn't here yet?" she yelled. Sonny was a lawyer, her sister's son and the best man.

"Should be here soon. He had that speaking engagement this afternoon," reminded her husband.

"That was supposed to be over by two o'clock. Hope he didn't have car trouble."

"Remember it takes four hours to get here."

Now John knew a bit more about the best man and did not feel any easier about a possible rival for Gina's attention. His self-confidence ebbed slightly. *How can a mechanic compete with a Philly lawyer?* Sometimes stupid thoughts can make one crazy and he knew it.

John decided he needed to escape for a breath of fresh air. He grasped Gina's hand and guided her toward the outdoors. There a few others were loitering about enjoying the crisp September air, smoking or holding a drink in their hands. No sight of Carlo, Dante or Joey for the time being. Hard to tell when the rascals would appear from nowhere brandishing their type of humor.

Perhaps at last he would finally be alone with Gina. He had often contemplated this very moment. They walked around aimlessly studying the starlit skies and making idle conversation. The smell of ripe apples coincided with the approach of autumn while Italian music filled the air.

The lilac bush and quince tree grew in a secluded spot away from the reverie. As they slowly approached, John could no longer contain his so often withheld passion. After suddenly embracing he pressed her slender body in his strong arms and inhaled the light fragrance of lilies of the valley. His steel gray eyes rested on her lovely face. Alone with her at last to kiss this gentle and beautiful creature that he desperately wanted to hold indefinitely. Neither spoke. There was no need to.

She was easily receptive to his strong body and buried her head in his chest. He kissed her on the forehead, hair, flushed velvety skin and then the full lips. They separated and smiled at each other. John had expressed his feeling, although briefly, and no Philly lawyer was going to abscond with her. They walked slowly back without speaking, hoping the happy glimmer in their eyes would not expose their stolen moment of bliss.

Upon reentering the kitchen it was obvious that no one was even aware of the short rendezvous under the quince tree, with the possible exception of Dolly who gave John one of her patented winks and left it at that. There was standing room only. Food was the priority. John and Gina made straight for the living room. Dante, Carlo, Joey and a few other young people occupied that space while listening to records and quite unaware of anybody going or coming. John and Gina sat on the couch for awhile and pretended to be totally absorbed in the new melodies.

"It's about time you got here; so what took so long, Sonny?" Madeline's voice announced her nephew's arrival and the clamor intensified with introductions and explanations.

"Do you think we should go out and meet the best man, John?"

"I guess we have to," was his wary reply.

Sonny was explaining something about being detoured and losing his way somewhere around Sellersville.

"Gina come over here and meet the best man. You too, John," commanded Madeline.

At last Sonny was no longer a figure of the imagination.

There he stood; a man of medium height, heavy set, in his late twenties, with a thin mustache and slicked down black hair; well dressed in a dark suit, with a watch and chain hanging from the vest pocket. Dark penetrating eyes that he probably used to seduce his adversaries seemed a bit frightening, yet his smile was pleasant. He spoke deliberately in a well-modulated voice. "I have been looking forward to meeting you Gina." They shook hands while John cringed.

"And this is her friend, John Sabatino."

Sonny was not intimated with John's stature but smiled in a genial manner as he looked upward. "It's always nice to meet a fellow Italian. Are you also from this village?" John wondered if he meant to display superiority as a city slicker confronting a small town resident.

"Yes. My parents arrived from Italy around 1883."

"What kind of work do you do?"

"I'm a mechanic for a railroad company." John stared him down with calm gray eyes and no smile.

"Many are the times I have yearned for the chance to work with my hands. But then every job has certain drawbacks."

"I guess you're right there." John detected a bit of patronizing by Sonny.

Ralph suddenly appeared and the discussion swung into the character of the town and the value of a close-knit community. Ralph left momentarily to meet the other guests. Rosa and Luigi joined Madeline who continued to entertain.

"Is Sonny going with any girl, Madeline?" asked Rosa.

"Yeah he's going with someone." Madeline's eyes looked fiery "He is supposed to be so smart and he goes with some redhead or rather orange head that my sister likes to call a 'putana.' She works as a clerk in the courthouse, smokes a pack of cigarettes a day, likes her drinks and reads the Hollywood magazines. Can't imagine her either as a mother or good wife. Tricky Harper is bad news for us. If my sister doesn't blow her stack then I will."

"It's always heartbreaking for a mother to see children get involved with the wrong person and unable to get through to them," interjected Rosa. "Maybe it will all blow over."

"Right now it's still going strong. Thank God he did not bring her along. That's because his mother will be here by morning and fireworks would go off for sure. Look at those pretty bridesmaids. Why can't he find a girl like any of them?"

"He no look for a cook and housekeeper. He got other things on his mind. Just you wait, he change." Luigi tried to be consoling.

John and Gina quietly slipped off to the living room again where a few couples were dancing the fox trot to the tune of records. They watched. John did not dance; Gina tried in vain to coerce him. "I don't want to make an ass of myself, Gina. Sometimes when there is no one around I might give it a try."

It was a cohesive group that ate, sang and engaged in loud discussions. Sonny and Luigi were the most vocal. Their views were on opposite sides of the political spectrum as they spoke in English and Italian. Sonny spoke perfect Italian while Luigi tried to connect with perfect Italian but often reverted to the Roseto dialect. One came to conclude that Sonny was intelligent as well a braggart. Luigi maintained his ground and held his own even with this self-assured Philly lawyer. By eleven o'clock the DeFranco home was quiet and ready for a night of rest.

*   *   *

Admittedly Rosa's widely known skills would have been an asset in any tailoring establishment or dress salon. All gowns styled and meticulously sewed for Marianne and her bridesmaids were exquisite and definitely comparable to those shown in any of the best shops. Dresses were in keeping with the mid-twenties styles. Marianne wore a satin gown adorned with small-simulated pearls on the neckline and wrist. A veil cascaded over her lovely face and back from a lace cap. Although the ladies all wore pumps only the bride's were plain. The attendants sported large decorative buckles in front of shoes that matched salmon-colored velvet gowns They wore black brim velvet hats with soft feathers matching the dresses, and carried huge bouquets of white roses and hanging ribbons.

Cars decorated with streamers of crepe paper (white

for the bride's car and salmon for the bridesmaids' cars) adorned the vehicles in keeping with the colors of the gowns. Gina and the bridesmaids preceded the bride as they slowly marched up the steps of the church on a bright cool Sunday morning to the awes and delight of the many who had assembled in front of the church. It was not yet traditional for a father to escort a daughter to the altar. The bridegroom, best man and male attendants waited before the altar to receive their partner. Men wore white shirts, white bow ties and black tuxedos with satin lapels.

Ralph watched with pride and joy as his bride, her face covered with veil, strolled up the aisle of the packed assembly to the traditional wedding march. No smiles were evident among any of the wedding party. It was a very serious church event and smiles were reserved for later.

After having exchanged the vows and with the conclusion of Mass they exited down the aisle and steps trying to evade showers of rice as well as being plunked by hard almond candy. The photographer's studio was the next stop and finally the DeFranco home.

John had been a keen observer from the extreme right section of the church. Understandably his eyes were chiefly focused on Gina throughout the ceremony. He watched with interest as she and Sonny followed behind the newly wedded couple. He was only slightly taller than Gina who as usual looked radiant. Sonny seemed to be delighted with her. John was not delighted with him. He made eye contact with Gina and they exchanged smiles.

Receptions were humble by today's standard. Nothing sophisticated but plenty of delicious food and gallons of wine served in the dinning room, living room and kitchen. The guests gelled well among much hugging and kissing, the latter definitely a natural Italian trait. Luigi and Rosa floated around in a joyful mood. Music was provided by three local musicians—a violinist, piano and an accordion player. Linoleum, which covered the basement floor, was adequate for dancing to rapid Italian music as well as the slow American dances. Several Philly girls attracted a fair number of spectators when they took center stage by dancing the Charleston. When the wedding party slowly descended the basement steps to join the action everything came to a sudden stop.

John did not lose sight of Gina even as the group exited the dining area and trotted down the stairway. Of course dancing was not on his mind. Gina was! He hesitated awhile but finally decided to follow. The rapid Italian dance "tarantella" was in full swing to the music of the accordion player. The wedding party waited for a slow dance before joining the dancers. Unobserved John retreated to a secluded spot, lit a cigarette and watched.

Minnie, a slender girl in her late teens, with short dark hair, a Philly guest and Ralph's cousin, approached him and focused her glimmering eyes on him. "Wanna dance, John?" She was one of the several who had exhibited their skill with the Charlestown.

"No, sorry, Minnie, but I don't dance," was John's instant reply.

She stared at him with eyes as dark as blackberries. "Tall and handsome and doesn't dance. What a pity! Don't think Gina would mind if we would at least give it a try." She placed her arm around John's shoulders and clutched his hand. "If you can count you can handle the slow rhythm of this recorded dance number. Just follow me I'll count and instruct. It will come easily." John stared at the eyes underneath the bangs. She was forceful. He followed, stumbled a few times and felt utterly stupid.

"I'm told you work hard. Sometimes you must also have fun."

"Minnie, this may be fun for you but not me."

"Relax you're as stiff as a piece of 'bacala' (dry cod). From this dark section of the basemen no one can see. Loosen those joints. Now that's much better."

"It appears you do a lot of dancing?" John tried to look comfortable.

"My friends and I belong to the Italian club. There is dancing every Friday night. Dixieland bands, local orchestras and often just records."

John could feel her vitality as she led him around in the close quarters stopping only with the end of the music.

"Listen! This next number is really slow. Wanna swing out there and shock Gina?"

He gave her a quizzical stare. Soon they slowly joined the other dancers. Eddy and Rita were the first to stop and glare in total disbelief. John wasn't aware of anybody. For him it was total concentration as Minnie kept encouraging him along.

"Let's head that way, toward Gina and Sonny. Wait till she gets a glimpse of you gliding around like an old pro."

Ralph and Marianne danced by. They were totally engrossed in each other and hardly noticed what was happening around them. Marianne had removed her veil earlier and looked radiant and relaxed. No doubt about it, this Philly gang knew how to live it up. Most were good dancers and a few sang while dancing. When they approached Gina, she was stunned to see John with a sheepish look making a brave attempt to take it all in stride. Fred Astaire he was not, but then who cared. It was fun time. Gina smiled at John while Sonny hummed. Minnie had succeeded where she had failed. Next came a jazz number so John disengaged himself. Sonny approached his cousin to dance after Gina excused herself. Most stopped to watch as they displayed their expertise. John was relieved to finally join Gina, clutch her hand and simply watched the fast stepping dancers.

"Refreshments are being served!" came the yell from the top of the basement steps. Gradually they all made their way up to the living room where a group had gathered around the piano to sing popular Italian melodies. Trays of cookies, cannolis, biscotti and you name it covered the table. A pile of paper bags lay there for the convenience of those who wished to take some treats for home use.

Weddings gladden the heart of all in attendance and at least for a few hours, raise the level of expectations This one was totally above par, well planned with heartfelt feelings of future success.

Festivities ended before nightfall. Goodbyes were saddened by tearful separations with the departure of Marianne and the Philly entourage. Friends remained a few hours longer to help restore the home to some semblance of order. John retrieved his jacket and with thick brown hair ruffled from carting furniture around, placed one last kiss on Gina's cheek and trotted homeward. By eleven he had fallen into a deep relaxed sleep.

*   *   *

The closing months of 1924 were memorable. Gina had naturally accepted John's offer for marriage. Luigi and Rosa as expected and without reservations gave their approval. June of 1925 was set as the wedding date. Gina received a diamond ring; a cluster of small diamonds in a white gold setting.

John purchased an eight-room brick home built in 1910 for $4,000.00. Some repairs and a modern plumbing system needed to be installed, much of which he expected to do himself. Mateo Martino who owned the home had accepted a position with the Philadelphia Symphony Orchestra as a violinist. He and his family had moved to Upper Darby in November.

Music was an integral part of the town. Professor Filippo Carrescia organized the Roseto Cornet Band that ably performed in Atlantic City, Washington D.C., New York City and Newark, New Jersey, and had an impact on the musical structure of the town.

Professor Ungaro, a few years later, taught the piano and various other instruments. He was well respected as a firm disciplinarian and a top music teacher; not one to withhold a few slaps on the hand for lack of concentration and preparation. That was enough for some young people to try and quickly hang it up. Most parents, expecting their children to be exposed to some music appreciation, squashed any such attempt and hence the lessons continued. Mateo enjoyed his music and did not require the parental push. He achieved his dream of becoming a celebrated violinist.

Victorian attitudes persisted almost worldwide although such restrictive notions seemed doomed during the flapper and gigolo decade of the twenties. Not so with the local families whose outlook on morals was much too deeply ingrained to suddenly accept new standards. Change would come but at a snail's pace.

As with most engaged couples John and Gina committed themselves to a state of virginity during their pre-nuptial months. John's emergence into teen years was once met with a dire warning by his undaunted mother. "Do not get yourself in trouble with a girl or I shall chop off your manhood." A gruesome feeling swiftly overtook him. Maria Giuseppe had a way of getting her point across on his young mind.

His friend Tony Bartoni did not similarly restrain his

emotions. When Emma Luski was pregnant with his child they eloped to Elkins, Maryland. His parents were furious. To have such shame thrust upon them was unbearable. And having a son forced to marry a "no good bastard" was a horrific blow. They relented in a short time. Emma bore him five children, was an excellent cook and made sure the husband and children were her top priorities. The respect she showed Tony's parents never wavered. To top it all she always addressed them as Mom and Pop. Italian parents did not particularly relish having to cozy up to a daughter-in-law or son-in-law who addressed them as Mr. or Mrs.

Preparations for Gina and John's marriage began in earnest. Gina wanted only a bridesmaid and best man. Eddie and Rita were their choice. Sewing only two dresses would be less cumbersome for Rosa. However, drapes and curtains were needed for their home. Gina had a number of items already stacked in her cedar chest. Crotched bedspreads, scarves, bedspreads and pillow cases designed with tatting were a few of the well-crafted items accumulated over the years as part of the hope chest.

John had been spending most of his free time reviving the newly purchased home. Early Saturday morning of the first week in June, he drove down to the Bangor Hardware Store to pick up s few supplies. After parking his truck in front of the store and heading for the entrance of the store, he saw a familiar figure darting up the street and waited for him to get closer.

"Whatta you know, if it isn't Elmer Snyder. You do get off that farm once in a blue moon. How are you doin?"

"I'm fine, John. How about you?" They shook hands and were obviously happy to meet again.

"Where did you park?" inquired John. "You seem to have walked a little distance?"

"A friend of mine gave me a lift. He had to turn off

down the street on his way to work. I'm having a little problem with the truck and had to bum a ride."

"So how are you getting back?"

"My cousin works at the feed store. I'll walk there and he will drive me home at noon. That's when he quits."

"I'll be glad to give you a lift."

"Hey thanks, John. I'll surely be grateful. Also you will finally get to see my farm."

The two meandered around the store for an hour. John purchased a clothes line and white paint. Elmer searched for different sized nails to complete the barn fence and an assortment of minor repairs in the home. Unusual tools drew their attention. They finally paid their bill at the register, jumped into the truck and John drove westward at twenty-five miles an hour on a country road.

A few scattered farms were visible along the short journey. As indicated earlier most of the land was owned by a few German farmers who provided a scenic landscape of neatly planted acres of corn and oats most of which was later harvested, stored in silos and fed to the farm animals during winter months. Roadsides were covered with wild flowers such as white and yellow daises, Queen Ann's lace, orange lilies and wild fern. John was always in awe of the local landscape with the ever-visible Blue Mountains in the background and as always enjoyed the view as they rode along.

"So how is the house coming?" Elmer broke the brief silence.

"It is in pretty good shape. A few minor things yet to be done but it will be ready for inspection when family and friends come to see the bed."

"What do you mean by 'come to see the bed'?"

"A few days before the wedding, friends and relatives pay a visit and are given a tour of the house, especially the bedroom. The couple's mothers make up the bed. Drawers are left open so visitors can admire the bride's needlework."

"That sure is a weird thing. Sounds a bit crazy to have to go see a couple's wedding bed which is a private thing." Elmer withheld his humor and merely smiled "Suppose they don't own a house?"

"Well then they set up in one of the parents' homes. No matter where they expect to sleep, that bedroom will be dressed up in satin and lace or whatever else they can afford. Drinks such as anisette or any such cordial, or even small shots of whiskey and locally made candy get served. Gifts for the couple are also dropped off at that time." Elmer could merely scratch his head and peer at John through his gold-rimmed glasses looking a bit confused.

"That part about the mothers making up the bed beats me."

"I often looked upon it as their stamp of approval to the marriage."

After crossing the highway and continuing westward, Elmer alerted John to the fact they were approaching his farm.

"Slow down, John, there she is on the left."

Typical of the area farms were neatly arranged rows of various crops. As John turned into a narrow dusty road leading to a white frame home he also noted a significant acreage of land with rows of potatoes and cabbage. A small garden in the vicinity of the home contained the more common vegetables such as a few tomatoes, celery and lettuce.

John parked his truck along the side of the home. When he was about to step out he was confronted by two squawking ducks ruffling their feathers seemingly on the verge of attack. Elmer got out of the truck and shooed them away.

The four-room farmhouse was at least a century old. Years later an addition had apparently been made. Apple, walnut and hickory trees cast their shade over the residence that was surrounded by a four-foot fence. Hollyhocks, lilac and other flowering bushes lined the fence. A shaggy golden-haired dog roamed inside the fenced area and excitedly greeted his master.

The noise alerted Emma who went outdoors to check out the commotion. Wearing a white full-length apron over a blue dress and a white cap with only a small portion of reddish hair visible, she appeared shy as her husband approached with a strange visitor.

After brief introductions they proceeded to walk into a large immaculate kitchen, the more recently built section of the home. The unmistakable odor of pork and sauerkraut cooking on the black wood stove permeated the room. A long oak table occupied the center of the room Water from the well was pumped into the deep slate kitchen sink. Recently washed large tin milk containers remained near the sink. Scattered about the polished plank floor were oval braided rugs. A worn old leather Bible lay on a tall wooden pedestal next to what seemed to be a comfortable cushioned old rocker. An array of clay and glass containers from many years past occupied open wooden shelves. Attached to the ceiling and hanging over the table was a kerosene lamp.

"This no doubt is where Emma spends most of her time?" John was intrigued by the vastness of the kitchen with numerous windows open to the outdoors.

"You've got that right. My Emma sure works hard." The remark brought an appreciative and docile smile from his wife and her fair velvety skin turned a bit crimson. "See that vessel near the cabinet? Well that is what she uses to churn the milk into butter. Customers stop in to pick up gallons of milk but some we keep for our personal use. Much is churned into butter."

"Do you know the Muellers?" inquired John. "They deliver our milk each morning about five A.M. with horse and buggy."

"Sure I know them. They have a dairy farm a few miles down the road."

"John, would you like to sit and have a cup of tea and fresh apple pie," Emma asked.

"Thank you, Emma, but I must be going soon. These are busy days for me."

"I understand you will be getting married in a few weeks?"

"Yes and to be truthful I'll be glad when it's over. You are both invited. The reception is at Gina's home. Take your son Jeremy along. By the way where is he?"

"Thank you kindly, John," responded Elmer. "We expect to be there. Jeremy is spending a few days with his grandparents. Before you go I want to show you around the farm."

"I'm looking forward to it. Emma, it was a pleasure meeting you. Hope to see you at the wedding."

"Thank you. We will certainly try to attend. God be with you."

The two men strolled back into the bright sunshine. John recognized Elmer's truck parked behind the barn and headed that way.

"Let me check your truck a minute, Elmer. Maybe I can find the trouble."

"Sure would appreciate it, John. Here let me lift up the hood."

John peered down intently for a few minutes. "You've got a loose wire near the battery. Got a mall plier?"

"You betcha. Right here in the back. I will fetch it for you."

After a few jerks with the pliers the wire was adjusted.

"There you go, Elmer. All fixed. Now that wasn't so bad." John carefully pulled down the hood.

"Thank you. Now come along and take a look at the rest of this place."

"Ready and willing."

Slowly the two strolled along while Elmer indicated various points of interest on the well-kept farm. There was a hen house with over a hundred chickens and a large noisy rooster. The odorous pig sty housed three huge hogs. Snoozing on the grass beside it were two beagles not particularly caring who was about. Not so with the herd of cows that crept closer to the edge of their enclosure as if trying to nosy in on the reason for the stranger's presence and appearing a bit intimidating.

"Looks like you have a job just milking these cows?"

"Twice a day; morning and night. See the fields out there? That's hay that will soon need to be cut. Got to pray for sunshine to get an abundant and fluffy supply. Animals don't like moist hay."

"Weather can sometimes be a curse to a farmer. Right Elmer?"

"Many times it is. You learn to take the good with the bad."

As the two friends continued their walk John recognized acreages of familiar plants. "Do I see fields of strawberries?"

"Sure do. Should be ready in a couple of weeks. People often prefer to pick their own berries and even beans. Pay less that way. Others will buy from the stand we place along side the road."

"I've picked many blueberries and strawberries during my young days especially wild blueberries." John smiled.

"My friends and I did plenty of that also. Saw a few of those Italian ladies carry pails of berries on their head. They sure did a good balancing act."

"It still amazes me to watch and never see a pail tumble."

Of course as with most farming areas the pungent odor of manure prevailed. Piles of it lay around the barn area. John pointed in that direction. "I guess that is spread and plowed into the fields."

"Yep! What cometh also goeth," Elmer was quick to add.

Overall John was impressed with the neatness of the barn and in fact the farm as a whole. "I have to hand it to you for doing a mighty good job with the land."

"No big deal, it's in my blood and I love it."

"Gotta be going, Elmer. Got lots to do. Thanks for the tour."

"Whoa! Here comes Emma with something for you."

It was a warm apple pie that she had placed in a small carton and gently handed over to John. "Hope you enjoy it."

"Thank you! I'm sure I will, Emma."

The two men walked to John's truck. Elmer held the pie as John slid into his seat, retrieved the pie, thanked him and placed it on the seat beside him. They shook hands and John headed for the highway leaving behind Elmer waving his Texan type straw hat. Emma remained beside him. Overhead honking wild geese winged their way toward a small lake.

* * *

No one was at home when John returned. The women had gone shopping and Lorenzo was doing some landscaping at the rectory. The doors were open as usual. Few Rosetans bothered to lock the doors. Lunch waited for him on the stove in the shanty. It was the usual Saturday menu of veal and peppers in tomato sauce and a mixed green salad. He cut a few slices of crusty Italian bread and poured out a glass of wine. The apple pie would be shared with his family.

After satisfying his lusty appetite, he rinsed the dishes and left them in the sink. Lucia and Grace preferred it that way; not always satisfied with his efforts. He then ambled inside the home, toward the parlor (never called living room), where he slumped into one of the two large leather rockers. The grandfather clock struck two. Mother and sisters would not return for several hours. Clothes shopping for his wedding was their main objective. In a few weeks all the planning and anxiety would cease and his life would enter a new phase.

This lifelong abode with its antique flavor would be revisited occasionally and always be a special part of his life. The dark varnished colonnades between the dining room and parlor, the round oak table with black leather seat chairs, china closet containing never used dinnerware, the beaded lamp on the long rectangular table, the player piano, silver spittoon, uncomfortable queen Anne type sofa, lace curtains and crotched doilies would live on forever. There would be the dark oval frames containing grandparents' pictures always seemingly mocking him when he was a rebellious youth. Only in recent years with the advent of recordings and radio had the two rooms been used and even free of the familiar musty odor.

The slam of the kitchen screen door startled him from a melancholy mood. Nina abruptly appeared in the doorway, smiling broadly and sporting a new look—bangs and a shingle.

"What happened to your hair? Half of it is chopped off."

"Come on, John, don't you recognize the flapper look?"

"All I see is a lot of beautiful long hair missing from your head. Now you look like my little nephew." Actually the style accentuated her eyes and full lips. "Who clipped you?"

"Sammy the barber."

"No kidding! He cuts mine and all the other guys too."

"So now he even cuts girls hair." Nina strode to the wall mirror to check out her hair again as she had done for countless times that day.

"Gotta hand it to you, Nina. You are always a step ahead."

"Trying to stay that way. Aren't the girls back yet? Julia told me they would be back by the middle of the afternoon."

"It isn't the middle of the afternoon yet. Why the hurry?"

"We go to confession at four o'clock every month you know."

"What sins do you commit?" as if John had to ask.

"Venial sins, like disobeying my mother, and maybe impure thoughts. I'll be sixteen soon you know."

John only smiled at this vivacious young woman who had always been like a sister. "You will be doing a lot of penance for that."

"Yeah I know. Father Montiani can be pretty tough. But do you know what? I feel better after it's over."

"Will you stop having impure thoughts?" John peered knowingly.

"Don't want to. It just happens. Hey I'll see you later."

With that Nina sped off but not before yelling, "Manny wants to come in."

"Let him in."

Manny was their large tiger cat, highly adept at conquering his prey. Actually he was named Emmanuel after the Italian king, Victor Emmanuel, and later it simply became Manny. John petted him gently while the cat purred and rested beside his extended long legs.

Loud chatter and excitement followed by Nina's return announcing the presence of a zeppelin in the sky prompted John to go outdoors and look up alongside the others in the neighborhood, to witness a slow moving silver aircraft. A two-winged plane would often draw similar attention. In school, with teacher's permission, children rushed to windows to stare in awe at the mere sound of a plane's engine.

Not all teachers were so inclined. A few overstepped the boundary of proper discipline. History in the making did not deter a few teachers from sticking to what they thought was maintaining order. Miss Axelrod, third grade, fit that group. She on one occasion slammed Freddy Lucci's head against the blackboard for chewing gum. It caused a sizable hole in the slate board that was later covered with black construction paper and remained so for a number of years. Fortunately Freddy did not suffer a concussion. He never told his parents. They would have added an extra blow for disobeying his teacher. Talking in the classroom brought on another favorite punishment. She covered the young culprit's mouth with a patch of white construction paper using white paste as the adhesive. Miss Axelrod was not exactly easy to love.

The gawking continued until the zeppelin had disappeared from view but the excitement remained unabated. Inventions of the twenties continued to amaze.

Meanwhile John caught a glimpse of his brother Mike's Jewett slowly motoring up the street. Shopping had been done and he was driving the ladies back home. When Mike turned off the ignition in front of the gate, Nina ran to greet the shoppers as they stepped out with a multiple number of bags and boxes. John followed not far behind her.

"I know what you people were staring at?" declared Grace. "We've been watching it too."

"Can't get enough of watching planes and zeppelins?" remarked Nina.

"Grazia Michele," Maria Giuseppe looking rather haggard from the shopping trip, thanked her son. John approached to help his mother step out of the car and then walked to the driver's side to chat briefly with his brother. Mike resembled his mother as far as facial features were concerned. He was shorter than John but stockier. He and his wife Louise had five children.

"Aren't you getting out?" John asked.

"Can't, I'm supposed to meet Sal at the fire house. Wanna come along?"

"Not today. Saturday you know. I'll be going over to Gina's."

"How's the house coming? Need more help?"

"I'm in pretty good shape. Thanks anyway."

"Well if you do just call."

"Will do."

Mike left and John returned indoors to join the women and a pile of shopping bags on the table. His mother sat on a chair totally exhausted and sipping a glass of water. The girls considered their shopping trip a huge success.

"We are ready for the big day."

"It sure seems that way, Julie. Looks like you girls

bought out the stores. By the way are you practicing the 'Ave Maria'?"

"I'm giving it my best, John." Julia was not as outgoing as her sister Nina but rather shy. Both were attractive Julie possessed a beautiful singing voice and was a member of the church choir. Her rendition of the "Ave Maria" was always inspirational.

"No doubt about it, Julie, you are the best."

"Thanks, John." Julie gave him the usual tender smile.

*   *   *

The last week of June climaxed hectic months of renovations. The house was finally ready for the influx of the Friday and Saturday stream of visitors to "see the bed" and, in this case, inspect the sparkling newness of the home. Maria Giuseppe and Rosa had "made the bed." Satin spread and matching drapes were in place. Family and friends visited during late afternoon and early evening. Gina and John received them graciously by dispensing candy, cordials and whiskey, as well as White Owl cigars for the men. It was Prohibition time so people made their own homebrew. Numerous wedding gifts were piled on the dining room table for display after the colorful ribbon and gift-wrap was removed.

The furniture in the dining area was cherry wood. There was a long rectangular table and six chairs. Fine dinnerware was displayed in the china closet. Light and cheerful, the furniture was a definite change from the oak or mission furniture of the past. A dark green sofa with matching chairs provided comfort in the living room, contrasting well with light beige walls. Coffee table and floor lamps were added accessories. A few small rugs covered shiny hardwood floors. Metal table and chairs plus a sturdy icebox sat in the kitchen.

It was an enjoyable day for John and Gina not withstanding the frantic last minute activities. Eddy and Rita had been among the last guests and were sitting around the kitchen table when the doorbell rang. John opened the door to a pleasant surprise; standing before him was a grinning Elmer and wife Emma.

"We came to see the bed, John."

"What a hell of a surprise! Come on in and join an old friend." Of course the men knew each other from the car shop days. The ladies were introduced. Eddy rose when the couple entered the kitchen and greeted them with genuine delight. "If it ain't my old buddy. Glad to see you got away from the cows."

"Sorry I'm a bit late. Had to milk them before coming here."

They sat round the table obviously happy to be reunited.

"Emma, your apple pie was tops. Don't be surprised if my sisters call to get the recipe."

"Will be happy to share it."

"Better yet," added Elmer, "why not drive them to the farm? Get your mom away from the stove for a change and bring her along too. Of course you two lovely ladies are also welcomed at any time" They thanked him and hoped to see the farm.

"Something tells me it would be a real education for all of them, Elmer."

"We will be most happy to have you and your family at any time, John. Now don't you forget it. Of course Rita and Eddy need no invitation."

The conversation shifted and within an hour they were prepared to leave. Greatly impressed with the home they expected to meet again the next day for the wedding. Together they all walked toward the door. Elmer gave John an owlish look and whispered into his ear, "Nice bed. Enjoy!!"

*   *   *

At six-thirty A.M. Sunday morning, Gina opened her eyes to bright sunshine and a light breeze fluttering the lace curtains. The long anticipated day of her wedding had dawned. The unmistakable aroma of Luigi's strong Italian coffee drifted throughout the house. He was always the first up in the morning; five-thirty A.M. He checked his garden while the coffee perked. Her mother followed a half hour later. You could set your clock by their routine.

Gina glanced at the familiar furniture—oak furniture painted mint green. Young women, especially, brushed pained on any type of wood that had been around for decades only to regret the goof years later. She had opted for a cheerful bedroom.

Dante and Carlo would no longer share a bedroom. One of them would claim possession of this one.

Gina rose quickly and walked to the mirror giving her brown hair a fast brush. She dressed with ever-increasing anxiety and walked downstairs. In several hours the place would be chaotic. Rosa was alone in the kitchen. The thought of having another daughter leave the fold had mixed blessings. Learning to do without both of them would be depressing. On the other side of the equation was the fact that they had chosen respectable men. And of course the likelihood of grandchildren loomed happily in the future.

"You are up early. Did you sleep well?" as if Rosa had to ask.

"I woke up a few times to check the weather. It's going to be a beautiful day, Ma. Thank God. Kind of worried about that."

Rosa looked at her beautiful daughter, fresh and vibrant with all the eagerness of youth. She would make an attractive bride and a devoted wife. Rosa had tried to instill in her daughters what she believed were proper values.

Luigi walked in and smiled at his daughter. " 'Buona matina.' Nice day, Gina. You maybe nervous a little bit?" Luigi glanced proudly at his daughter.

"Just a little, Pop. Soon it will be all over and then I can relax."

Marianne and Ralph didn't seem to be entirely awake as they sauntered into the kitchen and wearily greeted the family. As expected, their marriage was obviously going well, and to no one's surprise.

"Sit and I'll pour you a cup of coffee. Zia Maria Giuseppe sent a bushel of biscotti. They're wonderful." Rosa placed a dishful on the table.

"They look good but I can't swallow anything," responded Gina hastily.

The others dunked the hard biscotti in their coffee.

"The boys are still sleeping I take it?"

"I should wake them up, Ralph. They have a little decorating on the cars to do yet," replied Rosa.

Conversations from the not so quite awake family ended after a brief period and a few last minute details were ironed out. Following one daughter's recent marriage the routine for the second wedding seemed less hectic. A sunny and warm June day would give wedding guests the chance to enjoy the outdoors rather than lengthy and tiresome hours sitting around the crowded indoor tables.

*   *   *

Breakfast for John was in the shanty. It was vacation time! The shanty would once again be occupied for the summer. When he walked in parents and sisters were huddling together over their coffee. Biscotti and sliced almond toast were piled on a large wooden tray for home use. The large tins filled with cookies were destined for the bride's home.

"Good morning, John. Still a few hours to change your mind," Lucia needled him briefly,

"Wouldn't do that. This is my big chance to get away from you two and the usual complaints." He smiled briefly.

"We tried to train you, John," added Grace. "Now you will be more careful about leaving dirty socks and rolled up towels in queer places. Gina will appreciate that."

"Not to change the subject, but what the heck is that goop you spread over your faces?"

"We did it all for your big day Just trying to look beautiful."

A light film of skin cream covered their faces. Actually they had soft youthful skin but this was a special day and even though unnecessary they gave it the full treatment! The five and ten cents store featured many new items to enhance beauty.

"Doubt if it will help much." John relished teasing his younger sisters. He would miss it.

The parents were enjoying the exchange of sentiments.

"Figlio mia. We no want see you leave here. It will be hard for a while. But you do right thing." His mother wiped away tears.

Deeply proud of his masculine and assertive offspring, Lorenzo simply reaffirmed his wife's mixed feelings.

The conversation happily shifted to last minute concerns such as the expected arrival of Angelina's and Concetta's families. The others lived in the area and would head directly for the church. After an hour, they left to get dressed before they were detoured in any way.

When they reappeared at ten A.M., Maria Giuseeppe was wearing a gray dress, two strands of pearls and a lace mantilla on her head. Lorenzo, lean, refined and the picture of dignity followed. He wore a light gray suit and carried a straw hat in his hand.

The gradually swelling and excited gathering included the Bethlehem families. Having just arrived they reacted with smiles of delight upon witnessing their well dressed parents. Lucia and Grace were fashionable and to no one's surprise. Stylish brimmed hats covered straight black hair. The ends had been curled up with the help of the latest fad—the electric curling iron. Pale silk flowered dresses looked well on their tall frames. High-heeled white satin pumps added a few more inches to their height.

John and Eddy's sudden entrance brought down the house. And why not? Flashing pearly white smiles, looking like models in tuxedos and white bowties, they drew loud applause.

Slyly Nina inched her way toward the male focus of attraction. Looking every bit a sparkling picture in bright yellow, she kissed the two men on both cheeks. "But aren't these two just the most handsome guys around?" she yelled with outstretched arms. Her efflorescence kindled the group into loud applause and hearty laughter. The short trip to church followed.

When the bride's entourage arrived, Luigi and Rosa were the first to step out of the car. Rosa, in her late forties, looked stunning in a light orchid lace dress and matching straw hat Luigi wore a dark blue suit and blue tie. He helped his wife as they ascended the stairs. Bride and bridesmaid remained behind until all the guests had made their way inside. Their subsequent appearance ignited a massive appreciative response especially from the pre-dominately young ladies. They had fairyland dreams of their own Prince Charming carrying them away from the mundane life. Realistically it would carry them no further than Roseto and in most cases into the same type of solid but unromantic marriage they had witnessed with their parents.

As expected Gina looked as beautiful as the bouquet of lilies she carried in her arms. Her dress was simple yet worn gracefully over her slim figure. Rosa had put a great deal of effort on the cap-like head piece which was accen-tuated with many pearls.

The eleven A.M. Mass was filled to capacity. The bride walked slowly down the aisle to the music of the wedding march. Rita who wore a light aquamarine satin dress and matching cloche hat walked ahead. Gina later confessed to being oblivious to everything except the priest standing on the altar and John and Eddy standing in front of the first pew. Her bouquet shook slightly. Hard to deny the fact that like most brides, she was nervous. Only when John's arm reached to help her up the one step to the altar, did she breathe a sigh of relief.

Father Montiani performed the wedding ceremony be-fore the beginning of Mass. John placed the ring on her fin-ger. It was not customary for the groom to be the recipient of a wedding band. Rita lifted the veil from the bride's beautiful face. John could only offer a subdued smile. As Julia sang the "Ave Maria," tears welled in Rosa's eyes. One sensed the customary deep emotions from the faithful church members as well.

After slightly more than an hour the newly-weds walked down the aisle, arm in arm, and out into the bright mid-day sunshine amid showers of rice, candy and even nickels and dimes. Excited children picked up the loot in record time. And then back to the well decorated Jewett to head the parade of an assortment of twenties cars, with horns honking down Garibaldi Avenue and along the secondary streets. People rushed out to wave and wish them well. Then it was off to the local photographers before joining the guests, approximately one hundred in all, at the bride's home.

In a relaxed and joyful mood, families came together and were simply content to be themselves and celebrate the union of this happy couple. There were tears of joy, much embracing and as usual plenty of food.

Music and dancing were low-keyed when compared to Marianne's wedding. Rosetans were not exactly fast steppers. The "tarantella" was always a must and the vocalists who gathered around the piano kept the guests in high spirits. The wine did the same. Gina and John focused mainly on each other while attempting a good impression of the fox trot. Nina and a friend let loose with the Charleston. Elmer and Emma were participants in an unfamiliar ritual. Eddy and Rita were obviously a well practiced dancing couple. The best came when Maria Giuseppe and Rosa joined others on the crowded dance floor for a torrid take of the "tarantella." That really spirited the others into a "let loose" attempt of their own but not before everyone stopped to clap in appreciation of the older women's solid performance.

It was a highly enjoyable day that ended amid tears and good wishes, as the bride and groom left for a honeymoon trip to Niagara Falls.

*   *   *

"Our Lady of Mount Carmel," was the patron saint of

Roseto, Italy. Many Italian cities and villages have patron saints. On their feast days banners and statues are paraded through streets and avenues with the faithful walking in a procession of prayerful adoration. When the Rosetans settled in America they continued paying homage to their patron saint by naming the church in her honor and observing the religious and civil celebration on the last weekend of July. Actually the feast day is July 16. In Italy the farmers were away working in the fields during mid-July so the celebration was postponed until the end of the month.

In America this event has continued. Over a century of tribute, especially to the religious aspect, has not abated but in fact flourished. The civil celebration has shrunken from the decades of the twenties and thirties when the festivities had reached new heights. Those were the years of the bandstands. Dancing not only on the band platform but also in the Marconi Club, porches, restaurants, and pubs are now but a memory. The Italian and American flags flew above porches and streets. The population tripled when relatives came from varied distances to be reunited with relatives and friends and to share in the storied festivities. It was "The Big Time"; almost like Times Square on New Years Eve. Three nights of fireworks lit up the skies of the Slate Belt region and attracted numerous residents. Parking spaces were at a premium.

Carnivals offering varied attractions such as rides, shows and the unwanted gypsies made a profitable visit. Crowds queued before souvenir stands. Local sausage and pizza stands had record sales.

In 1926 an added feature was introduced—the queen of the celebration. To qualify a young lady is required to sell raffle tickets.

The one selling the most becomes queen. The other

contestants become princesses and attendants. Proceeds are used to pay church expenses.

The Roseto "Big Time," has given the town a great amount of publicity throughout the century.

Education, long on the back burner, gradually moved to the forefront during the latter half of the twenties as an increasing number of residents entered the professional field.

Several Rosetan doctors served the community. Their fees were meager. Two dollars for a house or office visit was the ongoing fee for a number of years. Sometimes the doctors had to be satisfied with a bag of vegetables. An increasing number of students entered colleges and universities until today the percentage of professional and business people exceeds normal expectations for a small town. Uneducated but wise and industrious immigrants took responsibility for their own lives and those of their children through rough times, worked hard and were well focused on the future.

Within a span of slightly over a quarter of a century the early settlers had established a borough, built a school, borough hall, fire department, post office, churches, textile factories, retail stores, social clubs, sports teams, playgrounds, Boy Scout troops and a bank.

*   *   *

The personal lives of the residents underwent gradual changes Many were happy events. Marianne and Ralph became the parents of three children, Donato, Madeline and Louis. Gina and John had two girls. Mamie Josephine was born in 1926 and Carmela Rosa (Aunt Zee) in 1928.

It was customary to name offsprings in honor of grandparents.

When a number of children in the extended family were already bearing their name, middle names were often used. "Mamie" was in memory of Rosa's unmarried sister who had died a few years back. Her middle name "Josephine" was respectful of grandmother Maria Giuseppe. Carmela Rosa was named for Lorenzo's mother and her grandmother.

The church frowned upon non-biblical names. Popular American names such as Heather and Debbie were beginning to infiltrate the Italian community. When arrangements for baptism were made, usually a week after the birth of a child, those names were apt to be deplored by conservative, tall and gray-haired Father Ducci who expected a biblical name instead. In some cases a compromise resulted. First names remained biblical and American middle names were tolerated; for example, Antoinette Heather Maroni.

*   *   *

Sorrows, such as deaths in particular, affected the whole community. As a member of the close-knit community the deceased were mourned as family.

When Nina excitedly rushed into Maria Giuseppe's kitchen on an early April morning in 1928 the expression on her face revealed despair.

"Zia Maria Giuseppe can you come over? Julia is sick."

"Que cosa e."

"She has bad pains in her belly. We were up all night."

"I come right away. I call the girls first." Lorenzo had already left for work.

Maria Giuseppe found Julia in the fetal position, moaning and gripping her stomach. Michalina sat in a chair beside her, tears rolled down her cheeks. Lucia and

Grace joined them in a matter of minutes and recommended a doctor be called. Nina had already called family members.

The doctor arrived within minutes and recommended she be rushed to the hospital. Julia was lifted from her bed, carried bodily into a car and driven to the Easton Hospital. She was diagnosed as having a ruptured appendix. Efforts to save her failed and she died three days later.

The funeral director picked up the body at the hospital, embalmed it and delivered the casket to the home for the viewing that lasted two days. Home viewings were customary until the late thirties when funeral homes became the logical place for them and where the mourning was not as demonstrative. At home the weeping and wailing was intense much as that seen among Mediterranean and middle-east women on television today.

The outpouring of sympathy for Michelina and her family, as expected, was enormous. Maria Giuseppe and her daughters seldom left her side. The two mothers sat together even through the night, consoling, a few periods of sleep, rising occasionally to weep over the body while Michelina whispered "Figlia bella" and back to the sofa. Only the howling of John's hunting dog, Nellie, broke the silence of the long night. Dawn came and the sunlight light cast eerie patterns through the shutters and unto the wall.

A stream of viewers continued uninterrupted through the day. When John and Gina approached Nina to offer condolences she was enveloped in Eva's arms and almost lifeless. John talked to her briefly but he himself felt shattered for he too, had lost a loved one. Lucia and Grace were in the kitchen accepting food and keeping the place in order. Lorenzo was in another room where the men had congregated.

Often there is a thin line between sadness and laughter. When Pepino strolled in to view the body, the mourners were confronted with a comical situation. He had replaced a missing black button with a white one in a place where such a button was bound to evoke a smile, even a subdued one. Poor Pepino he tried to take care of his needs as best as he could. In the days that followed one of the ladies would substitute the right button.

The funeral cars and marchers made their way towards the church. There the pallbearers, nephews of the deceased, hoisted the coffin, carried it into the church and placed it on the gurney. It was covered with a cloth bearing the cross and rolled toward the altar. The church was filled with a solid sea of mourners, all wearing black.

The children's choir was outstanding. A tiny bird had winged its way through an open window and rendered its own tune. Father Montiani was obviously filled with emotion as his voice cracked but managed to give an outstanding eulogy. The coffin was reopened in the vestibule for one last look at the angelic body. More intense weeping followed. Julia was buried in the cemetery adjacent to the church.

There the coffin was slowly lowered into the ground amid intense wailing. Nina fainted into James and Eva's arms.

*   *   *

The tumultuous and exciting years of the twenties were slowly coming to a close. Lindbergh's solo flight across the Atlantic in 1927 was the ultimate feat. It triggered worldwide acclaim for the popular and daring young hero. "Lucky Lucky Lindy" became a popular record. "Yes We Have No Bananas" and Italian records like "Compare" were spinning on the record players.

It was a mid-Saturday September morning in 1928. Maria Giuseppe was busy rolling out macaroni dough in the shanty with a long thin wooden pin. She expertly tossed the dough about and rolled it on a floured board until thin. After rolling up the stiff dough jellyroll style, she sliced it with a sharp knife and fluffed the spaghetti unto another board. There was enough to feed even the unexpected Sunday arrivals for the noonday meal. Rosetans always had their dinner exactly at twelve It included some type of macaroni, roast, salad, antipasti and plenty of wine.

"Good morning, Ma. I see you are getting ready for Sunday dinner."

"Giovanni, good morning, sit. I give you a cup of coffee." Maria Giuseppe quickly reached for the pot and poured it into a large cup she had placed before her son.

"Where is Pop?"

"He come right out. He get dressed and go to the bank soon. You all come to eat tomorrow?"

"Sorry can't make it, Ma. Marianne, Ralph and the kids are coming.

Lorenzo slowly walked in with an inkbottle, a blotter and a pen in his hand and as always glad to see his son. "Good morning, Giovanni."

"Good morning, Pop. Getting ready to write a letter to Zio Donato in Italy?"

"No, no I sign my check, then I go to the bank and put in my account." John was quite used to this pen and ink routine and immediately spread a piece of newspaper on the table. His father placed the paraphernalia down and reached in his wallet for his quarry check; representing two weeks work—exactly $38.42. He dipped his pen in the small ink bottle and with precision signed the check, blotted the ink and returned the check to his wallet. John removed the various items so that his mother could pour a cup of coffee for her husband.

"When are you going to stop working, Pop?" It was a question he had asked numerous times and always received the same answer.

"I feel good so I work yet."

His father was sixty-seven and had thick gray hair and a very lucid mind. His mother was sixty-two, vibrant, with hardly a gray hair and no wrinkles.

Lucia joined them as they debated the merits of a bank account.

John was a proponent of a savings account and receiving interest. Lorenzo had some mild reservations and Maria Giuseppe was not quite ready for banking. She had always placed her money in a coffee can behind the canned tomatoes stored in the basement. Over $500.00 including a gold coin, and five silver dollars had been saved through the years. She wanted to see her money.

"What are you girls up to?"

"Same thing. Work at the silk mill is slowing down. Some say the owners may even shut down the place and go elsewhere."

"What will you do then?"

"Probably try the other factories. Bangor Clothing is looking for workers." Lucia reached for the large pot and poured a cup of coffee, added a teaspoon of sugar and a small amount of milk.

"They make men's clothing, pants and jackets. You will have to learn a new job."

"There might not be a choice." Lucia dunked a slice of almond toast in her coffee. "Of course there are plenty of shirt and blouse factories around."

"Wanna bet they don't pay as much as the silk mills?" John took a long swallow of coffee.

"I know that, but I'll have to take what I can get, especially as a beginner. Not to change the subject but how are the children? We didn't get a chance to come over during the past two days."

"Mamie is always petting her baby sister. Carmela sleeps a lot. You and Grace have been a big help with the children."

"No big deal. We're glad to help when we can."

Grace walked in; a towel wrapped around her head. She had just washed her hair, and realizing John was visiting for only a brief time, decided to forgo the setting until later.

"You look just beautiful, Gracie," John teased. He was used to his sisters' Saturday routine.

"Thanks, you always say the nicest things. By the way are you enjoying the Nash?"

"We only use it on Sunday as you well know. That's when we ride around the countryside. Otherwise it stays in the garage covered with a huge sheet that Gina sewed. She doesn't want the car to get dusty. As for me I like the pick-up Ford truck but a family needs a car."

"After years of seeing only Model T's and other black cars, I sort of like the change. A green Nash catches the eye pretty quick." Lucia dunked another slice of almond toast as she joined in the conversation.

"Yeah, General Motors is introducing a lot of new styles and not usually black. What are you girls doing today?" John knew they always planned something for Saturdays.

"We are going to a movie to see Janet Gaynor and Charles Farrell in 'Seventh Heaven.' Nina is coming along." Grace poured herself a cup of coffee and squeezed in between her mother and Lucia at the table "She goes to the cemetery every single day after work. That's about

134

it—work, cemetery and of course church. After four months she needs a change or she will go crazy." Grace secured the towel on her head.

"It's been tough going for everybody. Michelina stopped by on Wednesday. She talked and cried but as you know never dull. Gina enjoyed the visit. You see her every day, don't you Ma?"

"Sure! No want her to be alone too much. It takes time but she be all right. Julia she always be close to the heart."

John checked the clock on the wall. An hour had elapsed. "I gotta get going. Need anything from the hardware store or Flory Milling, Pop?"

"No, Giovanni. Yesterday I go with Filippe after work. You can drive me to the bank and then I go do a little work at the rectory."

"Did you order the grape for the wine yet, Pop?"

"Forty cases. It will come in two weeks; about the middle of October."

"That's when we get all the fruit flies," Grace interrupted.

"If you want the wine, you must put up with the fruit flies," John countered, staring at his sister with his steely gray eyes.

"Giovanni, you wanna take home some pizza with potatoes?"

"I'll pick it up on the way back, Ma."

"Enjoy the movies girls. Hope you don't get crazy ideas from those Hollywood actresses."

Both men rose. Lorenzo reached for his weathered old gray hat and father and son walked slowly toward the truck.

*   *   *

The crisp autumn weather soon gave way to a long winter. The grapes had yielded two barrels of fine wine. By Thanksgiving the hog had been butchered and the fat rendered and stored in large clay containers.

The sausage which dried for a week in the attic was fried and placed into hot Mason jars, sealed and turned bottom side up until the fat rose to the top to preserve the contents. Jars of vegetables and fruit were neatly stacked in basement shelves and baskets of apples and pears were stored in cool cellars. Next on the agenda were preparations for the holiday season.

Every culture has its own unique traditions brought to America from the old world. Thanksgiving is basically an American holiday. On that day the Rosetan immigrants prepared the usual Sunday type dinners; macaroni, antipasti, roast of chicken and potatoes and for dessert mixed nuts and a bowl of fruit with cheese. Turkey dinners became popular in the thirties.

Squid, "baccala" (cod), smelts and eel dishes are not exactly what the Americans see on Christmas Eve dining tables. For the Rosetans and in fact for most Italians, those particular fish were and still are part of the traditional menu. Abstinence from meat on that day was a church rule and prompted the fish menu. When that church rule was abolished fish still dominated the evening's meal. Shrimp, lobster and scallops were added to pacify the new generation, many of whom have intermarried into other cultures. Non-Italian "Med-e-gan" mates are often turned-off by squid, "baccala" and the eel.

Several days before Christmas of 1928, a heavy snow blanketed the area. Children made it to school by stepping in the footsteps of adults walking ahead of them and enjoying every bit of the deep snow. There were no snow days. After roads were cleared, both children and adults brought out sleds and headed towards the steepest hills in town—"ou heela da soombeeta" (The Jumpers Hill).

On noon of the 24th Philip, Lorenzo and Maria Giuseppe's son, dropped by to visit and enjoy the specialty of the noonday lunch. His twelve-year-old son, Tony, accompanied him. Fish odor was overwhelming as they stepped into the closed-in porch. They dusted off the light snow from their clothing. Copulinis and gloves were removed stuffed into the pockets of sheepskin coats that were hung on the brass tree. Heavy clip-on boots were dropped near the old, worn, black leather sofa.

In the kitchen his mother and sisters were busy at the stove frying "zeppolos," a wet pizza dough wrapped around a piece of fish. It was lunch for anyone who dropped in. Most preferred to have them bagged and carried home to share with families.

"Merry Christmas everybody!"

"Merry Christmas!" came back the greetings in unison.

"Filippe, you come just in time. Antonio, come here near the stove. You look cold." Maria Giuseppe grabbed her grandson's hands in her own worn hands to warm them.

"Thanks Grandma. It sure is cold out there. After I have a few 'zeppoles' I will feel better." Tony was already as tall as his father; about five feet eight. He endeared himself to everyone with his conquering smile and comical disposition.

"Figlio bella, mangia, mangia. Lorenzo and your sisters they no come?"

Larry had to go with the Boy Scouts to hand out candy for kids and Mary Jo and Jennie are stringing popcorn for the tree. "They want us to bring them some 'zeppelos,' Grandma."

"Sure, sure! We make lotsa 'zeppolos.' Maria Giuseppe hugged him tightly.

"Where is Grandpa?"

"In the cellar taking out the ashes from the furnace," Lucia responded.

"Aunt Lu, don't forget to save your Christmas tree for me."

"A promise is a promise," replied his aunt with a broad smile.

"This year my friends and I expect to collect the most trees. So far forty-two are promised to us."

Collecting discarded trees after the holidays had become an annual event for the youths of the town. It was a spin-off from an old Rosetan event that honors Santa Antone. His feast day occurs on January 17. In Italy bonfires were often a means of expressing dedication to a particular saint. The faithful stood around the fire and said a prayer to the saint. Of course one had to wonder what the real motive was for youngsters like Tony dragging away old Christmas trees. No doubt the competitive nature became the chief driving force although they did remember "Santa Antone" in their brief prayer.

"I always worry about those fires, Tony, especially when they are big."

"There are always grown-ups around, Aunt Grace. And most of the time there is plenty of snow. We build them where there are no homes close by." Tony began to consume the "zeppolos" at a fast pace. "Grandma, I'm glad you made some without fish. I can sprinkle powdered sugar on them." When his grandfather suddenly appeared Tony ran to embrace him while Lorenzo gently patted his head. "Grandpa, I hope you didn't throw the ashes out in the street. We can't sleigh-ride if you do that you know."

"Naw, naw, Antonio I throw in the garden."

"Pop, you should be thinking about switching to oil

heat and radiators instead of shoveling ashes from that old furnace."

"I think about it, Filippe."

"We have been trying to talk him into doing it," added Lucia. "Looking down through the grate at the red glow of this furnace is always scary."

"Not to change the subject but will Angie and Concetta's family be coming in tonight?"

"Yeah, Angie called this morning. The roads between here and Bethlehem are pretty clear. They will all be coming and staying overnight," Grace responded as she began to clean up. "There will be forty-two altogether."

"Before I leave do you need help setting up the tables?"

"Sure would be nice, Phil." The girls appreciated any help they could get on these special days.

The door to the porch closed. It was Gina who was removing her boots. She opened the kitchen door. "Merry Christmas everybody!"

"Merry Christmas, Gina."

"Sure smells good in this kitchen." A plaid shawl covered her head and she wore a heavy brown coat and carried a shopping bag. She had gained a few pounds in recent years but her dimpled smile was still a winner. "I have the chestnuts, cut, and ready for the oven." Lucia reached out and placed them on the kitchen cabinet.

"Thanks a million. That is a big help. Take off your coat and sit awhile. Who has the kids?"

"Maryanne is there with her three so they are having a ball. John and Ralph are in the garage fooling around with the car."

"Gina come here and taste the 'zeppolos'."

"Thanks, Ma. I'm going to do just that. You must all be tired after the frying. I'll bet most of the fish for tonight's meal is cooked."

"We got up early, Gina. The squid in tomato sauce, the anchovy sauce, the 'baccala' salad and 'baccala' soup are now in the cold cellar. The baked eel will be prepared later, as will the fried smelts and the orange salad with the olives," Lucia continued. "Of course we will cook the five pounds of angel hair pasta at serving time."

"Wish I could have helped."

"You take care of babies. That's best job for you,"Maria Giuseppe added quickly.

The frying was soon completed and they gathered around the kitchen table for a brisk conversation and lunched on some leftover minestrone, provelone and bread with a glass of wine.

"Did John tell you about Mamie?"

"No we haven't seen John for a couple of days." They all appeared concerned.

"Well yesterday afternoon Mamie complained that she had a headache and kept blinking her eyes in a weird way. I got scared and called Zia Christina next door. She came right over and guess what?"

"Mal occhio'"

"That's right, Ma. She did the thing with the olive oil and water. In a few hours she was much better."

"She probably just had a little gas." Philip was a doubter. Most of the others were firm believers and had some experience with the effects of the "evil eye."

"Guido Nardo dropped off some tool he borrowed from John and I remembered that he said Mamie was a beautiful child."

"But he no touch and say 'God bless you'." Lorenzo beat Gina to the expected answer.

"That's right, Pop."

The conversation became lively as a few others related their own take on the effects and cure of the "evil eye."

After a half hour Gina pushed back her chair and rose. "Sorry but got to get going. Will see you again at five."

Grace helped Gina into her coat and shawl while Lucia handed her a brown bag containing "zeppolos."

"Thanks for everything. " She declined Philip's offer to drive her home while insisting the short walk would do her good.

The kitchen was cleaned as only Lucia and Grace the perennial spotless cleaners, performed that task. Tables for the Christmas Eve supper were set up in the dining room and parlor, and covered with white cotton tablecloths. Next came the dinnerware, an assortment of three sets of dishes redeemed from coupons plus a few cheap finds. The five and dime store was the source of the crystal-like glasses for water and smaller ones for the wine. The silverware wasn't exactly silver as expected, but some inexpensive metal. Certainly not fit for royalty but odds were the gourmet food was fit for a king.

Describing Christmas Eve is not an easy task. Let's just say it's a "happening" that lives on until this day. Wall to wall people and tight squeezes are usually the rule but no one minds it a bit. The spiked punchbowl and the wine lend themselves to a very merry evening.

Lorenzo and Maria Giuseppe, surrounded by children and grandchildren, were in their glory. All raved about the various dishes. The kids preferred the Angel Hair pasta swimming in oil and garlic sauce or anchovy tomato sauce; not yet having come to grips with the squid sauce, or many of the fish entrees—nine in all. No one has a clear understanding why nine types of fish are traditional. Roasted chestnuts, "ceci calzones" and the fried rosette pastry were the dessert.

At seven, amid the sound of bells and "ho hos" a big fat hired Santa and his helper emerged from the horse drawn sleigh. They hoisted two huge bags of gifts over their shoulders for the nineteen grandchildren who were looking forward to his arrival. A noisy welcome awaited them. They dropped the heavy bags on the floor, near the tall tree and gave out a resounding "ho ho ho!" Mamie cried a little but the older children enjoyed it thoroughly.

Lucia and Grace had spent a good deal of time planning for Santa's arrival. Home sewn flannel stockings were filled with small wind-up and other miscellaneous toys for the younger children. Older ones were given games. Everyone received a small box of red and green hard candy depicting holiday figures. Lorenzo and Maria Giuseppe gave each of their grandchildren a five-dollar bill. An appreciative hug was received in return. By ten most had departed for their home.

Christmas Masses were crowded as expected. Lorenzo and Maria Giuseppe attended the early morning service with children and grandchildren. Following the Masses, the faithful, hardly stymied by the frigid weather, milled about in front of the church to exchange greetings. A steady stream of family and friends filed through residences until noon.

As usual, dinner was at noon. Baked ziti, roast and antipasti were on Maria Giuseppe's menu. Only Angie's and Concetta's families remained to enjoy it. Holidays had to be shared with in-laws, so the rest met their obligation and had dinner elsewhere. It was a rather quiet holiday feast in contrast to Christmas Eve.

A steady snow fell on that New Year's Eve. At midnight a few firecrackers went off in the distance. More numerous were the clanking of pots, pans and lids with neighbors yelling, "Happy New Year." Times Square it was not!

*   *   *

Ominous clouds were gathering as the New Year 1929 emerged. Rural America was much less aware of impending economic disaster than Wall Street. The jazz age of the twenties with shifting morals had left its mark. Nation wide people were buying on credit in order to obtain the many products of that era. Cars, radios, automobiles and electrical appliances were high on the "wish list." The law of supply and demand would eventually exert itself.

Lorenzo worked only a few days a week during severe winters. Home repairs that had been postponed summoned his attention during off days. Feelings of guilt enveloped those early immigrants when they succumbed to idleness—almost like it was a major sin. When income slumped during less productive periods, they survived. Wages were meager but one must remember so was the cost of goods and services. Water, electric and tax bills were but a few dollars. And there was the stored food in the basement.

Maria Giuseppe filled her long winter days baking homemade bread, cutting macaroni, and tatting. Granddaughters were always eager to join her when she made "cavatelli." Little fingers mimicked her fast press and roll production as they gathered around the kitchen table. Watching her handle the dough made a lasting impression and one they unsuccessfully attempted to mimic. Their grandmother preached and gestured constantly on the need to learn all things, especially cooking, sewing and needlework lest someday a prying mother-in-law bemoan her son's choice of a "good for nothing" wife.

As always Mamie asked, "Grammy, do you need yeast?"

"Sure, sure Mamie, you and Carmella go to store and get yeast." Regardless of whether it was needed or not, she gave the girls a nickel to go to the store. Fresh yeast was three cents, the other two cents was used to buy penny candy. Maria Donata, the storekeeper, gave them the yeast plus a small bag filled with candy. The girls never forgot.

*   *   *

Spring follows even the harshest of winters. In rural America the tiny shoots emerging from the soil lift the spirits and hopes while the seasonal cycle is once more repeated.

Saturday morning in mid-April, 1929, Nina was walking around "The Block" in Bangor. She had opted to walk the one-mile from her home to enjoy the clear sunlit day and to purchase a few personal items and a small bouquet of flowers for Julia's grave. It was the third anniversary of her death.

A familiar voice called as she approached the florist's shop. She glanced back to see Victor Castellucci running up to meet her yelling "Nina. Wait up."

"Vic, you sure are a stranger. Haven't seen you around. Where have you been?" As he came closer she noticed he was wearing gray slacks and white long sleeved sweater over a gray sport shirt—no knickers.

"I've been around. You just don't look for old men."

"You're not letting me forget that I called you an old man. That was a few years back." Nina giggled pleasantly.

"Of course not. You broke my heart."

"Yeah I'll bet. Anyway you look much better now."

"What are you doing these days?

"About the usual thing—work, eat and sleep."

"And shop," added Vic as he looked down at her brown leather shopping bag.

"And shop, too."

They were in front of the Bangor Candy Kitchen when

144

Vic asked if she would like to stop inside for a hot chocolate or coffee. It was too early for ice cream. She agreed without hesitation. They stepped into one of the more elegant places in town. White tile floors with Greek island scenes depicted on the walls and crystal chandlers created a pleasant atmosphere. A Greek family owned the business. Rows of homemade candy were displayed on part of the one wall. A fountain and stools sat on the opposite side and plenty of booths in the back. Only two were occupied. Vic led Nina toward one of the closest booths. A young lady approached in a few minutes to take their order.

"What would you like, Nina?" inquired Vic.

"Hot chocolate please."

"How about a cinnamon bun?" Breakfast was not served.

"Just hot chocolate."

"Hot chocolate, a cup of coffee and a cinnamon bun please."

The waitress returned rather quickly with the steaming hot chocolate topped with a glob of whipped cream, coffee and a large gooey bun that rested on a separate dish.

"Won't you at least taste the bun?"

"All right. It looks good. Just a bite."

"How about four bites?" Nina watched as he slowly broke off a small section with large well-groomed hands that sported a high school ring and placed it in her hand. He broke off a piece for himself. Nina studied him carefully. He had thick black hair, dark skin and very blue eyes. The latter she had never been aware of before. Actually she never took time to observe him.

"Vic, you have the deepest blue eyes. Nice against the dark skin."

The unexpected compliment unnerved him only temporarily. Girls he knew tried to be more aloof with a most eligible bachelor. Nina did not exactly fill that bill. Certainly naïve, but refreshing, especially in that light green knitted coat sweater. He studied her carefully. Bangs and straight-shingled hair framed beautiful brown eyes and sensuous full lips. Her remarks were innocent and freely given.

"Thank you," he replied and tried to change the subject. "Did you get all the shopping done?"

"Have to get the flowers for Julia's grave yet." She sipped the hot chocolate very slowly.

"Haven't talked to you since the viewing when you were out of it."

"Must have been. I don't remember seeing you." Tears welled in her eyes.

"Tragic but you must let go. Your life is important too."

"My mother did a better job of handling it. I got real bitter. She tried to console me instead of the other way around." Nina tried to avoid Vic's eyes. And creased the napkin several times. "What's new with you, Vic?"

"I'm still working at the printing company in Easton. For over a year I did the night shift. About a month ago I went back to days and got a promotion. They did away with the night shift. Work has been slowing down a bit, so a few guys were let go. Are you still at the shirt factory?"

"Yes and probably will be there till I die."

"That's a dreary thought."

"How about Marie, your neighbor, single, eighty-two and still working at that sewing machine."

"Wanna bet that's not going to happen to you."

"I hope not. Did you notice the number of women with 'motors' in their homes? Mothers can't leave their children so the bosses have bundles of work brought to them."

"Can't miss that steady buzz when a neighbor is working at one. Got to do whatever brings in the dollar, Nina."

"Are you dating anyone in particular, Vic?" The change in subject matter was as unpredictable as the charming person sitting across from him.

"No one special."

He didn't have to ask how things were going in that department for her. That type of news got around especially among the male population. Any healthy man would have pursued her but she failed to respond to any of their approaches. He asked anyway. "What's with you?"

"Like I said before, work, eat and sleep. Some Saturdays we see a movie."

"Hard to believe, especially a fun person. Just you and your mom, right?"

"Just me and my mom." There were more creases in the napkin as she averted his prolonged glance.

"So you don't even go to the church dances on Saturday nights?"

"Did go a couple of times."

"Only a couple of times?"

"It was slow dancing and boring."

A smile appeared on Vic's face. He glanced at his watch. Almost forty-five minutes had passed since they walked into the candy kitchen. "I'm enjoying this, Nina, but I have to get going." He reached for the remaining small section of gooey bun, split it in half and fed it to Nina who was momentarily frozen by the gesture. "Can't waste this. We will continue this conversation some other time."

Nina drained her cup of the remaining hot chocolate, picked up her shopping bag and proceeded to exit the candy kitchen, until Vic led her toward the candy display case and ordered two pounds.

"Candy is for you, Nina, so choose whatever you like."

"Thanks, Vic, but you are much too nice." After giving him her most genuine smile, she selected chocolate covered finger pretzels, crushed peanut chocolates and small caramel chocolate covered squares. Vic paid the bill at the cash register while Nina gently placed the white box of candy into her leather bag. They walked out into the bright sunshine.

"Where to next before I drive you home, Nina?"

"You are going to drive me home?" She looked surprised.

"You don't think I'm going to let you walk?"

"The flower shop is my last stop."

They both walked into the small empty shop that was only several doors down the street. The sound of the bell alerted a young petite woman who appeared from the back room. She quickly recognized Nina who was a frequent customer since the death of her sister. After exchanging pleasantries Nina ordered a small bouquet of daffodils. The woman left and returned shortly with the flowers wrapped in green tissue paper. Vic attempted to pay for them but Nina thanked him and insisted this was her own private thing. She paid for the bouquet and they were back on Broadway and heading for Vic's car.

"There's my car on the other side of the street, Nina," It was a 1929 tan Studebaker. They waited for several cars to go by before crossing. Vic helped Nina into the car and then walked over to the driver's side, turned on the ignition, and began the short drive up the hill.

"This is a beautiful car, Vic, and new?"

"Got it about a month ago."

Nina observed his every move as he manipulated the clutch and brakes. She was happy to simply be sitting next to him and hoping the trip was a longer one. But it was soon over. He parked his car in front of her home and rushed out to help her out with the promise of getting in touch with her soon.

She was ecstatic and so was Eva who was hoeing around the bushes in her front yard and observed the unexpected event. Nina thanked Vic profusely and watched him drive off to his appointment. Eva was waving enthusiastically, a happy grin on her face and undeniably shocked. Nina matched it with her own state of elation and yelled, "Come on over."

"You bet your boots."

Nina watched as Eva dropped her hoe and ran over to share the obvious excitement of her young friend. Breathless and displaying her gold tooth smile she hugged her "What a nice surprise! Nice guy, Nina!"

"It was a fun morning. Come on in and I'll tell you about it."

They found her mother, Michelina with Maria Giuseppe, who was apparently ready to leave when they walked into the kitchen. Exuberance on the faces of the two younger women evoked a smile on their faces before being told of the reason. They found out soon enough.

"You will never guess who drove me home from Bangor, Ma."

Almost anything that brought a little sunshine into her daughter's life lifted her own spirit. "No got idea 'Figlia bella'."

"Vic Castellucci."

"Nice boy. Long time no see him."

"He works in Easton. That's the reason, Ma." Julia's death had cemented their relationship far beyond the usual mother-daughter relationship.

"You should have seen the car he has," added Eva. "A good-looking hard-working man with a beautiful car is a good prospect. He even helped her out the car."

" 'Buona familigia,' Nina. 'Buona fortuna.' " Delight

149

was apparent over Maria Giuseepe's face as she wished her good friend's daughter much deserved happiness.

They all extolled the young man's virtues until Nina reminded them that nothing might result from just a mere encounter. And for a moment reality began to settle in. Inwardly they all hoped for the best. A letdown could be devastating.

"Must go now. It is almost noon. God bless! Nina."

"Thanks, Zia. Tell the girls to stop over when they get back from Antonia's home."

"Sure, they come."

Nothing developed that following week. Grace, Lucia and Eva were highly excited about the possibility of a budding romance. Now Nina was not quite so sure. In retrospect she thought that perhaps she should not have made a big thing of the encounter. No telephone call. But then Vic was no fool. With four other people on the party line and ready to listen to other's conversations one had to be careful when speaking on the phone. The number of rings, one to four, was assigned to each telephone customer. At least that number of people was often listening.

Nina walked by Vic's parents' home during evening hours but no Studebaker in sight.

On the Friday night of the second week a call finally came. "Going to be doing anything on Sunday afternoon?" The voice was unmistakable.

"Nothing special." Nina tried to remain calm, hoping her voice would not betray her excitement.

"Will pick you up at two for a drive along the Delaware River and Water Gap. Is that all right?"

"That sounds like fun."

"One more thing, we will be double dating with friends of mine. You will find Bruce and Janet good company. Also your Mom may feel a bit better about safety in numbers."

"Guess what? She trusts you as much as I do."

"Just a good guy, right?"

"Right. I think so anyway."

"See you Sunday afternoon around two."

"Will be ready." Nina hung up feeling weak in the knees. After telling her mother about the call, she called the girls and Eva. Upon hearing all the minute details, they were almost as excited as she. The following week would not go by fast enough.

*   *   *

It was a clear Sunday afternoon in May. Nina peeked out the window for the first sight of the Studebaker. Instead a different style car slowly approached. The blue and beige 1929 Chevrolet Coup with a rumble seat was an unusual model. Vic stepped out the front seat and walked slowly to the front wooden gate of the white frame home. He was wearing light gray pants and white sport shirt. Nina opened the door after a short knock, smiled and ushered him into the living room where her mother sat on the sofa. Vic removed his cap and approached the mother.

"Zia Michelina, I haven't seen you in months. You look well."

"Not too bad Victorio and you?" Michelina was all smiles. The Castellucci family was well respected.

"I'm fine. Hope you don't mind if I borrow your beautiful daughter for the afternoon? I will bring her back safe and sound."

"I no worry, Victorio. You have a nice day."

"Thank you, Zia. Friends of mine will be with us. They will enjoy meeting Nina."

"Grazia Victorio."

Bruce and Janice were waiting beside the coupe when Vic reappeared with Nina beside him dressed in a light blue dress and white sweater. They both agreed that she was a pretty girl. Bruce pushed back the door to the rumble seat as they walked toward the car. Introductions were brief. Eva and the girls had ringside seats behind the lace curtains of the large window at Eva's home, sharing the excitement of the moment. Vic helped Nina into the open-air seat and then hopped in beside her. It was a tight squeeze but no complaints.

"Ready for a wild ride, Nina?" Bruce added with a smile.

"This is neat," she responded.

"Hold on to you hair, Nina, and be on guard; the guy on your left needs watching," Janice teased.

Nina quickly knew she would be in fun company. Janice, a nurse, and Bruce who worked with Vic were in their mid twenties and certainly more worldly than she.

They were off to a place she had heard about a great deal but never visited. It was only a ten-mile trip to the Gap but a memorable one. The light breeze was enough to ruffle the hair and encourage a feeling of freedom and exhilaration. They rode past farmlands until they came to a junction in the road, turned left at Mount Bethel and then to Portland and along the Delaware River. The first sight of the river was an awesome sight for Nina, whose world did not extend much further than the Slate Belt and a trolley or an auto-shopping trip to Easton. Vic took on the role of a tour guide as he pointed out various interesting sites.

The Delaware Water Gap was caused by a meeting of mountains and river that created a water gorge through the cliffs between New Jersey and Pennsylvania. When they arrived at the site of the national wonder, Bruce parked his car at a viewing area where a refreshment stand and wooden benches provided a convenient spot for observing the magnificent view. They all got out of the car and walked around the small area.

Above the cliffs and etched into the rocks, either by nature or man, was the famous Indian head with headdress extending into the mighty cliffs. The Indians once rode their canoes up and down the river and hunted in the area. They left behind archeological finds such as arrowheads and pottery. On this particular afternoon several sailboats were visible in the distance. The water level was quite high. Lack of rain during hot summer months often reduced the level to a point where sediment and rocks were exposed and the flow was reduced to a minimum.

"Do you think you would like to sail on this river, Nina?" Vic was watching the awe-stricken young girl who was as refreshing to look at as the panorama around him.

"Today?"

"No, but sometime in the near future."

"That sounds exciting but I can't swim. Suppose the boat overturns?"

"We'll put an inner tube around you to ease your mind."

"Hey Vic, why don't we plan a boating trip. We can rent a boat at Dockey's. I know you're all for it, Jan."

"Count me in anytime, Bruce," responded Janice who loved any activity involving water. She was an excellent swimmer.

"Tell me, Nina, do you ever do anything besides work?" Bruce asked her point blank.

"I like to dance."

"You would say that. Now do you think I could keep in step with you." Bruce was heavy set but not fat, jovial and a tease. He put Nina at ease. "You probably like the jazz bands? Do you do the Charleston, as if I should ask?"

"I try my best," she responded with a big smile.

"Vic will have to put on his dancing shoes, I can see that." They all turned towards him for his take.

"Come on, Bruce. I'm not a bad dancer. I might surprise Nina. By the way are we going to have refreshments. It's my treat."

"In that case I'll have the best they have to offer."

"Coffee, birch and root beer; vanilla, chocolate and strawberry ice cream. Take your choice. Ladies first."

Janice and Nina chose a dip of vanilla ice cream in a tall class of birch beer while the men had hot coffee. They sat on the wooden benches until ready for the next part of the trip.

"Back into the rumble seat again, Nina?"

"Where to next?"

"The Pocono Mountains."

"The Pocono Mountains! I've heard a lot about them. Friends of mine go up that way to pick blueberries."

"There is a lot more there than just blueberries."

"Plenty of bear and deer?" Nina looked around for an answer.

"Not the main focus of the day."

"Beautiful scenery?"

"Yes and a lot more as you will soon discover," added Vic. Nina was in for in a real awakening and he was happy that he had enough foresight to plan a trip that finally got her away from porch rockers on a Sunday afternoon.

"Just being with all of you is exciting enough for me."

"We enjoy your company as well." They all smiled in agreement. "By the way would you like a kerchief for your hair?" Janice reached for a white chiffon kerchief from her pocket. "You may mind the wind in that rumble seat." Janice displayed the nurse in her.

"I think I will be alright."

"Take it anyway and play safe." Nina accepted it graciously. Vic helped her back into the rumble seat as Bruce and Janice watched until they themselves sat in front to begin the westward trip to Stroudsburg and then continue north to the Pocono Mountains. Soon the river was no longer in sight.

After skirting by Stroudsburg and beginning the thirty mile drive to the top of Mt. Pocono Nina decided to fold the kerchief into a narrow band and wrap it around her head so that the ends draped down over her shoulder. The mountain air was cooler and a brisk breeze was stirring. Vic took stock of the youthful, fresh picture she portrayed in the white sweater and chiffon scarf and not forgetting the sensuous mouth. Nina felt comfortable next to him and told him so. That's the way Nina was—fresh as the Pocono breeze. He only squeezed her hand and smiled.

The coupe sped up the mountains past souvenir shops, restaurants, gasoline stations and billboards. Also there were plenty of reminders of the once proud Indians. Their pictures and tribal names decked the fronts of many public places including ski slopes, camps and local villages. When they reached the top of one of the highest peaks, Bruce parked the car off the road. They could thus get out and thoroughly admire the view and the magnitude of the virginal beauty of the land. Splashes of white dogwood could be seen on the lower elevation. Pine forests were everywhere. All was quiet and subdued so that whispering seemed appropriate.

Ten minutes later they were heading back down the mountain until Bruce turned right and drove a couple miles along a path that was barely sufficient for the width of two cars.

"Where to now?" Nina was surprised to note that they were heading into a thick forest along a gravel road lined on either side by honeysuckles. They had picked the right time of the year to enjoy the sweet fragrance of the popular wild flower.

"Wait a few minutes and you will see." Vic was enthusiastically anticipating Nina's reaction to the approaching sight.

"Look at that stone palace ahead of us. It's beautiful. And no woods but plenty of lawns."

"That is what is known as a Country Club and what you think are lawns is actually a golf course."

"Everything is so perfect, Vic."

The four of them got out of the car and walked around a small area but no further.

"It's restricted. We stay right here. Only members are allowed. It takes a lot of money to join and only a few are chosen," explained Vic.

"Most of these people are very rich and powerful, Nina. Some are heads of corporations like Bethlehem Steel. Many professional people like lawyers and doctors are members. A few more of these country clubs are beginning to sprout in the area but can't be seen from the highway," continued Bruce.

"Look at those old men with the golf clubs strolling along. Must be as old as the huge oak tree next to the club."

"Come on now, Jan, bet you they haven't even hit eighty. That tree is at least two hundred years old."

"Pretty close. The young guys with the tennis rackets coming this way are much more my type."

"Princeton?"

"Harvard, Dartmouth or maybe Yale but Ivy League for sure."

The young men who did not acknowledge the spectators walked to their white convertible parked off the road and made a quick getaway. Several women dressed in white straw hats and pastel dresses paraded around the premise.

"Time to head home and back to reality." Bruce started back toward the car and the others followed. Within the hour Vic was in front of Nina's home helping her out of the rumble seat. They walked towards Bruce and Janice.

"Thanks for letting me use the scarf Janet."

"Keep it, Nina, as a souvenir of our first meeting. Hope we have many more."

"Thank you very much. I enjoyed it a lot."

"No need to wait for me, Bruce. I'll be walking back to my place. Thanks! See you at work." They waved and drove off.

Michelina had already opened the door for her daughter and Vic before they stepped on to the porch. Gleaming with excitement, she welcomed them back as if they had been away more than a few hours "Come inside, Victorio. I make nice tomato salad, some cheese and a glass of wine."

Vic kissed her on the forehead and apologized. "Thank you, Zia; perhaps another time. May I visit Nina again?"

"You come anytime."

That he did. Nina and Vic were married in June of the following year.

*　　*　　*

The fall of 1929 was one not forgotten for many generations to come. Though the Rosetans did not jump out of windows as was destined for a few financiers and stock market manipulators, they too felt the pinch of the economic disaster. Whatever the reason for the depression, and there were many given by historians, the major worry was how to best feed a family without a job.

For most local residents, savings were only in the realm of a few thousand dollars. Nevertheless the dollars and cents saved over many years were gone when local banks failed. People like Lorenzo suffered quietly and repeated "It's just money." Luigi bellowed out his angry feelings for all to hear and blamed President Hoover and the capitalists for the nation's troubles. As for Maria Giuseppe she still had that coffee can of money in the cellar behind the tomato jars along with the garden produce.

There were no food lines in Roseto and generally none in any similar areas of the country during those bleak days. The cities bore the blunt of the hardships. Government programs like the WPA and NRA initiated by President Roosevelt were an effort to stimulate the economy. Residents were hired on local public jobs such as building parks and roads. Teens were often employed for summer jobs. Locally many were simply hired to break stones for public structures. Those who thought it would be like cracking nuts were quickly set straight. Local masons informed them that even stone cutting was an art form that had to be approached with a certain degree of expert knowledge. Happiness for them was returning to school in the fall.

Although the garment industry was depressed, a partial workweek was better than nothing. Instead of twenty dollars a week, women had to be satisfied with ten dollars. The slate industry fared no better and winter layoffs prevailed. Resiliency was an ingrained part of the local character and most survived the tough days with minor hardships.

*　　*　　*

A high school education became the norm during the following decades and many more students who could afford it were entering college. A few were attending universities and witnessed an unusual event during the late thirties and early forties. It was the building of oval metallic structure on campus next to the science building called an "atoms masher." The atom bomb came several years later.

Mamie and Carmela graduated high school but preferred to work in the blouse factory owned by their uncles Dante and Carlo. The girls were given management responsibilities. Like Grammy Rosa, sewing was in their genes.

It wasn't "all work and no play." Young people with access to automobiles traveled to local parks. Saylors Lake was but a few miles away. Swimming, fishing, picnics and dancing were the main attractions The large dance floor at the Lake House featured big dance bands on Saturday nights during the summer months. Louis Primo, Harry James and Tommy Dorsey were notable guests during the thirties and forties.

Older folks socialized as ever and enjoyed the radio, particularly anything Italian. When Primo Carnera fought Jack Sharkey and Max Schmeling in the summer of 1933, all ears were glued to the radio. The media was highly critical of his boxing style. No matter, the Rosetans embraced him even if it was for a short run and soon forgotten. With baseball Yankee greats, Joe DiMaggio, Phil Rizzutto and Yogi Berra the love affair was eternal.

*　　*　　*

The depression years were followed by the equally difficult war years 1941–1945. Military build-up boosted the economy. The women, including mothers, entered the work force in increasing numbers. Gina's brothers, Dante and Carlo, talked her into helping them put out military shirts urgently needed by the army depot. John was not particularly in step with that idea but finally agreed. A number of blouse and shirt factories were functioning in Roseto. Practically everyone had a relative who owned a factory. Jobs were there for the asking. They socialized and worked at the same time. Many remained until their mid-eighties. Earning money and being productive at an advanced age fed their ego.

Over two hundred and eighty soldiers from Roseto served their country during World War II. Eight gave their lives. The Martocci-Capobianco Legion Post was named in honor of two brothers, George and Carl Capobianco, killed during World War II, and John Martocci who was killed during World War I.

A Catholic high school, Pius X, and Our Lady of Mt. Carmel elementary school were erected due to the intense effort of Father Leone.

A budding economy, a flood of marriages because of returning veterans, an increase number of children, later labeled "baby boomers" shaped the years of the late forties and fifties. Domenic and Mamie as well as Carmella and Neil were married during the post-war period.

*   *   *

Roseto received a dose of fame in 1962. A medical research team from the University of Oklahoma headed by Doctor Stewart Wolf established an office in the town upon the advice of local physician Doctor Benjamin Falcone. He had over the years observed that the incidence of heart attacks was less prevalent among the Italian community than other ethnic groups in adjoining communities.

Clinics were set up, and physical examinations as well as sociological studies became part of the study. The results of the research reached both the national and international scientific world and indicated that indeed heart disease from myocardial infarction for those less than forty-seven years of age was one-third the national average and significantly lower than citizens of neighboring communities. Rosetans also lived longer, many reaching well into their late eighties. When a ninety-two year-old woman was asked to give her thoughts on why people in Roseto lived longer, she quickly responded by first pointing toward the heavens and then commented, "Love God, eat good, drink a glass of wine, work and rest too; have good family and friends."

"Eating good" meant enjoying garden vegetables, pasta, homemade bread, chicken, pork, eggs and a small amount of beef for meatballs and "bracioli" added to spaghetti sauce. Most had never tasted butter until they came to America. Cattle could not be raised in that mountainous area of Italy—only chicken, sheep and hogs. And even that meat only for special occasions. Beefsteaks and other beef products were never part of the their diet. Most certainly neither were pies, cakes and rich pastry. That came later. In Italy flour to bake bread and make macaroni was not refined. The wheat germ was intact.

Roseto was a close-knit community. That too was a consideration when the study was made. Support came into play when crises arose.

They were not a sedentary people but worked hard both at their employment site and around the home.

The genetic factor was never discounted. The Rosetans were aware of the families that were most prone

161

to heart disease. They accepted it as a heredity disease that could not be challenged.

Another survey in 1971 by the same team revealed an increase in heart problems. By that time the life style had changed dramatically. A sedentary life style prevailed. Residents drove the one-mile to work and sat to watch television when they returned home. Like everyone else in the country, they snacked on the wrong foods and had little time to squeeze around the kitchen table to talk and let off steam or to receive the sound advice and opinions of older family members. In fact the dinner table soon no longer became an important entity. Family members ate at different times. Sports, meetings and jobs were but a few of the culprits and practically all parents worked.

*   *   *

Pop music stars like Elvis Presley and the Beatles had introduced the nation to a new beat. The nation "rocked and rolled." Anti-war demonstrations became prominent. The assassinations of President Kennedy, Robert Kennedy and Martin Luther King didn't lift the spirits. Changes in lifestyle and attitudes by the "baby boomers" were unsettling for the older generation while the country as a whole saw changes that were comparable to the twenties but more destructive to family life. Divorce became more acceptable and morality was governed by one's own whim. Movies, news media and television pushed for freedom in all aspects of life. Though on a much smaller scale, the Rosetans went along with the trend.

Maria Giuseppe passed away at the age of ninety-four. Lorenzo died when he was eighty-seven. Their world of strict religious belief, moral and ethnic values passed away with them.

Part Three

1989

Beth and Nicole planned to spend a day in New York City before commencing the school year. After news of Dan's infidelity had sent the family into a tailspin, the trip was put on hold. Nicole asked only to be left alone. Besides there were lesson plans to complete for the first week of the 1989 school year. Beth pressed hard and finally convinced her that she needed to take hold of her life without delay if only for the sake of the children.

On the Thursday before Labor Day they were off to New York City, via Interstate 80, in Beth's red Toyota. A misty morning changed within the hour to bright sunshine. Beth brought down the sunglasses that lay on top of her head, and sped along at fifty miles an hour on the four-lane highway. Traffic was light, only slowing down for a minor traffic accident involving a pick-up truck and a car. Highway patrolmen were at the scene.

Nicole was clasping her hands on her lap, with a far away look, and seemingly checking out the landscape; her mind was elsewhere.

The boys had been told about their father. They spent most of the evening in their bedroom playing computer games, not wishing to communicate for any length of time.

An ambulance sped by.

"Will Pappy and Grammy be coming back tomorrow?"

"Yes, they called Mom. Aunt Lu and Aunt Grace also went on that seven-day trip to the Boston area. Wait until they hear." Nicole stared out the window. "I try to put my

165

finger on at least some little thing that may have driven Dan away but I come up blank."

"Don't even try. He simply lost his marbles. Some saucy dame must have blown his mind. Sure didn't expect him to be that weak."

"Whatever the circumstances, I feel cast aside like a rag doll. A chunk of self-esteem is gone. And now how do I face people?"

"Is it too early to think about a divorce?"

"Not according to Pete. He wants to begin proceedings immediately."

For a short period neither spoke. Nicole drifted back into her own world of uncertainty.

"There is a memorial mass tomorrow morning for Grand-pop Luigi and Grand-mom Rosa at eight A.M." Beth tried to break the lengthy silence.

"Yes I know. Saw the announcement in the bulletin," Nicole replied.

"Will you be going?"

"Yes. I hope to. They have been dead for twenty years. It's hard to believe. And then the way he passed away just two months after her death. Never could adjust without her. While seldom openly displaying any public affection for each other, nevertheless, their respect for each other ran deep. Dan was openly affectionate and see what happened."

"Old folks were that way. Just a matter of the times," replied Beth absently.

Passing by run-down neighborhoods and blighted areas of New Jersey, the Twin Towers of New York City were soon visible. Rising above the morning fog they were an imposing and reassuring sight, beckoning travelers into the city. East River boats honked their horns. Beth turned right on the way to the Lincoln Tunnel hoping they would not be mired in a bottleneck. Just wishful thinking for the morning traffic moved at a snail's pace.

Finally out of the tunnel and on the city streets Beth snaked her way through busy avenues and to the first stop—the Metropolitan Museum of Art on Eighty-third and Fifth Avenue. After an attendant at the garage parked their car, they walked to the front entrance and waited with a number of others for the doors to open. Their plans were to take in the featured exhibit followed by a leisurely walk down the avenue.

The gathering crowd showed no emotion about waiting. Some read the newspaper, conversed quietly or simply hung around. When the doors were flung open, they slowly entered the main floor of the five-story magnificent building. It was not a new experience for the sisters. Beth, an art major, had enjoyed many visits here, and a few with Nicole. They strolled past the ancient Egyptian artifacts, hardly hesitating for they had inspected them on previous occasions. They took the elevator and got out on the second floor.

Large imposing Renaissance paintings hung majestically on the spacious walls. Many were permanent fixtures. On the right side of the hallway were entrances to current exhibits featuring French Impressionists, including Monet, Pisarro, Degas and Renoir. Also several paintings by Manet, Van Gogh and Cezanne. Some they had seen before but always enjoyed. The place was beginning to get crowded.

An hour later, they were ready to hit Fifth Avenue but not before stopping in the ladies' room. Sitting on a bench in the long hallway was a woman who Nicole thought looked familiar. Perhaps not, but that smile brought back faint memories. Seconds later the woman stood. She was embracing Miriam "Micky" Shapiro. They had taken an education class together at Penn State.

"For the love of Pete, Nicole, what a marvelous surprise. You look beautiful as ever. Haven't seen you since happy days. What are you doing?"

"Teaching first grade back home, Mickey. And you?"

"Math; switched my major." Miriam was a head taller than Nicole, had a boyish haircut and a toothy smile. "I'm working at a high school in Newark."

"Married?"

"Heck no. Who would have me? You?"

"Married with three children. Micky this is my sister Beth." Nicole wanted to change the subject and hoping not to get into the Dan situation.

A Hispanic woman emerged from the ladies' room. Miriam called her friend, Natalie, and introduced her to Nicole and Beth. Natalie was also a teacher in the Newark school system. They chatted briefly and exchanged addresses. Miriam and friend left to keep hairdressers' appointments.

Next stop, the Museum of Modern Art on Fifty-third and Fifth Avenue. Quiet a distance but they chose to walk prompted by ideal weather, comfortable shoes and a desire to fuse with the spirit of the city. Of course the high fashion window displays were added incentives. Winter fashions were already out. Though making frequent stops they were soon approaching the bustling area surrounding the museum.

The main entrance was flush with the street. They walked into a huge spacious room with a mass of students from a variety of countries rushing to classes held in the building. Nicole and Beth chose to rest on the benches a few minutes before proceeding further. Beth then took the escalator to the second floor to check out the exhibits.

Nicole decided to explore the exhibits on the first floor. A huge canvas by Monet titled "The Lily Pond" covered practically one entire wall. She sat on a sofa to study it and rest her weary feet. This was definitely her type of art. An equally huge canvas covered with small curly lines and massive scribble hanging on the opposite wall drew her attention. She decided her students' works were equal to it. Beth joined her sister as Nicole was studying the painting and gave her opinion. "This I do not consider a work of art but an untalented artist who had no business sharing equal space with Monet."

"That's what modern art does. You react!" laughed Beth. Maybe for a while she forgot about Dan. "There is a collection of the works of some modern artists, such as Pollack, Chagall, Mondrian and Piccasso in other rooms."

"You know I have mixed feelings about Picasso. Some of his works are interesting. Remember the one with the wash basin and pitcher covered with a man's hat?"

"Sure. You thought it was something Grand-pop would do: drop a hat wherever convenient. Without a doubt, just by studying his canvases one comes to the conclusion that he was not only a prolific painter but also a sensuous man. A private collection bordering on pornography was supposed to be quietly circulating through European capitals."

"Never heard that, but I am not surprised."

The sisters continued their tour of the museum until they called it quits and were back on Fifth Avenue. Next stop was Saint Patrick's Cathedral at Fiftieth Street and Fifth Avenue, where they slowly propelled their tired legs up the steps and inside the dimly lit hall of the beautiful and impressive edifice. A few worshippers were scattered about, kneeling in prayer, intently lighting candles or sitting and meditating. Nicole wondered how many of them had serious problems, perhaps life-threatening illness, the loss of a special loved one, loneliness. Some might have personal problems like her own that might more easily be resolved than tragic death. After a short period of prayer and meditation they were back on the avenue and heading for Saks Fifth Avenue.

Crystal and everything lavish greeted them. They enjoyed admiring the beautiful jewelry but slowly skirted the aisles to more affordable departments. After purchasing some things for their children, they decided to get something to eat. It would be lunch on the mezzanine.

They chose the stairway and headed for the mezzanine, visited the ladies room and then waited for the hostess. She led them to a small round table with a view overlooking Fifth Avenue. They placed packages on an extra chair and literally flopped down into the comfortable leather chairs, heaving a sigh of relief. A small oriental waitress with a very friendly smile appeared with the menu. Soup for the day was chili. Without hesitation they returned the menu and placed the order—one large bowl for two and two tall glasses of ice tea.

The oriental girl returned minutes later with a small tureen of chili and a dish of corn chips and gently placed them in the center of the table. Iced tea followed. Nicole and Beth quickly reached for the tea and took a hefty swallow. No silverware was required; only chips to scoop the chili—a loaded chip for every mouthful.

Within the hour they were hailing a Yellow Cab for the drive back to the Metropolitan Museum. The driver helped them out when they arrived. Nicole paid the fare and tip. The driver tipped his hat in return. They stopped to buy souvenirs for their kids from vendors and then walked to the garage. By three-thirty they were out of the Lincoln Tunnel and heading home with little out-going traffic.

The cultural side of New York City, the large stores, great restaurants are but a few things that drew Nicole and Beth and millions to that city. The seedy side of drugs and crime also prevail and the cause for many to seek safer haven in the Pocono Mountain area. In Stroudsburg housing problems and an overcrowded school system have resulted from the suddenness of the movement.

After an hour of driving, Beth opened the car window and asked Nicole to do the same "Let's breathe in that fresh mountain air. We should be home in thirty minutes."

*   *   *

Early morning sunshine filtered through the picture window when Nicole pulled back the drapes on Labor Day. Great weather! Lucia and Grace were having their annual picnic. They and grandfather John were the only siblings still living. Grandparents, children and grandchildren would be attending. Aunt Zee and Neil were going to a family reunion in Easton. By last counts over one hundred and fifty of Neil's relatives were gathering at Bushkill Park.

John and Gina had visited Nicole on Saturday afternoon. There was deep concern, anger and shock, as had been the case with the other family members. They could only offer their granddaughter heartfelt support amidst tears and consolation.

Nicole prepared a casserole of baked beans for the picnic. Yesterday she had baked a tray of assorted cookies. Everyone brought something. While the children slept she decided to give the kitchen a good cleaning. The following day was the first of the school year.

*   *   *

Lucia and Grace maintained the homestead throughout the years. Still lean, both have dark-brown, dyed "permed" hair and dress well. A twenty-two-year-old Lincoln registering less than twenty thousand miles enables them to get around the immediate area. During an emergency the "boss" always knew that he could depend on them to help in the factory. In their early eighties, they are still referred to as "the girls." They are wearing slacks and cotton tops and ready to entertain the family for the yearly picnic.

Lawn chairs were out and two tables had been extended and covered with colorful tablecloths. Plastic spoons and forks as well as paper cups and napkins had been placed on a small table. A large coffee dispenser, sugar bowl and cream pitcher rested there as well. A huge maple tree provides shade. All the fruit trees were long gone—too much trouble having them trimmed and sprayed each year.

Animals, coupes, and back house are history. A small patch of ground is cultivated for a few tomato and pepper plants. The girls enjoy gardening and the outdoors. Throughout the years they made themselves available for baby-sitting nieces and nephews. A neighbor's son mowed the meticulously kept lawn for ten dollars a week but they continued to trim the evergreen bushes themselves.

At twelve-fifteen Domenic and Mamie arrived carrying a pot of sausage and peppers and a large wooden bowl of sliced melon and assorted fruit. Grace opened the "shanty" door and they placed the food on the refinished large oak table that dates back at least a century. The small air conditioner kept the room cool. Lucia placed charcoal into the grill for "burgers" and hot dogs.

"Aunt Grace, are you all tired out?" Mamie gave her aunt a tight hug. Domenic did the same.

"Never too tired for my family."

They went out to greet and hug Lucia.

"We heard you all had a wonderful trip."

"Very nice! We had never been up that way. Martha's Vineyard, Plymouth Rock and Boston were interesting—got a history lesson."

"As usual we were glad to be back in our own bed," said Grace. "A few days away from home is enough for me. Too old I guess. Where's Pete?"

"He should be here soon," added Domenic. "He was supposed to pick up rolls at LeDonne's Bakery."

Pete strolled down the walk minutes later carrying two large paper bags filled to the top with hard rolls. "Hi, my favorite aunts. Are you girls behaving these days?" He placed the bags on the table and hugged his aunts.

"No choice. How about you?" Lucia gave him the direct stare and a smile.

"I'm always good, Auntie."

" 'Bugiardo.' Lawyers lie a lot."

"Not me."

"That's why we love you so much."

Pete gave his aunt another hug. "You girls sure look sexy today. Must be the slacks."

"We try our best, Pete, but nothing works, not even tight slacks."

"Maybe I can help out with a couple of old guys I know."

"Forget it, Pete, young or nothing," teased Grace.

"Just a couple of fast babes. I should have known."

"Who bought Eva's old house?" John yelled as he and Gina walked toward them carrying more food. In their early eighties, they looked well. Both had gray hair. John's was cropped short to within an inch of his scalp. Gina wore an orchid pants suit. John wore blue denims and white sport shirt. "I missed something while we were away."

"We were surprised too. A young couple from New Jersey bought it according to Tony." He was Philip's son who had purchased Michelina's home when she passed away. "This is the second owner since Eva died five years ago. A number of New Jersey people are crossing into Pennsylvania to live. They say taxes here are lower." Lucia motioned for them to sit in the reed rockers.

"Lu, tell him about Pee Wee's house," motioned Grace.

"You know it was sold to strangers about a year ago and made into apartments?"

"Yeah, so what happened?"

"State cops were there yesterday. Somebody got caught with drugs."

"You're kidding. The old town ain't what it used to be, is it?"

"That's for sure." Grace looked downcast.

"Did you ever think Dan was going to drop a bombshell like he did? Nothing is the same including marriage. How a man can leave children and a wife at the blink of eye is a mystery to me. Thankfully he wasn't around at the time or I would have choked him." Pete's face burned with anger.

"You are a lawyer who faces this type of situation often and yet you are surprised. It is not easy for any of us. Learning to handle it requires some effort from all of us. His day will come." Domenic had been trying to hide his own feelings of hurt and dismay.

"Do we have to talk about it again?" Grace asked. They had discussed the whole sordid story yesterday at Mamie's and Domenic's home; Nicole wasn't there. The girls had yet to face her and the children. Mamie again shook her head in disbelief. Gina and John were visibly moved.

"Will Tony and Maria be coming over, I didn't see the car parked in front of the house?" John had enough of Dan.

"Supposed to be coming over later," responded Lucia. "They went to watch the parade in Pen Argyl. Our firemen are marching in it."

"Dad, I don't know if you read the obituaries several days ago and noticed that Elmer Snyder passed away."

"Yes, I did, Mamie. He was in poor health; had suffered a stroke about two years ago. It's a blessing for Emma who had to do everything for him."

"I knew he had sold the farm and was living in Nazareth."

"He hated to sell after having it in the family for over a hundred and fifty years. The Pennsylvania Dutch farmers owned all that land beyond the Slate Belt. When developers paid big bucks for the farms, a number of them sold." John cushioned his chin with his hand as he discussed his old friend.

"I always liked those two," Gina added. "They were as natural as the ground they loved so much. We had not seen them for at least five years."

"I think the last time we saw him he was walking with a cane."

A car parked and doors banged shut. Lori and Tom's unmistakable voices were loud and distinct. Beth and Pat had arrived with their children and more food. With them came a lot of youthful bubbling action.

Nicole's and her children's subsequent entrance produced a contrived state of normalcy. Andrew and Matthew carried bats and other sports paraphernalia. Lisa had a chocolate cake and Nicole brought her share of food and deposited it on the table. Lucia and Grace enveloped Nicole tightly between them for at least a minute without a word spoken. Their genuine love and concern was readily communicable.

Grandparents John and Gina became the initial object

of the new arrival's attention. After embracing each of them they proceeded to make the rounds. The children received some humorous ribbing. Surprisingly, things went well, although Gina was teary-eyed on more than one occasion.

Game time; Pat ushered the kids as well as Nicole and Beth to the outer limits of the lawn for a game of softball. Most of the others followed. Domenic attempted a turn at bat. Best of all was the sudden appearance of John who hit the ball well, to the utter amazement of his grandchildren. One attempt was all he could muster. He laughed and returned to his soft rocker.

"Nice going Grand-pop," yelled Pat. "You are definitely a candidate for my team."

"Just give me a call, Pat. First base is my favorite position. A bit weak in the other spots." They all laughed.

Lisa hit the ball into an evergreen bush and made it to third base. Nicole's hit brought her daughter home. When Beth came to bat, Pat deliberately pitched his wife way high, and as usual, she made a stab at it and missed.

"Not fair," she yelled.

"I'm sorry, try this." The ball practically hit the ground. She swung hard, and by a stroke of luck hit the next high ball past second base.

"There, I fooled you that time, Pat."

Pat registered a wide grin across his face. "I'll have to try a fast ball next time."

Burgers, hot dogs, baked beans, salads, sausage and peppers plus an assortment of other dishes were on the table. Grace yelled, "Come and get it."

Utensils and dishes were picked up and then it was choosing food from the buffet table. An hour later they were back playing other games, including quoits with real horseshoes.

Dessert time was at about six P.M. Then came the customary moment before the school year when Lucia called the nieces and nephews to stand before her as she distributed notebooks and pencils. While peering into their eyes she handed them out with the admonition, "And make sure none of you bring home bad marks or I'll stand you in the corner." They were amused, gave her a high five and promised to do their best. Grace gave each a crisp five-dollar bill.

*　　*　　*

The call came about nine-thirty P.M. Andrew, Matthew and Lisa were in bed. When Nicole picked up the receiver to answer the phone, a familiar voice came across.

"Nicole, this is your bitchy mother-in-law."

As if the voice of Stella Grasso needed identification! It was forceful and unmistakable. She had not heard from her since Dan's indiscretion and thought it strange that she had not called earlier to voice her opinion.

"Hi, Mom. How are you?"

"How am I? Sick about the whole stinking mess. I did not even have the courage to call you and apologize for what that 'carnuto' son of mine did. Sick and disgusted that he got himself shackled to a 'putana.' Not only that but to forget that he has children and a good, decent wife."

"You should not blame yourself, Mom. Doesn't a man of his age need to take responsibility?"

"Who can figure it out? So many things go through my mind. Maybe he is part of the sixties generation that got screwed up with the rebel message."

"I don't think so, Mom. More likely it was due to a woman who had the ability to let him forget all the values instilled in him."

"Nicole, you are putting it too nicely. He is a

son-of-a-bitch who fell for a slut, bum and a first class 'putana.' God help me! Mark my word he is going to live to regret it. Now how are my grandchildren?"

"As well as can be expected. They went to bed early—school tomorrow you know."

"Nicole, I don't want to lose them. Don't keep them from me."

"I wouldn't do that, Mom."

"I should know better. My son lost a decent wife. We all love you." Stella's voice cracked.

"I love you too, Mom. How is everybody back there?"

"Madder than hell, but healthy."

"Give them my love and regards."

"Will do. Lots of luck to you this new school year and my love to the kids. I'll keep in touch."

"Thanks for calling."

"Should have done it earlier."

With the final good-byes, Nicole felt a sense of relief. So far the Grasso family was supportive. She was ready for the new school year.

*   *   *

Pertinent decorations were in place. The janitor had cleaned the classroom. Everything sparkled. Workbooks were stacked on a separate table. Twenty-three students would be entering at eight o'clock. Her grandfather John often repeated the fact that there were sixty in the first grade when he attended the Columbus School and both parents lived at home. Today a sizeable number were reared in a single-parent family much as her own. Most often the effects of such arrangements were felt in the classroom.

Well-dressed six-year-old students began to stream in at the sound of the bell. Most looked apprehensive. One, accompanied by her mother, began to cry. Nicole advised the mother to leave; that she would be fine. A student grabbed her hand and led her to one of the tables that had replaced desks.

After the Pledge of Allegiance Nicole introduced herself. "Now, I am going to pass out clip-on cards with your names. Please attach them to your shirt or blouse. Raise your hand when I call out your name."

That completed, a round-faced cheerful boy raised his hand. "Yes, Benjamin." Nicole noted his name as she approached. He stood up as he was instructed to do in kindergarten. "Mrs. Grasso, do you see that kid there?"

"Yes, Benjamin."

"His name is Gus but his mom calls him 'Gusto' because he runs like a gust of wind. That's what his mom told me. I'm his neighbor." Gus had a wide proud grin. "And do you see that kid there?" Benjamin pointed to a well-dressed youngster. "That's 'Dude'." The young boy showed no particular reaction. The youngsters all laughed. Nicole noticed he was Arthur James Jones or A. J. as she later learned the parents called him. The father was attorney Daniel S. Jones. "That is very interesting, Benjamin. Thank you for telling me; however, in class we will call all by their proper names." It became apparent to Nicole that Benjamin would keep her well informed about many things.

Workbooks were passed out and short discussions followed. At eleven-thirty they lined up for lunch. Miss Hunt, the art teacher, took over from twelve-thirty until one P.M. Good time for Nicole to eat lunch in the teachers' room. Buses arrived before two-thirty P.M. and teachers left a half hour later. Nicole felt quite happy with the first grade class.

Her own children were home by three-thirty and excited about the day. Matthew was in the sixth grade, Andrew in eighth and Lisa in tenth. The telephone would occupy their time for the next hour. Homework and dinner followed.

At about five P.M. Domenic stepped into the kitchen. Mamie quickly pressed him onto action—to deliver a pot roast to Nicole. He was presently working as a cement finisher because Bethlehem Steel was no longer operational. A few years back he was forced to look elsewhere for work. When he arrived at Nicole's home she was waiting for him near the door ,and quickly relieved her father of the pot roast.

"Dad, I could have picked it up. You must be tired after a ten hour day."

"No more tired than you. Where are the kids?"

"The boys are at the computer playing a game. Lisa is on the phone talking to her girlfriend, with whom she spent most of the afternoon."

"That's nothing new. You and your sister did the same thing. How did your day go?"

"Not bad, but you can't judge much by the first day. The kids usually are at their best. One little girl cried but soon settled down after the mother left. Guess who called last night."

"Haven't a clue," said Domenic as he sat in one of the chairs.

"My mother-in-law. Mom probably didn't get a chance to tell you. I called and told her about it when I got back from school."

"Bet Stella feels bad about her son."

"I am sure she does."

Domenic's voice alerted the boys and they came in to greet their grandfather with hugs. "You guys happy about your first day?"

"It was okay. Good part is that we didn't get much homework." Andrew grinned.

"Can't learn much that way."

"Grand-pop, do you want to play the computer game with us?" asked Matthew.

"I'd like to, but I must get home to shower and supper. First I'll say hello to Lisa and then I'm off."

*   *   *

Nicole's second day at school started in a humorous fashion. Benjamin stopped at her desk before heading for his table.

"Mrs. Grasso, how old are you?"

"Can you keep a secret?"

"Sure!" he replied. An anxious smile covered his cheerful round face.

"Well, so can I." A sweet old lady once pulled that one on Nicole. "Why?"

"You are pretty. I might want to marry you someday."

"Something tells me you will be changing your mind and I will be disappointed."

Benjamin's friendly grin reappeared as he walked slowly to his table. Spelling books were opened and each word discussed individually. The following morning they would be tested.

For the second day Nicole was often met by a puzzling stare from Jesse a pretty little auburn-haired girl.

"Is there something you would like to ask me, Jesse?"

She simply nodded and continued the assigned work.

Lunch was in the teachers' room again. Only when she had lunch duty and had to monitor the children did Nicole grab a bite in the cafeteria.

Carol Keating, the fifth grade teacher, was having lunch when she walked in. About sixty, but looking at least ten years younger, attractive with short bleached-blond hair, she also had a youthful figure. A top-notch teacher, she was also a strict disciplinarian. Kids knew that even before they walked into her classroom. Divorced at least twenty-five years ago, she never remarried. Her only daughter, Sharon, married a doctor and they had three children.

"Nicole, I did not have an opportunity to talk to you yesterday. How was your summer?"

"Very nice until two weeks ago."

"What happened then?" Nicole thought everybody knew by now, yet nobody mentioned it even if they did know.

"Dan asked for a divorce quite unexpectedly."

"For heavens sake! I'm deeply shocked." She put down her unfinished sandwich.

Nicole felt free to talk to Carol. After all she was almost as old as her mother. And besides had experienced a share of marital unhappiness herself.

"He found someone he liked better, Carol."

"Wasn't he working for some pharmaceutical company?"

"Yes. He met this woman in Texas and now wants to marry her." Nicole did not tell her about the pregnancy.

"I am truly sorry, Nicole. I wish I could help you in some way. It must be a difficult time for you?"

"My family has kept me sane."

"You do have strong family ties so you will work it out." Carol finished her small carton of milk. "As you know I also went through somewhat the same situation."

"What happened in your case, Carol?"

"I married Paul at twenty-three. He was a very handsome man. That was his only asset. After a year in college, he had dropped out to take a political job. His family always managed to pull strings and eventually got him a job that did not last long, as is par for the course when there is a party shift. Meanwhile we had our daughter, Sharon, who was two at the time. I placed her in a child-care facility while I was teaching. He went from job to job. During one six-month lay-off he was satisfied with merely collecting unemployment benefits. The bottom line—he was simply lazy. We had our home mortgage to pay besides everything else."

"You were patient during all that time?"

"Maybe it was love. He enjoyed humiliating me. When he continued berating me because of his own low self-esteem my patience wore thin. Besides I was certain he was cheating on me." Carol began to fiddle with the milk carton.

"And you finally acted?"

"Nicole, I told him to get out of the house or I would."

"So he did?"

"No, I did. He was away one day. I hired a moving van and moved to an apartment with Sharon. I left him a bed and a few other items or what the law required." Carol registered a wide smile. She was obviously a woman who took control.

"What happened to him?"

"Sharon hears from him once in a while. He remarried twice and divorced both times."

"So now he has to work since he has no wife to support him?"

"My daughter tells me he is working in a department store in Maryland—in men's wear." Carol glanced at the wall clock. "Nicole, I would love to continue this conversation, but my class is due to return to their homeroom."

"It was a pleasure talking to you, Carol."

"Thank you! I'll listen anytime you wish to talk, Nicole."

The rest of the week went well and nothing of significance occurred. On Friday afternoon she was in her SUV looking forward to a restful weekend.

Saturday morning the children remained in bed until eight-thirty. Much of the housework was done before they were up. Lisa was the first at the breakfast table and settled for a bowl of cold cereal and orange juice. Their first football game was against Nazareth. Bangor felt confident about t winning. She promised to have her bedroom clean before leaving.

Matthew had a glass of orange juice and spent the next hour before the television. He expected to play with his friend Adam, ride their bikes and watch a movie that Adam's mother had rented. Andrew and his friend were going to the park and play basketball. Nicole planed to do grocery shopping. Matthew decided to go along. Chances of stopping at the drug store were good. They had a video he wanted and perhaps his mother would buy it for him. By eleven A.M. they were home. Matthew got his video.

Andrew had already left for the park and Nicole had just finished putting the groceries away when she heard a soft knock on the kitchen door. She opened to see her grandfather John smiling and carrying a package.

"Gramps, come on in. Here let me take that from you."

"It's a pizza with potatoes. Your grandmother just got it out of the oven."

"Thanks a million. We will all enjoy it as you very well know."

"She always aims to please," he said while giving his granddaughter a warm smile.

"I know that very well and am blessed."

"So am I," added John as his face beamed with pride.

Nicole was proud of her grandparents who were still active and very modern.

"Grand-pop, would you like a cup of coffee. It's fresh."

"No thanks, Honey. I have some things to get at the drug store and I must stop at the garage for gasoline and oil check. Need anything?"

"Since you asked, do me a favor and buy me a newspaper. I stopped there earlier but forgot it."

"No problem. See you later." John drove away in his 1987 black Chevy.

*   *   *

At two P.M. the telephone rang. None of he children were home. Matthew had eaten some pizza and grabbed an apple before going out to play with Adam an hour ago. Nicole immediately answered and recognized Lena Romano's voice.

"Nicole, from my window facing the park I saw a bunch of kids running around like crazy, laughing and a bit unsteady. It was too suspicious to ignore so I took a walk down there. I found several men already involved in trying to help. Upon checking things out I saw that Andrew was with them. It seems the kids were drinking wine. I don't know how they got it."

"Oh for heavens sake! Thanks for calling, Lena. I'll be right there." Nicole put both hands to her head. She was visibly shaken and rushed out to her car. Her grandfather was getting out of his car with the newspaper in hand. When she explained what had happened, he asked her to get in the car. They would go to the park together.

The scene that confronted them was not pretty. About eight boys were present. Several were vomiting. Others were just hanging around with silly grins on their faces. Tony Caiazzo and Al Russo were the two men trying to settle the boys. Nicole immediately ran to Andrew who was

185

sitting on the ground looking totally bewildered. John approached the two men whom he knew well.

"Where in the hell did these kids get the wine?"

"As far as I can understand from talking to one of the boys, John, they sneaked a gallon from 'Luigi ou longa's' cellar. He still makes a few barrels a year. He is a grandfather to one of the kids." The two men gathered around Andrew, John and Nicole. "He threw up," continued Al Russo. "He'll sleep it off."

"Do you know what it is?" added Tony Caiazzo "These kids are used to soda. They never drink wine; not even mixed with water, the way we drank it as kids. Just poured it down is what they did."

John nodded in agreement, but the explanation did not calm Nicole who looked at her son in dismay. Three other men were approaching, probably to get their sons. Andrew was helped into the front seat between his mother and grandfather and the three headed homeward.

Peter, on the porch when they arrived, was naturally puzzled to watch Andrew being aided out of the car. Without hesitation he ran to help fearing he had been hurt while playing.

"What in the devil happened?" Pete was shocked to see a sickly faced nephew.

"He and friends had a drinking party," replied Nicole.

"A what?" Pete stared as he helped and didn't know whether to laugh or be serious. He could not say he wasn't involved in similar situations as a youth.

"Can you picture a bunch of kids with a gallon of wine?"

"Holy cow! Grand-pop, unfortunately you had to witness it and probably get upset."

John responded quickly, "Especially when it's someone that is very close to my heart."

Andrew, too unbalanced to talk, simply dropped onto the living room sofa and fell asleep.

"I have got to get home or your grandmother will be worried, Nicole." John left, vowing to check on Andrew later.

In the meantime Pete explained what prompted his visit. He had started divorce proceedings for Nicole. The papers were on the table and needed signing. That done they sat around and had a cup of coffee.

"Want a slice of potato pizza, Pete? Grammy sent it over."

"So that explains Grand-pop's presence here at an ideal time."

"Yes. God bless him. He was such a big help and calming influence."

"If I won't deprive your family, I will gladly have a slice of pizza."

"There's plenty there. You know Grammy's pizzas."

"I still can't believe those kids did a thing like that."

"Nicole, you should know. After all you are a teacher and deal with youngsters everyday. True they are little and might get into only minor misdeeds, but when a bunch of older boys get together they will do the unusual just for kicks. Remember when Dad heard I was traveling with the glue-sniffing kids in my junior year in high school?"

"Do I! Never saw him so angry. Did you sniff?"

"Once or twice. Really didn't do a thing for me. Dad's calling down sure did." Pete took a healthy bite of pizza and chewed slowly. "I couldn't hang out with those guys any more. In fact, I'm sure you remember that Aunt Grace incident. She took frequent tours around Sammy 'the turtle's' neighborhood to make sure I wasn't getting mixed up with that crowd. People thought they did drugs. One evening Aunt Grace was investigating and a small fluffy dog began chasing her. She ran and lost her loafer. She had to retrieve it when the dog was back indoors."

Nicole began to laugh. "Aunt Grace did weird things in her efforts to protect us. And still quiet athletic for her age. She and Lucia made frequent stops at Mary's Luncheonette to check on us." "Mary Bert," who owned the place, was a popular grandmother and mentor for the high school kids who enjoyed hanging out there. Mary bridged the gap between the young and old with her colorful speech and personality.

Pete shook his head in as he recalled happy moments. He observed a relaxed look on Nicole's face and was glad. If only he could absorb some of her blows, even the soft ones.

The surprise came when Andrew strolled sheepishly into the kitchen.

"Hey there, fellow, we have some pizza for you and a glass of wine."

"Don't say that, Uncle Pete. It makes me wanna throw up."

"Pizza makes you sick?"

"No, wine does. I never liked it anyway."

"So why did you drink it?"

"You don't understand, Uncle Pete. It was part of the fun."

"I understand. I'm hoping it teaches you a lesson." He wanted to say, "Tow the line or else Aunt Grace will be checking up on you." But that would take some explaining. Pete's role in their lives as a father figure would be tremendous in subsequent years. He became a "cool" uncle to assume the place of a runaway dad.

"We are disappointed, Andrew. I hope it serves as a lesson." Nicole motioned for her son to sit down.

"I'm sorry, Mom."

"Apology accepted. Now do you want a glass of ginger ale? It might help?"

"Yes, please. That pizza looks good. I might be able to have some later."

"It is good. Grandma made it. Having it later is a good idea."

Pete glanced at his watch. "I think I better get going. There are a couple of things that need to be done. Nicole may I have those papers?"

His sister reached for the documents that were placed on the cabinet and handed them to him.

"Are you coming over for Sunday dinner, Nicole?"

"We plan to."

"Good. Aunt Zee and Uncle Neil will be there. See you tomorrow." He gave Andrew a high five and told him to lie down.

*   *   *

Nicole and children were waiting in front of church on Sunday morning for the early Mass attendants to exit. It was surprising to see grandparents Gina and John among the early worshippers who began to stream out. Gina was holding on tightly to her husband for fear of falling. Generally they attended a later Mass. The grandchildren caught sight of them and rushed to their side to greet them. Andrew looking a bit guilty, was the last.

"You seem to be a lot better today, fella. How do you feel?"

"Much better, Grandpa."

John gave him a pat on the back. "Be careful next time."

"Okay, Grandpa."

"Lisa, did your team win yesterday?"

"Yes, but I'm still hoarse from all that yelling." John then turned to Matthew and asked if he had a good time biking with Adam.

"Do you know what, Grandpa? We found a rabbit's nest with tiny babies but we didn't touch them."

"That's my boy. The mother rabbit might abandon them." John gave Matthew a tight squeeze.

"So why did you two attend this Mass?" inquired Nicole.

"Didn't I tell you we were going to Louise and Alfred's sixtieth wedding anniversary dinner?" Gina answered as she alternately hugged her grandchildren.

"Sorry, I completely forgot, Grandma. Too much on my mind these days."

"You don't have to explain, honey."

"Thank you for the pizza. It was delicious and easily devoured." Nicole gave her grandmother a peck on the cheek. "Have a good time at the dinner. We have to go in now or we will be late."

Nicole looked back at her grandparents while they were crossing the street, and lamented the fact that she would never have a relationship like theirs.

They were home by ten A.M. The Sunday paper was on the porch. The children changed into casual clothes and fought over the comics. Dinner at Nicole's parents was at noon—the traditional time.

Lisa brought her homework to the kitchen table. There was enough time to work on her biology notebook. Andrew and Matthew retreated to play a computer game.

Nicole leafed through the newspaper but her thoughts were elsewhere. In retrospect the incident with Andrew was unnerving. Undoubtedly many more were to be expected. The children were not talking much since their Dad left, but they must certainly be hurting. When Matthew fell from his bike the tears came much too easily. Were they tears of unhappiness because the father left? And was Andrew's stab at drinking another clue?

Soon Dan would be the father of five children. Although he had a good income, Nicole wondered how much financial support he could afford. Yet it basically always went back to the primary reason for the family break-up—something she pondered over and over again. Even blaming the sexual revolution. How often had she heard that no one should put up with a lot of garbage, so if you don't like your mate, well, then just leave. Perhaps that's what Dan did.

Was she starting to feel sorry for herself? And was her student Jesse staring at her because news of her separation already got around. Perhaps Jesse simply felt sorry for her.

Those hurt by a marriage break-up find their own way of handling the situation. Some looked for a pay back. A quickie remarriage often proved a disaster. Others chose higher grounds such as more college credits or any route to reestablish one's self worth. At the moment Nicole felt she had nothing to prove. Giving her family the attention they required was her primary interest. Hopefully the support from family and friends would see her through the maize of expected problems.

Eleven-thirty A.M. according to her wristwatch, and time to gather up her brood and head for dinner at her parent's home. Beth and her family, as well as Aunt Zee and Uncle Neil, would be there. It would be Sunday afternoon with the kids when Uncle Pete would initiate a game of touch football. Uncle Neil, now in his early sixties, also participated. He couldn't run very well, but when it came to throwing and kicking, he was adequate and in fact pretty amazing.

One mile was the distance between the two homes.

Within minutes they approached the familiar two-story brick home which had received several coats of thick white paint through the year, to cover red bricks that had proved to be of a sub-standard quality. Mamie and Domenic purchased the home thirty-two years ago from an elderly couple who had moved in with their daughter and husband. Much had been done to improve the one-acre property. It is now well landscaped, with a paved driveway leading to a two-car garage.

Nicole parked the car in the driveway. Neil's car was already parked in front of the garage. The unmistakable aroma of spaghetti sauce filtered outdoors. Carrying armfuls of assorted paraphernalia, it was but a short walk towards the back door and into a light and spacious kitchen where her well-organized mother had already set the table. After depositing their things, they marched into the living room to meet parents, uncle and aunt deeply engrossed in a television program.

"The gang's all here. Time to eat," shouted Uncle Neil as he rose to embrace them.

Aunt Zee dressed in gray slacks and black knit top followed. The loops in her ears dangled as she tightly hugged the young family members. Mamie and Domenic received a peck on the cheek from grandchildren.

"Pete isn't here yet?" wondered Nicole.

"Mass should be out by now. He will be here soon," responded Mamie.

"Mom tells me you guys will be going to California around Christmas to see Guy, Darlene and the grandchildren."

"It's time, Nicole; two years since we last saw them," replied Aunt Zee. "We will be there in time to celebrate Justin's tenth birthday which falls between the holidays. Amy will be eight the following June."

"Hard to believe isn't it?" asked Neil and at the same time he pulled Andrew close. "How's my boy doing?"

"Okay." No further explanation from Andrew who registered a rather guilty look. Uncle Pete's arrival was marked by the slam of his Audi. The boys ran to him as he entered the living room and gave him the high five. Lisa received a hug for her team's victory. He knew that they had faced a tough opponent. "I heard you were still the prettiest cheerleader of the crew."

"You always say that, Uncle Pete," was Lisa's usual response.

"I'm very serious, honey," added the uncle.

Lasagna was the pasta special and a roast of chicken and potatoes went with it. Aunt Zee had prepared antipasti. Nicole's chocolate cake with creamy vanilla frosting and a dip of ice cream was the dessert It was a far cry from the dessert of fruit, nuts and biscotti preferred by their ancestors.

For a change Mamie and Domenic relaxed as they sat next to each other at the dinner table. It would be a long, hard grind before accepting the undeserved fate of Nicole and her children. As Domenic remarked, "That too will pass."

The kitchen was cleaned. Dessert was postponed for later. While children were playing outdoors, the men were discussing the upcoming football game on television. At the sound of the doorbell Peter answered and found Leonardo Nezio taking up a collection for the annual memorial Mass in honor of Santa Lucia.

"Come in, come in, Leonardo." No longer were older people addressed as Zio or Zia. That had gone the way of the Model T Ford. Leonardo was a slightly built man, in his early eighties wearing ill-fitting clothes—at least a size too large.

193

Domenic and Neil stood and greeted him warmly. Peter led him toward a chair. "I haven't seen you for some time, Leonardo. How are you feeling?"

"My knees are not too good, Domenic. And I miss my wife very much."

Lucy Nezio had died over two years ago after a debilitating disease that lasted over ten years. While she was ill, Leonardo had pushed her wheelchair over the ramp he had built and thus maneuvered her outdoors. He had parked it under a tree while he worked in the garden. During the hot, humid days he covered her face with netting to discourage the bugs from attacking her helpless body. "A kind and virtuous man who is undoubtedly destined for heaven," concluded his neighbors. "No day goes by that he doesn't visit her grave."

Mamie and Aunt Zee graciously acknowledged Leonardo when they entered the living room. And as he had done many times before repeated, "I remember during the depression how your father handed me a ten-dollar bill so I could pay for my coal. It was hard with five kids. God bless him. How are they doing?"

"They are pretty well. Thank you for asking," replied Mamie.

"Is your aunt Marianne still living?"

"She is in a nursing home temporarily. She broke her hip about a month ago. Uncle Ralph died two years ago."

"May his soul rest in peace. One of his sons is a judge, right?"

"Yes. In a county near Philadelphia."

"Carmella, I don't see you much but once in a while I see Neil. Do you still work?"

"I help out when needed, Leonardo. Very few factories are still operational. A lot of the work is going to foreign countries where labor is cheap, you know."

"Not many factories and not much work in the quarries either. Nothing is the same," added Leonardo.

"How is your family these days?"

"They are scattered all over, Carmella. Charlie wants me to go live with them. As long as I can help myself I want to stay in my own home. Sometimes we old people get in the way. Young people especially don't always want us around. They don't like the way eat, doze or smell."

"Thankfully they are not all that way, Leonardo." Domenic wasn't in total agreement. "But then again, I'm sure some of the kids were obnoxious in your days too."

Leonardo laughed, disclosing well-kept teeth. "I'm sure you heard a few things before from your father-in-law. We were far from angels."

They all looked intently toward this gentle looking man who was admitting to sometimes straying from the right path.

"You've heard of 'The Rooster,' I'm sure. He was a real character, a clown to be sure. Also a special cop during the 'Big Time.' Saturday night of the feast, and in the midst of heavy traffic, he stopped cars and approached drivers with all the splendor of a special cop. With voice delivery implying great importance he asked drivers to show their licenses They obliged, he looked, returned the license and yelled 'go ahead.' The funny thing was that 'The Rooster' could not read."

"Well," continued Leonardo, "Halloween was a fun time for us also, but our generation expressed it in a different way. We sometimes overturned outhouses. One particular Halloween night I tagged along with some older boys who decided to do that to the 'The Rooster's' special domain."

Now the family became mesmerized to think that this

kind man would accompany a bunch of hoodlums on a mission of this sort.

"I can picture that night as if it were today. We sneaked through gardens and dark paths until we came close to that well-kept outhouse." Leonardo had on a happy face. "Cautiously and silently we got closer until we were within a few yards of the small wooden castle. Within sight of it and prepared to get a grip on the toilet 'The Rooster' exploded from inside the outhouse. He was ready for us with a heavy baseball bat in his hand. We never ran so fast!" His audience laughed. "A sixty-year-old man could never catch up with us."

"Leonardo, tell me how is your neighbor Rosaria?" asked Zee. "Aunt Lucia told us she fell and at eighty could have had a broken hip."

"She is alright, Carmella. She got a small bump on her head."

"What happened?"

Leonardo was a bit reluctant to discuss that matter and shyness overtook him, but these were adults so he proceeded to relate the incident. "Her husband Paolo was chasing her around the kitchen table and she took a spill. Poor Rosaria!"

"Why would he chase his wife, whom he loves," asked Zee.

"Because he loves her, Carmella." His face turned crimson. He wished they would understand without further explanation.

Peter understood fully. "She had a headache and he ignored it, Aunt Zee."

"Holy cow. Pretty good for an old guy," added Zee as they all tried to subdue their laughter. Leonardo was happy to end it in a subtle way.

They were enjoying Leonardo and his easy way of

holding their attention when Nicole, who was outside with her children, made an entrance. She knew Leonardo quite well. He was Celia's grandfather, and she had often been in his home with her good friend.

"Leonardo, glad to see you. I hope you're well."

"Not bad at all for an old man, Nicole."

"And Celia?"

"Fine too. She is still living in Allentown with her three children and husband. How about you and your family?"

"You don't want to know."

"If you talk, I'll listen."

"Dan left me for another woman."

This immediate response shocked her family for she had been reluctant to talk openly about her failed marriage.

Leonardo looked bewildered as if not knowing what to say. His pink translucent skin seemed to suddenly turn gray. He fixed his eyes on her, at a loss for words. Clutching his hands and in a soft deliberate tone said, "The devil is about more than ever these days, Nicole. Like a hawk swooping to snatch his prey so this abominable creature continues to snare even the best of people."

Nicole smiled warmly at the little old man. She realized that he was deeply moved. He rose and turned to them and said, "I must be going now." The men reached into their pockets for a generous donation in honor of Santa Lucia and handed it to him. He thanked them and was prepared to leave but not before approaching Nicole; he gathered her hands in his, and kissed them. "Pray for the intersession of Saint Anne, patron of mothers, to guide you and your family. I will do the same." Several days later, Nicole received a Saint Anne medal from Leonardo, delivered by her father.

Before watching the football game and having dessert,

the family went outdoors to spend time with the children. It was a bright, sunny September day. The women sat on the chairs and watched while the less than fit men made a feeble attempt at keeping up with the excited kids. It was a laugher when measured in terms of adult physical endurance.

*   *   *

An invitation to a wedding had arrived by mail in mid-September of 1989 from their Canadian cousins. Mamie, Aunt Zee and their families were invited to attend the wedding of their cousin Louisa. The ceremony was to take place in Toronto in mid-October. Canada was less restrictive than the United States in its immigration policy. Therefore, during the fifties, many Rosetans emigrated from Italy to that country hoping for more opportunities and a better way of life.

*   *   *

In 1975 Mamie, Aunt Zee, Domenic and Neil had toured Italy with a group arranged by an association of local factory owners. They traveled by chartered jet and arrived in Rome during the first week in July. Rome, Venice, Florence, Padua, Pisa, Naples and Capri were among the cities visited. It was a luxurious twelve-day trip. Roseto was not part of the itinerary, however, since a number of the travelers were interested in visiting their ancestral town, a special bus was engaged for a day.

The bus left at five A.M. and sped southward on the main highway and a few hours later reached the agricultural south, past tobacco fields and rows upon rows of vegetables as well as fruit orchards. The bus finally turned eastward toward the Apulian peninsula amid mountains that are part of the Appennine range. The people who lived by the lush Pocono Mountains were a bit surprised by the brownish mountains of southern Italy that nurture only a few pines.

The bus traveled through small villages like Castellucci, Abruzia and Biccara, places that were familiar to the Rosetan travelers. As they approached their destination, the driver suddenly stopped at the base of a mountain and parked in front of a small country store. The tourists got out to stretch their legs and upon entering the store found only a limited inventory, but were fortunate to buy cool drinks and snacks. After a fifteen minute rest, the bus continued up the narrow steep mountain road that was once a donkey path.

Obviously the Roman bus driver had never driven in this area for he made frequent stops to ask for directions and pertinent information. Eventually they reached their destination. In the distance on the very top of the mountain, nestled in a valley could be seen the village of Roseto and the homes with the red tile roofs. However another obstacle soon confronted them. A narrow section of the road with a dangerous steep decline both sides of the frightened the passengers. The bus was barely able to continue and appeared on the verge of rolling down the mountainside. The travelers decided to walk the short distance, while the driver bravely proceeded to safer grounds. The passengers then reentered the bus.

Their entry into the village created mass excitement. It was like the triumphant return of Julius Caesar from a distant battlefield. In a brief time the people emptied out into the town plaza asking about cousins or other relatives who left the town. There was an exchange of names and often a perplexed look. Only when family nicknames were given was there any hint of recognition. Assigning nicknames is

a unique phenomenon. Nearly every family has been sad-
dled with one. "Michele ou Soppa" (Michael the Cripple)
or "Basilio Spalia Vasca" (Basil with the low shoulders) are
examples of nicknames handed down for generations.

Visitors inquired about relatives or friends and were
gradually reunited.

Mamie and Aunt Zee announced that they were looking for a cousin, Filomena, whose only daughter Pina, op-
erated a bakery shop with husband Marco. No problem for
no one in the town is a stranger. The residents gladly accepted the honor of being a tour guide. A short heavy-set
man wearing an old gray hat immediately obliged to accompany them and their husbands to the bakery. They
walked up the hilly ancient cobblestone road that even resembled the main street in Roseto, U.S.A.

From a distance came the aroma of freshly baked
bread. When they entered the hot bakery several men were
removing the crusty loaves from the brick ovens with large
wooden spatulas. Certain that the pretty, tiny, dark-haired
young woman at the counter was Pina, Aunt Zee, flashing a
wide smile, slowly approached and asked in Italian if she
was Pia. The cousin smiled back but there was no recognition.

"Si," she replied curiously.

"We are your cousins from America."

The shock in her face was monumental. Introductions
followed. Pina spoke English fairly well so they began a
bi-lingual conversation and intervals of hugging and kissing. Marco, fair of skin, thin and of medium height was introduced. Pina suggested that she and the other American
cousins walk to her mother's apartment.

It was but a short distance and like other tourists they
looked about and studied the old buildings made of sand
and mortar. Painted a dark ochre, green or white they con-

tained apartments accommodating four to six families, perhaps the forerunner of the modern condominium.
Filomena was waiting on the small porch and gestured excitedly when her American cousins appeared in the distance. As they ascended the concrete stairway to her
apartment, the short full-figured woman of about fifty with
a delightful round cheerful face extended her arms and enthusiastically embraced each one. A telephone call had informed her to expect company from America. Her
grandfather and Maria Giuseppe were siblings.

Following the initial meeting they were led through a
bright kitchen containing light modern furniture and into a
comfortable cool living room. Conversing solely in Italian
they tried to bridge the gap of decades of separation when
mail had been the only means of contact and so much had
been left unreported.

Filomena hurriedly began to prepare lunch. It included homemade pasta in marinara sauce, antipasti of
cheese, roasted red peppers and prosciutti. A small basket
containing slices of freshly baked white and whole wheat
bread was set on the side. Maria Giuseppe had often remarked that while in Italy there was no white refined flour
but only whole-wheat flour, milled locally from the wheat
grown in their fields and used for bread and macaroni.
Only when she came to America was white flour more
commonly favored.

A delicious meal for hungry American cousins was
immensely satisfying. The homemade wine was outstanding, as were the fresh figs and apricots.

Filomena lived in Naples with her husband but spent
the hot summer months in the cool mountains of Roseto.
Her husband, Michele, was employed by the city and
joined his wife on the weekends.

A television set and appliances purchased in Foggia

were proud possessions. As elsewhere the installation of electricity had ushered in a new lifestyle. Following lunch, and after returning to the living room for a brief time there came a tour of the town.

Women in black mourning clothes were quite visible—maintaining one of the few remaining traditions. A sizable number of people were fair-skinned with blue eyes. Roseto is closer to the east coast of Italy. The effect of the immigration of fair-skinned Slavic people who crossed the Adriatic Sea into Italy and intermarried the olive-skinned Italians was apparent. Armies from other European nation that traversed Italy throughout the centuries also left physical and cultural reminders of past history.

The short tour revealed the presence of several ancient churches, a modern school, a decent small inn to accommodate overnight tourists and a jewelry store. Flowers cascaded from balconies and potted plants adorned the town. To obtain high quality hospital care, it was necessary to travel to the city of Foggia where there were also excellent schools, restaurants, hotels and the usual modern services found in any large city.

The impression formed was that though this was not a prosperous village, it was still much better than the one left behind long ago by grandparents who lived in the damp basement levels of humble apartments and also left behind a legacy of uprisings. In 1860 seven men were put to death after rebelling against an ancient feudal system that had restricted them to a peasant lifestyle. In 1882 the militia had to be called to restore order. a talented, brave and vigorous people could not be enslaved forever. Though difficult to leave families behind, the decision was made to seek a better life and many had immigrated to America.

Saying good-byes to their cousins were difficult but promises were made to meet again. An invitation was extended to their Italian cousins to visit them in Roseto, U.S.A.

The bus left at twilight and cautiously made its way down the slopes through small towns and farms with vineyards and fig trees. The driver had been advised to take a less hazardous road for the return trip. After heading south toward the flat areas of Baria that sparkled with the evening lights, the bus sped westward to the main highway and north to Rome with some very happy but tired Rosetans.

The homeward flight was full of praises for what they had experienced during their trip. Rome with its magnificent churches, Sistine Chapel, and historic sites could not be absorbed in mere days. Florence with its David in the Uffizi gallery was an unbelievable cultural experience. The outdoor restaurants would be missed. The food excelled and the fresh fruit and fine wine were top grade. Yet to have embraced never-before-seen cousins and villagers from their ancestral town was a heart-warming experience that would forever be cherished.

*   *   *

The invitation to attend the wedding of their Canadian cousin Louisa, was accepted and the reply forwarded. It was learned that Filomena, Pina and Marco would also be attending. The plan was for a three-day stay in Toronto. Domenic and Neil took vacation days from work. Arrangements for motel accommodations were made and road maps for the trip had been attained.

At six-thirty A.M. Friday morning the four travelers headed toward the New York border, Buffalo and Toronto, Canada. It was a perfect time of the year. The colorful autumn foliage was at its peak. They stopped occasionally to enjoy the scenery and rest. Seven hours later they arrived at Niagara Falls.

The enormity and powerful force of these celebrated falls could be felt for miles. During the twenties and thirties it had become the favorite site for a honeymoon. In fact this is where their parents, John and Gina, honeymooned. The souvenirs they had brought back are still around. After briefly walking about the area they stopped and joined a group led by a guide who recited some interesting facts. American and Canadian falls are separated by Goat Island. The American Falls are 183 feet high while the Canadian falls are 168 feet high. a glacier swept through the area 12,000 years ago and the surge from Lake Erie covered the Niagara Falls area.

The time spent at the falls was hardly enough to fully appreciate their magnitude. They decided to stop for a longer period on the return trip. Presently they were looking forward to a brief rest and supper.

The spaciousness of the city of Toronto is extraordinary when one compared to New York and Philadelphia. Its history dates back to the early eighteenth century, but Mississauga Indians lived there long before that time. Within the past century it had become one of the most multicultural cities in the world with a population of over two and one half million. Tall modern buildings, museums, schools, colleges and wide highways gave credence to the fact that it was quickly becoming one of the most important cities in Canada.

The Roseto foursome left the motel a nine A.M. and stopped at a small shop for a light breakfast of toast and coffee. They were sure to be overfed the rest of the day. Their first destination would be Giuseppe and Maria Fillippa's home. They are the bride's grandparents; also the parents of four children—Maria, Antonio, Giusepina and Filomena.

A telephone call the previous night informed them of their arrival and to expect them about ten A.M. Maria Fillippa and Giuseppe were not strangers, having visited Roseto several times during the week of the "Big Time." Their American cousins were invited to stay with them during the short visit, but chose the motel rather than present an extra burden on a hectic day.

Giuseppe, Filemona, Fausto, Donato, Michele and Annina were siblings. All were in their seventies, with the exception of Annina who was eighty-two and lived in Montreal. The men settled in Toronto in the late forties, got jobs with the sanitation department of that city and sent for their wives. They were now retired with good pensions, beautiful homes and well-educated children.

Neil drove to the address on Mississauga Street and parked in front of the two-story brick home where the cousins anxiously waited.

Smiling and waving as soon as they were sighted, the Canadian cousins rushed to greet the Americans before the car was parked. Warm greetings followed by a few tears marked the joyful reunion.

"But why you no come here last night? You know we got plenty of room." Maria Fillippa showed displeasure in their decision to stay at a motel.

They thanked her for the invitation, but reminded her that this was not the time to present them with additional work.

"No mind work when family come from Roseto," added Giuseppe.

Although their cousins had been in Toronto for nearly fifty years they were bilingual and still felt more comfortable speaking Italian; there were mingling phrases from both languages.

In the living room they sat on comfortable blue sofa and chairs. a picture of Jesus hung on the beige wall. The animated conversation that continued for at least an hour included inquiries about the health of American relatives. Giuseppe wanted to hear about their parents, Gina and John and also, aunts Grace and Lucia. There was the usual discussion about gardens. Giuseppe reminded his cousins that the Canadian growing season is short due to the colder climate. They talked about the year's harvest. The vineyard had produced good grapes and many tomatoes were canned.

Finally, they were led into a bright kitchen with a long maple table. Giuseppe was an excellent host, and escorted them to captain style chairs. He, like the other males in the family, was short, stout, reddish face, light eyes and had a bulbous nose. In fact he very much looked like the Russian president, Gorbachev. Maria Filippa, on the other hand, was a bit taller with black hair and eyes, and had a vivacious personality.

Fine white and maroon dinnerware, beautiful silverware, and crystal wine glasses were set on a lace tablecloth. The luncheon consisted of melon topped with prosciutti, linguini with pesta sauce, supresso and mozzarella, a tossed salad with arugala and romaine lettuce. Dessert was a wedge of ricotta pie. The cousins received top-notch treatment. They sipped their wine slowly while the conversation continued.

"Has Filomena arrived from Italy?"

"Si, she come Thursday, Mamie. She and Pina stay with Fausto and Maria Donata."

"We're anxious to see them," added Aunt Zee.

"We see everybody at reception. We all sit together," was Maria Filippa's quick response.

"Neilo, where your parents come from?" asked Giuseppe.

"My parents were born in the United States. My grandparents came from Naples."

"Ah Napolitani."

"They had a reunion about a month ago, Giuseppi, when over one hundred people came together. They know how to celebrate," Aunt Zee added.

"Nice men my cousins married."

"Yes, most of the time. I guess we'll keep them." Aunt Zee smiled and winked. Mamie simply smiled and nodded.

"And your son?"

"He is in California with his wife and two children. We expect to fly there during the Christmas holidays."

"He works with the FBI," added Neil with obvious pride.

"And your family, Domenico."

"I have no relatives in Italy. Most are in this country. Now about my own immediate family, that's a different story."

"Not everything is well," responded Mamie before Domenic could answer. Obvious pain registered in her face.

"Whatsa matter?"

"Nicole's husband left her and the children."

" 'Managga lo cucco and e l'accetta.' Bad, bad thing." Giuseppe looked shocked.

"Madonna mia, Madonna mia," was Maria Filippa's anguished response.

"He is a salesman in Texas. Got mixed up with a woman who is having his twins besides."

By now, the two Canadian cousins were beside themselves.

"Bad for everybody but especially kids. How they do?"

"They don't say much but of course they hurt." Domenic shrugged.

"Poveri figlia bella." Maria Filippa wiped her eyes.

This discussion was followed by a discourse on the evils existing in the world today. Mariucci, "a seca" (the thin one) lost her grandson to drugs two weeks ago. He was only nineteen years old. Marriages don't last. Women worked, made good money and were getting sexually involved with men in the workplace. Family values were eroding and the kids were the scapegoats—a commonly held notion particularly by their generation and the "doilie mothers." "Get with it, Grandma and Grand-pop. Times change," was the ongoing rhetoric among the young.

"It's time to break up this interesting discussion," Domenic said as he checked his watch. "The wedding is at four P.M. I'm sure Maria Filippa and Giusseppi have things to do."

"No, no, we got plenty time."

Mamie and Aunt Zee rose and began to clear the table. The men left to check out what was left of the garden, mainly winter lettuce.

Before returning to the motel, Neil asked if they needed a ride to the church, but they expected to ride with their daughter and son-in-law.

*   *   *

It was less than a mile to St. Mary's Church. After parking the car they began the short walk to the entrance. Aunt Zee wore a light brown dress and high-heeled shoes to match. Mamie wore a gold woolen dress and brown shoes. The men were well groomed in dark suits. No complaints about the weather; seventy degrees and a bright sunny day. Grandparents and parents of the bride arrived within ten minutes.

The bride soon made her entrance and strolled to the altar with her father followed by the maid of honor and four bride's maids, dressed in autumn gold. The customary expressions of delight were heard as the couple made their appearance. The bridegroom met her at the altar, and walked forward while the attendants sat in the first row of reserved seats. Extraordinary music by a vocalist and accompanying violinist provided an emotional experience. The ceremony lasted slightly over an hour.

Splashes of rice greeted the newlyweds amid photographers who took numerous shots.

Relatives began to converge on the Roseto guests. Filomena and Pina were among the first to meet them and excitedly embrace them. Many who introduced themselves were unfamiliar. Maria Filippe, looking quite attractive in a blue lace dress, was joined by Giuseppe who led other relatives for an introduction. It was another unforgettable event.

Dinner was at six P.M. in a huge hall with high ceilings and crystal chandeliers. Bride, groom and the others in the wedding party as well as parents greeted the guests. Luisa was a pretty brunette and clearly resembled her mother Maria. The tall groom, John Hamilton, had light hair and blue eyes. Luisa was a nurse; John, an accountant. The bride's father, Nicolas Ronco, was born in Canada but his parents emigrated from Italy. While the orchestra played soft music, the guests were directed to assigned tables. Senior relatives sat at the same table and talked at a fast pace. A Roman feast followed a short toast.

Anyone who has attended a Canadian Italian wedding

would recognize this type of dinner—a multiple course meal with no end in sight. Dessert was a huge wedding cake, accompanied by all types of cookies and Italian pastry. You name it; you would find it. Breakfast often followed.

The Canadians enjoyed dancing and they really "kick up their heels," though not necessarily good dancers; even the novice pretended to be Fred Astaire. Aunt Zee and Neil wowed the guests with their expertise. Most wondered out loud how their cousin Carmella, wearing high-heeled shoes, could possibly keep going. Mamie and Domenic did well but only with the slow tunes.

Another dinner followed at Faust and Maria Donato's home at noon on Sunday. This time it was homemade "cavatelli" macaroni, stuffed veal pocket, salad, and for dessert cherries in brandy. Children and grandchildren were there en masse. Carmella and Maria the daughters had a real estate business in Toronto. All the children were well educated and industrious.

Tearful good-byes and promises to meet again ended the brief visit. These relatives enjoyed traveling and flew to their ancestral town in Italy rather frequently.

It was back to the motel, a good night's sleep and the long trip home.

The following morning seven suitcases were packed in the trunk and Neil was at the wheel of his Volvo. Mamie and Aunt Zee sat in the backseat—several bags of snacks beside them. Never let it be said that they would be sacrificed to starvation by relatives!

The trip home, though tiresome, was uneventful. They stopped briefly at the Falls and picked up a cup of coffee at a drive-in. Then it was back on the scenic New York and Pennsylvania highways until the sight of the Pocono Mountains meant they were back on home turf.

Home was a beautiful sight! Neil parked in the driveway removed the luggage from the trunk, and helped carry it indoors. "See you later." Neil and Zee made the short drive home.

Mamie called Nicole. It was four P.M. She was expected to be home. Lisa answered, happy to hear her grandmother's voice.

"Hi, Grammy! You're back! We missed you."

"Glad to be back, honey. How's everything?"

"Nothing unusual. Aunt Nettie and Aunt Tessie visited yesterday and were sorry to miss you." (They were Domenic sisters who lived in Allentown.) "They will call during the week."

"Did your team win on Saturday?"

"Yes we did. Uncle Pete, the boys and Mom came to the game and then we all went out for pizza. Grammy, before I forget, we had a bomb scare at the high school and had to evacuate the building."

"Some people need to have their heads examined."

"Real idiots, that's for sure. Here's Mom."

Nicole came to the phone and asked, "How was the trip?"

"It was a long ride but meeting all the relatives was worth it. They just couldn't do enough. Anything new?"

"Lisa told you about Aunt Nettie and Aunt Tessie. They are upset about my marriage but couldn't get here earlier. Beth and her family also visited for the afternoon. We all missed you. How was the wedding?"

"Couldn't ask for anything nicer. Luisa was a beautiful bride. Her husband seemed very nice and there was plenty to eat and drink."

"What time did you get back to the motel?"

"About one A.M."

"Did you have time to travel around the city?"

211

"Uncle Neil drove us around for about an hour. Not nearly enough time to see everything. You wouldn't believe the number of Rosetans who are living there and doing well."

"Hope I get the opportunity to visit some day."

"Wait Nicole, your father wants to talk to you." Mamie waited for her husband as he was coming down the stairway and handed him the receiver.

"Nicole, how did your weekend go?"

"Hi, Dad. It was pretty decent. I'll bet my paycheck you will be glad to sleep in your own bed tonight."

"You better believe it. Yet I enjoyed the trip."

"Aunt Nettie and Aunt Terssie spent Sunday afternoon with us. Don't know whether or not to believe all the funny tales they related about the old days, but they sure kept us in stitches. Beth's family encouraged them to keep going; especially Pat. He thought their humor was even better than Irish."

The father's sisters were aware of the trip to Canada. It was all about spending premium time with Nicole and bringing some laughter into her life.

"I'm not surprised. Just give them center stage. When Aunt Zee is with them, it's pretty wild."

"Won't keep you any longer, Dad. Going in to work tomorrow?"

"I expect to."

"Okay! Get some rest. See you soon."

Domenic walked toward his favorite lounging chair and reached for the newspaper. The phone rang.

"Dad, just checking to see if you were back. How was it?"

"We enjoyed it very much, Pete. Where are you?"

"I'm still at the office, but expect to stop at the Chinese restaurant and pick up an order. Tell Mom not to prepare

212

anything for supper. Will see you in a little better than a half hour."

Domenic and Mamie Donatelli were happy to be home again.

*   *   *

Nicole was in school early Tuesday morning. Yesterday she had arranged the reading groups according to ability. It was the "Blue Birds," "Robins" and "Blue Jays." Benjamin and Arthur were among the top students and in the "Blue Birds," Jesse was included in that group. She was an excellent student who worked diligently but seldom smiled. Always well dressed, one wondered what fermented the sadness in those beautiful pale green eyes. During the past six weeks of school she maintained that same quiet composure and was often lost in her own world.

The school bus was expected to take Nicole's first grade class, as well as two other classes, to a pumpkin patch on a local farm the following day to prepare for Halloween. Children chose a small pumpkin to decorate in class. Next to Christmas this was a most exciting time of the year. There exists the secret over costumes to be worn, a parade and best of all there is very little schoolwork.

Halloween morning was rather cloudy with a feeling of rain in the air. However by noon the sun began to peek through dark clouds, revitalizing the emotions of the youngsters who were looking forward to an exciting day.

At noon homeroom mothers arrived carrying desserts and snacks. Unquestionably they were of immense help with the children's costumes. Witches, fairies, pirates and aliens were everywhere. Arthur J. Jones carried himself with dignity while masquerading as President Lincoln. Benjamin was dressed as a gorilla and fortunately did not behave as one. An uncommon smile emerged on Jesse's face. She was a beautiful princess and for a change looked happy. The parade was long. One had to marvel at the creativity of the youngsters and their make-up artists Clean-up time and the end of the school day was soon announced. Kids were obviously tired and so were the teachers. Still wearing their costumes they headed home.

More serious business followed in successive days. First report cards were readied and appointments were arranged with parents to discuss their child's progress. Nicole was looking forward to that quarterly discussion between parent and teacher; perhaps shedding light on individual problems. Jesse was certainly not a problem, but an enigma.

Parent-teacher meetings began and were completed during the first week of November. Jason Michaels, Jesse's father, kept his four P.M. appointment on Friday, entering the classroom exactly at the designated time. A rather tall, thin young man, about thirty, he had well-trimmed light brown hair. After extending his hand to Nicole he introduced himself.

"It is a pleasure to finally meet you, Mrs. Grasso. Jesse speaks highly of you."

"Well thank you. She is a very good student and well-disciplined."

"I try my best."

Nicole noticed he used the singular noun and said, "You and your wife must spend time with her."

"Unfortunately my wife, Jesse's mother, left us in August."

Nicole assumed she had died. "Was she sick?"

"Oh no! She did not want to be married any longer and returned to New York."

"And Jesse?"

"She became my responsibility. My wife works for a publishing house. You see, Mrs. Grasso, we moved into Mount Bethel three years ago. East Stroudsburg University hired me as a math professor. It was convenient for my wife to commute to New York while I taught at the University. She hates rural areas; I felt raising Jesse in this vicinity was safer. Besides living conditions are more affordable. I grew up in Quakertown. My parents are German."

"What happens with Jesse when you are not home?"

"My hours afford me the opportunity to spend time with her. Also a neighbor has been of tremendous help."

Nicole by now was mentally confronted with a terrible scenario. How can a mother abandon her child to the care of even a loving father?

"An elderly widowed aunt will be living with us. She has gladly offered her service. It will also lift a financial burden from her life."

"Is there anything that you might want to discuss about Jesse's school work or any problems that she has had while in school?" Nicole was relieved.

His eyes for a brief moment seemed to stray and all at once he was so pitiful. "My only hope is that she is loved. It is hard to compensate for the loss of a mother's love or even her indifference. As for schoolwork, I am totally satisfied with her progress. You are an excellent teacher."

Nicole agreed to be ever watchful and to communicate with him about any aberrations. He thanked her knowing she would be most cooperative. How could she be other-wise when she understood the situation so very well? Extra efforts would be taken to somehow bring a bit of sunshine into Jesse's life.

On Monday of the following week Natalie, one of her pupils, told Nicole she was having her birthday party the following Saturday. Linda Kransky, her mother, worked in the school cafeteria. Natalie, quite outgoing, was excited about the coming event. All the girls in the class were invited. She shared her enthusiasm with Jesse who even smiled and thanked her for the invitation. Perhaps Linda had some insight into Jesse's life.

On her next trip to the cafeteria Nicole subtly began a discourse on the birthday party and the excitement generated by it.

"Mrs Grasso, I have four children and it seems there is either a birthday for one of mine or some other's that they must attend. Of course they look forward to them."

"Jesse was excited about the invitation. She is so laid back. To see her smile is a genuine pleasure."

"How can that poor child smile? Her mother doesn't want to be bothered and left it up to her husband to raise her; pretty selfish if you ask me. No grandparents or anybody around. My daughter is the only one she told. That mother is a stinker and deserves a swift kick."

"Yes, her father told me all about it during our parent-teacher meeting. Seems like an aunt is going to move in with them."

"Oh thank God for that! I told Natalie to bring her home once in a while. They can even study together."

"Natalie and Jesse are two of my best students."

A big smile appeared on Linda's tired face. "Thank you Mrs. Grasso. They have a good, kind teacher."

"Thank you, Linda. I can only try. They must cooperate you know. As far as rejection, especially by a mother, well that's not easy for Jesse to overcome. Take it from one who knows."

"That's true, Mrs. Grasso." Sadness covered her face. "You've had your bad time. Thank God you have a nice family to help you. Would you like some fresh fruit salad?"

"I would love it. Thank you so much."

*   *   *

It was Saturday afternoon; two weeks before Thanksgiving. Nicole was on a lounge chair reading the newspaper, feeling thoroughly relaxed. Lisa had not returned from her great grandparents' home, where Grammy Gina was putting the finishing touches on a dress for the Thanksgiving dance at the high school. It was an affair much anticipated by Lisa and one that had the girls on the telephone.

Earlier Matthew and Andrew had left with their Uncle Pete and Uncle Neil to see a Flyer's hockey game in Philadelphia. The sound of the telephone woke her from a near snooze. She lifted the receiver and quickly recognized her sister-in-law's voice.

"Did I interrupt something, Nicole?"

"Absolutely not, Maggie!"

"You and the family are well, I hope."

Nicole proceeded to fill her in on the family and asked about her family.

"Everyone is fine, thank you. Angelo is in New York on business today. Did Mom call you?"

"A couple of weeks ago. I was surprised to hear from her."

"I'm sure you will be hearing from her again soon."

"What makes you say that?" Nicole was puzzled.

"Well because of some major developments."

"Major developments?"

"Yes."

Nicole wished that Maggie would get to the point.

"Dan's girlfriend had a miscarriage."

Nicole hesitated momentarily before speaking. "That is too bad, Maggie. It's tragic. I really don't know what else

217

to say." Only mixed feeling swept through Nicole's body. "When did you hear about it?"

"Last night. Dan called Frank. They call each other occasionally. Mom was calling, but when Stacy answered the telephone Mom hung up. She hasn't talked to Dan for over a month."

"So how did Mom and Dad react upon hearing about it?"

"Mom reacted as expected—she couldn't care less according to Angelo who walked over to tell them about it. Dad simply walked away without commenting. Has Dan made any more attempts to get in touch with the children?"

"He wrote to them. They have not acknowledged his letters. He has been very faithful about sending support checks. Hopefully they will come around but the hurt is very evident, Maggie."

"Can't really blame them. It takes time to heal. Listen I'll keep in touch with you about any new developments. Stay well."

"You too, Maggie. Give my love to all."

"Will do."

Nicole fell back in her chair and pondered the ramifications of this development.

"Mom are you home?" Lisa had returned home while she was deep in thought. Nicole rose to meet her as she deposited a package on the kitchen table. "Grammy made my favorite cookies. Mom, it's getting cold out there. I think I better get out my heavier coat."

"How is the dress coming?"

"Only some minor adjustments to be made. Nina and Victor Castellucci are visiting and staying for supper. Guess what? Nina wants me to meet her grandson. She is so funny."

Nicole smiled at her daughter as she removed her

school varsity jacket. Her lovely face was crimson from the cold. "I've met him several times. He's quite a good-looking guy."

"He's a senior at Easton High and has been accepted at Temple University. He wants to be a dentist. It's interesting to hear the old folks talk about the bygone days."

"As they age, many seem to dwell a lot more on the past."

"Do you remember ever placing candles on graves the eve of All Soul's Day?"

"No, but your Donatelli grandparents did mention it quite often. Before the fifties, the section of the graves where the person was buried did not have sod. Candles, often as many as fifty, were placed over the gravesite in memory of loved ones. Prayers were offered. The cemetery became one glowing, spectacle and a fire hazard since the grass around the graves was dry during late October. Eventually that particular tribute to the dead was banned."

"Nina placed flowers on her relatives' graves two weeks ago. Today she and Victor returned to pick up the vase."

"Julia, her sister, was only nineteen when she passed away. It must have been devastating. Nina never forgot." Nicole looked at her young daughter and shuddered at the thought of such a tragic loss for a mother to have to bear. The death of a sister or any other member of a close-knit family was equally difficult to accept.

"That is very sad, Mom."

"Now to another topic. Aunt Maggie called about a half hour ago."

"What did she have to say?"

"Stacy had a premature birth and the twins did not survive."

Lisa stared quizzically at her mother, and then

219

shrugged her shoulders. "I don't know what to say, Mom. Perhaps it's poetic justice. Anyway the babies are angels in heaven."

"Since your brothers are unaware of that aspect of the ordeal, we will say nothing to them about it."

Lisa agreed it was for the best.

The phone interrupted their conversation. It was Aunt Zee calling to say the boys would not be home until about seven P.M. They were stopping for something to eat after the game. Nicole suggested she join them for cheesesteak and a salad. Aunt Zee readily accepted and arrived by five P.M. The sound of her Chrysler was unmistakable. She parked it in the driveway. Lisa met her at the kitchen door and embraced her.

"Cold out there. It almost feels like snow weather. My car heater isn't working."

"I'll bet that's not the only thing not working! How old is that car Auntie—at least fifty?" Lisa enjoyed teasing her aunt.

"I stopped counting, Honey. Why complain when the old buggy still does its 'thing'," she replied while removing a black print kerchief from her head, sticking it into the pocket of her red wool coat and handing it to Lisa. Her hair had been recently dyed, a bit more auburn than usual and worn page-boy style. A cluster of fake gold dangled from her ears.

The table was set for three with a platter of carrot sticks, celery and olives in the center. Aunt Zee reached for a carrot stick, carved out a quick bite, and placed the rest on her dish. "Spent an hour or so with Aunt Lucia and Aunt Grace this afternoon. Aunt Grace sprained her ankle this morning."

"How did she do that?" inquired Nicole.

"While pushing a wheel barrow in the yard; her foot slipped into a chipmunk hole."

"Still going strong at eighty-one."

"Nothing stops her. Aunt Lucia got her to a doctor who told her it was only a sprain." Aunt Zee took another bite of carrot. "She'll finish the job in a couple of days."

Nicole completed frying the steaks and onions, placed sliced cheese over the top and turned off the heat after covering the whole thing with a lid. In a few minutes it was ready for the crisp, hard, steak rolls.

"So what else is new?"

Nicole and Lisa looked at each other. "You're going to be surprised," responded Lisa.

"Try me."

After a bit of hesitation Nicole broke the news. "Dan's friend had a premature birth and lost the babies."

Aunt Zee wasn't one to get easily taken off base but her dark eyes registered emotion. "It's too bad. What did my favorite actor, Clark Gable, say in that famous movie *Gone with the Wind*?"

" 'Frankly my dear, I don't give a damn.' " Nicole rekindled her aunt's memory.

Aunt Zee was tall like her grandfather Lorenzo but had the spirit of her grandmother, Maria Giuseppe "I have no pity for that 'puttana.' But losing babies is another thing."

"We feel the same way, Aunt Zee. And my father is part of that whole rotten affair," Lisa added. Nicole nodded in agreement

"I thought your Dad had the guts to meet temptation head on. I was wrong. Many times we pay for those stupid mistakes." Nicole served the hot steaks, and poured hot coffee into the cups. Lisa settled for water. "Looks like Grammy baked a batch of her favorite cookies. By the way is she finished with the dress?" Aunt Zee chewed on the steak and reached for a stick of celery.

"Only a few minor adjustments need to be made, Auntie."

"One more week and you will be the belle of that shin-dig."

"I'm excited. It will be my first school dance. Do your remember yours, Auntie?"

"I sure do. We had about ten teachers around to chaperone the affair. They made us play stupid games like 'spin the bottle.' Never did get the chance to dance with my handsome classmate, Cliff Edwards. Instead I found myself dancing with 'Shorty' Kneeler. He was a head shorter but a terrific dancer. No way could I dance cheek to cheek with 'Shorty'!"

"Did he escort you home, Auntie?" Her niece found the whole thing amusing.

"Are you kidding?" Your Grandpop picked us up. He didn't trust the new generation of high school kids."

"Uncle Pete is picking me and my friends up after the dance."

"You girls are only sophomores so that's the way to go," added Aunt Zee. The chit-chat continued for another hour. This time they dwelt upon all the modern conveniences that made the working mother's life supposedly easier.

"What would I do without a washer and dryer? What if I had only a washboard to wash clothes?"

"Nicole, they would not use a towel once and then throw it in the hamper. The early generations took weekly baths and there were fewer clothes to wash. Mothers were home. They washed on Monday, ironed on Tuesday, baked on Wednesday, cleaned bedrooms on Thursday, living room and kitchen on Friday and Saturday. The shopping list was short. Sunday was always a day of rest. Who rests today in spite all of the conveniences?"

"Don't forget the soccer, baseball, basketball and football games that the parents must attend, while maintaining a full-time jobs." Nicole felt the tension merely discussing it.

Aunt Zee checked her watch and decided it was time to go. Within minutes she had slipped back into her coat, covered her head with the kerchief and was back at the wheel of her Chrysler.

*   *   *

Thanksgiving was cold with snow flurries. Bangor-Pen Argyl High School football game was scheduled for one-thirty P.M. It was a high voltage game for two rival teams. No love was lost between them. The usual bonfire was held the previous night as well as some spray painting of the enemy turf. Both were competing for district championship.

Mamie, Domenic and Aunt Zee stayed home to prepare dinner. All the other family members dressed warmly not only to see the game but also the cheerleaders, especially Lisa of course, put on the best performance of the season. Nicole wasn't exactly at ease watching her daughter get flipped around. Bangor was victorious in a hard fought game—final score was 14–7. Cars paraded through the Slate Belt while honking the horns.

Gina, John, Lucia and Grace were already there when they returned from the game. Carrying dessert, Beth, Pat and children joined them about the same time.

Dinner with turkey and all the trimmings was at five P.M. There was no pasta dish for Thanksgiving, and no one really missed it. That too went with Maria Giuseppe.

Christmas and New Years came and went with the usual amount of celebration. Aunt Zee and Uncle Neil were sorely missed but they and the rest of the family called to extend good wishes. As for Dan, that situation was not completely resolved. However, he did send gifts to all the children. Nicole insisted they send a Christmas card with a thank you note.

*   *   *

The invitation came through the mail in mid-February—a wedding to be held at the Gaylord Opryland Hotel in Tennessee. Francis, grandson of Ralph and Marianne Martucci and son of Judge Louis Martucci, was going to marry Sheri Wilson of Knoxville, Tennessee. It was the second marriage for both. He was a professor at a small college. She was studying for a doctorate in education and the mother of twin twelve-year-old daughters by a previous marriage. Francis had a daughter and two sons also by a previous marriage. Relatives decided it would be an opportunity to spend time together, besides participating and sharing in "a celebration of love" marriage ceremony.

Reservations for plane tickets and hotel accommodations were made several weeks in advance. Luggage was packed and then it was off to the Philadelphia International Airport in three separate cars. Beth and Patrick with their two children drove from Bethlehem and met them at the terminal. The eight P.M. two-hour flight to Nashville was smooth and the weather was clear. John and Gina were among the passengers who joined their children and grandchildren.

The plane taxied onto the runway shortly before ten P.M. Judge Louis and Francis, the prospective bridegroom,

224

met them at the terminal and were greeted enthusiastically. Next was a short walk to a small bus, the several mile drive to the hotel and tearful reunions. Marianne, with the use of a cane, was among the first to meet her sister Gina and the others; although not having visited since early December, they phoned each other frequently.

Laden with luggage they boarded the escalator of the luxurious hotel and headed for a section of rooms reserved for the group. Nicole and her family had twin queen-size beds in a spacious bedroom; Matthew and Andrew slept in one and Nicole and Lisa in the other. Leather chairs with reading lamps, television set, telephone, a large bureau with drawers completed the package. Mathew immediately turned on the television expecting to see the channels he watched at home. Such was not the case. A soft knock on the door and Andrew opened to see his cousin Ralph, who was about fourteen. He walked into the room and the three began plans for the following day. Nicole gently reminded them that taking off on their own was out of the question.

Meanwhile there was a steady flow among the rooms to check each other in this meeting of the clan. Well after midnight they finally scattered to their own quarters.

Breakfast was at "The Cracker Barrel" restaurant only a mile away. Some walked while others climbed into the shuttle bus for the short trip. Southern hospitality, casual dress and a country atmosphere prevailed. They felt quite at home. Fresh orange juice, bacon, sausage, eggs, pancakes, waffles and biscuits were on the menu. Grits was a southern dish they had heard about but never tried. First taste was not promising, but the waitress advised them to add a bit of maple syrup and butter. It worked!

After briefly meandering around the country store, everyone headed outdoors. Threatening dark clouds covered the skies and the promise of rain seemed inevitable. Under roof, Opryland within its circular compound was a perfect retreat. Brick paths lined with tropical trees, plants and waterfalls led to dining quarters, cafes and retail stores.

John and Gina had already taken the escalator to their room to freshen up and rest. Marianne and her daughter, Madeline, followed within the hour. Aunt Zee, Neil, Mamie and Domenic soon joined them. Madeline's husband, Rick, was in South American for his company and unable able to attend the wedding.

"Mom, did you and Pop pack your boots and hat?" Mamie teased her parents. Country attire was expected for the evening dinner.

"We have jeans but no boots," replied Gina.

"How about a cowboy hat, Pop?" asked Neil.

"Will a Yankee cap do?" responded John.

"Do you want to get killed?" teased Neil. "Let's take a bus to town. Maybe we can pick up some country attire."

"That suits me fine," added Madeline. Unlike her sister the years had taken its toll on her. Yet she was a game person at eighty-four. Her thick gray hair was cut short. She claimed it was an easy style to maintain by a broken down woman.

"You're my kind of gal, Aunt Madeline. Love you!"

"Love you too, Carmella."

A soft knock on the door and Judge Louis and his wife Barbara entered the near crowded room. The judge was tall, refined and genial. He had gained some weight through the years. His wife, Barbara, had also put on a few pounds. She had short reddish hair, pure Irish and a good sense of humor. They had three children but had hoped for at least eight. A hysterectomy after her third child dashed those hopes.

"Where is the rest of the family?" inquired Judge Louis.

"At the moment Beth and Nicole, accompanied by Patrick and children, are taking a walk. There is plenty of open space out there. Of course you know Peter couldn't make the trip," Domenic explained.

"He had a case in court I understand."

"That besides acting as a godfather for a friend's child."

"And how is Nicole handling her situation?"

"She doesn't say too much, Louis, but I know it hurts," responded Domenic, while Mamie simply shook her head. "Neither of us expected to see her subjected to divorce."

"It hurts," added Barbara. "I never expected Francis and Dotty to break-up. Marriages seem to go sour a lot quicker these days. My husband is a constant witness to ugly divorces."

"Change is not easy for us folks to accept. When hatred and divisiveness conquer understanding, it is often best to call it quits. Sadly, children bear the scars of that constant bickering as well as divorce. As to what's best for the kids, it's six of one and a half dozen of the other. And don't forget the bodily harm that might ensue because of hatred."

"Nicole and Dan didn't display any of that, Louis."

"Mamie, his was a case of uncontrollable lust. Satan, you know." The judge smiled knowingly.

"Bastards, that's what they are," interrupted Aunt Zee. "Call me intolerant but I don't accept Nicole's situation very easily."

"None of us like it," added Barbara, "but we all pray for the best."

"How are you feeling, Uncle John?" inquired Louis.

"Ready for the new millennium. Technology will offer

many exciting new inventions. However the years for me are quite limited."

"Keep that positive thinking, Uncle John. I admire it. Mom is not as optimistic about the future, especially family life," added the judge.

"It scares me to see the families pulled apart. They can't even find time to eat together." Marianne was adamant in her attitude.

"Mom, I'm with you there, but you must learn to adjust to some of the changes. It's not always possible to cling to all of your customs. People have jobs and kids have schedules. I wish we could all eat together every single night. Forget it!" Madeline and her mother had many discussions about clinging to the past.

"It's a matter of reaching a compromise. Learning to accept what works best for all concerned, but family life should never suffer," said Domenic.

"Hey how about getting off this subject and hitting the downtown area," suggested Neil. "Maybe we can even stop at the Ole Opry House."

"It's a go with me," the judge added with enthusiasm. "We'll hire a bus to take us around. Are you game, Mom?"

"Of course, Louis, you don't think I would miss that."

*   *   *

The bus trip to Nashville was short. Nicole, Beth and families joined the entourage. As they approached Center City Gina and John thought the area was comparable to the main street in Allentown or Easton. Marianne, who sat next to them, thought it was decidedly more 'country' than Philadelphia. The bus driver was told to picked them up at the same location in exactly two hours.

After walking a short distance, they crowded the foyer

of the old Opry House where all types of memorabilia were on display. Here were CDS by such country heroes as Dolly Parton, Loretta Lynn, Johnny Cash and many more. The theatre section was closed. After an hour of checking out the place, they settled for souvenirs and recordings by the artists.

Next was a visit to various shops. The family, after a short conference, split into two groups. Domenic, Mamie, Aunt Zee, Neil, John and Gina were among the group entering a shop featuring country specialties—boots, cowboy hats and belts. The proprietor greeted them with a wide smile and a big dose of southern hospitality as he invited them to look around and enjoy themselves. They freely accepted his invitation.

Neil approached the hat racks with anticipation and lifted a ten-gallon hat to his head. With the exception of Marianne, who sat in a comfortable chair, the others clowned as they also tried hats and made a few purchases. Next came the shoe department. Neil bought a pair of pointed black boots, and for a final touch a black belt with silver metal. No denying the fact that he stood tall and handsome. Aunt Zee warned him to stay away from the cowgirls.

The judge looked refined in a large black hat while Domenic evoked a few laughs with various styles and finally settled for a light brown hat turned up at the sides. Domenic also purchased a pair of boots. The event was pure comedy. They stopped to pay the bill where the proprietor gave them a wide smile and asked where they lived.

"Pennsylvania!" replied Aunt Zee.

"Where in Pennsylvania, Ma'am?"

"Roseto." Aunt Zee hesitated thinking that Roseto was certainly not in his vocabulary.

"Roseto? Now that sounds mighty familiar."

"Eighty miles northwest of Philadelphia," added Aunt Zee. "It is a little Italian town near the Pocono Mountains."

The proprietor scratched his head momentarily. "Now that ain't the place where people live a long time, is it, Ma'am? Seems I read something about that place in a journal." He peered through his horned-rimmed glasses perched on the tip of his nose.

"That's the place," replied Aunt Zee, surprised he had read about Dr. Wolf's study.

"Now tell me, Ma'am, is that study all it's cracked up to be?"

"There is some truth to it. See those folks there?" Aunt Zee pointed to John and Gina. "They are my parents, in their early eighties and still going strong." The rest of the family began to gather around the counter and check the ongoing conversation.

"You don't say." He extended his hand to congratulate John and Gina. "Now, tell me what is the reason for the reported longevity?"

And as John and others had done so many times, smiled and replied in a very simple sentence—"Good genes, close family ties and friends who support each other, hard work and good food." Finally John whispered in his ear, "also a couple of glasses of fine wine."

"Now you don't say." Then he whispered back, "But we Baptists don't drink, Sir."

"Then you better have good genes," teased John.

Everyone found the conversation quite amusing and several also began to express their own views to this southern gentleman.

"Resiliency—always hanging in there," added the Judge.

After paying for hats and boots and extending farewells and good wishes, they walked out into what appeared to be a few drops of rain. The next stop was the guitar store. Upon entering a long narrow music shop a block down the street, a tiny lady greeted them and asked if she could be of help.

"If you don't mind we would like to look around," responded Domenic.

"You go right ahead," said the little lady as she checked out the large group of strangers.

Domenic was the only one who knew anything about guitars. During his high school years, he had played with a band that entertained at school assemblies and country picnics. Many were the times he envisioned himself as a country singer. In fact he had often made a stab at singing with the familiar southern nasal twang. He still had that yen for a guitar! Prices of the instruments ranged from a few to thousands of dollars. "Country pop stars often chose to have jewels placed on their guitar," explained Domenic. "Naturally they paid a good price for that service and of course could afford the extra embellishment." It was another learning experience for the visitors, who studied the instruments and admired the workmanship for a brief well-spent period of time.

Domenic stopped at the counter to thank the lady for the privilege of browsing about. "I wish it was possible to spend much more time here. You have an impressive inventory."

"Thank you," she replied.

The final stop was a corner ice cream and soda parlor, momentarily empty of patrons. Chairs and tables beckoned the tired travelers. Gallons of ice cream in a variety of flavors lay in the glass cases. An attractive young lady, in a starched white uniform stood ready to scoop it into cones or paper plates. Dry pallets were gradually refreshed, and tired feet finally found relief. Groups of studious looking young people from nearby Vanderbilt and East Tennessee Universities eventually began to stream in giving the lady behind he counter a dose of anxiety.

As the Rosetans walked outdoors into a light rain, a bus was parked at the pre-arranged corner and right on time. The other half of the family had already boarded to escape the rain that was getting heavier by the minute. A simpatico bus driver from Nigeria, offered to give them a brief tour of Nashville although torrents of rain obscured a clear vision. Vivid discussions of his African roots, and important city sites combined to hold the attention of the front seat occupants, Judge Louis, Domenic and John.

They learned the Nigerian had lived in the United States over twenty years, returning for an occasional visit to see family and friends. His favorite African dish was snake meat. That drew a bit of disgust from the threesome until John reminded them that it was probably as delicious as eel. The Nigerian continued in a well-modulated voice, sounding every bit an intellectual and going one on one with the Judge, stopping frequently before landmark buildings for short periods. His candor and pleasant nature was rewarded with a generous tip. They finally returned to the Hotel parking space about four-thirty P.M. in time to prepare for the western style dinner.

*   *   *

Aunt Zee and Neil appeared in the dinning room with the self-assurance of western cowhands while other guests gawked and then clapped to show their approval. John and Gina looked every bit like aging Roy Rogers and Dale Evans, when they strolled into that wing of the Gaylord Hotel. Domenic, wearing a large badge, strutted like the sheriff of Silver Creek County, and regretted that he had left his guitar at home. Mamie, wearing jeans, winter boots and a plain straw hat held on to the arm of her husband. Beth and Patrick came in with their children—all looking comfortable as a western family. Nicole appeared happy as she entered behind Lisa and the boys. It was fun for everyone.

The bride's family was less inclined to submit fully to the western theme but nevertheless seemed excited about joining the mayhem and establishing warm relationships.

Judge Louis and Barbara, as well as the bride's parents, gathered in one corner with their son and intended daughter-in-law. Marianne sat with son Donato and wife Laura, who had made the trip from Florida where they were presently residing, and not far from their aging uncles Carlo and Dante. The latter's grandchildren had factories in Mexico, and shuffled between Florida and the Yucatan peninsula.

Dressed in white western clothes, Sheri, in her early thirties, was introduced to the Roseto relatives by Francis. Soft spoken with a refreshing personality, she was easy to love and engage in conversation. All agree that the pair seemed well suited for each other. It appeared their children, who sat at a table with the other young guests, would be comfortable with the union.

Dinner was at seven; a mixed salad and a choice of the entrées that featured roast salmon, spinach filled ravioli, filet mignon and chicken Marsala. Baked potato or rice and asparagus were served with it. Dessert was cake and ice cream. There was a generous supply of wine to suit the taste, and add to a very happy evening.

Next day, Saturday afternoon at two P.M. the guests were ushered into the beautifully decorated pavilion of the Gaylord Opryland Hotel. Set up neatly were white folding chairs on both sides of the aisle with large white bows hanging on the back. Violin music filled the air. Dressed in a white taffeta dress with full skirt, the bride, looking like a graceful swan strolled down the white-carpeted aisle to join her prospective groom under a stately large gazebo.

Daughters in pastel pink gowns followed as attendants; one of them scattered rose petals along the way. A tall gray-haired Baptist minister officiated at the brief ceremony that concluded with a solo rendition of "Amazing Grace." It was an impressive ceremony. A cocktail hour followed on the terrace. Dinner and dancing in a large ballroom put the final touches on a magnificent wedding day.

"Top grade and refined!" said Nicole who's appearance in a long black gown with a long red scarf draped down the sides invited praise throughout the evening. Tired but happy from dancing with relatives and new acquaintances from Sheri's family, she had an enjoyable evening.

"Amen," replied her father who with Mamie plus Nicole and Beth's family sat at one of the large oval tables. Aunt Zee and Neil sat with parents John and Gina, although much of their time was on the dance floor.

The ballroom was empty of its weary guests by eleven-thirty P.M.

*   *   *

Saint Joseph's Church was an eight-minute drive from the hotel. A small bus drove early risers to nine A.M. Mass. They returned to the hotel within the hour and found many of the relatives in the lobby. After consuming muffins, cinnamon buns and bagels, juice and coffee, they finalized last minute details, paid hotel bills and completed packing.

Two P.M. was lift-off time from the runway at Nashville. The weather was in their favor. It was sunny but brisk. Next stop—Philadelphia International Airport.

Marianne's family had flown into Nashville a couple of days before the wedding, however, they all took the same return flight. John, Gina and Marianne buckled-up in adjacent seats and chatted all the way. The three-thirty P.M. landing was perfect. Saying good-byes was not. Tears flowed and there was much hugging before they separated to drive home.

*   *   *

At seven P.M. Peter was helping his parents with luggage while getting a charge at seeing his father wearing a cowboy hat. "You look like a real cowboy, Dad. Just looking at you two tells me you had a good time."

"Everyone enjoyed being together. It was a terrific weekend. Sorry you couldn't be with us."

"Not as sorry as I am."

"Everything okay here?" asked Mamie. "How was the baptism?"

"The baptism went fairly well, although the baby cried through part of the ceremony. Father Leone took it in stride. Brunch was at the Stroudmoor with an assortment of food too numerous to detail. My court case should wind up by the end of the week."

Peter and Domenic wrestled with the luggage, finally placing it in front of the stairs to the second floor until they got their second wind. Mamie checked out the house to see if everything was in order—not that she expected otherwise. It was simply a force of habit for a meticulous mother.

"Did the kids have a good time?"

"Everybody had a good time, Peter. By the way you kept this place pretty clean." Mamie smiled gratefully at her son.

"Now, Mom, did you for one minute think I would

leave a mess? Anyway I only came home to shower and sleep."

"So what else is new—death, births or whatever?" continued Mamie.

"It was a quiet few days."

Domenic reached in the refrigerator for a cold beer. He was still wearing his cowboy hat. "Peter, they had a western style dinner that you wouldn't believe. You should have seen your mother looking like she was born a real cowgirl." Mamie smiled a bit sheepishly. Domenic proceeded to describe the beauty of the guitars in the music store. Peter was overjoyed at simply watching his parents buoyed up after a memorable trip.

"So nothing much happened while we were away?"

"I forgot to tell you. Stefano, 'the cucumber', sold his house."

"Who bought it?"

"No one we know. I did hear the new owner is going to make four apartments."

"You know what that means. Hopefully he will use some discretion and be selective in renting them out. After 'Rich' DeVito sold the old homestead you remember what happened, Pete."

"How can I forget? The new owner turned the place into apartments. One of the renters threw his beer bottles out the window. Police were called plenty of times—drugs and fights."

"Actually it hasn't been so bad. Most of the newcomers are decent people trying to raise their families in a quiet area with good schools. They usually improve the single homes enough to make the town proud."

"Think I'll run over to see the kids. I missed them." Peter glanced at his watch.

"Shall I cook some macaroni before you leave?" asked Mamie.

"Not for me, Mom. Aunt Lucy and Aunt Grace served me a banquet at noon. I'm not a bit hungry."

"I'm having a prosciutti and provelone sandwich, a few olives and a glass of wine, Mamie."

"That sounds good. I think I'll have the same."

Peter put on his overcoat and left immediately.

*　　*　　*

June 8 was the last day of school. Nicole was looking forward to the summer vacation. Plans to take a couple of education courses at Lehigh were postponed. Her children were going to spend a couple of weeks in Hoboken with their grandparents.

Scanning the happy faces on this last day, she once again realized how much she would miss this group who helped sustain her through a transitional year. Heartaches and happiness were also apparent in their lives. Jesse had become much more outgoing since her aunt came to live with them. A.J. Jones, a very bright boy, should eventually find success. "Gus" was a live wire and would make an excellent running back for the school football team. Benjamin, personality plus, would always have plenty of friends because of his natural humor and friendliness. Yesterday he cancelled his offer of marriage.

"Mrs. Grasso, I can't marry you any more. I think Jennifer likes me and I like her."

"Got to do what is right for you, Benjamin."

"Whatever 'floats your boat.' Right, Mrs. Grasso?"

"That is correct, Benjamin." Nicole wondered how he came up with these catch phrases—probably from his older brother.

"You are a cool teacher, Mrs. Grasso."

"Thank you, Benjamin."

Nicole wished them all a happy summer and received "high fives" in return. Summer months this year required serious soul-searching and planning.

Part Four

1996

In 1996, much like other recent years, Nicole's focus was largely on her children's education. June 2 was noteworthy since it was the date of Lisa's college graduation from East Stroudsburg University with a B.S. degree in Education and a major in Special Education. After making the Dean's List during the four years, a job was assured in the Pocono area. Andrew had completed two years at Villanova University, and like his Uncle Pete, aspired to become a lawyer. Matthew graduated high school and was accepted at Lehigh University for the fall session. Mechanical engineering was to be his major. Like his grandfather, John, he had a natural ability for that vocation.

College education for three children required financial sacrifice. Nicole had often thought about the expected difficulties. Fortunately the task went along much more smoothly than anticipated. Dan had contributed regularly to their support and college education. Peter became the father image, offering stability and financial assistance with a modern insight. Domenic and Mamie remained healthy and involved. Aunt Zee was heavy-handed in dealing with anyone straying far from the narrow path. John, now in his early nineties, remained in fairly good health. Gina, Lucia and Grace were still quite active. The latter had taken a liking to TV cartoons, probably the effects of a lifetime of baby-sitting.

Exactly what thoughts may have crossed Dan's mind during his children's special occasions, Nicole could not know. He had mailed congratulatory cards and gifts. His children had thanked him and wished him well. They had not totally forgotten the way he had distanced himself from their lives. He was not around when Andrew was in a car accident, or when Matthew received sports honors. The children had lukewarm feelings for their father.

Nicole was outside, conversing with her neighbor Gloria on a Friday morning in late June when the phone rang continuously. She excused herself and ran inside to answer. "Okay, I'm coming. Hold your horses," she whispered as she lifted the receiver with a blunt "Hello."

"Nicole!"

"Maggie, what gives?"

"Did I take you away from something special?"

"Not at all—just some backyard talk with my neighbor."

"Are you alone?"

"Yes."

"I have to report some disturbing news, Nicole."

"Who died now?"

"Not that final but a very tense period for the Grassos. Dan was rushed to the hospital with chest pains overnight. He has to undergo heart surgery."

"Oh for heavens' sake!" Nicole was stunned.

"Mom, Pop, Angelo and Frank are making plans to fly there today. The operation is scheduled for tomorrow morning. As you know they haven't seen each other since the sad event seven years ago."

"Perhaps this will connect them again." Nicole tried to emphasize the positive.

"Too bad it has to be like this. Hopefully he'll make it." Maggie did not sound upbeat.

"Coronary operations have become much more successful in recent years, Maggie. You know that. Besides, Houston has some top-notch hospitals."

"Guess we can only pray, Nicole."

"Wait! Do you happen to know the name of the hospital?"

"No, but I'll let you know as soon as I find out; also, any other pertinent details that may arise."

"Thanks, Maggie, I'll be waiting for your call."

Nicole went into a dither wondering what to do first. None of her children were around. Matthew was taking an entrance examination at Lehigh. Lisa was headed for the bakery to pick up an order for Aunt Lucia. Andrew left with his Uncle Peter to look at used cars. Calling them on the cell phone was the first reaction but decided to wait until they returned home.

Shortly before twelve she heard Peter's Audi in the driveway. Andrew was getting out while the motor was still running. Nicole motioned for Peter to come in. He turned off the ignition and both joined her. Andrew was a head taller than his uncle and resembled Dan, tall, handsome and a beautiful smile. Deeply tanned skin was the result of a week at the shore.

"Something happen? You look unraveled, Mom."

Peter agreed and asked for a reason. Nicole gave a quick resume; Maggie would call back to give an update.

"Shocking to say the least," was all Andrew could utter.

"Never had any symptoms according to Aunt Maggie; of course he may have chosen to ignore them." The discourse continued until Nicole asked them to sit and have something to eat. They had stopped at "Joe's" stand for a couple of hot dogs and a Coke and preferred to simply sit and talk.

Looking upbeat, happy and vibrant as usual, Lisa

walked in about a half hour later, seemingly ready to explode with laughter. "You will never guess what our dear aunts were a party to."

"Tell us. We can always use a good laugh. Nothing they do surprises me."

"Aunt Lucia made me pick up her order—two large loaves of bread and rolls at the bakery."

"So what?" Andrew didn't particularly look interested.

"So what!!" echoed Lisa. "Well let me tell you." Her lovely face was radiant and her eyes gleamed. "That bread I picked up wasn't for them."

"Then who for?" Nicole was baffled by her daughter's prolonged discourse.

"They were for Nina."

"Nina usually calls in her order and picks it up herself when she comes to Roseto," added Nicole.

"Not this time. Do you want to know why?"

"Not really, Lisa, but get to the point." Andrew was getting a bit impatient and in no mood for this type of talk after just hearing the news about their father.

"Do you want to know who else was there?"

"Santa Claus," teased Uncle Pete.

"Not even close. This guy was tall, brown hair and handsome. He probably wanted to give out a 'ho ho' when he became aware of the plot."

"A plot? What is this, a mystery?"

"A very obvious one. When I walked into the kitchen Nina was sharing chamomile tea with our aunts. All looked very pleased with themselves. This guy with the long outstretched legs was Nina's grandson, Ray Thomas, her daughter Julia's son. He is a third year student at Temple Dental School. Nina had tried to match us up for some time. She finally pulled it off. Shades of the times when

Grandma Maria Giuseppe did that sort of thing a century ago, wouldn't you say?"

"Better than arranging a blind date like we often do today. At least you got to see the guy," interjected Andrew. "Something tells me you wouldn't mind hearing from him. Right?"

"I'll be disappointed if I don't. He is a real 'hunk' but then maybe he already has a heart interest."

"What about your friend Jeff?" asked Uncle Pete.

"Raymond is much nicer. Jeff is okay that but it was never a real relationship."

"So why string him along?" Andrew stared at his sister.

Nicole interrupted the conversation and said there were more serious matters to discuss at the moment. "Some unsettling news to report, Lisa."

Lisa looked about and for the first time became aware of a strain on their face. Reacting with sudden panic she simply asked, "What happened now?"

"Dad was rushed to the hospital," replied Andrew.

"Why?"

"Aunt Maggie called moments ago. He is scheduled for heart surgery," Nicole informed her rather bluntly.

"When?"

"Tomorrow morning. I'm expecting Aunt Maggie to call back with more information."

"Wow! What do we do now?"

"Just hope and pray, Lisa," added her Uncle Peter. "Do you have any suggestions?"

Nicole intervened and asked them to wait for Aunt Maggie's call. It was not long in coming. The Grasso's had made flight arrangements and expected to fly from JFK airport in New York to Houston by nightfall. Motel reservations were made. The children wondered if this might be an opportune time to be reunited with their estranged father. Nicole hoped they waited for the result of the operation before making a final decision.

Angelo called on Saturday morning to report that everything went well. Four arteries had to be replaced. Dan was recuperating in the intensive care unit. When he heard that the children were seriously considering making the trip to Houston he was elated. Dan had asked about them while under sedation. Back and forth calls followed until they reported that they planned to fly down on Tuesday morning, and hopefully find their father progressing. Angelo announced that reservations would be made and paid for a flight from Newark—the airport most convenient for them.

* * *

Peter drove Lisa, Andrew and Matthew to Newark Tuesday morning. Nicole accompanied them. It was a bright sunny morning. They arrived within an hour and picked up the tickets at nine A.M. The flight was scheduled for ten A.M. Nicole had anxiety pangs seeing her offspring board the plane while praying the flight would go well. The pilot lifted off the runway smoothly announcing that they would arrive in Houston at twelve-ten P.M., and expected no major weather problem.

Meanwhile Peter and Nicole stopped at a coffee shop for a light breakfast of coffee, orange juice and Danish before returning home.

"I wish I could see the children and Dan when they meet for the first tine in seven years." Nicole spoke as she tried to swallow the pastry.

"You will get a minute by minute description from Lisa. Trust me."

Nicole simply smiled and knew that she would accomplish nothing that day, but wait for Lisa's call.

*   *   *

Low clouds appeared as they flew over Texas. The pilot announced the weather in Houston was misty and hot. There was an hour difference and watches had to be adjusted. "Please set your watches for eleven A.M." The city soon came into view through the light mist. Slowly the jet glided down the runway. The landing was a bit bumpy but on target. They stopped to thank the pilot for a safe trip as they walked over the ramp. After retrieving their flight bags in the huge airport, the sight of their uncles Angelo and Frank wearing broad smiles brought sunshine to this misty day. The reception was warm as they continued embracing and kissing. Only two weeks earlier the Grassos were in Roseto to celebrate Lisa's and Matthew's graduation.

Angelo quickly relieved Lisa of her bags. Dan's condition was naturally the focus of their conversation as they slowly walked to the rented car. Twenty minutes later Frank parked the car in the Desert View Hotel. Waiting outside to greet the grandchildren stood Stella and Vito Grasso. They had been anxiously waiting and rushed to greet them as they emerged from the car. The meeting was tearful. Neither grandparent could subdue their emotion. Lisa held their hands as she walked between them.

Uncles and nephews carried the luggage. After stopping at the main desk to get the keys, they continued down the lengthy beige carpeted hallway and assembled in Vito and Stella's room. The cool, comfortable motel was sheer delight after escaping the humid, hot outdoors.

Two bedrooms had been arranged; one for Lisa, and

247

the other for her brothers. Luggage was deposited in their rooms.

"And how was your flight?" asked Vito. In his seventies, he looked quite hearty and a bit on the heavy side. The hair, what was left, was gray.

"It was pretty smooth, Grand-pop. It seemed like we were here in no time," Andrew replied.

Vito and Stella thought he looked so much like Dan that the grandparents were mesmerized by the resemblance.

"Now let's hear about Dad." Uncle Angelo and Uncle Frank had given a few details but the children were anxious to hear more.

"How does he look?" asked Matthew.

"Not too great, but a lot better than he did on Sunday," commented Frank. "When will we be able to visit?"

"At three o'clock, Lisa. We are only allowed to stay an hour," answered Angelo.

"I can't wait. Does he know we are coming?"

"Yes, we had to tell him, otherwise the visit might be a shock."

"Have you seen Stacy yet?" Lisa was anxious to hear all about her.

"Yeah we saw that 'putana'," replied Stella. She was still wiping away tears of joy at having her grandchildren near her.

"I thought you were going to try and think of her more kindly," interrupted her son.

"Angelo, I only said that I would treat her nice. That's what I promised God if Dan would recover. I didn't promise to love her."

"But aren't we supposed to love everybody? That's what you taught us." Angelo enjoyed teasing "the coach."

"That might take time. Right now she's a fly in my soup."

"Or a fly in your spaghetti sauce," added Vito with a smile.

"Lisa, do you want my assessment of Stacy, from the male viewpoint?"

"Sure, Uncle Frank."

"She's a good-looking, selfish babe."

"Yes she is," added Angelo. "Both frontal and posterior views can turn a man's head and sometimes his senses."

" 'Va fa gula,' you guys are all alike. You gotta look inside the woman sometimes. Matthew don't listen to your uncles. They can be a bad influence," suggested Stella.

Matthew simply smiled. Why not? A popular quarterback on the high school football team, he was the recipient of more than a few female favors. Not quite six feet, he was handsome, muscular and broad-shouldered. Stella was in step with young men's behavior. She had raised four strapping sons. Yet Matthew's innocent looking smile was rather angelic according to Stella's assessment. Grandmothers sometimes think that way.

"I didn't hear a thing, Grandma."

"Yeah, yeah!"

Vito glanced at his watch. "It's almost twelve-thirty. Do you think we should all freshen up and go out for some lunch?"

All agreed and headed for their rooms reassembling a half hour later. Lunch was at "Mario's Bar and Grill," within walking distance and claiming the best pizza in the city. The clouds had lifted and a hot, muggy day was the forecast. A parking lot filled with cars suggested a definite wait for seating accommodations. They entered through the electronic doors and stood in what seemed an endless line of hungry customers. When the waitress yelled, "Table for eight," Angelo raised his hand and responded, "How about seven?"

"Come right this way, sir." and led them to a large corner table in the softly lit corner of the cool dining area. The crowded bar was on the other side. A small dark-haired Spanish waitress approached and distributed menus. Another filled the glasses with water.

Although they had made their choices in advance, they nevertheless glanced over the menu to see what the place had to offer. It included an assortment of pizzas and the usual fast-food items plus a lengthy list of alcoholic drinks. The waitress came back five minutes later with her small tablet and a toothy smile.

Frank gave the order. Two large tomato pizzas—both topped with mozzarella, one with sausage meat, and a small anchovy pizza. Vito and his sons had wine. The others had iced tea or lemonade. As they waited for their order they became engrossed with the family at the next table—parents and two small blonde girls about six and eight. The mother was a blonde while the father was dark, either Italian or Spanish. The youngest of the girls had a good portion of the tomato pizza on her face and occasionally the mother would dab the child's face while the child resisted.

"Why doesn't she just let that kid eat in peace?" remarked Matthew.

"Because the mother wants her to look pretty and not sloppy," shrugged Lisa at her brother's annoyance.

Angelo had a mouthful of anchovy pizza when he nearly flipped upon detecting a figure, familiar even in the dimly lit room. It was Stacy at the bar with two gentlemen, one on either side of her. One appeared to be a short bald-headed man, the other a tall gentlemen. Both wore business suits.

He turned to Frank, sitting next to him and whispered, "Do you see who's sitting at the bar?"

"Holy mackerel! I wonder if she even made a trip to the hospital this morning."

Stella was taking a long drink of iced tea when she saw her sons deep in conversation and staring across the way. "What's got you guys so rattled?"

"Do you recognize anybody sitting at the bar?" asked Angelo knowing his mother might rupture a blood vessel at the sighting. Her round full face turned a fiery red. A few quality Italian names began spewing out of her mouth besides "That son of a bitch! There's your 'faccia brutta,' stepmother guys." All eyes turned towards the bar.

"Let's keep our composure and handle this with common sense. Remember we are in a public place," suggested Angelo. "Suppose we wait until they are ready to leave. Then I'll approach, greet her, and ask if she would care to meet Dan's children."

"I believe that's the best way," concurred Vito. "Stella, it's best that you just keep asking God's peace." His wife gave him one of her not so lovable stares.

The grandchildren were sophisticated enough to handle the situation with dignity although their first encounter with Stacy was in a bar. Every generation has its own way of evaluating similar circumstances. Lisa grabbed her grandmother's hand and squeezed it tightly, understanding the nature of her feelings.

When Stacy slung her purse over her shoulder and apparently was ready to leave, Angelo decided it was time to confront her. He began the slow and deliberate approach.

"Hello, Stacy!"

She turned around. Surprise was written over her face. "Hi, Angelo. Looks like you too are here for a fast bite to eat?"

251

And don't forget the booze, thought Angelo, but only replied, "Yes, they have delicious pizza."

"Meet business associates of mine—Harry Katz and Sidney Mooney. This is my husband's brother, Angelo Grasso." Hands were extended and a short meaningless conversation followed.

"Will you be going to the hospital again this afternoon?"

"Yes, we hope to."

"I called him this morning. His voice sounded much stronger. Hopefully I'll visit this evening."

Damn you, thought Angelo, who felt like saying, "Why didn't you at least make a quick visit this morning?" Instead his dark eyes turned to her. "I would like you to meet Dan's children. We are sitting at a back table."

"I was looking forward to meeting them. Dan told me they were flying in today to join you." She then turned to her companions. "I'll see you back in the car."

The Grasso family watched as she and Angelo walked toward them. Everything looked well on her. The white linen suit with the black top was no exception. The blonde hair was trimmed slightly shorter than usual. Smiling with utmost sincerity or seeming so to the family, she looked toward Stella and Vito. "Good afternoon, Mr. and Mrs. Grasso, and you too, Frank. Finally I get to meet Dan's children."

"Good afternoon," they replied almost in unison.

Andrew and Matthew immediately rose and shook hands following the introductions. Frank and Vito stood up but did not shake hands, since they had already met at the hospital. Stella remained seated but Lisa rose to greet the older woman with a slight bow and forced smile. Everything was done almost casually.

She stared at Andrew momentarily stunned by the

likeness to Dan. "I can't believe how much you resemble your father. And you, Matthew, are the well-built and popular quarterback I've heard about."

The boys thanked her. Andrew gave his stepmother the fast look and decided she was well put together. Matthew gawked and gave his winning smile. Lisa was non-committal, but Stacy was certainly aware of the dark-haired beauty that sat next to her grandmother. Three grown attractive people were not what Stacy had envisioned.

"I am definitely astounded to see the difference compared to photos that Dan has in his wallet. Certainly he will be surprised as well." Stacy continued to give her best pitch. After all she was a saleswoman and tried to come across as the sophisticated blonde beauty. "I am so sorry that I cannot spend more time with you at the moment. Hopefully we will get together before you leave. Right now I have an appointment." Stacy glanced at her watch and then Dan's children "It was so nice to meet you, Andrew, Matthew and Lisa. I will try to see you all again before you leave." Eyes turned toward her as she passed through the aisle and made her way to the car.

"So what do you think of your stepmother?" asked Angelo with a grin, anticipating some blunt remarks.

Matthew got up and gave a comical performance much as he had done in the all-male school play. Using his arms in the most feminine way and with a distinct wiggle, he mimicked Stacy. "It has been a pleasure to meet you all. Do hope we get to see each other again." He brought the family to an outburst of laughter and concluded, "Do you know what? She is a fake."

"No doubt about it, but she is an attractive woman," added Andrew with a shrug.

"And self-centered; that's for sure." Lisa was still

amused by Matthew's dramatic take. "Grandma how come you remained so cool?"

"Lisa, when I can look around and see my wonderful children and grandchildren and the way they handle themselves, I thank the Almighty God. Why should I let out with some appropriate Italian words and embarrass you all?"

Vito agreed with utmost enthusiasm. "Thank God, Stella, for a change you acted like a woman."

"Take a hike, Vito, before you get to see the real me again."

"That never floors me," added her husband while placing a kiss on her chubby round cheeks.

"What say we get started? We still have an hour before visiting hours; suppose we do a little sightseeing around the city prior to the hospital visit?"

"Sounds good, Uncle Angelo," replied Lisa as she began to rise from the chair. A white sleeveless sheath dress hugged her youthful body.

Vito stopped at the register to pay the bill and get a few mints. Angelo waited for him and together they walked outdoors into the oppressive heat. It was already beginning to look like a day destined to be packed-full of activity. After returning to the motel for a few minutes to freshen up, they called a "limo" for sightseeing and the hospital visit.

As the moment approached for the children to finally meet their father after a long time of minimum communication, anxiety prevailed. The driver stopped in front of St. Thomas Hospital and assisted them out of the limo. Pick-up was arranged for four-thirty P.M. They walked through the door, flush with the front walk and into the spacious entrance room adorned with huge plants. Two elderly women sat at the desk probably volunteers. Angelo already knew the procedures and asked for permission to visit the patient in room 408, Dan Grasso. No problem.

Everything seemed relatively quiet as they entered the elevator. Frank pushed the button for the fourth floor. Two young nurses who had entered with them got out on the second floor. When the elevator stopped on the fourth floor, Stella uttered a quick prayer. Lisa held on to her grandmother's hand as they continued down the lengthy white tile corridor until they stopped in front of room 408. The family decided not to enter in unison and present an overpowering experience for Dan. The door was wide open—a good sign thought Stella. She was the first to enter with Lisa squarely behind her—almost hidden. Stella was a big woman.

There he was—sitting in a chair, in blue and white pajamas, anticipating this momentous occasion. Gaunt, salt and pepper hair, and naturally weakened by the operation, he looked up at his mother as she planted a kiss on his cheek. She was careful not to injure the incision on his chest. When she stepped aside Lisa and father looked at each other in total forgiving love. She embraced him carefully, withdrew and looked into his eyes. Happiness erased the pain of a long and bitter separation. He gathered her hands in his. "How is my precious and vivacious cheerleader? I missed you all very much."

"We missed you too, Dad."

Stella withdrew toward the hallway and asked the boys to go in. Grandparents and uncles observed from a short distance away. Dan looked up as they came slowly toward him, barely able to contain himself. Never had he been able to properly envision the sight of these strapping and handsome young sons. Strong arms circled his shoulders. Tears began to roll down his cheeks. Lisa wiped them away with her tissue.

An attractive young nurse walked in, smiling broadly and peered into his face. "How are you doing, Mr. Grasso?"

"Right now I have no pain." Dan proceeded with introductions.

Pointing to Andrew, she said, "This one resembles you a great deal."

"Thank you, Miss Jenkins. I'm deeply thankful and undeserving of the three of them." Tears welled in his eyes.

The nurse monitored his blood pressure, smiled again and left after a "Nice to have met you all."

Andrew eyeballed her as she departed. "Not bad." The others smiled and were grateful for the slight break of tension. Dan was happy for a couple of healthy guys.

The other Grassos joined them after the nurse gave her okay. Sentimentality had obviously overcome them as well. Stella was still dabbing her eyes. She relaxed in a convenient chair.

"Now tell me, Dan, did you ever expect your kids to be so good-looking?" "They owe it all to their mother, Frank. Most important, they are decent, healthy and well-educated children."

"Your influence during our formative years was also important, Dad; financial help was greatly appreciated," said Lisa who tried to smooth the situation and downplay the difficult years when she wanted him out of her life.

"Thank you, Honey. You are much too kind. How is your mother?"

"Never stops, feels well and looks well, just like the others in the clan."

"How are they doing?"

"Well, Grandpa John said he wants to live to be a hundred but only if Grandma Gina is with him. Grandmother Mamie and Grandfather Domenic are hearty and well. Uncle Peter is a gem and really seems to be interested in this new girl he is dating."

"And Uncle Neil and Aunt Zee?"

"They still like to go dancing on Saturday night. Aunt Zee never stops giving her advice. We agree solely to get her off our backs."

"How about your two old aunts, about ninety I guess?" Dan was beginning to feel comfortable.

"They are still around and make sure we always have enough to eat, especially when Mom has to go someplace," added Matthew. "Sometimes they do goofy things. Dandelions are out by early April. Aunt Lucia took her old car and she and Aunt Grace, paper bag in hand, decided to go out in the country to gather a few for a salad. Aunt Grace spotted an old nemesis while picking the dandelions—a dog; a harmless beagle, probably the pet of the farmer who owned the property. She slipped down the bank in a hurry to get away. Lucky she didn't pull her back out of place again." Mathew loves to tell funny aunt stories which are exaggerated and embellished.

Dan laughed and then held his chest at the slight pain.

"Does it hurt, Dad?" asked Lisa, appearing deeply concerned while she smoothed his hair.

"Only slightly, Honey. They give me plenty of pain pills."

"How long will you be staying here?"

"Several more days, I think. I'm looking forward to going back home. You can bet on that."

"Who will be taking care of you?" asked Stella.

"We have a housekeeper who comes in to clean for us once a week, Ma. She has agreed to spend a few hours each day with me until Stacy gets home from work."

His mother's stomach began to churn "acido." *The "bitch" can't even stay home and nurse him a short period*, she thought but restrained herself from agitating her son. When alone with her sons that night, she again brought up the subject but she was thwarted. "Ma, stop living in the middle ages. She has a job. Besides they can afford the necessary care. Don't be a dinosaur," was Angelo's curt reply.

Hospital visits continued until the return flight home scheduled for Friday. They met Stacy at the hospital one afternoon. An invitation to visit was extended. They thanked her but declined due to a tight schedule.

Before they said their good-byes Dan looked at his daughter. "Lisa, may I ask one big favor of you?"

"What's that, Dad?"

"May I have the honor of escorting my beautiful daughter down the aisle on her wedding day?"

"It would make me very happy, Dad." She kissed him. "But first I must find the right guy."

"Shouldn't be much trouble, Honey."

It was a tearful separation. To be reunited with his children for only a brief time was exhilarating. But watching them as they left the room that final afternoon was a real downer. It was all hugs, kisses and promises to meet more often.

*　　*　　*

At five-twenty P.M. Friday, their jet taxied down on the Newark Airport runway. Nicole and Peter were there to meet them. The children had telephoned home several times, but now the ride home would be full of interesting revelations. After picking up the luggage they joined mother and uncle—all exhibiting smiling faces and happiness.

"How was your flight?"

"The best, Uncle Pete," Matthew was the first to answer. "Going and coming." They hugged, kissed their mother and headed for Peter's Audi.

"Man, it's great to get back to cooler weather. It was

over a hundred in Houston." Relief was apparent in Andrew's face.

After the placement of luggage into the trunk, all piled in for the ride on Interstate 80.

"So how would you guys grade the reestablishment of your relationship with your dad?" asked their uncle.

"Definitely 'tops,'" was Andrew's immediate response.

"I'll go along with that," added Matthew. "His feelings were pretty much there for us to see."

"That's for sure," agreed Lisa. "You might also be surprised to hear that he asked to 'give me away' if and when I marry."

"Who would marry you?" said Matthew with an impish grin.

"Some smart, good-looking guy with good taste," replied Lisa as she pretended to land a blow to his ear. "By the way, Mom, he wanted to thank you for the get-well card."

"Thought I would do my good deed for the month. I am surprised to hear he wants to be part of your wedding."

"I didn't expect him to have the courage to revisit his past," said Peter.

"No, I believe he would definitely want to assume that pleasure in light of what has just transpired." Nicole maintained quite reservations about having to face him again.

"Hey, by the way, what about Stacy?" asked Peter

"Just another beautiful self-centered iceberg," answered Andrew. "You wouldn't believe where we first met her."

"Where?"

"In a bar and grill where we were having lunch with our grandparents and uncles. She was at the bar with a couple of business associates."

"Can't blame her for a short break."

"Neither can I, but my grandmother isn't that liberal-minded. Darts were flying plus a few unmentionable words were probably brewing. Fortunately she kept them to herself." Lisa evoked some laughter with her remarks.

"Even I know the meaning of those words. And they ain't pretty," interjected Matthew.

The siren from a trooper's car or ambulance was audible. Peter checked his rear view mirror and his speedometer—sixty miles an hour. State troopers were racing to an emergency scene a few miles ahead where several distraught ladies waited beside their steaming car.

"Mom, did I get any telephone calls while we were away?"

"Not one, Lisa. Raymond didn't call, sorry."

"Forget it. How much do you want to bet that he has a steady doll in his Philadelphia apartment right now? Maybe someone he met at Temple." Andrew could be a bit merciless.

"Do you think Nina would push the match if he had a steady friend?"

"Get real, Lisa. You know darn well that couples even live together without going public about the relationship. Telling their grandmothers, who are clinging to old rules, only incurs their wrath."

"So we'll just wait and see," countered Lisa.

"Yeah, why don't you do that?"

Peter and Nicole remained relatively quiet. Their generation began the sexual revolution and experienced the relaxation of Puritan values.

Andrew dozed off. He wanted no part of the conversation. His siblings reverted to discussing their visit to Houston and the happy relationships fostered by the trip. They crossed the Delaware River Bridge and then entered the town of Mount Bethel. They would be home in ten minutes.

*   *   *

June had been a comfortable month but July turned up the heat. Nicole was taking an education course at Lehigh. It meant an increase in pay. Matthew was a lifeguard at the pool, while Andrew was working at his uncle's law office for the summer months. Lisa had not heard from Raymond. Lucia and Grace told her that he was taking a course at Temple. Nina and her husband were visiting relatives in Ohio so information from that source was stifled. Lisa, hoping for something better, had decided to call off her lukewarm relationship with Jeff.

A faculty meeting for the new teachers was scheduled for that morning at the Mansfield Middle School. It was to be a short get-acquainted event prior to the superintendent's vacation. Lisa was looking forward to getting a glimpse of the guidance room and meeting a few of the faculty members. Boredom had begun to set in. She had called her father a few times during the last two weeks; he was doing quite well. By nine A.M. she was driving fifteen miles north to get an inkling of her first real job.

Seven new teachers had been hired—all were recent college graduates. The meeting lasted an hour. A sparkling clean room with modern furniture was waiting for her—inviting enough to spur Lisa's ambition to start working.

Next stop was a bookstore where while sifting through a pile of paperbacks, she looked up to see a familiar face. "Find something interesting?" It was Martha Trays from ESU.

"Hi, Martha! Thought I would stop here a minute before heading home. I was at Mansfield for a brief meeting."

Her friend was a heavy-set girl with a high I.Q. and had graduated "cum laude." "Any new developments with you?"

"An interview at Mount Pocono in about two hours. There are a couple of openings in the middle school."

Lisa was positive her friend would easily land a job. "Let's head for the coffee corner."

After a brief time with each other, Lisa returned home via the mountain road and made a last minute decision to stop at her great grandparent's home.

Gina in a lightweight floral housedress met her at the door when she heard the sound of the Volkswagen and the slam of the car door.

"How did your meeting go?" The family was on top of each other's schedule.

"Not bad. I got to see my room and love it, 'Grams.' Where's Grand-pop?"

"In the kitchen having a bite to eat. There's enough for you too." Lisa followed her through the old but well kept rooms. Fans were used to cool the house on this hot July day. Windows were kept closed. Her grandparents did not like air conditioning.

"Hi, Grand-pop."

"Hi, sweetheart. Come sit and join us for a little lunch. Your grandmother made some breaded zucchini flowers."

"I'm in time to eat one of my favorite dishes. You know how much I like zucchini flowers." Lisa hugged him. "Grandma, please sit I'll get my own dish." Gina was quickly thwarted as she walked toward the cabinet.

Beside the zucchini there was a fresh tomato salad, sliced provelone, and John's all time favorite, fried peppers; also fresh Italian bread to soak up the succulent garlic flavored olive oil in the salad. That menu had not changed through the century.

Lisa lifted the crisply fried zucchini with her fingers, relishing every bite, and then helped herself to some of the other food including a small glass of wine. Her great-grandparents watched adoringly.

"How is that knee doing, Grand-pop?"

"Not much change from day to day. The pills dull the pain but I'll be taking the bad knees to my grave. How did you make out at the school?"

"It was short and sweet." Before she proceeded further she heard the heavy click of heels outdoors and when the kitchen door opened, to no one's surprise in walked Aunt Zee carrying a small package and a container of blue berries.

"Lisa, I never expected to see you. I thought you were supposed to be at a faculty meeting."

"Went and got back already, Auntie. And in time to get my fill of zucchini flowers."

Aunt Zee reached in the cabinet for a dish and sat down at the table. "Everything go okay?"

"Sure it was a thirty minute meeting and a first look at the room where I will be spending my work week."

Aunt Zee helped herself to some tomato salad and began to plunge the bread into the olive oil. "I see you are beginning to get tomatoes from those few plants you have, Pop. Nothing like freshly picked ripe tomatoes."

"Did you notice the garlic I pulled out?"

"How could I miss? It's spread out and drying on the back porch." She had walked the short distance from her home and entered through the rear door.

"Where is Neil?"

"He spent most of the morning at the Fire House with the guys." Aunt Zee had a helping of zucchini flowers. "How many of these things did you fry, Ma?"

"Thirty-two. Your father had to contend with the bees while picking them this morning."

"They enjoy them like any other flower," added John.

"Ma, did you notice, I got the yarn? It's on the countertop. Now you can complete that afghan. How's your dad doing, Lisa?"

"Pretty well, Auntie. We called last night. He has slight pain but goes outdoors to enjoy the yard."

"Did you read the obituary section in the Express this morning?"

"Yes I did Pop. Mike Pulli passed away. The hospital kept him hooked up a long time. It's best this way. He will be cremated; always claimed it was more sanitary. Neil's uncle was cremated. During the Memorial Mass the urn containing his ashes sat on a table in front of the altar. It was so final."

"This is getting depressing. Let's talk about happy things," pleaded Lisa. She wanted to ask if they knew anything about Ray but perhaps that too might invite gloom. Her grandparents were old and didn't seem to mind talking of death. In fact they always said they were ready whenever God called. Funeral arrangements were formulated years ago. "I heard you were at the Jersey mall yesterday. Did you get the coat you wanted, Aunt Zee?"

"Yes, a burnt orange light-weight coat for autumn. You may also be interested in knowing that senility is beginning to affect your great aunt."

"I would never have guessed," answered Lisa displaying her sparking smile. "What makes you say that?"

John and Gina looked surprised to hear such an admission from their still perky daughter.

Aunt Zee picked up another zucchini flower, dipped it in the remaining salad in her dish and chewed slowly. "That mall, as you know, is huge and generally crowded and yesterday due to the sale, it was even more so. After parking the car, I began what seemed like a mile hike to the stores. For a change I wore sneakers. Thank God for that!"

"You must have really been tired, Auntie?"

"Yes, Lisa, but that is not the gist of the story." Aunt Zee took a long swallow of iced tea. "Carrying a big coat box and a shopping bag of other sale items is pretty tiresome, even for a big woman like me especially for the long walk back to the car."

"Don't tell me you dropped everything?" Gina looked somewhat anxious.

"No, Ma, I didn't know where I parked the car or what direction to go."

"Isn't the place alphabetically laid out?" John could not believe his self-assured daughter could have been so absent-minded.

"Sure, but who looked? In desperation I approached a young man and asked for help. It's a 1975 Chrysler I told him."

" 'Lady, with that type of car it's no problem,' he said while grabbing my packages. The car was located within minutes.

"After thanking and tipping him generously, I heaved a sigh of relief, praised God and headed home."

"Did you tell Neil?"

"No, Ma, you know darn well he would never let me forget it."

The foibles of the large malls were discussed at length until John excused himself, hobbled over to his lounge chair in the living room and turned on the television. Gina checked out the yarn. Aunt Zee and Lisa began to clear the table and wash dishes. The phone rang Gina picked up the receiver on her portable. It was Mamie who called her mother to report that the Canadian cousins would not be

265

coming for the "Big Time." Maria Filippe had undergone minor surgery and several of the others were spending the month in Roseto, Italy. The special bus would not be making the usual trip. Gina was clearly disappointed as were the rest when she hung up and relayed the message. Somehow their absence would diminish the gaiety of that annual event.

*　　*　　*

A heavy overnight thunderstorm had blown out electrical power. Nicole was up before seven A.M. Microwave and clocks were out. Fortunately the telephone lines were still intact. July was prime month for electrical storms in the area. Nicole decided to call her parents They were notoriously early risers. Mamie answered the phone.

"Mom, do you have lights?"

"No, Nicole, but your Dad was outside talking to some neighbors. They claim a transmitter was hit by lightning. Met-Ed's trucks are in the area so power should soon be restored. Television is out also. Are the guys up yet?"

"I can hear the water running; Andrew is taking a shower. The other two are still sleeping. I was planning to go shopping this morning but the stores too are probably out of power. I'll play it safe and postpone it to this afternoon."

"I miss my coffee which I have first thing in the morning. Lucy next door has a gas stove. She called me over so I'll visit for a short time I'll call back later, Nicole."

"Okay, Mom. Say 'hello' to Lucy for me."

"Will do."

Andrew walked into the kitchen as Nicole hung up the receiver. "No power Mom?"

"The storm knocked out a transmitter in the area."

266

"I didn't realize we had a storm; slept like a log."

"Can't brew coffee, Andrew."

"No big deal. I'll only have orange juice. Later in the morning I'll take a break and go over to Rosie's for coffee and a couple of eggs and bacon."

"Watch those cholesterol packed foods, Andrew, especially in light of what happened to your dad."

"We have good genes, Mom. Now look at the Decenti family. They are plagued by heart disease."

"They are not the only ones so plagued. Your Grasso grandparents are fine, yet the son became a victim. Diet is a factor too, Andrew."

"Could be Stacy is also a factor. Tension brings on plenty of diseases. It's a fast, tense life, Mom. Families don't just sit around cracking nuts and squeezing their bodies around the kitchen table to talk like they did when 'Mamona' Maria Giuseppe raised her family. Those days are part of history. Today it's eat or be eaten."

"And live on fast foods, drugs, and all kinds of pills."

"You are intelligent, Mom. You know what's happening. It's a hard fight. I'll see you around four-thirty this afternoon."

Nicole knew all too well. Life is a battle. She was thankful for her family. How else could she have battled through rough times. The lights went on at exactly nine-eleven. She hurried to adjust the clock, microwave, and plug in the coffee pot. Lisa walked in shortly after Andrew left. She was dressed in white denim pedal pushers and sleeveless top to match.

"Good morning, Mom. Power outage hit us?"

"We had a horrendous thunderstorm." Nicole poured herself coffee in a mug. "Did you sleep through it?"

"I was aware of it but sleepy enough to ignore it.

Knowing how they frighten you, I presume you walked the floors."

"That I did. The power went off about five so I lit a few candles. Would you care for coffee, Honey?" Nicole sipped hers while standing.

"No thanks. I'm having orange juice and cereal. By the way are we going shopping?"

"Shall we go this morning while the temperature is still comfortable or wait until later in the day?" Nicole sat at the table with her coffee mug.

"I am all for going now."

It was the right decision for they found the stores relatively quiet and were able to get what they wanted in record time. Purchases were put away and by eleven A.M. Lisa curled up in a comfortable chair with one of the paperbacks she had picked up in Stroudsburg.

Nicole was sweeping away the debris of leaves left by the storm when a black car approached slowly, as if not familiar with the area. He checked the house number and turned off the ignition. A tall young man with reddish brown hair, wearing tight blue jeans and a white sport shirt walked briskly toward her. The friendly smile conjured up a feeling that perhaps they had met before.

"Are you Mrs. Grasso?"

"Yes I am," was her immediate reply.

"My name is Raymond Thomas, grandson of Nina Castellucci. Hope that rings a bell." He extended his hand and held hers a minute or so. A broad smile appeared on Nicole's face.

"Why of course it does, family connections go way back." This sudden appearance of her daughter's dream man was bound to send Lisa for a loop. *She was right, he is a "hunk,"* thought Nicole.

"I have already come to that realization after meeting

Aunt Lucia and Aunt Grace," replied Ray. "Quite an usual pair those two, especially after learning they were approaching their nineties. A couple of romantics I think."

Nicole laughed and agreed that her greats aunts looked at the world through rose-colored glasses.

"Mrs. Grasso, I am sorry to come here without first calling, but our telephone lines are down because of the storm. Hopefully you will not mind if I talk to Lisa a few minutes. By the way is she in?"

"Yes she is, just follow me." Nicole wondered if Ray's sudden appearance might not "freak out" her daughter and cause a loss of composure.

She led him through the back entrance, into the kitchen and then the living room. There her daughter was still curled up in the chair, deeply engrossed in the book and not even bothering to look up until she heard her mother's voice, "Lisa, Ray is here to see you."

An expression of shock, thrill and dismay for not looking her best covered Lisa's face as she desperately struggled into her sandals to greet Ray.

"Telephone lines were down. Since Ray had to come up this way he decided on a personal visit."

"Actually I had to come up and pick up a couple of tomato pies at the bakery." Ray smiled and enjoyed the naturalness of Lisa's appearance.

"I'll leave you two alone."

"Please don't, Mrs. Grasso. I am only staying a few minutes."

"Would you care for a cup of coffee?"

"No, but will gladly take a rain check."

"Happy to oblige," replied Nicole.

Lisa was secretly elated hoping that might suggest a return visit. The three talked about relationships and his grandmother's young years in Roseto, and how she had continued the friendships over the long span of time.

"Nina and my grandfather, John, go back a long time," added Nicole.

"After hearing some of my grandmother's stories, that does not surprise me."

"You will be graduating soon from Temple Dental School?" asked Lisa trying to collect her emotions.

"In January of 1997 to be exact. I've been taking one of the more complex courses during the summer so I can breeze through the final semester. July in Philly is no picnic."

"Do you live on campus?" inquired Lisa, while giving him an A+ dental smile.

"No, I have a tiny apartment off campus but close enough to make a quick dash to school." Finally Ray came to the point of his visit. The stage-show "Late Night Catechism" was being presented at the State Theater in Easton on the following evening, Saturday night, and he asked Lisa if she was interested in attending.

"I would love to," was her enthusiastic response, as she tried hard to maintain her equilibrium.

"Great, I'll pick you up at six P.M. Time of the show is at eight P.M." Ray rose to leave. His grandmother was expecting the tomato pies to feed a hungry bunch of grandchildren. Lisa led him to the door—same way he came in, not taking chances on incurring bad luck by using the front door.

Euphoria reigned supreme as Lisa gave out a cheer. Nicole was happy for her daughter. So were Andrew and Matthew upon hearing the news. But like many brothers pretended to remain low-key. "Curtains it will be when Ray really gets to know you, Lisa."

"Get lost," was her only response.

Within hours the news had circulated among the clan.

Gina and John were not surprised. Neither were Lucia and Grace.

*   *   *

A telephone call came from Ray about five P.M. Nicole answered and called out, "Ray is on the phone."

Lisa rushed in, fearing a postponement of the date.

"Hi, Ray."

"Lisa, would it be all right if I picked you up about fifteen minutes earlier?" came Ray's low voice.

"That will be just fine." Relief was written over her face.

"My Mother and Dad would very much like to meet you. Okay with you?"

"It will be a pleasure."

"Great! See you soon."

Lisa showered, brushed her hair and applied a light touch of rouge and lipstick. After selecting a simple sleeveless black dress from her closet and a pair of high-heeled shoes, she was ready for the evening. Ray was tall. A couple of extra inches helped. Lisa was not a novice at this sort of thing, yet this was different. She was not relaxed. After one last glance in the full-length bedroom mirror she listened for the doorbell.

A nagging thought kept creeping up. What if Ray was dating her just to satisfy his grandmother? Aunt Lucia and Aunt Grace could also be part of the conspiracy. The sound of the doorbell put a halt to that morose thought.

"Good evening, Ray," came her mother's voice.

"Good evening, Mrs. Grasso. How are you this evening?"

"Just fine, thank you. I think Lisa heard the bell but let me make sure." She returned quickly and Lisa followed, exchanged simple greetings, bid Nicole goodbye and walked toward Ray's black Ford. He held the door for Lisa and hustled towards the driver's side. Before turning on the ignition, he looked down on her and merely smiled and said, "You look very pretty."

Ray looked handsome in his light summer suit, but she decided to forgo any suggestion of flattery for the time being. She simply gave him a sweet smile and said, "Thank you."

"My parents are looking forward to meeting you. Hope you don't mind?"

"Not one bit. And in fact I'm very honored. Will your Grammy also be there?"

"Wouldn't put it past her. You're smart enough to know that in her own subtle way she was instrumental in having you deliver that bread to your aunts' home a few weeks ago. When I saw you enter that kitchen and then looking at those innocent faces I wanted to tell them, 'Who do you nice old gals think you're kidding? You set this up.' "

"I too got the message," laughed Lisa, "especially since your Grammy was aiming to introduce us."

Smiling he turned to Lisa and said, "Since I saw a beautiful girl there were no complaints."

The twenty-minute drive was quite pleasant and they were soon approaching Jefferson Drive. They parked in front of a two-story, colonial home with tall white columns.

"Here is our home, Lisa." Ray helped her out and they walked the path to the front door.

Julia was the youngest of Nina and Victor's children. A woman in her mid-fifties, she married David Thomas and became the mother of Raymond and an older son, Eugene (Gene) who was married and had a son and daughter—nine and eleven.

Julia had waited anxiously for the sound of Ray's car

and when she saw them, ran to open the door. "So glad to finally meet you. I have visited your grandparents a number of times but never saw you there. Ray couldn't let me down." Lisa recognized the striking resemblance to her mother including the outgoing personality.

After embracing, they entered the spacious living room where David Thomas rose to shake her hands and introduce himself, "I am Julia's 'Med-e-gon's husband' " the often used slang humorously used to identify a non-Italian or American. Dave was a solid, tall beefy man with a great sense of humor who worked as a superintendent on structural steel buildings. He always earned good money so that Julia became a housewife devoted only to her husband and boys.

"It's a pleasure to meet you. Back home they will be happy to hear that Ray was kind enough to have me meet his parents." Lisa, now feeling very much at ease and looking beautiful, easily found favor with Julia and David Thomas.

Small talk about the Roseto relatives continued briefly until Ray looked at his watch and reminded them that they had to leave.

"Hate to see you go so quickly."

"Mom, you know we have dinner and theater tickets."

"Okay, I won't push you this time." His parents kissed Lisa and asked her to convey best wishes to her relatives. Nowhere was Nina to be seen. Julia called immediately after they departed and did the briefing.

*   *   *

Dinner was at the "Copper Kettle," a popular dining spot because of the fish menu. They sat at the bar for a cocktail while waiting for their order. It was a twenty-minute wait before they were led to a candlelit table. A platter of breaded shrimp, scallops, steamed clams and mussels were the entrée. Fries and spiced cabbage went with it.

Conversation was about school and jobs. Ray focused on his lovely date with the full red lips and decided that sometimes old folks have excellent taste. For the time being she was a "ten."

The State theatre, sitting atop of Northampton Street, had been renovated, but did not in any way lose the symbolic beauty of times past when movie theatres were ornate castles. They were havens during the depression years of the thirties and early forties. People escaped from dreary realities into a magnificent edifice and for a few hours watched as Hollywood carried them into dreamland. No longer a movie house, popular entertainers, plays and personalities are featured stars at the "STATE."

Every seat in the theatre was occupied. The show commanded a capacity crowd. Ray and Lisa had excellent seats and became thoroughly wrapped up in the performance of the woman playing the part of a nun. There was plenty to discuss while homeward bound.

Ray parked the car in front of the Grasso home twenty minutes later and turned off the ignition and headlights.

"Isn't the celebration in two weeks?" asked Ray.

"Yes it is the last weekend in July," responded Lisa.

"I would like very much to come up on Saturday night and escort you around the carnival and watch the fireworks with you."

"And I would love having you, Ray."

"My course will be complete that Friday. It's going to be all studying for me until then. When I get back I'll give you a call."

"Have you ever been here during the feast?"

"Yes, a few times with some buddies. I expect to enjoy it a lot more this year." Ray gave Lisa a pat on her hand and stepped out of the car to help her out. They strolled up the dark walk to the door. Only a dim light from the living room brightened the way. Lisa reached for her keys from a small black purse. Ray took the key from her, opened the door, handed it back and pecked her on the cheek. "Thanks for a lovely evening."

"I enjoyed it thoroughly. Thank you, Ray."

*   *   *

Three blasts of aerial fireworks marked the opening of Our Lady of Mt. Carmel Celebration at twelve noon on July 27,1996. Absent was the influx of relatives from distant areas. Those who did come stayed at motels. In years past such a decision would have been unacceptable. There was always room for visitors, even if it meant family members relinquishing their beds temporarily for floor mattresses. Although much less of the past was obvious, the spirit of a century old tradition was not lost.

Motorists were already beginning to latch on to parking spaces. Before nightfall spaces would be unavailable. Cars were parked on both sides of the streets throughout the borough. Sausage and pepper stands began what would be a busy night. The weather forecast was favorable making for decent crowds at the carnival grounds and for the fireworks displays.

Following the pattern of the past seventy-five years the "Queen of the Celebration" would be crowned at six-thirty P.M. That title rested on the head of the young lady who sold the most raffle tickets. Several other girls who vied for the honor but fell short became princesses. Active church members who were seniors at Pius High School, across the

275

street from the church, and Bangor High School were eligible to become members of the court.

Beth called about eight-thirty A.M. on Saturday morning. Nicole had already prepared desserts for the weekend festivities. Sunday dinner was at the parents' home as usual, while the afternoon would be spent at their grandparents' home. The route of the religious procession down Garibaldi Avenue took it past their home. Family members, most of them senior folks, watched from porches and lawns.

"I am on the way to the Farmers' Market, Nicole. Anything you need for the weekend?"

"Nothing I can think of at the moment. I stopped at Miller's farm and picked up a few fresh fruits and vegetables. What time will you be here, Beth?"

"About three. The kids want to join their friends there and get an early look at the carnival. We will be sleeping at Mom's overnight. How did Lisa's date go?"

"Evidently quite well. I'll probably hear more after she gets up."

"Great, I'm anxious to get the low-down. See you in a few hours."

Lisa walked into the kitchen about nine-thirty A.M. Nicole had the morning paper stretched out across the table and periodically took a sip of coffee.

"Morning, Honey. Did you sleep well?"

"After an hour of tossing and turning, I finally dozed off." Lisa reached in the refrigerator for orange juice, poured herself about half a glass and sat down.

"So, what's your assessment of Ray now?" Nicole already knew the answer. Her daughter's radiant face spelled out the answer.

"Exceptionally nice, well-mannered. Sorry the evening ended as soon as it did. We stopped at his parents' home before dinner and theater. Julia looks and acts a lot like her mother." Lisa smiled broadly.

"Why do you say that?"

"Mom, you know Nina. Tells you exactly how she feels. You can't help liking her. Also she is very affectionate. Her daughter is the same."

"The death of a sister, Julia, many years ago was a tragic loss. She named her daughter after her."

"I never knew that. In any event, I enjoyed the meeting. Ray's father is a big man with a good sense of humor. It was as if I had known them a long time."

"I take it the dinner and play went well?"

"Just a perfect evening, Mom. I'll be seeing Ray again this evening. We are going to the carnival. Don't cook. We will eat there. Andrew and Matthew will want sausage and peppers."

"They already told me to forget about cooking supper."

*   *   *

Nicole, her mother and daughter walked to the church for the queen ceremony and joined a large crowd of other interested spectators. Father James Prior, the pastor, was already on the podium. He was one of four brothers who became priests. The speaker joined him as the band readied the instruments for the appearance of the queen and her court. Strings of decorative flags were whipped about by a light breeze. Photographers were already clicking their cameras. Friends, some arriving from distances, joined the camaraderie. Anticipation heightened with the ever-swelling crowd.

With the first blast of music came the appearance of the princesses and senior high students, each beautifully gowned and individually introduced as they paraded from the school, across the street and up the circular steps to take their positions amid loud acclamations. Next appeared the queen in a white gown looking as regal as a Victorian queen. Her satin train was held by two pageboys, who were no more than five years old.

The crowning of the queen by the previous year's queen followed the main speaker. Each spoke briefly. The artistically decorated, bearing congratulatory bouquets of flowers, soon came into view. A young gentleman in evening attire escorted the queen and members of her court to the float which paraded down the main street behind a marching band. The pastor and mayor's car and a string of convertibles chauffeuring the young ladies followed. Spectators lined the streets and applauded as the parade passed by, thankful that the weather had cooperated fully.

Nicole and Lisa had joined a group of friends for a brief chat then steered toward Lucia, Grace and Mamie standing a few feet away.

"Did you and Aunt Grace attend the evening Mass, Aunt Lucia?" asked Lisa.

"Yes, between the fireworks and traffic, we don't expect to get much sleep. We can stay in bed longer in the morning." Lucia peered into Lisa's eyes as Grace approached with her familiar grin.

"Now what do you think of Ray?" Grace could not wait to ask.

"He is very nice and so are the parents." Lisa tried to be non-committal. "Too early to really tell."

"He's a good catch, a dentist and good-looking. We are praying to St. Anne that it works out."

"You are too much." Lisa was confident that her dear aunts already knew a lot more about the date than they pretended.

Mamie told her daughter that she would be going

home with Lucia who had parked the car in some friend's driveway for lack of street space. Nicole and Lisa decided to walk and take time to chat with friends who were visiting relatives for the weekend.

The atmosphere around their rancher was much more subdued with no traffic of significance. Only one car was parked in front of their home and Lisa realized it belonged to Ray. He had come an hour earlier than expected. She found him in the back sitting with Matthew and Andrew enjoying a cool drink. Ray rose as they approached and apologized for the early appearance. "You see I had a good deed to perform for my grandmother." Hardly looking repentant and smiling broadly, he continued, "She instructed me to deliver a package to your grandfather. Not quite sure about the address, I left home early."

"Ray, it's fine. You're welcomed at any time," said Lisa happily

"Mrs. Grasso. How are you this evening?"

"I'm fine, Ray, thank you, but would you please just call me Nicole."

"Glad to oblige."

"Now about that package, I have a strong suspicion about the contents. A big ripe tomato, right?"

"Now how did you know that?"

"Because Nina and my grandfather have this thing about tomatoes. They like to claim bragging rights to the first and the prettiest of the season," said Nicole. "It goes way back in time. Perhaps a form of continuity indicative of a close friendship," Nicole explained while everyone looked amused.

"He and your grandmother insisted I sit while they opened the neat little package tied with a red ribbon. I must admit it was a pretty tomato." Laughter followed. "Perhaps my grandmother has carried the tomato saga a bit further this year. By the way John and Gina are a wonderful old couple."

"Yes, very devoted to each other. Priceless in this age!" Nicole analyzed it often. Her children knew what circuited among her brain cells.

"Is it all right if I go freshen up a bit?" asked Lisa.

"You look great as you are," added Ray.

Andrew and Matthew wanted to add a few teasing remarks but let it go. They thought Raymond was pretty nice and did not wish to diminish the stature of their sister in his eyes. Besides there was always the chance that someday they would be the recipients of free dental care. Actually they loved their sister very much.

Lisa reappeared on the patio a half hour later looking exuberant and attractive in a sleeveless white denim dress. She was surprised to find her Uncle Peter and his friend Marion among the family gathering. He seemed much more interested in this friend in contrast to former dates.

Peter had taken on the role of the male guide to his sister's children during the past seven years. Now that they had grown into adulthood, he felt more inclined toward a serious relationship.

Peter approached his niece, gave her a tight hug and whispered, "Never saw you look more beautiful."

Lisa blushed and thanked him. "Are you going to the carnival?"

"Hope to walk up there and join the crowd."

Ray began to have a clearer understanding of the uncle's role in their lives.

"She is very special. I'm encouraged to see her choice for tonight's date is also very special." Peter glanced at his watch. "It's almost nine. Perhaps we should think about starting out Marion."

"I'm ready."

"Ray, do you and Lisa care to walk along with us? We will let you alone after that."

"It suits me fine," Ray responded while trying not to let Lisa's nearness cloud his stability.

"We will probably see you around. We expect to come up later," said Andrew. Nicole and her parents planned to view the fireworks from the patio.

The crowds thickened as they approached the carnival grounds. Familiar food odors filled the air. The clamor of rides and the loud barking of workers selling their wares echoed through the warm July evening. The foursome watched as a group of teenagers tried to spike balloons and hopefully be rewarded with a stuffed animal. Everywhere long lines of young people waited to get on rides. Noticeably missing over recent years was the sound of the merry-go-round. The Ferris wheel remained popular but the teenagers favored the fast and exciting twirling new rides.

Following a slow walk around, Peter led the group towards the food. The pepper and sausage stand was checking in with record sales and so was the "pizza fritta" stand. After a general survey of the area they settled for sausage and peppers plus drinks. Friends stopped for brief conversations as they meandered about and enjoyed their food.

"Hey guys, do you see who is sitting over there engrossed in the sounds of that Italian music group?" asked Peter. They all turned to the section with about fifty folding chairs.

"It's Aunt Lucia and Aunt Grace. Hate to bother them. They look like they are in another world," suggested Lisa, "but let's do it anyway, Uncle Pete."

"Those gals are probably reliving past 'Big Times'," said Ray as he held Lisa's hand and walked toward them. Pete and Marion followed.

Aunt Grace was the first to spot them. "Lu, look who's coming this way," she whispered excitedly.

All the love they bore in their hearts for these young people was clearly etched in their weathered old faces as they looked up to see them approaching.

Lisa kissed them and so did Marion.

"Isn't this past your bedtime?" asked Peter.

"We never miss the Saturday night celebration, Pete. Now you know that." Although it was quite warm they both had sweaters over their shoulders.

"Ray, you are here too. How nice," said Lucia as if she didn't know but smiled, peered down at their clasped hands, looked up and smiled again.

"And how's your grandmother, Ray?" asked Grace. They kept in touch with Nina but right now she didn't know what else to say.

"She and my grandfather are still going strong. Must be that Roseto blood. You both seem to be enjoying the music."

"Nothing is the way it used to be, Ray," said Lucia. "Years ago the fifty-piece Roseto Cornet Band furnished the music from a big bandstand. The queen and princesses sat along side. Carnivals had side shows and plenty of rides."

"Yeah, how about the belly dancers? They looked so nice on the outdoor stage with their flimsy robes. Our sister Angie got fooled. She bought tickets and led her three kids into the tent. When the dancers came on stage without their robes, Angie was embarrassed grabbed her kids and walked out. They were 'hoochie-koochie' girls, with pale bodies who wiggled around with sparkly tiny pieces covering certain spots and not a show for little children." Ray laughed out loud. The others had heard the story before.

"Grace, how about all the New York vendors selling balloons, Italian nougat, strings of hazel nuts and all kinds of souvenirs? They made things exciting. But I didn't like the gypsies. They thought we were dopes who would give them our jewelry to have our fortune told."

"Let's face it," added Lucia, "we miss those 'Big Times' when all the relatives visited. American and Italian flags flew everywhere. The beer joints were crowded. People danced on the streets and verandas."

"So why the downtrend?" asked Ray.

"Today every town has carnivals. People have cars and travel to different amusement places, like Disneyland. They fly all over the world."

"Don't forget television. Now they want to watch their ballgames. Oh well, we change too." Grace was getting philosophical. "Marion I'm glad you came up. How are you doing?"

"I'm well, thank you. Both of you seem happy. Always admire your 'ready to go spirit.' "

Marion was well liked by the family. She was a pretty, down to earth girl, in her late twenties who worked as a secretary for a county judge.

"At this age we take it from day to day," replied Lucia.

"Are you staying for the fireworks?" Lisa asked her aunts.

"No, Honey, we can see them from home," replied Lucia. "Anthony will drive us home."

Conversation continued until Peter reminded everybody that he and Marion were returning to Nicole's home to see the fireworks. Domenic, Mamie and a few others would also be there. However, he could not leave before picking up a batch of "pizza fritta" that he had ordered to take with him. Ray and Lisa expected to stay on the grounds until the first blast signaled the rush toward the church for perfect fireworks viewing. They would meet again on Sunday at her grandparents' home after the religious procession.

Ray and Lisa gave the Aunts a final hug and continued a slow stroll amid the crowd.

"Lisa suppose we live dangerously and take a spin on the wheel. Wanna give it a shot?"

"I haven't been on one since I was a teenager. I'm all for it."

Ray purchased the tickets and both stood in line until ten minutes later when they were strapped into their seats. He placed his arm around Lisa's shoulder. It was slow going until all were systematically ready for the steady rapid twirl, woozy stomach and the screams of a few. With another long line of young people waiting for their turn, the ride was much too short.

At eleven-fifteen they decided to walk up the hill and join the crowd who were beginning to position themselves for the fireworks display. The church steps were practically all occupied but enough space remained to squeeze in. Lawns were covered with young people, parents and children. Only a few street lamps shed a dim light into the total darkness. The first blast summoned the throngs, and a steady flow of people exited the carnival grounds and gradually blended into the surging crowds on the church plaza.

At exactly eleven-thirty, the skies of the Slate Belt region were filled with the blasts of pyrotechnics. The final few blasts seemed to shake the ground and signaled everyone to head home. And so began the stow trek home amid the rumble of auto engines that lasted well into one A.M.

Lisa and Ray, hands clasped, followed suit and were walking along when they were caught up in her grandfather's headlights as he and Mamie were leaving Nicole's residence. He stopped the car, rolled down the window and greeted them. "Isn't it past your bedtime?"

"Hi, 'Gramps' and Grandma. Just in time to meet Ray."

"Heard a lot of nice things about you. So nice to finally meet you," said Domenic with the usual pleasant smile.

Mamie leaned over her husband to get a better view. "Hello Ray, I've been looking forward to meeting you. Did you two enjoy the festivities?"

"Yes," replied Ray immediately "Of course, your granddaughter's company made it extra pleasant." Happy smiles verified their verbal expressions.

"According to reports we expect to see you again at Grandpa's after the procession," added Domenic.

"I'm looking forward to it," said Ray.

They said their good-byes and drove off.

Within minutes Lisa and Ray were walking down the side of the house and onto the lighted patio where a number of family friends were still gathered.

"Hi, everybody! Did you all enjoy the fireworks?" Lisa approached with Ray behind her.

"A lot better than last year," yelled Matthew. He and several of his friends had just returned and were consuming their sausage and pepper sandwiches. Out of the back door came Aunt Zee and Neil preparing to leave.

"Aunt Zee and Uncle Neil come over here and meet Raymond," called Lisa.

Introductions were quick and so was Aunt Zee's immediate reaction.

"So this is Nina's grandson? You are one hell of good-looking guy. How come she kept you in hiding?"

"I've been in town before, Mrs. Piccone. Sadly we just didn't cross paths."

"Look, Ray, please call me Zee. None of that Mrs. Piccone stuff."

Ray was momentarily surprised. She was definitely as earthy as described. His grandmother Nina told him she had the spirit of her grandmother Maria Giuseppe—tough but with a heart of gold. Mamie favored Lorenzo and Rosa in her approach to life.

"Don't try to fight her, Ray. She can be pure dynamite," added Neil. "By the way, you can drop the Mr. I'm just plain Neil and the husband of my favorite woman."

"Don't believe him, Ray. Many are the times he wanted to feed me to the sharks but he was afraid I would strike back." Zee put her arms around his waist. "He is really a pretty good husband. Wouldn't trade him for anything."

"You are easy to read," replied Ray. "I gathered as much."

"Before you think I'm too soft, let me tell you one thing: I'll beat the hell out of you if you mistreat this little honey of mine. Zee peered into his eyes, reminiscent of Aunt Lucia searching look.

"Aunt Zee, I wouldn't even think of hurting this kitten." Ray put his arms around Lisa's shoulders.

"Carmella, you've got Ray scared to death." Neil hardly believed his remark to be true.

"Yeah, just like I scare you." Zee gave Ray a big smile and hug, practically stabbing his face with her dangling ear loops. "Hey, sorry I can't stay longer. Have fun. Hope to see you after the procession." She gave Lisa a hug and both left after bidding everyone good-bye.

Four-thirty P.M. Sunday afternoon under a hot July sun, the procession dedicated to Our Lady of Mt. Carmel made its way down the Garibaldi Avenue. It followed the same route as the queen parade. A school band led the way, followed by the Knights of Columbus in their medieval attire, and the float with the statue of Mary. The queen and her court walked behind the float. Next came the church choir, sodalities and the faithful reciting the rosary. The great number of participants was testimony to the fact that the religious significance of the celebration had not been affected by a secular society.

Nicole, Beth and Lisa walked together. The afternoon heat kept the older folks at home. Paper cups filled with fresh water were dispensed in front of the firehouse. From those on porches to those standing along the sidewalks, an air of solemnity marked the occasion.

"Hi, kitten!"

Lisa looked up to see Ray flashing a broad smile. "I thought I would surprise you. Haven't marched in a procession since I was an altar boy. Actually I felt a bit guilty about watching instead of participating."

"Just for that you will be going straight to heaven," whispered Lisa, shocked but thrilled to see him.

"I'd like to think it's a form of penance. Truth is I wanted to spend more time with you, instead of sitting at your great grandparents' home waiting for you to join us. My grandparents came up also. They can't help but notice the positive effect you have on me."

"You are just a top-notch guy, Ray," whispered Lisa in his ears.

"I tried to tell you that last night but you didn't believe me."

"Perhaps you just didn't read me," whispered Lisa.

Ray said hello to Nicole when he finally became aware that she too was walking with Lisa. After gracefully acknowledging his greeting she introduced him to Beth who, unnoticed by Ray, followed with thumbs up.

In less than an hour they returned to the church where the crowd slowly dispersed. Ray and Lisa walked to the parking lot where he had parked his car. Nicole and her sister headed to their grandparents' home in Beth's car.

Backyard picnics under the shade of trees or tents had become traditional. John and Gina's home were on the procession route and attracted a good number of guests. Mamie and Zee oversaw preparations. Family members brought casseroles of food. As usual no one went hungry.

John, Gina, Nina, Victor, Lucia and Grace were still sitting on rockers, rosaries clasped in their hands, when Nicole and Beth followed by Lisa and Ray arrived. Domenic, Neil, Patrick, Andrew and Matthew sat at one of the tables enjoying cool drinks with their cousin Anthony and wife Maria. All had watched the procession from this vantage point. A few of the teen youngsters were huddled together in another section.

Lisa and Ray were the biggest attraction. Their first stop was towards the exuberant grandparents and aunts. Domenic approached and guided them to Patrick who had not yet met Ray; the others had already been introduced.

Nicole and Beth collapsed in a rocker. Zee who was filling large paper cups with cold lemonade walked towards them.

"Looks like you girls have had it. Pretty hot under that sun?" she said while filling their glasses.

"Ninety-five degrees according to the thermometer in front of the Legion," said Beth as she wiped her face and arms with a tissue. "Let's relax a bit before serving the food."

"Ten minutes and then we serve or those kids will start yapping," replied Zee as she moved on with cold drinks. John and Victor had walked over to a small table and were enjoying a glass of wine, fresh figs and provelone. They declined the sugared drinks.

"Looks like you two are in a serious mood," said Peter as he sat beside them.

"Hello, Pete. I am just telling your grandfather that I pulled out my garlic. This year's crop was pretty good. He tells me that his was good too."

"Right weather for it," concluded Peter. "Not to change

the subject, Victor, but I must tell you I am impressed with your grandson."

"I am proud of him, Peter. He works hard and is going to be an excellent dentist. My instinct tells me that he likes Lisa."

"Of course you guys had nothing to do with it, right?" asked Peter with a smile.

"Just a little, Pete, just a little," replied Victor with a wide grin as he reached for a fig. "You young fellas know that they have professional matchmakers. We have a better insight and did it for free. By the way do you need any help?"

"No thanks, Victor, I can manage that," laughed Peter.

"That's what I thought but decided to ask anyway."

Gina and Nina slowly approached, almost undetected, and carefully sat at the table.

"So what has you guys so wrapped up in conversation that you didn't even notice us?"

"Very simple, Nina, I merely asked these wonderful men what single factor was responsible for their good health at this time of their lives. Do you want to know what they said?"

"What did they say, Peter?"

"It is all due to their wives' loving care."

Nina gave him a devilish look and smiled. "I doubt very much that they would actually admit it. Anyway I will tell you the reason, Peter. It's because we always made them happy."

Peter, John and Victor had a hearty laugh.

"It was ninety percent you gals and ten percent them?"

"Not exactly. We were lucky Peter for marrying hard working family men. If we had to do it again we would definitely marry these same guys." Gina smiled docilely and bowed her head in agreement.

Part Five

1998

The invitations for Lisa and Raymond's wedding were stacked neatly in a long shallow box ready to be mailed. On Saturday June 21, 1998 the wedding was scheduled to be solemnized in Our Lady of Mt. Carmel Church followed by a reception at the Spruce Hill Country Club in the Pocono Mountains. Approximately 300 guests would attend.

Raymond had opened his office in Easton and already had a sizeable clientele. Lisa enjoyed her work at the Mansfield School where the school year ended June 9, three weeks before the wedding. It had been an exceptionally busy year. Lisa tried to achieve a balance between formulating wedding plans and working. Happily everything turned out well thanks to the 'action group' surrounding her. As usual both families were there merely for the asking. She and Raymond had purchased a home in Washington Township, with easy access to their work.

On Friday night, May 9, Nicole was seated on the living room sofa waiting for the doorbell to ring. Looking attractive in a light green suit with matching pumps, she was expecting Mr. Luca, the high school principal. The sophomore and junior dance was scheduled for that evening in the school auditorium.

Carl Luca knew Nicole quite well, not only because her children were students in the school but also because of numerous faculty meetings. During the last meeting held a few weeks back, he asked her to help chaperone the dance. She had agreed treating it as an obligation rather than a date. Carl Luca was a widower. His wife had passed away four years ago. A man of about fifty, he had a married son who lived in Albany, New York.

Andrew and Matthew were in their bedrooms, not too excited about meeting Mr. Luca. They remembered him as a disciplinarian and a no-nonsense guy. When he had unexpectedly entered a noisy classroom, he simply stared, often as long as ten minutes without uttering a single word. The ensuing silence was almost overwhelming. Students were never too thrilled about crossing his path.

Having never come under his scrutiny while in school or seen the inside of his office, they nevertheless decided to watch TV in their rooms instead. Lisa remembered him as a pretty good-looking man and a good dancer.

When the doorbell rang, Nicole greeted him and asked if he remembered her daughter Lisa. Wearing a light weight brown suit that matched his thinning brown hair he appeared jovial and friendly.

"Of course, how could I forget one of our best cheerleaders? Your mom told me you will be getting married soon, Lisa."

"Yes, in a month. Some of the teachers will be attending the reception. I wouldn't mind at all having you join us."

"Thank you, Lisa. I shall certainly give it some serious thought. Are you enjoying your work at Manchester?"

"Very much so, Mr. Luca." As they began to leave she wished them a fun evening hardly forgetting they were chaperones.

"We will try our best. I expect to twirl your mom around the dance floor a few times if she will let me."

"Go to it. She needs to brush up on her dancing."

As Nicole and Carl drove off Matthew and Andrew joined their sister and asked if he was still the "offensive coordinator." Although Matthew would be a junior at Lehigh in September, and Andrew had been accepted at the University of Pennsylvania Law School, both remembered him well.

"Now cut it out," replied Lisa. "Even principals can be pretty nice guys. I must admit though, it was a bit strange watching Mom being escorted out the door."

"I suppose in our secret dreams we always wished that Mom and Dad would someday be reunited," said Matthew wistfully.

"Banish all such thoughts," replied Andrew. "We're lucky she didn't freak out during that bust. She was a real trooper."

"Even if Mom could, she would never take him back. He really threw her a devastating curve ball and knocked her to pieces. Take it from a woman's point of view. As for Dad, I'm not quite sure he has had second thoughts," remarked Lisa.

"It will no doubt be an awkward situation for them to finally meet again after nine years," said Matthew.

"It has to be. Meanwhile excuse me while I write out a wedding invitation for Mr. Carl Luca."

*   *   *

Raymond and Lisa's home required very little renovation. With the exception of a fresh coat of paint throughout the house it was in excellent condition. Floors were polished and the furniture was to be delivered on Monday. Grandparents were unaware that they were already beginning to spend weekends together. Naturally Nicole never revealed it. They certainly would have objected and been deeply hurt. Modern day couples did not necessarily wait for the wedding night to consummate their marriage. If grandparents preferred to use blinders, so be it. Nicole would not disillusion them. Lisa and Raymond were very much in love and she was thankful for their happiness.

Carl Luca had asked Nicole to be his guest when he and another couple planned to visit the Pennsylvania Dutch countryside on the last Saturday of May. It would be a two-hour drive to Lancaster County. Nicole had never been there and Carl thought she might enjoy the Amish countryside, and a first-hand look at their austere lifestyle.

He was in front of her rancher by nine A.M. and Nicole was waiting. He opened the door of his black Chevy for Nicole and introduced her to Leland and Jennifer Roland, who owned a garden supply store in Mount Bethel. They were in their late forties or early fifties and a very pleasant couple.

May in Lancaster is a busy season for the Amish farmers who still live as their ancestors did centuries ago. After fleeing religious prosecution in Germany during the seventeenth century they traveled to Switzerland and finally arrived in America where many settled in the Dutch country of Pennsylvania.

Here they still follow "the old ways." Modern facilities are strictly banned which means no electricity in the homes. Chemical fertilizers and sprays are prohibited on farmlands and everything is organic. They can be seen in their familiar black garb shopping in town or selling their produce at stands. Their horses and buggies often snarl traffic.

Carl headed south for Route 22 and then they would be on 340 between Bird-in-hand and Intercourse. It was a scenic drive of well-kept farms, barns with hex signs and farmers behind horse drawn plows.

"Nicole, do you think you could ever live this simple life?" asked Carl as he turned to her.

"I have often yearned for simplicity but as for actually accepting it is a long term way of life, definitely no," was Nicole's firm response. "My great grandparents lived that way as did yours. However each generation has adapted to change."

"I can certainly go along with that, Nicole," added Jennifer who was pouring coffee from her thermos. "Would anyone like coffee?"

"Strong as usual I hope?" asked Carl.

"Exactly as you like it." Jennifer poured him a cup. Nicole was the only one who declined but reached for Carl's cup. A busy stretch of highway lay ahead. When the lights turned red at the intersection, he drank half of it and returned the cup to Nicole's outstretched hand. "The genetic implications of marrying within their own group has come under scrutiny even among their own people," continued Jennifer.

"It seems they have looked into joining another Amish group to offset that possibility," added Carl and then turned to another topic for discussion. "Leland, no doubt your type of business functions well in this environment."

"It probably does, Carl. Catalogues, like Sears, also provide knowledge of current modern farm machinery. Not all Dutch farmers are Amish so modern technology is highly sought."

The clip-clap of horses' hoofs, buggies and the plain people were highly visible as they entered Lancaster. Tour buses dropped off their travelers closer to center city and then headed for parking lots.

Saturday morning was the busiest of time for the region's farmers. Asparagus, vegetable greens, lettuce and spring flowers were the current products. Potatoes, apples and tomatoes were leading fall crops. Fresh cider was also available at that time, as well as homemade sauerkraut.

Quilts, and all types of needlework elegantly done by the Amish women were highly sought and brought a fair income.

Carl found an easily accessible parking space and the group walked among the friendly folks past small shops and restaurants featuring home-style meals. Well-supervised children in Amish clothes held onto parents and relatives.

Nicole and Jennifer stopped to admire the needlework at one of the booths. An adjoining stand featured paintings by a young local artist who appeared to be in his early twenties. An Amish farmer working in the fields was the subject of the painting that attracted Nicole's attention. After some deliberation, she purchased it for thirty-five dollars.

Carl and Leland were busy admiring tools, and they stopped to watch a tall blond woman wearing a Dutch cap and a white apron make funnel cakes. Fresh doughnuts, hot cross buns, corn muffins and shoofly pies were also on sale. Leland was tempted to buy a shoofly pie but decided to first consult with his wife. She consented without hesitation. Nicole bought muffins and a shoofly pie.

Several hours later they were sitting at a table in a quiet, spotless small restaurant placing their order. The home-style meal consisting of roast pork, mashed potatoes covered with brown gravy, peas and carrots and a small dish of spiced cabbage was served within a short time. Warm apple pie with a dip of vanilla ice cream was the unanimous dessert.

"Perhaps if we all lived this way, there would be no fears of a nuclear war or any type of war for that matter. It might be a peaceful world," wondered Jennifer.

"Unfortunately all cultures do not adapt easily, or have

land that can be cultivated to sustain their people," said Leland.

By three P.M. they were back in the car and homeward bound.

"This was an enjoyable and educational trip for me," said Nicole. "It's but a two-hour drive, yet I have never gotten down this way."

"I was certain you would appreciate an introduction to a different lifestyle," said Carl as he turned to observe the grateful expression on her face. "We all need to get away from the routine and pepper-up our lives a bit. You can share the experience with your young students."

"That's for certain," added Nicole. Only another teacher would make that very pertinent suggestion. She wondered how that kind face could stare a class into complete silence.

Leland and Jennifer, under the spell of rolling farmlands and grazing cows, were unusually quiet. Carl thought they were grabbing a few winks until Jennifer suddenly asked what crops were growing along the route.

"Mostly fields of wheat, oats, corn and hay planted in early spring," replied Carl. The countryside was definitely relaxing.

By five P.M. Carl parked his car in front of Nicole's home.

"It was a real pleasure, Jennifer and Leland, for me to spend the day with you."

"Thank you! It was ours as well. Don't forget we expect to have you and Carl share a Sunday afternoon with us after the wedding," reminded Jennifer. "We will keep in touch."

"I will look forward to it."

Carl helped Nicole out of the car and walked her to the front door where Nicole thanked him for a beautiful day.

"My pleasure. I will see you at the wedding. I should be back from Albany in two weeks. I will call to check and see that you are not stressed out from the busy days ahead."

*   *   *

And stressful days they were. The wedding had been a year in the planning, hoping that all loose ends would be in place at least a few weeks prior to the special event. A prospective bride never feels completely secure that such is the case. Lisa was no different.

Since cooking the dinner is no longer a personal responsibility but rather one allocated to the reception hall, one might expect a lighter burden for the family. However that was not necessarily the case. The custom of baking trays of assorted cookies for the reception served in conjunction with the wedding cake lingered. At least a dozen varieties of cookie dough is prepared in advance. Wednesday was chosen as the time for the cookie brigade to assemble at Mamie and Domenic's home to bake and package these delicious gems.

As anticipated, the seniors were the first to arrive. John, Gina, Lucia and Grace, were early risers—five A.M. to be exact. The Dontelli home was less than a mile away and John was still able to drive that short distance. He picked up his sisters at seven-thirty A.M. Nicole, Lisa, Beth and Aunt Zee arrived shortly. Mamie had already begun the process by setting the oven at the required temperature. Baking board and trays were out and there was a large pot of coffee brewing on the stove.

John was of no particular help but resigned himself to watching TV in the living room and reading the morning paper. All shapes of cookies—round, square, rolled were deftly shaped and baked without a huge mess in the kitchen. Lucia and Grace, with their 'mapines' (dish towels) were on constant watch for any spilled ingredients. Washing and drying cookie sheets was also their responsibility. Past performance made them good bets for the job.

"Grammy, did you have cookies at your wedding?" asked Lisa as she spread icing on the round vanilla cookies and dipped them in coconut.

"Honey, we had exactly three types of cookies; biscotti, sliced almond toast and the ones you are icing now. The Betty Crocker cookies came later."

"Where did you have the reception?"

"At the Marconi Club where we passed around large wicker baskets filled with prepared sandwiches. There were plenty of drinks and lots of dancing. Local orchestras furnished the music. We even had a wedding cake." Mamie enjoyed comparing her wedding with present day country club extravaganzas.

"Where did you have your reception, Aunt Zee?"

"In a small old movie theater on Chestnut Street. Receptions were all about the same with plenty of beer and soft drinks."

By one P.M. twenty-five small trays, one for each table at the reception hall, were filled with cookies, covered with cellophane, gathered at the top and tied with white ribbon. A few extra trays were prepared for home use.

Domenic and Neil walked in about that time carrying two large tomato pizzas and an anchovy rolled pizza. The kitchen was clean and a wooden bowl filled with salad greens, sliced cucumbers, chopped radishes, cubed provelone, and fresh scallions lay in the center of the long kitchen table set for ten. Lisa had left early for her home in Washington Township.

"You made it just in time," said Aunt Zee. "We are tired

of looking at cookies and craving some solid food. Did you get the work done at the Legion?"

"There is still a few more things that need attention but that will wait for another day," said Neil. He and Domenic were veterans of World War II having served in the European theater; they were active members of the Martocci-Capobianco Legion Post.

While the men washed the women completed minor details in the kitchen. Cookie trays were stored in a basement refrigerator.

"So where are your guys, Beth?" asked Neil always ready to get a charge from his wife's niece.

"I was thinking of sending them over to you to inflict a taste of teenage crap," replied Beth as she began to serve herself some salad.

"As if I didn't know better. You're lucky they're great kids."

"I owe it all to their dad," pretended Beth as she reached for some anchovy pizza.

"You got that right," continued Neil with a wide smile.

"Don't let that 'foo-foo ladda' (teaser) rattle you," broke in Aunt Zee.

"Oh I know better I love him just the same," winked Beth. John and Gina enjoyed the give and take. Domenic and Mamie found it amusing as usual. Neil and Aunt Zee were in high spirits. Their son, his wife and grandchildren would arrive for the wedding Friday.

When Peter dropped in, conversations became livelier. "I came for Marion's dish of cookies." The two had married over a year ago. "She couldn't get the day off."

"We didn't forget," replied Mamie.

"You should know by this time that Mom doesn't overlook her favorite son," teased Beth.

"Hi, Aunt Lucia and Aunt Grace. What have you two lovely maidens been up to?"

"Nothing exciting, Peter," replied Lucia.

"Did Mario come over to fix that small hole in the walk?"

"No we got some ready mix and fixed it ourselves," answered Grace rather proudly.

"And saved yourselves a couple of bucks, right?"

"Right!"

"Not to change the subject, but what's the latest on your love life, Nicole? Is Carl back?"

"I think he should be back this evening. And besides it is only a platonic relationship." Nicole's face turned a bit crimson.

"Whatever it is, enjoy. It's time you think about yourself," continued Peter. There was total agreement.

"Lisa is getting married and the boys will be going back to college in the fall. I have been telling Nicole it's good to socialize and have a little fun," advised Gina, as she looked lovingly at her granddaughter.

"I have been lucky to have you all around. It was never a hardship." Nicole reached for a piece of melon from the bowl placed on the table by her mother.

"Maybe it wasn't such a hardship," suggested Aunt Zee, "but I hope you don't think all guys are cads, although there are plenty of bums out there. They say this guy is pretty straight. He better be if he is a principal; so let go of the past and get out once in a while."

Nicole stared ahead. "I can't forget that easily, Aunt Zee. It's difficult to forget the hurt. To his credit, Dan has never forgotten his children as you well know."

"Something tells me Dan is aware of the terrible mistake especially when he looks at his grown children and knows he wasn't around to take a bit of the credit."

Domenic spoke softly. "He may also be suffering. It's time to get on with your life."

"Domenic, I hope to hell he is suffering," said Aunt Zee as she slowly chewed on a slice of pizza.

"We all make mistakes, Carmella. Let's look forward and try and forgive," added Domenic in his usual philosophical stance. "What do you think, Pop?"

"You all said it for me. There is nothing more I can add. All I want is to see my granddaughter happy," shrugged John. Gina and Mamie shook their heads in agreement.

"Where are all the guests staying this weekend?" asked Beth.

"Most have reservations at motels. Madeline, Louis and Barbara are staying with us," replied Mamie. "Gone are the days when we put mattresses on the floor for our out of town relatives."

"Since my family is flying in I can't help in that department," added Zee.

"Angie and Concetta's families are returning to Bethlehem after the reception."

"Sorry to have to cut this short, but I must leave. Thanks for the cookies, Mom. My wife will eat most of them." Peter left. The others were homeward bound by late afternoon.

Mamie had made a big pot of tomato sauce and placed salad greens in plastic bags for Beth and Nicole. That evening supper would be spaghetti and a salad for her daughters' families.

The eight P.M. telephone call for Nicole was from Carl. He had returned home from Albany. "Just checking to see if you are still in one piece," was his initial remark.

*   *   *

Following the Friday night church rehearsal, the wedding group headed for Giovanni's restaurant. Lisa's roommate, Andrea Jennings, was her maid of honor. Raymond's friend, Keith Edwards from Dental School days was the best man. Beth's children, Lori and Tommy, were in the wedding party as well as Andrew, Matthew and cousins Dana and Dina Grasso and Justin and Amy Piccone.

Nicole was at home taking care of loose ends until finally succumbing to the lounge chair, thankful for a brief respite from a hectic day. It was short-lived; the telephone broke the silence. After the second ring, she picked up the portable phone on the end table beside her, and recognized the caller immediately.

"Nicole, this is Dan."

The shock was immense, and the sound of his voice for the first time since he left nine years ago unnerved her.

"I recognized your voice immediately. Lisa is having her rehearsal dinner. I'm sure you want to talk with her, Dan," already feeling it was a stupid answer.

"No, Nicole, I want to speak with you if I may." His voice was subdued. "First of all, how are you bearing up under the pressure?"

"No problem. There is plenty of help. Have you recovered fully from the heart operation?"

"I am almost at one-hundred percent and thankfully working full time."

"Glad to hear that. Where are you now?"

"At a hotel in Stroudsburg. We flew into Newark where Frank and Maggie met us. We came in with them. Most of the family, including Mom and Pop, are staying in this hotel."

Nicole wondered if he was calling from his room. She was certain Stacy was not around.

"Lisa is happy to have you all here."

"I wouldn't have it otherwise. The basic reason for this call is to apologize for any hurt I have caused you. I am truly sorry! For years, and especially after being reunited with the children, I have hated myself for having been an idiot. It is something I must bear for the rest of my life." Very few clan members would disagree. "You certainly did not deserve that treatment. I was a weakling who got lost in a fantasy world." There was a lull as if he could not proceed further.

"Admittedly Dan, it was tough going." Nicole thought she would help him regain his composure.

"It is highly unlikely that the wedding day can present a moment to properly discuss this."

"The years have gradually healed the hurt, though certainly not thoroughly, the end of what I thought was a good marriage. I appreciate your call and accept your apology. The welfare of our children is important to us. I hope to share their interest in a friendly way."

"Thank you for being so candid, Nicole. This is a great load off my mind. Hopefully it will be a more comfortable day for both of us."

"I am sure it will be a proud one."

"Looking forward to seeing you again and praying for a happy union for Lisa and Raymond. Good night, Nicole."

"Good night, Dan."

Shocking and yet a step in the right direction, thought Nicole as she hung up while reeling from the unexpected call.

*   *   *

Bright sunshine greeted Nicole as she stepped outdoors to pick up the morning paper. A mother robin and her two chicks floundered about on the grass. They had left their nest in the evergreen bush near the porch and would soon be on their own. A coincidence, she thought, just as she too would see Lisa, leave the nest to make her own life.

Understandably Dan's call the previous night occupied her mind. She spread out the newspaper on the kitchen table while the coffee was brewing. Sunday's issue would carry a photo of the bride and groom. They were a happy couple. She prayed it would be a long lasting joyful marriage. Her mind wandered back to Dan. Undoubtedly eyes would be scanning their reactions upon the initial encounter and throughout the event. She was determined to keep it low-keyed, friendly and distanced.

The silence of early morning belied the importance of the day. Her children were still sleeping as she absent-mindedly sipped her coffee, and continued leafing through the newspaper. Moments later she was outdoors watering hanging potted flowers and feeling edgy.

Gloria, her neighbor, wearing a long robe, walked over from almost nowhere, smiling and aware of the enormity of the day. She had married off a daughter two years ago and was already a grandmother.

"Good morning, Nicole."

"Morning, Gloria."

"Butterflies in your stomach?"

"Yes, plenty of them."

"Anything I can do?"

"No, thank you, Gloria. Just having you and Jerry around during the ceremony and reception will be calming."

Gloria walked up to Nicole, hugged and kissed her as she had so often done during trying times. "You will be fine."

They talked briefly. Gloria gave her one more hug and left. The church bell beckoned the faithful to the seven A.M.

307

mass. as Nicole returned indoors to await the first sound of an awakening household.

*   *   *

Beth, Pat, Lori and Tommy arrived about ten A.M. carrying clothes on hangers and in suitcases. Dana and Dina Grasso joined them shortly after that time. Aunt Zee dropped off her granddaughter Amy who was also a bridesmaid. From then on it was telephone calls, florist delivering flowers, the arrival of the maid of honor, bridesmaids and Mildred, their hairdresser and family friend.

Tiny rolled sandwiches, champagne cocktails, and fruit as well as an assortment of cookies were on the dining room table.

A narrow silver crown headpiece was placed on Lisa's head while Mildred arranged the hair around it. Makeup was lightly applied; Lisa's smooth skin was flawless. The white satin wedding dress was finally carefully pulled over her head. She was a picturesque princess. Small diamond earrings were Raymond's birthday gift several months earlier. The engagement ring was sizable.

Bridesmaids wearing royal blue gowns flitted about rather nervously. Nicole looked at her daughter with pride. "You look absolutely beautiful, sweetheart."

Lisa placed a kiss on her mother's cheek. "So do you, Mom. Looks like you are going to give me some competition. You never looked more lovely." Lori approached her aunt, kissed her. "That is exactly what I was thinking."

Nicole thanked them. Her brown hair had been highlighted with blond streaks. A mid-calf length orchid chiffon dress covered a slim figure.

Beth, dressed in a light blue well-fitted gown, walked

in from the bedroom. Following behind her was Patrick, looking refined as ever in a navy suit and tie.

Andrew, Matthew and Tommy dressed at Aunt Zee's home. Raymond, his best man and his brother were driving directly to church from Easton.

At one-thirty the tulle was arranged neatly over her Lisa's head and face. The chauffer-driven limousine waited outdoors.

Nicole and Beth helped Lisa to the limo while the rest of the wedding party followed. After they were all settled, Patrick held his car door open and helped Beth and Nicole enter. Mildred, the hairdresser, remained behind to put things in order. She would join them at the reception.

As they approached the church, they saw cars lined along streets and in the packed parking lot. They parked in the reserved space and waited for the bride.

Dan had been waiting in a room beside the vestibule when he was alerted that the bride had arrived. Looking handsome and refined, he straightened his tuxedo and walked down the dozen concrete steps toward the limo. When he spotted Nicole with Beth and Patrick, he headed that way.

Understandably he looked rather awkward as he approached Nicole, planted a kiss on her cheek as well as on Beth's, then shook Patrick's hand. Time had not aged him, although there were a few more gray hairs. Conversation was subdued with a prolonged glance at his ex-wife.

"Lucky to have such a beautiful day, aren't we?"

They all realized that time was too short to engage in conversation. The bride was waiting; Nicole, Beth and Patrick had to be inside before the bride made her entrance.

Andrew, smiling broadly, waited for his mother. She took his arm and was ushered to the front seat. Domenic and Mamie as well as John and Gina were already seated.

Raymond and the best man stood before them Lisa and her father began the stroll down the aisle to the strains of organ music. The groom gently took her arm and led her to the altar. The maid of honor and best man followed. Bridesmaids and ushers took their respective places as Father Prior began the marriage ceremony and then the Nuptial Mass.

Nicole watched as Dan retreated to the other end of the pew and join the blonde woman, his wife Stacy. For just a fleeting moment the agony of the past nine years was relived. Lisa's wedding took precedence; yet there was the concrete evidence and actual finality of a broken marriage. She had come to terms with the situation and harbored neither love nor hatred.

The wedding ceremony lasted an hour. Then began the exit of the happy couple followed by the wedding party and the family. Cameras popped up everywhere. Dan and Nicole stood side by side during family shots.

Spruce Hill Country Club is in ski territory. Since Raymond and Lisa were avid skiers, it was among the familiar sites researched for their wedding reception. The large reception hall sold them. Grandparents Nina and Victor were reminded of their first date riding in a rumble seat and looking over that part of the Pocono Mountains when it was still virgin territory with a few exclusive country clubs.

The guests gradually arrived in cars and limousines that accommodated guests who preferred not to drive after a party. Traveling off the main highways, over macadam mountain roads, they finally arrived at the large stone structure that could easily impress even those with discriminating tastes. Sparkling glass doors and deep cushioned rugs greeted the incoming crowd as they were led to a paneled room with large mirrors, paintings, mahogany bar and small round tables. Young waitresses, dressed in white aprons over short black dresses, served a large assortment of hors d'oeuvres and all types of drinks. Many thought that this was actually the favorite portion of any reception, and dinner was secondary. Unquestionably it was an ideal time for walking about and socializing. A few, especially the elderly, preferred the comfort of chairs and tables.

John, Gina, Nina, Victor and the "girls," all well dressed, sat together along the mirrored wall of the dimly lit room. Endless numbers of guests approached to offer their congratulations to them as well as to the Dontaelli and Grasso grandparents who sat at the next table. Waitresses provided excellent service and attention. They marveled at the elderly grandparents' humor and companionship.

"We go back a long time," whispered Nina in the ear of one of the waitresses, still playful, "but honey I'm not telling you how far."

"All in your seventies, I'll bet," the waitress replied quite seriously.

"Late eighties and early nineties is closer," smiled John still displaying his own teeth.

"My Grammy is seventy-eight and sure shows her age," continued the waitress while hoping she wouldn't be caught loitering.

"Anything else I can order for you?" she asked as she brought out a pad and pencil from an apron pocket.

"Another glass of that good wine and a small dish of those stuffed mushrooms," said Victor whose gray hair had thinned considerably during the past ten years. Nina watched over him like a mother hen.

The rest gave the same order while the "girls" asked for some tiny hot dogs wrapped in pastry.

Making friendly contacts fitted the occasion. Eyes continually shifted toward Stacy, who made no effort to fraternize but remained standing near the open bar talking with several male guests who hung onto her every word. In her late thirties, she looked attractive in a black gown. The wedding group was expected to make an introductory entrance into the reception hall. Earlier when asked to join them, she had replied "I don't belong there." For a change she and Stella Grasso were in total agreement!

Recent arrivals included Carl, Leland and Jennifer, plus a few schoolteachers. Occasionally someone recognized at least one of them and stopped briefly to engage in brief conversation.

Aunt Zee and Neil introduced son Guy and wife Darlene. Many had never met them. Guy was tall like his parents and resembled Neil. Darlene wearing a long red beaded dress was a bit shorter and thin. Straight black hair with ends brushed upward framed an ivory skin. Outgoing with a contagious laugh, she obviously enjoyed walking around and meeting people. Judge Louis and Barbara were equally up to the task and made the rounds with them.

Bethlehem and local cousins sought relatives whom they had not seen in years. Antoinette's extended family came in from Long Island. None of the Canadian relatives were able to attend; a cousin was getting married that same afternoon.

At four P.M. doors to the reception halls were opened and the guests gradually began streaming in and seeking designated tables while awaiting the imminent arrival of the bride and groom. Waiters and waitresses were highly visible around the huge ballroom.

With the arrival of the wedding party came appropriate music. Introductions by the master of ceremonies, ovations for bridesmaids, ushers, maid of honor, best man and parents of the bridal couple followed in that order. Obviously none was more tumultuous and prolonged than that reserved for the happy couple as they headed for the dance floor.

A prayer and a toast with champagne were followed by a sumptuous meal that featured antipasti, fettuccini Alfredo and a choice of beef, mountain trout or chicken.

Soft violin music during the dinner did not stifle conversations. Rock and roll dance music would come later.

The closest relatives sat in front of the bridal table. Nicole joined Mamie, Domenic, John, Gina, Lucia, Grace, Beth, Patrick, Peter and Marion at one table. Raymond's parents, Julia and David, grandparents Nina and Victor sat with their family, at least for a brief time. Nina would not be tied down. She frequently darted to talk with John and Gina. The Grassos including Vito, Stella, Angelo, Maggie and Frank sat at an adjoining table. Dan and Stacy sat there as well. The latter maintained a reasonable distance from her mother-in-law. Stella uttered a prayer of thanksgiving.

Wine flowed and conversations gradually became louder.

"So you survived the anxiety period, Nicole. How was it?"

"I'm glad Dan called last night. After the first meeting, I found myself relaxing a bit. Actually he was nice and I had no feeling of animosity or attachment. It's hard to believe but true, Beth. Our children are happy so I'm happy." Nicole looked at Beth and smiled.

"Wanna know something?"

"What?"

"That's exactly how I figured it would be."

The waitress came between them to fill the water glasses.

"Really?"

"Yeah, really?"

"Why?"

"Because you just seem more together these days."

"Lisa is married, Andrew and Matthew are in college. I am content."

Beth patted her sister on the hand, and whispered, "I am mighty happy for you."

The orchestra was preparing to play, guests were table hopping, laughter and loud talking prevailed. The wine was having its effect. The bride and groom were the first on the dance floor. Others followed including Dan and Stacy. Peter asked his sister, both excellent dancers, for the first dance. They swung around like pros as did Beth and Patrick. When they returned to their table Marion congratulated them and smiled broadly. She preferred to see her sister-in-law on the dance floor for that first dance. Next dances would be Peter's and hers.

Nicole planned to walk around and see friends but Lori stopped for a brief conversation. Andrew and Matthew were chatting with their father and the Grasso relatives. Stacy was absent and a rough scan located her at the bar.

Nicole made a sudden turn after a tap on her right shoulder.

"Ma'am, may I kindly have this slow dance?"

She turned to face Carl. Grinning and dressed in white trousers and black jacket and tie, he looked impressive.

"I may just think about it a few seconds," she said.

"Certainly not that long," he whispered in her ear.

He held her hand and they were soon dancing to a familiar tune they had shared at the school dance. Just as then, Carl hummed along with the orchestra as many, including Dan, watched and wondered. He wanted to ask his sons who he was, but there seemed no point to it.

Later while on her way to the ladies room, Aunt Zee

stopped at Nicole's table to congratulate her for choosing a good dance partner, friend and whatever else he meant to her. "Nice going for two school teachers," she said with a wink.

The ladies room was deserted with the exception of someone in a dimly lit stall with an open door, leaning over the hopper and vomiting.

"You okay?" It was Stacy!

"Never felt better in my life," she replied slurring her words noticeably. "Who the hell are you?"

"My family calls me Zee."

"Hi, Zee Zee." Stacy looked up, her face a yellow-greenish color. Aunt Zee looked down with hand on hip, to watch a drunken wretch lean over the toilet. There was a mighty urge to dunk her blonde head into the bowl.

"Can I do something?" Zee couldn't believe she said that.

"Hi, Zee Zee. How old are you, Zee Zee?"

"Old enough to know a drunk when I see one."

"Ha, ha! Nice earrings, Zee Zee," she slurred and asked, "Do you like weddings?"

"Most of the time."

"Wanna know something? I hate this one."

"Why?"

"None of your damn business. Zee Zee, where did you get the earrings?"

"Salvation Army depot. Want me to help you get to the chair?"

"I can do it myself," she said while wiggling her long slim finger at Zee. Unbalanced efforts were useless and Zee helped her to a large white leather chair. Stacy's head fell backward and she closed her eyes. Zee left shortly after that and returned to Nicole's table to get her advice.

The Grassos including Dan were doting on Andrew

and Matthew and probably unaware, or did not care, where Stacy was. Nicole, on her way to stop at the various tables, told her aunt she would discreetly talk to Maggie about it.

Her first stop was with Stella and Vito, and then Maggie. She quietly disclosed Stacy's situation and then resumed a tour of the tables. After waiting several minutes, Maggie excused herself and left for the ladies' room. Finding Stacy with an attendant, she left it at that for the moment.

Nicole briefly conversed with the teachers then tried to give some attention to other guests. Aunt Zee's table also included Aunt Nettie and Tessie, Domenics sisters. They were having a hilarious time as expected when that group got together. "Mission accomplished," she told her aunt.

After socializing a bit longer, she walked back to her table where Raymond and Lisa were charming family members and having their photos taken with the various relatives.

They stopped at the Grasso table again where a teary-eyed Dan embraced his daughter for a sustained time. "Thank you for giving me the generous privilege of giving you away. I love you dearly, Honey. May you both be very happy," he said when he shook Raymond's hand. He then motioned for Nicole to join them for photos. She gladly agreed to pose with him and the bride and groom. Andrew and Matthew joined them for more family shots.

The wedding cake was about to be cut. The music was more rapid. The chicken dance drew a significant number of dancers followed by more numbers for the young 'rock and rollers.' Guests enjoyed the cookies placed on the tables by waitresses.

Lisa and Raymond quietly eased themselves away to spend the night in a lodge and then would be off to the islands the following morning.

Dan found Nicole standing by her table, and before she sat placed his hand on her right shoulder and said, "Thank you for being so forgiving and making this a perfect day. Of course, I expected nothing less from you."

"Glad we both helped in some measures, Dan. Everything turned out well. Do stay in touch with our children."

"Indeed I will." He kissed Nicole on the cheek and left to collect Stacy.

In two years, the clan would enter a new century. Many of the old attitudes and cultural differences had already eroded. One could only hope that the close family ties would persist and help maintain that resiliency and comfortable lifestyle so dominant in their lives.